COMMAND

COMMAND

BY

WILLIAM McFEE

GARDEN CITY   NEW YORK
DOUBLEDAY, PAGE & COMPANY
1922

This book is inscribed to those commanders under whom the author has had the honour to serve, who have achieved firmness without asperity, tact and sympathy without interference, and appreciation without fuss. It is inscribed to these gentlemen because while they lack the gift of self-advertisement, they have contrived, in spite of the trials and exasperations of a seafaring existence, to engage the respect and affections of their lieutenants.

PREFATORY NOTE

This tale is an original invention. It is not founded upon fact, nor are the characters herein described portraits of actual persons. The incidents and topography are imaginary.

W. M.

COMMAND

COMMAND

CHAPTER I

SHE was one of those girls who have become much more common of late years among the upper-middle classes, the comfortably fixed classes, than they have ever been since the aristocracy left off marrying Italian *prime-donne*. You know the type of English beauty, so often insisted on, say, twenty years ago—placid, fair, gentle, blue-eyed, fining into distinction in Lady Clara Vere de Vere? Always she was the heroine, and her protagonist, the adventuress, was dark and wicked. For some occult reason the Lady Rowena type was the fashion.

Ada Rivers was one of those girls who have come up since. The upper-middle classes had experienced many incursions. All sorts of astonishing innovations had taken place. Many races had come to England, or rather to London, which is in England but not of it; had made money, had bred their sons at the great public schools and universities and their daughters at convents in France and Belgium. These dark-haired, gray-eyed, stylish, highly strung, athletic, talented girls are phenomena of the Stockbroking Age. They do things Lady Rowena and Lady Clara Vere de Vere would not tolerate for a moment. Outwardly resembling the wealthy Society Girl, they are essentially quite different. Some marry artists and have emotional outbreaks. Some combine a very genuine romantic temperament with a disheartening sophistication about incomes and running a home. They not only wish to marry so that they can begin where their parents leave off, but they know how to do it. They can

1

engage a competent house-maid and rave about Kubelik on
the same afternoon, and do both in an experienced sort of
way. They go everywhere by themselves, and to men whom
they dislike they are sheathed in shining armour. They can
dance, swim, motor, golf, entertain, earn their own living,
talk music, art, books, and china, wash a dog and doctor him.
And they can do all this, mark, without having any real
experience of what we call life. They are good girls, nice
girls, virtuous girls, and very marriageable girls, too, but they
have a superficial hardness of texture on their character which
closely resembles the mask of experience. They are like the
baggage which used to be sold in certain obscure shops in
London with the labels of foreign hotels already pasted on it.
It follows that sometimes this girl of the upper-middle, comfortably fixed class makes a mistake in her choice. Or rather,
she credits with heroic attributes a being of indifferent calibre. She realizes in him some profound but erratic emotion,
and the world in which she moves beholds her behaviour and
listens to her praise of her beloved with annoyance. They
speak, not of a mistake of course, but of the strangeness of
girls nowadays, and incompatibility of temperaments. But
perhaps the most remarkable aspect of these affairs is the
blindness of the girl's friends to her frequent superiority over
the being whom she adores. She isn't good enough for him,
they say. The fact is, at the time of this story, fine women
were cheap in England, and gentlemen of indifferent calibre
were picking up bargains every day.

Mr. Reginald Spokesly, a case in point, was accustomed to
use this very phrase when in a mood in which his egotism was
lying dormant. "*I've* picked up a bargain," he would say to
himself as he leaned over the rail and watched the millions of
tiny facets of the sea reflecting the sunset. "A bargain," he
would whisper in an awed voice, nodding gravely at the
opposite bulkhead, as he sat in his room with his feet in a
bucket of hot water, for this was his way with corns. And
Mr. Reginald Spokesly was intensely preoccupied with
women. He had often sighed, on the bridge, as he reflected
what he might do "if he only had the means." Perhaps,

when he got a command . . . He would halt short at this, suddenly remembering the bargain he had picked up.

But it must not be for one moment imagined, when I speak of Mr. Spokesly as being at that time a gentleman of indifferent calibre, that he was so regarded by himself or his world afloat or ashore. Indeed, he was a rather magnificent person. He played his cards very well. He "kept his ears open and his mouth shut," as he himself put it. He had once confided to Mr. Chippenham, the third officer, that "there was jobs goin' just now, soft things, too, if y' only wait." The third officer was not directly interested, for he knew well enough that he himself stood no chance in that gamble. But he was impressed by Mr. Spokesly's—the second officer's—exquisite fitness for any such jobs. Even the Old Man, taciturn, distant, and dignified as he was, was not up to Mr. Spokesly. Who had so slow and so deliberate a walk? Who could treat the common people of the ship, the sailors, the firemen, the engineers and wireless boys, with such lofty condescension? It was a lesson in deportment to see him stroll into the chief engineer's room and extend himself on that gentleman's settee. It was unfortunately true that some of those common people treated Mr. Spokesly, not as a commander *in posse*, not as one of those select beings born to rule, but as one of themselves. Mr. Chippenham remembered with pain one incident which showed this only too clearly. They were watching a destroyer coming into port, her decks lined with bluejackets, her three funnels belching oil-smoke, her semaphore working. As she swung round astern of them, Mr. Spokesly, who had been pacing to and fro paring his nails, joined the little group at the rail, nodding in majestic approval.

"Ah," he remarked in his loose-lipped, husky drawl, "I sh'd like to 'andle one o' them little things meself."

And to this the third engineer, his greasy arms asprawl on the rail, had looked over his shoulder and remarked:

"You! I'd like to see you! You'd pile her up on the beach before you'd had her five minutes, that's what *you'd* do."

It was a vile, gratuitous insult, the third officer had thought hotly, and he had watched Mr. Spokesly do the only thing possible, walk grandly away. That was the worst of those beastly engineers. If you gave them an inch they'd take a mile. And he made a mental note of what *he* would would do when he attained to command—some twenty years ahead.

But this was, I am glad to say, an exceptional incident. Circumstances as a rule favoured the development of Mr. Spokesly's *amour propre* and he brooded with intense absorption upon his own greatness. Now this greatness was a very intricate affair. It was inextricably tangled up with the individual soul known as Reginald Spokesly, Esquire, of Thames Road, Twickenham, England, and the unit of the Merchant Service known as R. Spokesly, second officer, S. S. *Tanganyika*, a member of what is called "the cloth." Perhaps it would be better to include another manifestation of greatness, which was Mr. Spokesly's tremendous power over women. His own explanation of this last phenomenon was that he "kept them in their place." To him they were mere playthings of an idle hour. Perhaps his desire was most aroused by stories of Oriental domesticity, and he almost regretted not being born a pasha, where his abilities as a woman tamer could have had more scope. However, he did not read a great deal. In fact, he could hardly be said to read at all. He patronized a book now and then by falling asleep over it.

In the early days of the war, Mr. Spokesly's light had been hidden for some years in the Far East. Indeed, when I think of the sort of life he was gradually subsiding into out there, I sometimes wonder if he would ever have attained to such a capacity for moral effort as he afterwards displayed unless the war had evoked the illusion that he ought to go home and enlist, and so had opened to him the wealth of bargains to be picked up in England. That, at any rate, had been his ostensible reason for quitting the peculiar mixture of tropical languor and brisk modernity which had been his life for nearly four years. Perhaps it was not so much love of country as personal destiny, for Mr. Spokesly had a very real belief in his destiny. Here again his greatness, which was of course the warp and woof of his destiny, showed a pattern of perplexing intricacy. He regarded himself with approval. He was putting on weight. A vigorous man of thirty-odd, coming thousands of miles across the ocean to fight for his country! He read the roll of honour each week in the papers that met them on the homeward voyage, and the page blurred to his sight as he gazed through it into the future. You might almost, he reflected, count out those who were wounded and missing as well! Whether he had ever had any genuine intention of becoming a soldier I do not know. He had a remarkably strong instinct of self-preservation; but then many soldiers have that. As the liner neared home, however, Mr. Spokesly's thoughts centred more and more truly about himself and his immediate future. The seraglios he had quitted in Singapore and Kobe and Rangoon were, in his own words, "a thing o' the past." The time, "the psychological moment," as he phrased it without in the least knowing what the word meant, was come when he would have to marry or, at any rate, become engaged. He was not, he told himself, "pertickler." He reckoned he could fall in love with almost anybody who wasn't too old or too ugly, and providing always that she had "a dot." He was a stern believer in a dot, even though he did not know how to pronounce it. Looming behind the steep hill leading to a command were the happy mountain valleys of a comfortable independence. To marry money! Now he came to think of it, it had been the pervading ambition of his life. And here was his chance. He pulled down his vest and settled his tie as he thought of the golden future before him. He had a vision of an England full of consolable fiancées, young ladies of wealth, beauty, and position, sobbing gently for departed heroes, but willing to be comforted. . . .

It did not turn out that way, of course. Indeed, his first experience on arrival was of an England of brisk, determined young women making munitions, clipping tickets, and conducting street cars, and he was angered at the unwomanliness of it all. Woman's place, he had always believed, was in the harem. He had held, when lying in his hammock out East and lazily reading the home news of suffrage riots, that the Government "ought to have tied some of 'em up and horsewhipped 'em." But he left the Metropolis behind as soon as possible, and went down to stay with his family at Twickenham. And it was here, on a perfect day in late autumn, that Ada Rivers, living with her married sister at Richmond, brought balm to his wounded spirit.

From the very first day, spent in a punt at Kingston, she had struck the right note of adoration. He had been telling her how his last ship had been sunk by the *Emden*, and was going on to say he had providentially left her just before, when she broke in ecstatically: "And you went through it all?" He hesitated for a moment, and she followed this up with, "How glorious! You *have* been doing your bit!" She leaned back on the cushions and gazed at him with shining gray eyes as he poled her gently along, his large hairy arms, one of them clasped by a wrist watch, outstretched above her, as though in some mystic benediction, his loose mouth and double chin pendulous with the delicious flattery. For she was a fine girl—he realized that immediately his sister had introduced him. She made him feel his masculinity. He liked to think afterwards of how deliberately he had made his choice.

He floated for a time in a dream of sensuous delight, for she was one of those girls who will obey orders, who like orders, in fact, and whose proud subservience sends a thrill of supreme pleasure through the minds of their commanders. They were soon engaged.

There was not as much difference between this courtship and that of an average coal or ice man as one might suppose. Mr. Spokesly's emotional output so far had been, if I may say so, limited. But this was all grist to Ada's mill. It was put down to the strong, deep, English sailor nature, just as his primitive methods of wooing were credited to the bluff English sailor nature. She was under an illusion all the time. All that her married sister could say was useless. The married sister was married to a man who was a woman-tamer

himself in a way. He was now at the Front, where he had
won a medal for extraordinary bravery, and his wife was
dreading the day of his return. She used the interval of
peace and quiet to warn her sister. But who can fight against
an illusion? The married sister had to shrug her shoulders,
and point out that Mr. Spokesly was throwing himself away
on a silly chit. She admired Mr. Spokesly herself, to tell the
truth, and liked to have him in the house, where he was often
to be found during his six weeks' vacation. It was she who
told him his was "a man's work" in a low contralto voice with
a thrill in it. This was really unfair to the husband in Flanders who had displayed extraordinary bravery in holding an
isolated post for goodness knows how many hours. It would
not do, to assert that Mr. Spokesly ever played with the idea
of consoling a possible widow who already admired him. He
had not sufficient imagination for this. And Ada herself was
quite able to hold up her end. She made Mr. Spokesly feel
not only great, but good. It was she who led him to see
where his weakness lay, a success possible only to a clever
girl. Unconscious of her promptings, he came to the conclusion that, to do himself justice, he must make an effort
and "improve his education." When he heard the sisters
rattling away in a foreign tongue he made a mental note that
"he must rub up his French." The London School of
Mnemonics, however, did the trick. It was just what he
wanted. This school had a wonderful system of memory-
training which was endorsed by kings and emperors, merchant princes and famous mezzo-sopranos. By means of
this system, learned in twelve lessons, you trebled your
intellectual power, quadrupled your earning power, and quin-
tupled your general value to yourself and to the world.
The system was comprised in twelve books of aphorisms, slim
volumes in gray-green paper covers, daintily printed and
apparently addressed straight to Mr. Spokesly's heart.
First, he was told, he was capable of anything. He knew
that, and with an almost physical feeling of pleasure he read
on. Second, came a little story about a celebrated philosopher. Mr. Spokesly was charmed.

It must not be supposed, however, that this was all bunkum to Mr. Spokesly. It was, on the contrary, deadly earnest. Like many Englishmen of his day, he knew there was something wrong with him. He was aware of people in the world who used their brains and held clear notions about things and ideas, very much as a man groping along a foggy street is aware of a *conversazione* in one of the mansions. To him the London School of Mnemonics was a sound commercial proposition. In twelve lessons, by correspondence, they offered to develop his memory, stimulate his will power, and increase his salary. He had picked up the first half-dozen pamphlets in his fiancée's home. The husband of the married sister had taken the course as far as Number Six, which was: "How to Dominate Your Friends," with a chatty essay on Hypnotism and Matrimony, before leaving for Flanders and glory. Mr. Spokesly read them with an avidity unknown to him since he had spent a month in London many years before studying for his master's license. He felt on the highroad to success. He joined the London School of Mnemonics. He bought an engagement ring for Ada and a handsome bracelet for the married sister. He left them for a while, he said, "to join up." He meant to do it, too, for there is something pathetically appealing in the atmosphere of late autumn in England. It goes to the heart. It is not quite so piercing a call as the early spring, when one's very soul goes out in a mystical passionate union with the spirit of the land, but it is very strong, and Mr. Spokesly, without understanding it, felt the appeal. But at Paddington he stopped and had a drink. For all his years at sea, he was a Londoner at heart. He spoke the atrocious and barbarous jargon of her suburbs, he snuffed the creosote of her wooden streets and found it an admirable *apéritif* to his London beer. And while the blowsy spirit of London, the dear cockney-hearted town, ousted the gentler shade of England, Mr. Spokesly reflected that neither the army nor the navy would have any use for a man of commanding powers, a man whose will and memory had been miraculously developed. The army would not do, he was sure. The navy would probably put him in charge of a tug; for Mr. Spokesly had no illusions as to the reality of the difficulties of life in his own sphere. And he had been long enough at one thing to dread the wrench of beginning at the bottom somewhere else. This is the tragic side of military service in England, for most Englishmen are not adaptable. Mr. Spokesly, for example, had gone to sea at the age of twelve. Unless he won a lottery prize he would be going to sea at seventy, if he lived so long. So he reflected, and the upshot was that he applied—quite humbly, for he had not as yet developed any enormous will power—and secured a billet as second officer on the *Tanganyika*. He told his people and Ada that there was "a chance of a command," which of course was perfectly true. "It is a man's work," she thrilled softly, echoing her sister, and she closed her eyes to enjoy the vision of him, strong in character, large in talent, irresistible in will power, commanding amid storms and possibly even shot and shell. . . .

*   *   *   *   *   *   *

Having kept the middle watch, which is from twelve to four, Mr. Spokesly was sitting in his cabin abaft the bridge of the *Tanganyika*, his feet in a white-enamelled bucket of hot water, contemplating the opposite bulkhead. He was thinking very hard, according to the System of the London School of Mnemonics. The key of this system was simplicity itself. You wanted to remember something which you had forgotten. Very well; you worked back on the lines of a dog following a scent. From what you were thinking at the present moment to what you were thinking when you came in the door, which would lead you by gentle gradations back to the item of which you were in search. Very simple. Unfortunately, Mr. Spokesly, in the course of these retrograde pilgrimages, was apt to come upon vast and trackless oceans of oblivion, bottomless gulfs of time in which, as far as he could recall, his intellectual faculties had been in a state of suspended animation. The London School of Mnemonics did not seem to allow sufficiently for the bridging of these gaps. It is true they said in Lesson Three, with gentle irony, *Remember the chain of ideas is often faulty; there may be missing links.* Mr. Spokesly, who on this occasion was determined to remember what he was thinking of at the moment when the Old Man spoke sharply behind him and made him jump, was of the opinion that it was the chain that was often missing and that all he could discover were a few odd links! He lifted one foot out of the grateful warmth and felt the instep tenderly, breathing hard, with his tongue in one corner of his mouth, as his mind ran to and fro nosing at the closed doors of the past. What *was* he thinking of? He remembered it attracted him strangely, had given him a feeling of pleasant anticipation as of a secret which he could unfold at his leisure. It was . . . it was . . . He put his foot into the water again and frowned. He had been thinking of Ada, he recalled—— Ah! *Now* he was on the track of it. He had been thinking not of her but of the melancholy fact communicated to him by his own sister, that Ada had no "dot," no money until her father died. Now how in the world did that come to react upon his mind as a pleasant thing? It was a monstrous thing, that he should have capsized his future by such precipitate folly! Mr. Spokesly comprehended that what he was looking for was not a memory but a mood. He had been in a certain mood as he stood on the bridge that morning about half-past three, his hand resting lightly on the rail, his eyes on the dim horizon, when the Old Man, in his irritating pink-striped pajamas, had spoken sharply and made him jump. And that mood, the product of some overnight reflections on the subject of will power, had been rising like some vast billow of cumulous vapour touched with roseate hues from a hidden sun, and he had been just on the brink of some surprising discovery, when—— It was very annoying, for the Old Man had been preoccupied by a really very petty matter, after all. (The word "petty" was a favourite with Mr. Spokesly.) It had, however, broken the spell, and here he was, a few hours later, hopelessly snarled up in all sorts of interminable strings of ideas. The business of thinking was not so easy as the London School of Mnemonics made out.

Lifting his feet slowly up and down, he reached out and took Lesson Number Five from the holdall (with his initials in blue) which hung above his head. As he turned the richly printed pages, a delicious feeling of being cared for and caressed stole over him. *Never despair*, said the Lesson gravely, *Nil Desperandum. Just as the darkest hour is before the dawn, so victory may crown your toil at the least likely moment.*

And so it was! With a feeling of sombre triumph, Mr. Spokesly "saw the connection" as he would have said. He saw that the importance of that lost mood lay in the petty annoyance that followed. For the Old Man had called him down about a mistake. A trifle. A petty detail. A bagatelle. It only showed, he thought, the narrowness of mind of some commanders. Now *he* . . .

But with really remarkable resolution Mr. Spokesly pulled himself up and concentrated upon the serious side of the question. There had been a mistake. It was as though the Old Man's quiet sharpness had gouged a great hole in Mr. Spokesly's self-esteem, and he had been unconsciously busy, ever since, bringing excuse after excuse, like barrow-loads of earth, in a vain attempt to fill it up. It was still a yawning hiatus in the otherwise flawless perfection of his conduct as an officer. He had made a mistake. And the London School of Mnemonics promised that whoever followed their course made no mistake. He felt chastened as he habituated himself to this feeling that perhaps he was not a perfect officer. He took his feet out of the lukewarm water and reached for a towel.

It will not do to laugh at such a discovery on the part of Mr. Spokesly. Only those who have had responsibility can be fully alive to the enormous significance of self-esteem in imposing authority upon a frivolous world. And it must be borne in mind that to Mr. Spokesly himself, at that moment, to fail in being a perfect officer was a failure in life. It was part of the creed of his "cloth" that each of them was without blemish until his license was cancelled by the invisible omnipotence of the law. It was, if you like, his

ethic, the criterion of his integrity, the inexorable condition
of carrying-on in his career. This ideal perfection of professional service resembles the giant fruits and immaculate
fauna depicted on the labels of the canned articles—a
grandiose conception of what was within. Just as nobody
really believes that apples and salmon are like that and yet
would refuse to buy a can without some such symbol, so Mr.
Spokesly would have found his services quite unmarketable
if he had discarded the polite fiction that he was, as far as
was humanly possible, incapable of improvement. It was
the aura, moreover, which distinguished him and all other
officers from the riff-raff which nowadays go to sea and ape
their betters—the parsons and surgeons, the wireless operators and engineers. They were common clay, mere ephemeral puppets, without hope of command, minions to take
orders, necessary evils in an age of mechanism and high-
speed commerce. It was an article of Mr. Spokesly's creed
that "the cloth" should stand by each other. He was
revolving this assumption in his mind as he rubbed the towel
gently to and fro, and it occurred to him in his slow way that
if he were to adopt the modern ideas of the London School of
Mnemonics, if he were to devote every fibre of his being to
forging ahead, gaining promotion, proving himself a superior
article with a brain which was the efficient instrument of
an indomitable will, then the obsolete idea of professional
solidarity would have to go overboard. And just at that
moment, with the consciousness of that petty mistake casting
a shadow on his soul and the sharp rebuke of the Old Man
rankling below, Mr. Spokesly was quite prepared to jettison
anything that stood in the way of what he vaguely formulated
as "his gettin' on." Mr. Spokesly's conceptions of advance-
ment were of course largely but not entirely circumscribed by
his profession. His allusions in conversation with Mr.
Chippenham to "soft things" were understood to refer to
shore jobs connected with shipping and transport. At one
time the fairy-tale fortune of a shipmate who had married a
shipowner's daughter had turned his thoughts that way.
But not for long. Mr. Spokesly had a feeling that to marry

into a job had its drawbacks. He felt "there was a string to it." And come what might, in his own hazy, amorphous fashion he desired to be captain of his soul. Had he the power at that moment of calling up Destiny, he would have made quite modest demands of her. Of course, a command, a fine large modern steamer, twin-screw, trading for choice in the Pacific, where as he knew very well a commander had pickings that placed him in a few years beyond the reach of penury at any rate . . . Ada could come out. She would do justice to such a position out East. And when the war was over they could come home and have a little place up the river at Bourne End . . . nothing very great, of course, but just right for Captain and Mrs. Spokesly. The dream was so very fair, so possible yet so utterly improbable, that his mouth drew down tremulously at the corners as he stared at the bulkhead. His eyes grew tired and smarted. Ah! Money! How often he had mouthed in jest that sorry proverb about the lack of money being the root of all evil! And how true it was, after all. Suddenly he stood up and became aware of someone in the alleyway outside his window. With a sense of relief, for his reflections had become almost inconveniently sombre and ingrowing, he saw it was someone he already knew in a friendly way, though he still addressed him as "Stooard."

There is much in a name, much more in a mode of address. When Archy Bates, the chief steward of the *Tanganyika*, turned round and hoisted himself so that he could look into Mr. Spokesly's port, their friendship was just at the point when the abrupt unveiling of some common aspiration would change "Stooard" into "Bates" or "Mister." For a steward on a ship is unplaced. The office is nothing, the personality everything. He may be the confidential agent of the commander or he may be the boon companion of the cook. To him most men are mere assimilative organisms, stomachs to be filled or doctored. Archy Bates was, like another Bates of greater renown, a naturalist. He studied the habits of the animals around him. He fed them or filled them with liquor, according to their desires, and watched the result.

It might almost be said that he acted the part of Tempter to mankind, bribing them into friendship or possibly only a useful silence. It is a sad but solid fact that he nearly always succeeded.

But he liked Mr. Spokesly. One of the disconcerting things about the wicked is their extreme humanity. Archy Bates liked Mr. Spokesly's society. Without in the least understanding how or why, he enjoyed talking to him, appreciated his point of view, and would have been glad to re-pay confidence with confidence. He was always deferential to officers, never forgetting their potentialities as to future command. He respected their reserve until they knew him intimately. He was always willing to wait. His discretion was boundless. He knew his own value. Friends of his had no reason to regret it. That third engineer, a coarse fellow, one of the few irreconcilables, had called him a flunkey. Well, the third engineer paid dearly for that in trouble over petty details, soap, towels, and so forth. But with "gentle-men" Archy Bates felt himself breathing a larger air. You could do something with a gentleman. And Mr. Spokesly, in the chief steward's estimation, was just that kind of man. So, in the lull of activity before lunch, he came along to see if Mr. Spokesly felt like a little social diversion.

"Busy?" he enquired, thrusting his curiously ill-balanced features into the port and smiling. Mr. Bates's smile was unfortunate. Without being in any way insincere, it gave one the illusion that it was fitted on over his real face. A long, sharp nose projecting straight out from a receding brow nestled in a pomatumed and waxed moustache, and his eyes, of an opaque hazel, became the glinting centres of scores of tiny radiating lines. His chin, blue with shaving, and his gray hair carefully parted in the middle, made up a physiog-nomy that might have belonged either to a bartender or a ward politician. And there was a good deal of both in Archy Bates.

To the enquiry Mr. Spokesly shook his head. The steward gave a sharp look each way, and then made a complicated gesture that was a silent and discreet invitation.

"Oh, well." Mr. Spokesly shrugged his shoulders and pulled down the corners of his mouth. The face at the window tittered so violently that the owner of it nearly lost his balance and put up a hand to support himself.

"Come on, old chap. I've got half an hour to spare."

"Oh, all right, Bates. Sha'n't be a minute."

The face, like a satiric mask, suddenly vanished.

Mr. Spokesly put on his socks and slippers and, lighting a cigarette, prepared to go along. He liked the steward, and he felt lonely. It so happened that, quite apart from his intrinsic greatness, Mr. Spokesly was very much alone on the *Tanganyika*. Mr. Chippenham was too young; the chief officer, a gnarled round-shouldered ancient, was too old; the commander too distant. There remained only the chief engineer, a robust gentleman who conversed hospitably on all subjects in a loud voice but invited no confidences. And it was confidences Mr. Spokesly really wanted to give. He wanted to impress his ideals and superior views of life upon a sympathetic and receptive mind. Most men are unconscious artists. Only instead of working in stone or brass or pigment, instead of composing symphonies or poems, they hold forth to their kindred spirits and paint, in what crude words they can find, the god-like beings they conceive themselves to be. Indeed, when we call a man a "hot-air merchant"; when we say "he does not hate himself," what is it save a grudging tribute to his excessive artistry? He is striving to evolve in your skeptical mind an image which can appear only by the light of your intelligent faith and liberal sympathy. He claims of you only what all artists claim of the critic —understanding. He seeks to thrill you with pleasure at the noble spectacle of himself blocked out against a sombre background of imperfect humanity. But to get the very best out of him you must become one in soul with him, and do the same yourself.

CHAPTER II

YOU will be pleased to hear, sweetheart, that I have already got promotion, I am now chief officer, next to the captain. I dare say, in a short time your only will be coming home to take a command. I am persevering with the Course you gave me, and I find it a great assistance. Of course I have a great deal more to do now, especially as the last man was scarcely up to his work. . . . While as for the captain, I may as well tell you . . ."

And so on. Mr. Spokesly wrote this letter from Alexandria, where the *Tanganyika* was discharging rails and machinery. He wrote it to Ada, who was staying with her family, including her married sister, in Cornwall, because of the air raids. She read it by the low roar of the autumnal seas round the Cornish coast and she was thrilled. Having written it, Mr. Spokesly dressed himself in discreet mufti and went ashore with his bosom friend, Archy Bates. His commander, walking to and fro on the bridge with his after-dinner cigar, saw them disappear between the tracks and the piles of freight. He frowned. He was no snob, but he had most explicit views about a ship's officer's relations with the rest of mankind. It was, in his opinion, *infra dig* to associate with a steward. He had mentioned it pointedly yet good-humouredly one day, and at his amazement Mr. Spokesly had replied that he would please himself in a private matter. Captain Meredith had been so flabbergasted at this wholly unexpected turn of the conversation that he said no more. Later he put it down to swelled head. Yet what else could be done? Mr. Spokesly had a master's certificate and the third mate had none at all. Captain Meredith began to muse regretfully upon the loss of his chief officer. For although Mr. Spokesly had omitted to mention it, the im-

mediate cause of his promotion was the sudden death at sea
of his predecessor.   That gnarled and taciturn being, whose
round moon-face had relapsed with age to the consistency of
puckered pink parchment, had been for many years "taking
care of himself."   In that remote epoch when he was young
it may be doubted whether he had done this, for he bore the
marks of a life lived to the very delirious verge.   That was
long before Mr. Spokesly had got into short pants, however.
Mr. McGinnis took care of himself day and night.   He had
achieved a miraculous balance of forces within his frame, a
balance which enabled him to stand his watch on the bridge
and give orders to the bo'sun, but no more.   He would pass
with a stealthy quietness along the deck and into his room,
and there sit, his claw-like hands on the arms of his chair, his
emaciated form encased in a diamond-patterned kimono,
his pink jaws working noiselessly on a piece of some patent
chewing gum, of which he carried a stock.   Sometimes he
read a page or two of a quiet story, but usually he switched
off the electric and sat chewing far into the night.   At a
quarter to four one morning, the Asiatic sailor who came to
arouse him discovered him hanging by his arms to the edge
of his bunk, as though crucified, his appallingly thin limbs
sprawling and exposing tattooings of astonishing design and
colouring, his jaw hanging, his sunken eyes staring with sense-
less curiosity at a spot on the carpet.   The Japanese sailor
went back to Mr. Spokesly, who was on watch on the bridge,
and reported impassively, "Chief mate all same one stiff."
Mr. Spokesly was incredulous, though he knew from experience the uncanny prescience of the Oriental in such
matters.   "What? Sick?" he inquired in a whisper.   The
Japanese, a diminutive white wraith in the profound gloom of
the bridge, replied, "No sick. All same one stiff. No can
do." This was his final word. Mr. Spokesly hurriedly
aroused the captain, who came out on the bridge and told
them to go down together. They went down and Mr.
Spokesly had a violent shock. He told Archy Bates afterwards he had "had a turn." He did all that a competent
officer could do. He spoke sharply the man's name. "Mr.

McGinnis!" and Mr. McGinnis continued to regard the spot
on the carpet with intense curiosity.   He felt the breast, held
a shaving glass to the lips of the silent McGinnis, and realized
that the Oriental who stood by the door, his dark face impassive and his gaze declined upon the floor, was perfectly
right. As Mr. Spokesly raised the stiffened arms the kimono
fell open, and he had another violent shock, for Mr. McGinnis
had evidently been a patron of the art of tattooing in all its
branches.   His arms and torso formed a ghastly triptych of
green and blue figures with red eyes.   Contrasted with the
pallor of death the dreadful designs took on the similitude of
living forms. With a movement of hasty horror Mr. Spokesly
laid the body on the settee and went away to call Mr. Chippenham and the chief steward.

The conjectures which followed were most of them beside
the mark. The fact was, intelligence has its limits. The
miraculous balance of forces had been in some obscure way
disturbed, and Mr. McGinnis, like the one-hoss shay, had
simply crumbled to dust at the appointed time. Captain
Meredith was sorry, for Mr. McGinnis had been what is
known as "a good mate."   And Captain Meredith, whether
from mere prejudice or genuine conviction, was unable to
discern the makings of a "good mate" in Mr. Spokesly.   It
was almost miraculous, he reflected, how the work of the ship
had got balled up since the invaluable McGinnis, neatly
sewed up in some of his own canvas, had made a hole in the
Mediterranean.   It should be understood that Captain Meredith was a humane man.   He was also a seafaring man.
The fact that McGinnis had been excommunicated from the
church of his baptism did not deter Captain Meredith from
reading the burial service over him.   And his annoyance at
seeing his new chief officer and the steward "as thick as
thieves," as he put it, was really a humane feeling. He had
served in ships where the commander had been utterly at the
mercy of some contemptible dish-washer who had wormed
himself into his superior's confidence, acting perhaps as a
go-between in some shady deal.   He had seen a veteran
ship-master, a man of fine presence and like no one so much

as some retired colonel of guards, running ignominiously along the quay to fetch back a dirty little half-breed steward, who had seen fit to take offence and who knew too much. Captain Meredith had seen these things, and though he kept them locked up in his own breast he did not forget them. He was perfectly well aware of the precarious hold most of us have upon honour. He knew that a certain austerity of demeanour was the only practicable armour against many temptations.

But of course Captain Meredith couldn't be expected to understand Mr. Spokesly's state of mind. Mr. Spokesly didn't understand it himself. It was scarcely sufficient to say that his promotion had carried him away. Far from it. He regarded this step as merely a start. What had inspired him at the moment to "stand up to the Old Man" was nothing less than a wave of genuine emotion. You see, he really liked Archy Bates so far as he knew him then. They were real chums, telling each other their grievances and sharing a singularly identical opinion of the Old Man's fitness for his job. There are more unions of souls in this world than materialists would like us to believe. What Captain Meredith mistook for harsh and ill-timed impudence was really a thickness of utterance and a sudden vision of injustice. Once done, and the Old Man reduced to an amazed silence, the incident took in Mr. Spokesly's mind a significance so tremendous that he hardly knew what to think. He had "tackled the Old Man"! He had broken the spell of a lifetime of silent obsequiousness to a silly convention. After all . . . And, moreover, it took will power to do it. He was improving. The London School of Mnemonics had achieved another miracle. He went over it all again in Archy Bates's cabin, Archy's ear close to his mouth, door shut, curtains folded across the window. You never can tell who's listening on a ship. . . . "I turns an' says to him, 'Look here, Captain' . . ." Archy listening with intensity, his shoulders hunched, his opaque, agate-like eyes glittering on each side of his long sharp nose, while his thumb and forefinger slowly and repeatedly thrust back his pomatumed and waxed moustache from his lips, and breathing "Jus' fancy! . . .

And you told him that? . . . Goo' Lord! . . . Well,
I always knew 'e 'ad no use for me. . . ." Mr. Spokesly
pulled Archy Bates close up to him so that his lips were actually funnelled in the other's ear and breathed back:' *Take it
from me, Archy, he ain't fit for his job!*"

Archy Bates had risen, just then, to get the corkscrew. He
was profoundly moved, and actually found himself trying to
open a bottle of whiskey with a button-hook. He showed
his idiocy to Mr. Spokesly. "Jus' fancy. I don't know
what I'm doin', straight." And they both laughed. But he
was profoundly moved. He was preoccupied with the
possible developments of this tremendous affair. Mr.
Spokesly, by virtue of that last insane whisper, had of
course delivered himself over, body, soul, and spirit, to the
steward, but Mr. Spokesly was a friend of his. He had quite
other plans for Mr. Spokesly. He stared harder than the job
warranted as he put the bottle between his knees and hauled
on the corkscrew. Pop! They drank, and the act was as
a seal on a secret compact.

And it was that—a compact so secret that even they, the
parties to it, were scarcely conscious of the pledge. But as
the days passed, days of hasty clandestine comparing of
grievances in each other's rooms, days of whispering apart,
days followed by nights of companionship ashore, each realized how necessary was the other to his full appreciation of
life. Archy Bates found Mr. Spokesly a tower of strength
and a house of defence. If any complaint sounded in his
presence concerning stores, Mr. Spokesly was silent for a
space and then walked away. Only that vulgar third engineer was insensible to the superb reproof. "There goes the
flunkey's runner," he remarked, in execrable taste, and Mr.
Spokesly was obliged to ignore him. On the other hand,
Mr. Spokesly found in Archy Bates a sympathetic soul, a wit
that jumped with his own and understood without tedious
circumlocution "how he felt about it." More precious than
rubies is a friend who understands how you feel about it.
He found in Archy a gentleman who was master of what was
to Mr. Spokesly an incredible quantity of ready cash. At

first Mr. Spokesly had apologetically borrowed "half a quid
till to-morrow, being short somehow," and Archy had scorned
to split a sovereign. In some way only partially understood
by Mr. Spokesly as yet, certain eddies of the vast stream of
gold and paper which was turning the wheels of the war
swirled into the pockets of Archy Bates. He had it to burn,
as they say. It was bewildering in its variety. British,
American, French, Italian, Greek, Egyptian, and Japanese
notes were rolled into one inexhaustible wad. More bewildering even than this was Archy Bates's uncanny command
of gold. It was extraordinary how this impressed Mr.
Spokesly. At a time when sovereigns and eagles and napo-
leons had practically vanished from the pockets of the private
citizen, Archy Bates had bags of them. And like his paper
currency, it was of all nations. Ten-rouble Russian pieces,
twenty-drachma Greek pieces, Australian sovereigns, and
massive Indian medals worth twenty dollars each, chinked
and jingled against the homelier coinage of France and England. "Business, my boy, business!" he would explain with
a snigger when he met Mr. Spokesly's rapt gaze of amazement. Very good business, too, the latter thought, and sighed.
But there was one point about Archy which distinguished him
from many owners of gold. He spent it. There lay the
magic of his power over Mr. Spokesly's mesmerized soul.
He spent it. Mr. Spokesly saw him and helped him spend it.
Those princely disbursements night after night in Alexandria
postulated some source of supply. And night after night
Mr. Spokesly, pleasantly jingled with highballs and feminine
society, felt himself being drawn nearer and nearer the mysterious source from which gushed that cosmopolitan torrent
of money. Mr. Spokesly was in the right mood for the revelation. He was serious. He was a practical man. He
needed no London School of Mnemonics to teach him to cul-
tivate a man with plenty of money. When he and Archy
Bates had walked quickly away from the ship and passed the
guard at Number Six Gate, they could scarcely be recognized
by one who had seen them an hour before, Mr. Spokesly silently munching his dinner under the Old Man's frown,

Archy in his pantry, encased in a huge white apron, bending his sharp nose over the steaming dishes, and communicating in violent pantomime with the saloon waiter.

Now they stood side by side, brothers, magnificently superior to all the world. A dingy carriage rattled up and Archy waved it away impatiently. Another, with two horses and rubber tires, was hailed and engaged. "Might as well do the thing well," said Archy, and Mr. Spokesly agreed in every fibre of his soul. And it was the same with everything else. "My motto is," said Archy, "everything of the best, eh? Can't go far wrong then. He-he!" The third engineer, vulgarian that he was, would have laughed a shrill, derisive cackle had he heard that speech. The third engineer was under the illusion that only the virtuous have ideals. He was wrong. Archy Bates's profession of faith was sincere and genuine. He had an instinct for what he called the best, which was the most expensive. What else could be the best? A love of elegance and refinement was very widespread in those days of high wages and excessive profits. Archy's wife (for he had a wife and three children in a suburb of Liverpool) was rapidly filling her instalment-purchased home with costly furniture. Only a month ago a grand piano had been put in, and she had had the dining-room suite re-upholstered in real pigskin. Mr. Spokesly knew all this and it almost unmanned him to think that he was on the way to this eldorado. One night, soon after their arrival in Alexandria, Archy had hinted there was no reason why he, Mr. Spokesly, shouldn't be "in it," too. This was late in the evening, when they were seated on a balcony high above the glitter and noise of the Boulevard Ramleh, a balcony belonging to a house of fair but expensive reception, of which Archy was a munificent patron. Archy, after two bottles of whiskey, had become confidential. He had hinted that his friend Reggie should be "put next" the business which produced such amazing returns. Reggie had waited to hear more but, with amusing inconsequence, Archy had changed the subject, relapsed indeed into a tantalizing dalliance with a lady friend.

But to-night, in sober earnest, for Archy had had little besides a bottle of gin since rising in the morning, he proposed that they should join a business friend of his, and have a quiet little dinner somewhere. Mr. Spokesly was all eyes, all ears, all intelligent receptiveness. He enquired who the business friend might be, and Archy, who had his own enthusiasms, let himself go. His friend, Jack Miller, had been out there for years. With Swingles, the ship-chandlers. Occupied, Archy surmised, a very high position there. Had worked himself up. Plenty of skippers did business with Swingles simply because Jack was there. If he liked to leave, Archy hadn't any doubt he'd take a good half of Swingles' business with him. Knew all the languages, French, Greek, Arabic, and so on. Kept his own hours, went in and out as he liked. Archy only wished he had Jack Miller's job!

Mr. Spokesly listened greedily. As they debouched upon the great Place Mohammed Aly, with its myriads of lights and sounds, its illuminated Arabic night signs, its cracking of whips and tinkling of bells and glasses, its gorgeous, tessellated platoons of café tables, he took a deep breath. He felt he was upon the threshold of a larger life, inhaling a more invigorating air. It seemed to him he was about to quit the dreary humdrum world of watch-keeping and monthly wages for a region where dwelt those happy beings who had no fixed hours, who made money, who had it "to burn," as they say.

And Jack Miller, whom they met that night and many nights after, was a magnificent accessory of the illusion. He was a dapper little man in fashionable clothes, a runner for a local ship-chandler, who introduced them to half-a-dozen ship-captains of a certain type, and together they went round the vast tenderloin district of the city. Mr. Spokesly was conscious of a grand exaltation during the day when he recalled his nightly association with these gentlemen. There were others, dark-skinned Greeks and Levantines in long-tasselled fezes, who joined them in their pursuit of pleasure in the great blocks of buildings behind the Boulevard Ramleh and their jaunts, in taxicabs, to San Stefano. They were, as Archy put it, over whiskey and soda in his cabin, gentlemen worth knowing, men with property and businesses. And it was one of these, one evening on the balcony of the Casino at San Stefano, who mentioned casually that he often did business with Saloniki and that if Mr. Spokesly ever had any little things to dispose of on his return, he would be glad to make him an offer, privately, of course. He often did this with Mr. Bates, he added, to their mutual satisfaction. Mr. Spokesly was charmed.

And Captain Meredith, walking the upper bridge and seeing a good deal more than either Mr. Spokesly or Mr. Bates imagined, wondered how it would all end. Indeed, Captain Meredith did a good deal of wondering in those days. He saw the wages going steadily up and up, and discipline and efficiency going, quite as steadily, down and down. Here was this young sprig Chippenham, his acting second officer, a boy of nineteen with no license and no experience, pertly demanding more money. Captain Meredith recalled his own austere apprenticeship in sail, his still more austere gruelling as junior officer in tramps, the mean accommodation, the chill penury, the struggle to keep employed, and he smiled grimly. He had his own private views of the glory of war; but apart from this, he wondered greatly what the final upshot of it all would be for the Merchant Service in general and Mr. Spokesly in particular. For he could not help regarding his chief officer as a brother of the craft. He himself had received no illumination from the exponents of modern thought. He had never been impressed by the advertisements of the London School of Mnemonics, for example. He was so old-fashioned as to imagine that to get on, a man must work hard, study hard, live hard, and stand by for the chance to come. Mr. Spokesly, he knew quite well, had been through the same mill as himself, only some ten years or so later. He regarded him, therefore, as he could never regard Mr. Chippenham, for example, who had never been in sail and who didn't know an oxter-plate from an orlop-beam. As far as the natural shyness and taciturnity of Englishmen would allow him, he was anxious for Mr. Spokesly to do well. The man was singularly fortunate, in his opinion, to be chief mate so soon. In nine or ten years, perhaps, he would have the experience to warrant the owners' giving him a command. Provided, of course, that he stuck to his business and took an interest in the fortunes of the firm. It will be seen from this that Captain Meredith was a hopeless conservative and reactionary. One of his brother-captains whom he met at dinner ashore one evening actually told him so. "Why," said this gentleman as he held a match to Captain Meredith's cigar, "why, my chief officer told me to my face the other day that there was nothing in experience nowadays. One man was as good as another, he said, so long as he had his master's ticket. Yes! A fact!" Captain Meredith was aware, too, that his ideas concerning conscientious achievement and enthusiasm for one's employers were equally archaic. The young men of to-day seemed to regard their jobs with dislike and their employers with suspicion. Their sole obsession seemed to be money. He had had pointed out to him an intoxicated youth who was causing a disturbance in a hotel bar, a youth going out East to a ship as third officer at two hundred dollars a month, they said. And the tale was received by every junior officer in the harbour with hushed awe, although it was obvious that the object of their envy would probably be laid aside with delirium tremens before he could reach his billet. Captain Meredith noticed, too, that men who were engrossed in their work were rated "queer" and as back numbers. Even among captains he sensed a reluctance to discuss a professional problem. The third engineer, a skilled mechanic with a tongue like a rasp, and the second, a patient old dobbin who ought to have been promoted long ago, were examples of an older school, but the good captain was hardly in a position to appraise them professionally.

It was different with Mr. Spokesly. If anything happened to Captain Meredith himself, a sudden weight of responsibility would roll upon Mr. Spokesly that would, in the captain's opinion, crush him. For it must be confessed that licenses, diplomas, certificates, or whatever you call your engraved warrants to ply your trade, are no guarantee of character and nerve. Nor does efficiency in a subordinate capacity imply success in command. Just as some men are stormy and intractable nuisances until they reach the top, when they immediately assume a mysterious and impregnable composure, so others deliberately avoid rising above a comfortable mediocrity, conscious of their own limitations and well satisfied that some other human soul should endure the pangs of the supreme decision. Others there are, and Captain Meredith believed Mr. Spokesly was one of them, who lack knowledge of themselves, and who have not sufficient intelligence either to carry the burden or to refuse it.

This, of course, was not Mr. Spokesly's opinion as time went on. On the contrary, he had come to the conclusion that it was no use being a smart officer "if the captain wouldn't back a man up." He told Archy Bates that "the Old Man was doing all he knew to do him dirty." And Archy riposted at once with evidence that he himself was the victim of a foul conspiracy between the Captain and the crew over the grub. Mr. Spokesly would go out on deck from these pow-wows feeling very happy, for Archy never failed to open a bottle. Mr. Spokesly would sway a little as he walked forward to see how the work was going on in the forehold. The *Tanganyika*, having discharged most of her cargo, was now reloading a great deal of it in obedience to orders from certain invisible but omnipotent beings higher up. He would sway a little, and hold on to the hatch coaming, looking down upon the toilers below with an air of profound abstraction. Then he would move gently until he could raise his eyes and sweep a casual glance in the direction of the bridge. Sometimes he would see the Old Man's head as he strode to and fro. On one occasion he "caught 'im at it," as he told Archy. "Yes, he was spying on me. Watching me. See his game? I tell you, Archy, it makes a man sick. Fancy havin' to work under a man like that. Watchin' me. Now he'll write home to the owners in his confidential report. Well, let him. Thanks to you, I got more than one egg in the basket. Sometimes, I feel inclined to go and demand my discharge. I would, only it's war time. Got to carry on in war time."

Archy Bates nodded over his glass and dipped his long sharp nose into it before making an audible reply. "Me, too!" he said, setting the glass down empty. "Me, too! If it wasn't for the war and everybody having to do their bit, I'd swallow the anchor to-morrow."

And they sat for a moment in silence, each honestly believing the other, and thinking poignantly of home. Over the steward's bunk, stuffed into a corner of the frame that enclosed his wife's portrait, was a photograph of a girl, stark naked save for a wrist watch and a feather in her black hair, sitting on Archy's knee. From behind this Mrs. Bates's thin face and flat bosom peeped out, and her eyes seemed to be fixed thoughtfully upon the two exiled patriots who sat with uplifted glasses before her.

And on one occasion, Mr. Spokesly, who was spending the evening on board because steam had been raised for sailing, and because the owners had a tyrannical rule to that effect—Mr. Spokesly had a dream. He confessed to Archy that in common honesty he didn't know whether he was awake or asleep. A sort of vision! He was lying on his bunk with one of the manuals of the London School of Mnemonics in his hand which he was, he imagined, reading. It was an essay on "Concentration," and perhaps his thoughts had wandered a bit. . . . Anyhow, as he lay there, in among his thoughts slipped a new and alien impression that there was somebody in the room. He didn't turn his head, but just lay on in contemplation of this possibility. Perhaps he had half-closed his eyes, for the instructions how to concentrate included a note that the brain worked better if you lay down and shut out the distracting phenomena of existence. Everything was soft and hazy at the time. The notion that someone was there and yet not there intrigued him. And even a physical change, a faint movement of the air caused by somebody altering his position in space, a faint access of minute sounds entering by a cleared doorway, did not rouse his suspicions. On the contrary, he must have dozed, he told Archy solemnly. For the next thing he remembered with any approach to coherence was a figure with its back to him, standing by the toilet shelf, holding up an empty glass and smelling it. . . . A figure he knew. Yes, he nodded to Archy, who clicked his teeth and threw up his head, it was the Old Man. And as swiftly as it had come, it was gone. Mr. Spokesly found himself up on one elbow, pressing thumb and forefinger into his eyes, and then peering from the brightness of the light above his head into the rose-shaded twilight of the cabin. There was no one there. Everything was just the same. The glass was still there on the mahogany shelf, exactly as he had left it after taking a tot of whiskey before lying down. Now wasn't that a curious experience, he demanded?

But Archy was no votary of psychic phenomena. He waved everything of that sort clean out of existence. What time was it? Quarter-past eight? Why, he saw the Old Man himself sneaking up the saloon stairs to the chart-room about that time. Of course it was the Old Man. Just the sort of game he would be up to. It was revolting. Only the other day he had given orders for his own supply of spirits to be put in his bedroom instead of leaving it in Archy's charge. Never said a word to *him*, mind you! Told the second steward to tell the chief steward. See the game? Couldn't speak out like a man and say he'd missed a bottle or so. Justice? There is no such thing as justice when you work for an underhand, sneaking, spying . . .

Archy Bates had stopped short in his catalogue of the captain's deformities as though he had been suddenly throttled. A bell was buzzing in the pantry. They looked at each other. Archy put down his glass, listened for a moment, hissed venomously, "That's him!" and slipped out. Mr. Spokesly sat still while his friend was away answering the summons, and nursed the rage in his heart to a dull glow. At times it died out and he shivered as before a blackened fire, the dead ashes of a moody disgust of life. One of the tragedies of mediocrity is the confused nature of our emotions. We are like cracked bells, goodly enough in outward form and fashion, but we don't ring true. Our intelligence shows us many things about ourselves but fails to evoke a master passion. In Mr. Spokesly's case, his great desire to have riches did not obscure from his gaze the austere beauties of rectitude and the slow climb to an honourable command. Neither did it narrow down his interests to the sordid goal to which he aspired. The boding apprehension which was rising like a black cloud at the back of his mind, that he was neglecting his work, only reflected and magnified the blaze of his resentment. What encouragement had he, he would like to know. Here he was, slaving away, and no satisfaction. Nothing he did was right. Spied on! Ignored! Treated like a dog! Well, he would see. If this little business of Archy's came off, he would see if he was going to be trodden on by any shipmaster. Archy. . . .

For a moment the clear vision of Archy obsequiously waiting on the captain, getting him some hot water perhaps, or laying out a fresh suit of underwear, troubled the darkness of Mr. Spokesly's ruminations. A clear vision, such as even the mediocre have at times. And close to it, as though another miniature in another oval frame, a sharp, clear-cut memory of Ada Rivers looking up at him with gray adoring eyes, the proud tremble of her passionate mouth, the curve of her white throat. . . .

Mr. Spokesly rose to his feet and he caught sight of the naked girl sitting on Archy's knee, and of the bourgeois little face looking out from behind it. Archy's wife! A long dizzy wave of revulsion made Mr. Spokesly feel momentarily faint and he clutched the edge of the bunk board. For a moment he stood, slack-mouthed and moody-eyed, gazing at the photographs. Then he turned away and crept softly along the corridor.

Archy was surprised, on his return, to find him gone.

CHAPTER III

MUCH of the diversity and nearly all the bitterness of our lives are due to the fact that only rarely do we encounter our exact contemporaries. In any sphere where all start at a prescribed age, as in great universities and public services, there is a tendency to become standardized, to be only one example of a prevalent type. Ambition is coördinated, jealousy is neutralized; and the hot lava-flow of individualist passion cools and hardens to an admirable solidity and composure. One's exact contemporaries are around in throngs. One has no misgivings, no heartburn, no exasperation with fate. The fortunate being whose destiny lies this way takes on the gravity, the immobility, and the polish of an antique statue. The common people pass him as they pass the Elgin marbles—without emotion; but they are aware subconsciously of the cold pure beauty of outline, the absolute fidelity to type, which is the melancholy justification of his existence.

But the common people themselves are not like that. They quit their exact contemporaries at school and thenceforth are out upon the sea of life with men of all ages and breedings and nationalities around them and pressing them hard. They act and are reacted upon. Most of them nurse a secret grievance. Very few of them have any code of honour beyond law and decency. They are very largely needy adventurers, living by their wits, and are ready to pay money to those who profess to show them how they can increase their incomes, or obtain a pension, or "better their positions," or cure themselves of the innumerable physical disabilities which their fatuous ignorance and indolence have brought upon them. They love to decipher word competitions, football competitions, racing competitions. They

have the high-binder's passion for getting something for
nothing, his dislike to real work.   And this lack of contempo-
rary associates, this rough-and-tumble aspect of the world,
induces them to regard their vices as virtues and themselves
as oppressed helots struggling under the iron heels of those
whom mere luck and cunning have placed in authority over
them.   The London School of Mnemonics was making a
hundred thousand pounds a year net profit out of these people
in England alone.   Even the grim witticism of the company
promoter, that there is "a sucker born every minute," seems
inadequate to account for so monstrous a simplicity of soul.
The fact is, the very boldness of the trick rendered it easy.
You paid your guinea, and in due course, in due secrecy, and
under duly sworn promises to divulge no hint of their contents to a living soul, you received a number of refined-looking
pamphlets containing a couple of thousand words each.   You
thrilled as you joined in the game.   Even Captain Meredith,
sitting in his chart room and looking through Number Four,
which Mr. Spokesly had inadvertently left on the table, was
tickled by the subtle atmosphere of the style.   This, he
divined, was the newly discovered rapid-transit route to the
Fortunate Isles, and his expression hardened to rigid attention as his eye fell on the testimony of "a ship's officer."
This gentleman had risen from the humble position of fourth
officer to the command "of one of our largest liners" in the
miraculously brief period of eighteen months, and ascribed
this success entirely to the lessons of the London School of
Mnemonics.   Captain Meredith felt he would like to have a
talk with this person; but his mind became preoccupied with
another aspect of the case.   Here, he felt, lay the explanation
of a good deal of Mr. Spokesly's recent behaviour.   Captain
Meredith was fully aware of the perilous nature of an un-
married man's life between thirty and forty.   He himself had
married at thirty-four, having been frankly terrified by the
spiritual difficulties which he beheld surrounding a continued
celibacy when combined with a life of responsible command
at sea.   And as he sat back on the settee of his chart-room
and looked out over the top of Pamphlet Number Four at the

steel-blue waters of the Mediterranean, he became dimly aware of Mr. Spokesly's condition. He could not have set down in ordered phrases the conclusions at which he was arriving; a ship's captain in time of war has not the leisure to reduce psychological phenomena to their ultimate first principles; but he was not far wrong in muttering, inaudibly, that "the man was rattled." It was this tendency to try and understand his officers which lay at the back of his leniency towards Mr. Spokesly, a leniency which Mr. Spokesly himself, in later, saner moments, found it difficult to comprehend.

Mr. Spokesly had "pulled himself together," as he expressed it, when they went to sea. Archy Bates tacitly retired into the background. Archy himself was fully aware that the bosom friendliness of the days and nights in harbour could not continue at sea, and Mr. Spokesly ceased to share the never-ending refreshment without which Archy could no longer support existence. Mr. Spokesly felt better at once, for alcohol had no real hold upon his system. He toiled laboriously through the astonishing physical exercises which the London School of Mnemonics artfully suggested were an aid to mental improvement. He practised Concentration, Observation, and something the pamphlets called Intensive Excogitation, which nearly made him cross-eyed. Incidentally, he gathered incongruous scraps of information about Alcibiades, Erasmus, Savonarola, Nostradamus, Arminius Vámbéry, and Doctor Johnson. It was while he was busy carrying out their instructions for accurate observation, that Captain Meredith asked him, calmly enough, if he had noticed that the binnacle of Number Two lifeboat was smashed and useless. Mr. Spokesly assumed a mulish expression and said, No, he hadn't. Well, in future, he was to have the boats not only made ready, but *kept* ready, quite ready, all the time. Mr. Spokesly, looking still more mulish, said he'd attend to it.

With the gimcrack little sheet copper binnacle in his hand, Mr. Spokesly made his way to the chief engineer's room. He felt rather bitter. Here he'd been going along nicely for two whole days and now this happens! Spoken to like a dog over a little petty thing like this. As if it was *his* fault the blamed thing had got smashed. Did he notice it! As if the chief officer of a ship had no more to do than moon round the deck, looking at things. . . .

If Captain Meredith had told Mr. Spokesly that he himself had achieved a rung in the ladder by the simple process of paying very strict attention to his boats, it would have been the bare truth, but Mr. Spokesly would not have seen the point. He found the chief engineer standing before his desk in some deshabille, filling a black briar. His broad, hairy torso was almost naked, for the scanty singlet was torn under the arms and ripped across the bosom. His high-coloured features and reddish moustache were smeared with black oil, and he was breathing in heaves as though he had been running. When Mr. Spokesly presented his broken binnacle the chief glanced at it with a scarcely perceptible flicker of his bushy eyebrows and continued to fill his pipe from a canister on the desk.

"Well, Mr. Spokesly," he remarked in a voice suitable for addressing an immense open-air meeting. "Well, what is it now?" And he struck a match and lit his pipe.

Mr. Spokesly explained that he wanted it mended.

"Oh, you want it mended. Well, why don't you ship a tinker, my fine fellow? Eh? Why not indent for a tinker? You've got a carpenter and a lamp trimmer and a bo'sun and a squad of quartermasters. What's a tinker more or less?" And sitting back in his swivel chair and blowing great clouds, he looked maliciously at Mr. Spokesly. The chief was a man with an atmosphere. He had an immense experience, which he kept to himself save at the hour of need. He had an admirable staff who did just what he wanted without any rhetoric. Save at times like the present moment, when Mr. Spokesly, though he was quite unaware of it, was very much *de trop* owing to a breakdown in the engine room, the chief was a tolerant and breezy example of the old school. Just now, with the sweat cooling on his back and a battered binnacle offered to him for repair, he took refuge in dry malice. He studied Mr. Spokesly mercilessly. He was, or

at any rate he looked, perfectly aware of the extreme unfitness
of Mr. Spokesly's bodily frame, for Mr. Spokesly had done no
real work since he had passed for second mate eleven years
before. The chief himself was inclined to obesity, for he
verged on fifty and his frame was of the herculean type, need-
ing much nourishment and upholstery. But there was a
difference between the huge, red-freckled and hirsute masses
upon his bones and the soft puffiness of Mr. Spokesly's fatty
degeneration. The latter's double chin was in singular contrast with the massive and muscular salience that gave the
chief's face an expression of indomitable vigour. He sat
there, tipping himself slightly back in his swivel chair, looking
quizzically at Mr. Spokesly through the tobacco smoke. Mr.
Spokesly was annoyed. The chief had always been a decent
sort, he had imagined, and here he was jibbing at a little
thing like this. After all, it was the engineer's business to do
these things. He, an officer, couldn't be expected to attend
to petty details. . . . A short figure with a towel over
his naked shoulders appeared abruptly out of the engine
room and passed along the alleyway. The chief called in
his stentorian tones, which issued from between twisted and
broken teeth, "Hi, Mr. Tolleshunt, here's a job for ye.
Mate wants a binnacle fixed." And Mr. Spokesly's mind
became easy. A voice from behind a slammed door said that
the mate could take his binnacle and chase himself round the
deck with it, and the chief cackled. Mr. Tolleshunt came
out of his room again on his way to the bathroom. He was a
young man with a thick white neck, and black eyes set in a
dirty, dead-white face which bore an expression of smouldering rage. This, however, was merely an index of character
which, like many such indexes, was misleading. Mr. Tolleshunt was not ill-tempered, but he had a morbid passion for
efficiency. He was an idealist, with a practical working
ideal. He was not prepared to accept anything in the world
as an adequate substitute for achievement. He had seen
through Mr. Spokesly at once, for your idealist is often a
clairvoyant of character. And as he passed along to his bath,
his black eyes smouldered upon the chief officer, who re-

membered the many insults he had swallowed from this dirty engineer, and hated him. Suddenly Mr. Tolleshunt paused, with his hand on the bathroom door, and looked back. His dead-white face, the firm modelling of cheek and chin curiously exaggerated by the black smears of grease, broke into a grim smile as he spoke.

"Say, d'you know who I am, Mister?" he asked, and added, "I'll tell ye. I'm the Thorn in the Flesh," and he disappeared into the bathroom, whence came the rumble of water being boiled up by steam. Mr. Spokesly's eyes returned to the burly gentleman who was regarding him with amusement. Mr. Spokesly threw up his hands.

"Well," he said, looking stonily at nothing, "there it is. I was told to get it fixed, an'——"

"Fix it then," said the chief quietly. Mr. Spokesly almost bridled.

"Not my work," he muttered.

"Oh, I see; it's mine, you mean!" surmised the other in a tone of assumed enlightenment.

"It's engineer's work," said Mr. Spokesly irritably. The chief made no reply for a moment, merely studying Mr. Spokesly intently.

"See here, Mister," he began, and reached out a huge hand to close the door. "See here, Mister, you're under a misapprehension. Now I'll tell you the whole trouble. You heard Mr. Tolleshunt just now. D'ye know what he meant when he said he was the Thorn in the Flesh? It's a joke of ours in the mess room. He meant your flesh. And the reason for that is that you men up on the bridge are in a false position. Ye have executive power without knowledge. Ye command a ship and what do ye know about a ship? To whom do ye come for help, whether it is steering or driving or discharging or salving or anything? You want the same consideration and power that you have on a sailing-ship, where you know all about the gear and make out yourselves. Here, you just have to stand by while we do it. And on top o' that, you come down here with your silly damn breakages and expect us to be tinkers as well. You think Mr. Tolleshunt is sadly deficient in respect, I dare say. But what of his side o' the question? He's been up all night and all morning on a breakdown. So's the second, who's still at it. So have I, for that matter. We've all three of us got just as good tickets as you. Ye never heard about it? Of course not. What could ye do for us? When ye've pulled that handle on the bridge and heard the gong answer, you're finished! Ye're in charge of a box of mechanism of which ye know nothing. Ye walk about in uniform and talk big about yer work, and what does it all amount to? Ye're a young man, and I'm, well, not so young, and I tell ye friendly, Mister, ye're a joke. Ye're what the newspapers call an anachronism or an anomaly, I forget which. Ye'll never get men like young Tolleshunt, men who know their work from A to Z, to treat ye seriously unless ye take hold and study a ship for what she is, a mass o' machinery. Ye'll have to get shut o' the notion that as soon as ye become officers, ye must lose the use o' your hands. Now there's just as much engineerin' about that binnacle as there is in a kettle or a rabbit hutch. Put one o' your young apprentices to it, and if he can't, make him learn. I've been with old-time skippers who could do anything, from wire-splicing to welding an anchor shackle. They learned in the yard before they went to sea. Your young fellers can do nothing except slather a hose round the decks and ask for higher wages. Now don't be sore because I'm telling ye the truth. We're busy and we're tired. We've all sorts o' trouble you can't understand, vital matters that mean speed and safety. Suppose, after a spell on the bridge in fog, ye were to come down to yer room and find me there with some ash-bags to sew up, eh? Imagine it! Just imagine it!"

He sat there, looking sideways at Mr. Spokesly, his pipe between his enormous thumb and knuckle, asking Mr. Spokesly to imagine this fearsome thing. But Mr. Spokesly's imagination was for the time being out of commission. He was scarcely conscious of the request, so intensely preoccupied was he with the ghastly cleavage between his own estimate of his position and the chief's. Back of all these frank insults to his dignity, Mr. Spokesly scented the sinister prejudice of his commander. As he strode, in severe mental disarray, back to his room, he discovered a conviction that the chief "had been pumpin' the Old Man." Not that he needed any pumping, of course. It would be only too like him to blab to an engineer about his own officers. Well, there it was! Mr. Spokesly pitched the hapless binnacle on the settee and turned to the wash-stand. Perhaps it was due to the course of the London School of Mnemonics, the course in tracing the association of ideas, that when his eye fell on the tumblers in the rack he should think of that abominable trick of the Old Man sneaking in and smelling the glass to see if he, Mr. Spokesly, had been drinking. Couldn't trust him that far! Do what he would he could give no satisfaction. He would ask to be paid off to-morrow as soon as they dropped anchor in Saloniki harbour. That would be the best way. Just pull out of it. They would realize, when he was gone, the sort of man they had lost. The flame of indignation died out again and he sat moodily pondering the difficulty of commanding an adequate appreciation. Command! The word stung him to bodily movement. If only he could once grasp the sceptre, he could defy them all. He would have the whip-hand then. And there were ways, there were ways of making money. Some he had heard of on this run were quadrupling their incomes. Archy had whispered incredible stories of skippers and stewards working together . . . working together. Perhaps it would be worth while to stick to the ship for a voyage or so, even if he did have to put up with this sort of thing. They would reach Saloniki in a few hours, and then they would see.

It frequently happens that moods which would logically drive men mad, moods which seem to have no natural anti-dote, are broken up and neutralized by some entirely fortui-tous event. It is not too much to say that Mr. Spokesly's grievances were inducing one of these moods, when the wholesome activity of affairs on the forecastle-head, the keen autumn wind blowing across the bony ridges of Chalcidice, and the professional criticism evoked by the ships outward-bound, blew the foul vapours away. Captain Meredith, whose reflective and unchallenging blue eyes were visible between the weather-cloth and the laced peak of his cap, made a mental note that "the man was doing himself justice." Of course Captain Meredith did not perceive how very wide of the mark his sensible phrase led him. Mr. Spokesly always did himself justice. What he was eternally hunting for, in and out of the maze in which he spent his life, was justice from others. Captain Meredith did not realize that a middle-aged man with a grievance is like a man who has been skinned—to touch him causes the most exquisite agony. Nay, merely to exist, to permit the orderly march of every-day routine, chafes him to the verge of hysteria. It was nothing to Mr. Spokesly that he was serving his country; nothing to him that he was in imminent peril by mine and torpedo. During the voyage he had scarcely noticed the occasional formal slips that came from the wireless house informing them that an enemy submarine was operating in such and such a position, so many miles ahead or astern as the case might be. Mr. Spokesly had never seen a sub-marine and he didn't want to. The whole business of war in his eyes became a ghastly farce so long as he was not appre-ciated at his true worth. It might almost be said that at times he was indifferent to the outcome of the gigantic struggle. A horrible unrest assailed him. The world was heaving in a death grapple with the powers of darkness and he was as nothing in the balance.

But as he walked the forecastle-head and the *Tanganyika* passed through the bottle neck of Kara Burun into the wide waters of the gulf-head, he was restored to a normal atten-tion to the cut-and-dried duties of his calling. There was exhilaration in the thought of foregathering once more with Archy, of going ashore in a new port. And there would be letters. He drew a deep breath. Ada would write. Un-consciously he straightened up. A warm glow suffused him as he recalled her dark-gray, adoring eyes and the deep tremble of her voice as she called him her sailor sweetheart. After all, he was that. He was understood there, he thought, and was comforted. Rung by rung he climbed up out of the dark dank well in which he had been dwelling until, when the compressors had been screwed up tight and the *Tanganyika* was swinging gently on her eighty fathom of cable, he was recapitulating the heartening words he had last read in his "course" in the London School of Mnemonics.

Think well of yourself and your ability, it ran. *Get the habit of believing in your own ambition. This is only another way of saying that faith can move mountains. But remember that to be satisfied with what you are is to lose grip. If you are standing still you are slipping back. This paradox will be shown.* . . .

It was some hours later, after dinner, that Captain Meredith sat at the desk in his room looking out of the big side-scuttle at the blood-red and purple of the western sky beyond the Vardar delta. It was such a sunset as one may see across Lake Pontchartrain in the fall, or looking up some aisle of the dark silent forests that fringe the swamps of the Georgia coast. It has the opaque glamour that comes from the dense vapours rising from a marsh, the tangible beauty of a giant curtain rather than the far glories of miles of ambient mountain air. But Captain Meredith was not occupied with esthetic musings. In his hand he held a letter from the superintendent in London, and he sought seclusion, as was his wont, in looking out towards the immense polychrome of the sky. For the letter contained orders which might involve him in some difficulties. He was instructed to file, in an enclosed form, precise particulars of all his officers' records, and return them accompanied by his own opinion as to their fitness for promotion. It would be necessary, he was informed, to engage a large number of additional officers for a fleet which the company had purchased all standing, and the directors were anxious that those already in their employ should have the pick of the billets. It was important, he was warned, that he use care in recommending any man, as the directors proposed to act upon these suggestions, and the failure of a nominee would react unfavourably upon the prestige of the commander responsible for the report.

Like all men who have grown up inside the protecting walls of tradition and routine, Captain Meredith was unable to view a situation without prejudice. Some small portion of free and independent judgment he had, or he would never have become master; but the bulk of the decisions which he had to make were obtained by unconscious reference to rules, written or unwritten. This order, however, involved just that small part of his mental equipment which made his work of interest to him, his imagination if you like. It forced him to take a far wider view than was ordinarily advisable. He was aware of the popular legends which have grown around great commanders—legends of their genius for selecting subordinates, their uncanny aptitude for appraising a man's powers at a glance. Not so easy, Captain Meredith had found it. Like most of us, he had in time cultivated a habit of suspending judgment, a habit of discounting the dreadful efficiency of the new broom, the total abstainer, the college-graduate, and the newly married. What he waited for time to reveal was the man's principle. Without the main girder and tie-ribs of principle, all was as nothing. And yet what comprised this principle Captain Meredith would have been sore put to it to explain. It was not enthusiasm, nor was it will power. It was not even intellect or civil responsi-bility. It was deeper than any of these, a subtle manifes-tation of character as elusive and imponderable as a beam of light or the expression on a man's face. Somewhat to his surprise Captain Meredith's reflections showed him that not even compatibility of temperament had much to do with it. He and old McGinnis had never been warm friends, had even had frequent differences on minor details of executive routine. Neither of them would have invited the other to his home, had the opportunity served. That did not mat-ter. He had had some experience of officers quite different from Mr. McGinnis, clever, gay young men, "good mixers," passengers' favourites, and he had discovered that a man may be a brilliant social success and a useless incumbrance at the same time. To state the problem to himself was difficult, but it was forced upon him irresistibly when he endeavoured to formulate his mature conclusions upon the subject of Mr. Spokesly. His chief officer was his chief concern. Of the others he was able to set down a fairly just and intelligible estimate. Young Chippenham was a bundle of amiable possibilities. He would have to get his certificates before the company would make him or break him. The chief engineer was at the other end of the scale. His name was made. Behind him was a career of solid responsibility, of grave crises met and mastered with cool generalship and unbeatable energy. He was one of those men who carry in their own personality the prestige of a race, a nation, and a learned profession. Of the others it would be safe to take his verdict. Mr. Spokesly, therefore, remained the chief source of anxiety. For it was not a simple question of bearing witness to Mr. Spokesly's ability as a seaman, as a navigator, or as a desirable junior officer. The tremendous responsibility from which Captain Meredith shrank was twofold. On the one hand, he had to accept the onus of recommending his chief officer for a command. On the other lay the grave danger of injustice to a brother professional. Mr. Spokesly was a man no longer in his first youth, no doubt engaged to be married, with ambitions and aspirations with which Captain Meredith had the deepest sympathy. It was no small matter to stop a man's promotion. He remembered how he himself, piqued at some ungenerous act of the company, had talked of resignation, and his commander had taken him by the arm and muttered contemptuously, "And spoil yourself for life, eh?" And when asked "How?" that same shipmaster had drawn a brutal picture of a man throwing up a billet just as he was getting a name, entering another employ as a junior, spending years working up to chief mate again, only to find about a score of active, intelligent, and experienced officers on the list ahead of him, and gradually resigning himself to the colourless existence of an elderly failure. Captain Meredith was not the man to condemn a brother officer to such a fate without an overwhelming conviction. Rather would he . . .

But his thoughts refused to travel that road. He sat looking out at the sombre beauty of the sky, noting the long rigid black bar that divided sharply the dark swamps from the shining pallor of the roadstead. He tapped his teeth with his pencil. No, he was not prepared to jeopardize his own prospects. He had a family. He hoped to spend more time with them later . . . after the war. He was beginning to think sea life was narrowing. One got out of touch with so many phases of human interest and activity. . . . One toiled and moiled, and suffered agonies of anxiety and defeated vigilance; sleep and leisure went by the board for days; one found fault and made mistakes; superior young men in warships asked sarcastic questions during the small hours; and all to what end? After all, one only earned for all this the salary which a successful barrister or surgeon would pay his chauffeur. It was preposterous, when one came to regard it. So Captain Meredith's thoughts ran on, with a sort of light bitterness, sharpening their flavour and inclining him to charity. In more senses than one, he and Mr. Spokesly were in the same boat. He put his papers away in a drawer, picked up his cigar to take the air on the bridge. Without registering any final and irrevocable decision, he had made a mental note that "unless the man made an ass of himself" he would not stand in his way.

The sun, concealed behind a distant range, threw up a ruddy and vigorous glow as from an open cupola, but the roadstead lay in a profound shadow whose edge began to sparkle with coloured lights of a singular distinctness and individuality. It was like watching from the depths of space a congregation of blessed yet still intensely personal spirits on the heavenly shores. They stood in clusters or apart, in long lines or zigzags far up the mountain side. At times they were obliterated by trolley cars—gently moving glares which bore on their foreheads flashing blue-white gems. At other times a fountain of sparks indicated an otherwise invisible puff of smoke from a locomotive, and whole galaxies of shining points would vanish while an ammunition train moved laboriously across the city. But no knowledge of the actual causes could destroy the illusion that the lights were informed with an intelligent vitality. They winked and quivered with mysterious emotions. They went on journeys among other fixed stars of greater magnitude. They came out in boats over the dark water as though possessed with a passion for exploring, and then, losing heart, would go back in a hurry, or else expire. They raced along country roads and vanished in folds of the hills. They danced and were smitten with idiotic immobility. They were born, and they died sudden and inexplicable deaths. They were shocked, or were filled with calm content. Low down on the edge of the shore, where an open-air cinema was working convulsively, the lights had collected in some excitement around the screen. Captain Meredith, raising his night glasses to inspect this novel portent, imagined himself watching a square hole in a dark spangled curtain, through which a drama of inconceivable brightness and rapidity could be observed. It was, the captain imagined whimsically, like watching a huge brain at work, if such a thing were possible. He occasionally took refuge from himself in such reflections. Without any pretence to originality, he occasionally found himself in possession of thoughts for which custom had provided no suitable phrase. With the humility common to those of gentle birth who have followed the sea, he kept the results to himself. Even in letters to his wife, he adhered to the conventional insipidity that makes an Englishman's letters home one of the wonders of the world. He had become somewhat fearful of originality, even in others, during his honeymoon, when he had tried timidly to interest his wife in a novel he was reading. It was a novel about sailors and the sea, of all things in the world, and Captain Meredith had been so intrigued with the notion of a story written about sailors without distorting them out of all recognition that he couldn't keep it to himself. And he had been completely nonplussed when his gentle, blonde, and slightly angular young wife had displayed not merely a tepid lack of interest but downright dislike. "I don't like it," she had said acidly, and returned to her own book, an interminable tale of gipsies and highwaymen in masks, and a "reigning toast" with forty thousand pounds. They had been married some time before he realized just

what it was she didn't like in the story. And when he realized it, he put the thought from him in trepidation, for he
was prepared to sacrifice everything for her sake. She embodied for him all that he craved of England. She was
typical, as she bent over their one child, a flaxen-haired little
girl with incredibly thin limbs. And he was typical, too—as
he thought of them and their setting at Ealing—the modern
Englishman who has given intellectual hostages to fortune.

CHAPTER IV

MR. SPOKESLY once said in so many words that he disbelieved utterly in premonition. There was, he said, nothing in it. If there were, he remarked, we should be different. When pressed, he admitted freely that if we could read the signs we might get adequate warning of impending events; but by the time we have gotten the experience we are too old to bother about the future at all. This, of course, was when the war was finished and Mr. Spokesly, with the rest of the Merchant Service, had slipped back into that obscure neglect from which they had temporarily emerged. The gist of his remarks, therefore, seems to bear out the view that he had not the faintest notion, when he went ashore that evening in Saloniki with the gifted and amusing Mr. Bates, that he was on the brink of a fundamental change in his life. Looking back, he was almost induced to imagine that it was someone else who came ashore with Mr. Bates, a sort of distant relation, say, who had borrowed his body for the evening. And he was inclined to admit that, assuming what the philosophers say is true—that the only use of knowledge is for the purpose of action—it would preserve our idealism if our subconscious adumbrations could only be induced to function in a more emphatic manner.

The reason for interjecting this sample of Mr. Spokesly's later mentality is to be rid of any possible ambiguity. If Mr. Spokesly had been nothing more than Mr. Bates's boon companion his story would not be worth telling, there being obviously so many other more interesting people in the world. We have seen that Mr. Spokesly himself was aware of his real value, and had appealed to the London School of Mnemonics to elucidate his latent self from the commonplace shell in which he strove. The London School of Mnemonics

45

responded nobly according to its doctrines. It supplied him with an astonishing quantity of intellectual fuel, so to say, but omitted to indicate how it was to be ignited. Indeed, it is very singular how public and commercial organizations continually lose sight of the fact that in the spiritual world spontaneous combustion does not exist. And it is also true that the stark and secular desires of a man's soul, however powerful they may be to achieve a multiplicity of base ends, can do nothing for the man himself unless they are illuminated and shot through by some grand passion, whether of friendship, religion, or love. Which of these, depends upon the man. Some fortunate beings are the exponents of all three. Most of us, and Mr. Spokesly was one, are destined to know very little of either friendship or religion. So much might have been postulated. He was under no illusions as to his emotional resources. His remark that he could fall in love with almost any girl, so long as she had a bit o' money, was really a very fine declaration of extreme modesty. The virtuous are less humble. They lay extravagant claims to the privilege of having an ideal. Mr. Spokesly, as he sat beside Mr. Bates, who was smiling to himself in the darkness, watched the flashing lights of the Place de la Liberté grow larger and larger; and, as the din of the traffic reached his ears, experienced that feeling of pleasant and passive receptivity which he learned in time to know as the inevitable precursor of some momentous change.

Not so Mr. Bates, who smiled in the darkness. Mr. Bates was one of those human beings who manifest the shadowless and unwinking intelligence of the lower animals. The past, to Mr. Bates, was a period in which he had done well. The future was a period in which he would do well. Between these two delectable countries Mr. Bates moved gently along, a slightly intoxicated optimist. The perils of the sea and of war, the hatred of man or the wrath of God made no conscious impression upon Mr. Bates at all. Any of them might crush him at any moment, but he proceeded steadily upon his predatory way very much as a spider crossing a path proceeds until some careless but omnipotent passer crushes it beneath his heel. His attitude towards the gigantic engines of human destiny, which preoccupy most of us so much, was expressed in the pussy-cat smile in the darkness—a smile unseen and undesired.

"We'll go into Floka's first," he remarked, as the boat bumped the marble steps between the kiosks of the Place. He stood up, and his smile was illuminated by the sizzling glare of the arc lights along the quay, a smile that was, as we have said, fitted on over his face, and which bobbed up and down in obedience to the rhythmic undulations of the boat in the water. They waited for a moment until the Greek had made fast, and then stepped ashore.

"Why, is that a good place?" enquired Mr. Spokesly.

"Oh, yes. The *best* place. My friend, he goes there often. By and by, of course, we'll go along and see the talent. I'll show you, my boy. Believe me. . . ." They crossed the car lines and walked towards the café which Mr. Bates's friend honoured. Floka's was full. The little tables outside were thickly populated with gentlemen engaged in the national pastime of cigarette-smoking and coffee-drinking, and the grandiose interior, as severe and lofty and dirty as a Balkan politician, was thick with smoke and murmurous with conversation and the consumption of food. Mr. Bates led the way to a far corner where a long thin man, his frock coat falling away open from a heavily brocaded vest with onyx buttons, and his scarlet tarboosh on one side of his head, was lolling on the crimson plush cushions. In one hand he held the stem of an amber-mouthed *narghileh*. On the table was an empty coffee cup and a glass of mastic. Across his long thin thighs lay a Greek newspaper. He was reclining completely inert, gazing moodily across the crowded restaurant. The alteration in his demeanour when he became aware of Mr. Bates standing before him was dramatic. It was as though he had suddenly seen a very funny joke and had been subjected to an electric current of high voltage at the same time. He sprang to his feet with extraordinary animation, and his face was contorted from a sombre melancholy to what seemed to be an almost demoniac joy. It would be a solecism to say he looked as though a fortune had been left him. No one was at all likely to leave Mr. Dainopoulos a fortune. No one had ever left anything of value within his reach without regretting it extremely. It will suffice to say that his features registered a certain degree of pleasure upon seeing Mr. Bates.

"Why, my dear friend!" he exclaimed in a sort of muffled scream, and he wrung the honest hand of Mr. Bates as though that gentleman had only that moment rescued him from a combination of drowning and bankruptcy. "And how are you? Sit down if you please. What will you have to drink? You must be—what you call it?—dry. Ha-ha! Sit down. This is good luck. Your friend? I am very pleased. Sit down please. Here!" He clapped his hands with frightful vehemence, and held up a distracted waiter who was in full flight towards a distant table with a loaded tray. Mr. Dainopoulos, gently pressing Mr. Bates and Mr. Spokesly into two chairs, addressed the waiter as Herakles and gave him an order which sounded to his guests like a loose board being ripped forcibly from a nailed-up box. Mr. Spokesly, sitting immediately opposite this monster of hospitality, was not favourably impressed. Mr. Dainopoulos rarely impressed people favourably at first. The long emaciated face had the texture of the uppers of an old buckskin shoe. The blood-shot brown eyes in their reddened sockets seemed in danger of falling into the great pouches of loose skin below them. The mouth, full of sharp yellow teeth and open as though about to yawn, had been slit back to the salience of the jaw at some time and had been sewn up in a sketchy fashion indicated by a white zig-zag scar like a flash of lightning. As he talked this scar worked with disconcerting vivacity. Mr. Spokesly turned with relief to the whiskies and sodas which appeared, borne by the industrious Herakles.

"And how is business?" asked Mr. Bates, having lifted his glass and set it down empty. Beyond three or four sherries and bitters and a glass of gin and vermouth, before coming ashore, he had drunk nothing all day. He was thirsty. "And how is business?"

A simple question. And yet Mr. Dainopoulos did not render a simple answer. He regarded Mr. Bates for a moment and then turned his head cautiously to right and left. Preserving an impressive silence he caught Mr. Spokesly's eyes and smiled, taking a suck at his *narghileh*. It was at this juncture that two French naval officers, seated at a distant table and smoking cigarettes in long ivory holders (to keep the smoke from their beards), exchanged opinions upon the folly of their British allies in permitting the officers of ships to come ashore in civilian attire.

"You are quite sure, of course, that they *are* officers of a transport?" said the elder, observing with attention.

"Quite, my commandant. From the *Tanganyika*, arrived to-day. The little one I know well. The other I observed upon the forecastle as she anchored."

"But what are they doing in company with *him*?"

The lieutenant raised his shoulders.

"I imagine, my commandant, that they do a little business in hashish. But in any case it is not what you imagine. The English do not spy."

"But Dainopoulos may use them, eh?"

"Impossible, my commandant. You do not know them. I do. As you are aware, I was in the Crédit Lyonnais in Lombard Street. If Mr. Dainopoulos attempted to enlist their services they would batter his head in with his own *narghileh*. They have no compunction about robbing their government by peculation, but treachery is not their *métier*. And our friend knows it quite well."

"Business," observed Mr. Dainopoulos suddenly, "is very bad."

Mr. Bates seemed very amused at this and leaned over the dirty marble-topped table.

"Count us both in, my friend here and me, for the same as last time. How about it, eh?"

"Oh!" Mr. Dainopoulos pulled his extended frame up and put his elbows on the table, his eyes blinking quickly. "Oh, that's all right. Yes, certainly. But I mean to say business is very bad. You would not believe me, Mister, but the chances that are going, and all for a little management, are lost! Incredible! Only this week"— here he lowered his voice so that Mr. Spokesly, who was listening with undivided attention, scarcely gathered the words—"only this week, I could have made—ah, much money—if I had with me an Englishman who knows the business. Ten thousand drachma, easy as that!" Mr. Dainopoulos snapped his fingers without a sound and looked depressed.

Mr. Bates did not look depressed. His smile evaporated and he looked down his nose into his moustache with an expression of ruffled propriety.

"I must say——" he began, and added, after a pause, "'Course we hadn't arrived, but I should 'ave thought, seein' we was due here, you might have counted on me."

Mr. Dainopoulos regarded Mr. Bates as though he were sizing him up for the first time and found him to amount to an almost negligible quantity. And then he shook his head.

"No," he murmured in a muffled tone. "That's not what I meant. What I wanted—too late now, of course—was a Kapitan."

Mr. Bates, touching Mr. Spokesly's foot with his own, emitted a snigger right in the face of Mr. Dainopoulos.

"And what about it?" he queried, impudently. "My friend here's got a master's ticket. What's the matter with him? I'm surprised——"

He was. To Mr. Bates it was unpleasant to discover that Mr. Dainopoulos should doubt his ability to cope with any situation which involved a financial reward. That gentleman, however, was not exclusively preoccupied with Mr. Bates and his emotions. He turned immediately to Mr. Spokesly who sat quietly twisting his glass of whiskey on the marble table. The pale, prominent, and bloodshot brown eyes examined Mr. Spokesly with passionless attention. Mr. Dainopoulos had filled many posts in his career. Quite apart from his participation in what he discreetly alluded to as "the wars," he had rendered some slight assistance to the builders of the Panama Canal as stoker on an excavator, he had worked iu a felt-hat factory in Newark, New Jersey;

he had been a waiter in a Greek café near Franklin Square, New York; he had held the position of clerk in the warehouse of a Turkish tobacco importer in London; and he had also been an assistant purser in one of the Roumanian Lloyd mail steamers which used to run from Costanza to Alexandria. He was one of those people who, as the saying is, "could write a book," which means they can do or have done almost everything except write a book. Such people are rarely of a literary turn. Mr. Dainopoulos certainly was not. But he had one faculty which, if literary people only knew it, is of use even in literature. He could size a man up. By a natural turn of judgment, so necessary to success in his business as a "general merchant and exporter" coupled with ceaseless practice, he had acquired a skill in sizing up which seemed as effortless and intuitive as the driving of a fine golfer or the wrist-work of a professional billiard player. The London School of Mnemonics could teach Mr. Dainopoulos nothing about practical psychology. He might even have given them some useful hints. In the present instance he was not at a loss. He waited, however, for Mr. Spokesly to make some comment.

"That's right enough," said the latter, leaning forward and smiling. "But I'd have to know a little more of the game, you understand? There's a war on, you know. Can't be too careful."

"True," assented Mr. Dainopoulos reflectively and keeping his prominent eyes fixed upon Mr. Spokesly. "You do not wish, then, to take a chance?"

"Oh, a *chance!*" Mr. Spokesly achieved a certain irony as he emphasized the last word. "Your ideas of a chance and mine might be different. S'pose we have another drink."

The watchful Herakles came near as Mr. Spokesly lifted his hand, and took the order.

The fact was—and it may be presumed that Mr. Dainopoulos perceived it sufficiently well to make allowance for it—that Mr. Spokesly, as he sat beside Archy Bates and listened to the conversation, had experienced a sudden access of caution. Archy was not drunk, and as far as was humanly known, never would be really drunk; but he was sufficiently saturated to raise a certain distrust in the mind of a perfectly sober man. It may even be said that while Mr. Spokesly had no clear intention of deserting his chum Archy, he was beginning to wish that Archy were not indispensable in any scheme that might be proposed. And the occasional looks that various British and French officers cast in their direction made Mr. Spokesly uneasy. He suddenly realized the other aspect of making money in a shady fashion: that one has to do business with shady people. Mr. Dainopoulos, for example, looked extremely shady. Archy Bates, his long, sharp nose buried in a fresh whiskey and soda, his hat pushed back revealing the oiled graying hair parted in the middle and slicked back above his ears with their purple veins; Archy, picking dreamily among the pieces of fish and beetroot which had been served on little dishes with the drinks, looked extraordinarily like a rat picking at garbage. All very well, Mr. Spokesly reflected, to buy hashish and sell it in Egypt at four or five hundred per cent. profit, so long as the business could be transacted in a gentlemanly manner. But this new development—he did not see his way clear to accepting Mr. Dainopoulos as an employer. He was not fastidious— he had worked for a Chinese ship owner—but the officers at the other tables, in their inconceivably correct uniforms and polished harness, made him uneasy. Mr. Spokesly knew perfectly well that these people did not consider him as one of themselves. Even amid the noise and chaffering of a Saloniki café, rubbing shoulders with the uniforms of French, Greek, Serbian, Russian, and Italian officers, these men of his own race, he knew, never forgot the abyss that separates the seafaring man from themselves, the social *crevasse* which even Armageddon was powerless to abolish. Nevertheless, he felt he could never abandon for ever the possibility of entering, some day, the magic circle. It is this peculiarity of the English temperament which so often paralyses its victim at the very moment when he needs to be in possession of all his faculties, when the chance, perhaps of a lifetime, suddenly appears at his elbow.

But Mr. Dainopoulos, as has been said, could size a man up. He was intuitively aware that he had made no great impression upon Mr. Spokesly. And he had a special desire, now that chance had thrown them together, to engage the interest of a skilled navigator. He had received an offer which might result in a very large profit indeed. The business to which he had been referring, a mere matter of running a small cargo of canned goods down to a certain island and transferring it to an Austrian submarine, was a trifle. One could do that every day, right under the noses and beards of a dozen French naval officers. This was a much bigger affair. It involved the sale, at huge profit, of one of his little steamers which he had purchased for a song from the French early in the war, but it also involved the safe conduct of the vessel into an enemy port. His friends in Anatolia might compensate him ultimately for the destruction of his ship by an Allied warship and the crew could look out for themselves; but if the captain lost her by grounding, it would be a disaster of the first magnitude. All this passed through the nimble mind of Mr. Dainopoulos while Mr. Spokesly waited for further light on the nature of the service required. He saw the difficulty and, knowing the English character, he took his measure accordingly. He smiled.

"You come to my house and have some supper?" he remarked. "My wife would be pleased, I'm sure."

Mr. Spokesly looked at Archy Bates. That gentleman was no longer paying attention. In his own peculiar fashion he had arrived at some sort of intuitive recognition of the fact that Mr. Dainopoulos had no intention of letting him in on this affair. Well, that was all right, Mr. Bates reflected in one of those appallingly clear and coherent moments which suddenly open in the mentality of dipsomaniacs. That was all right. They were making a lot of money. Big risk for him, by Jove! but he was willing to shoulder it. By Jove! That last time in Port Said, when the police rushed into his cabin not five minutes after the laundryman, who also took his rake-off, had carried the stuff ashore in a boat-load of dirty sheets. It was a near thing. Two hundred quid he had netted over that, paid in Turkish gold. And they had found the bit of burlap in which it had been wrapped. He saw the chief of police now, standing there, in his bright red fez, and white uniform, legs apart, holding the thing to his nose. Hashish, by Jove! A close call! "What's this?" Mr. Bates jumped and made the table shake. Mr. Spokesly was speaking. For a moment he had forgotten where he was. Little beads of sweat stood out on his forehead. He smiled with relief.

"Shall we go?" repeated Mr. Spokesly. Somewhat to his surprise, Mr. Bates shook his head. He was still smiling with relief, for that brief moment, during which his consciousness had slipped back a couple of months, as it were, and reënacted the scene in his cabin, had been very real. Five years in an Egyptian penitentiary missed by five minutes and a quick-witted explanation! While he shook his head and smiled into Mr. Spokesly's face he was thinking that he would take twice as much this time, and he knew where to hide it. Moreover, and he smiled more like a cat than ever, the millions of lines round his eyes deepening, he reflected that if Mr. Spokesly went in on this there was practically no risk at all. Nothing easier than to say—— Eh, what? No! He was going along to the Amphitryon, to see a little friend of his. See them later. Aw—ri!

It was a notable feature of Mr. Bates's temperamental failing that it never affected his legs. In earlier years, as a saloon waiter, he had often astounded his shipmates by getting as drunk as a lord before dinner, and yet going down the long dining saloon of a great liner, a plate of soup in each hand, and depositing them in front of passengers in evening dress, without ever an accident. Perhaps his demeanour was a shade more deliberate, his attention a trifle more abstracted, on these occasions; that was all. And now, as he rose and went towards the door of Floka's, after a dignified farewell to Mr. Dainopoulos, although an occasional wandering eye fastened upon him for a moment, Mr. Bates never betrayed himself. He paused courteously at the door while a major with his brigadier in tow passed in, monocles reflecting the light in a blind white glare so that they resembled Cyclops, and then he walked out gently himself, and was immediately lost in the noise and bustle of the Place.

Mr. Dainopoulos looked at Mr. Spokesly and thrust a thumb into the armhole of his coat.

"Your friend," he began in a low mutter, "him and me we do big business—you understand?—but all the same he drink too much highball. No good, eh?"

"Well," said Mr. Spokesly, "he's his own master, and he can please himself about that. To tell the truth, though, if there's anything in—what you were speaking of, I'd just as soon he wasn't in it. You see what I mean?" Mr. Dainopoulos nodded and drew at his *narghileh.* "He's a friend of mine, and very good friend, too, but we got to draw a line somewhere." Again Mr. Dainopoulos nodded as he leaned across the table.

"And another thing!" he remarked in his muffled tones, and he held the mouthpiece of the *narghileh* just in front of his lips as though it were a speaking tube and he was engaged in conversation with someone at the other end. He even cast his eyes down, and seemed to abandon Mr. Spokesly entirely. "And another thing. Mr. Bates, he very fond— you know—very fond of the *mademoiselles.* That's all right. If you like them, very good. But Mr. Bates, he comes all the time to me. Want me—you understand? Now, I do no business in that line, none at all. I don't like it. Plenty men tell you, 'Oh, yes, you come with me.' You understand? But me, I got my family to think about. *Now* you understand?"

"It is not respectable," added Mr. Dainopoulos in a deep tone, and relapsed into silence and the *narghileh.*

Mr. Spokesly did not reply. Even when they had left the café and were being driven along the *quai* in the direction of the White Tower, on their left the dazzle and noise of *cafés-chantant* and cinemas, on their right the intense darkness of the Gulf, he did no more than acquiesce in what Mr. Dainopoulos was saying. For to tell the truth, Mr. Spokesly was making certain readjustments within himself. Neither Mr.

Bates nor Mr. Dainopoulos was of vital importance to the growth of his soul, yet they come in here. They were backgrounds on which were silhouetted combinations novel to him. He had to find room in his mind for the conception of a shady person who cultivated the domestic virtues. Mr. Spokesly might be a man of inferior calibre, easily swayed by the prospect of easy money, but his mind swung naturally to the equilibriums of respectability. "All that," as he called it, "was a thing o' the past." He was tired of the shabby and meretricious byways he had frequented, in moderation, for so long. With more knowledge of introspection he would have known this as one of the signs of coming change. Coming events are very often a glorified reincarnation of dead desires. Dreams come true. Fortunate men recognize them in time.

"Your family?" said Mr. Spokesly, and the man beside him turned towards him and said:

"When I say 'family' I mean 'my wife.'"

Mr. Spokesly had no definite image in his mind of the domestic arrangements of a man like Mr. Dainopoulos. The scarlet tarboosh on that gentleman's head leaned the Englishman's fancy to a harem. In any case, the Island Race imagine that every Levantine who wears a fez is a Turk, that every Turk is a polygamist, and finally that polygamy implies a score or two of wives locked up in cupboards. But the tone in which Mr. Dainopoulos uttered the word "wife" precluded anything of this sort. It was a tone which Mr. Spokesly immediately comprehended. It was the tone in which Englishmen refer to their most valued possession and their embodied ideals. There is no mistaking it. There is nothing like it in the world. It is a tone implying an authorized and expurgated edition of the speaker's emotional odyssey.

"And so," he went on, "you can see how I don't want to get mixed up in any of these here places." And he opened his hand towards the subdued glare of the cafés and dance halls. Mr. Spokesly saw. He saw also, in imagination, Archy Bates sitting, hand to moustache, amid the chalk-faced hetairai of Saloniki, second-rate harpies who had had their day on the

Parisian *trottoirs*, and who had been shipped by a benevolent government to assuage the ennui of the *Armée d'Orient*. He saw them from time to time with his physical eyes, too, as they came to the doors of their refuges and, setting off to visit confederates, flung a glance of shrewd appraisal towards the passing vehicle.

"Yes," he muttered. "I see, Mr.— Mr.——"

"Dainopoulos," said that gentleman.

"Mr. Dainopoulos, I'm no saint, y'understand, but all the same—well, a man wants something, y'understand? Besides," added Mr. Spokesly, " 'twixt you an' me an' the sternpost, I'm engaged."

"You don't tell me!" exclaimed Mr. Dainopoulos in that peculiarly gratifying fashion which seemed to imply that this was the first betrothal announced since the Fall of Constantinople. "You don't tell—and I bet you what you like she's English, eh?"

"Yes, she's English all right," said Mr. Spokesly, feeling somewhat embarrassed by his friend's triumphant cordiality. "Pretty safe bet, that," he added as the carriage stopped in front of a black, solid wooden gate in a high yellow wall.

"Safe enough?" laughed Mr. Dainopoulos, not quite seizing the point intended. "Why, sure! Englishwomen are the best of all. I ought to know. Ha-ha!" and he slapped Mr. Spokesly's knee while his other hand sought the price of the ride. Mr. Spokesly failed to appreciate this approval of Englishwomen. A suspicion shot through his mind. He looked at the dark gate in the yellow wall. What, precisely, did this man mean by that last remark? Was all this talk of family and so forth a blind? Was he, Mr. Spokesly, on the brink of an adventure? It must be confessed that he would not have objected to that; but his gorge rose in spite of him at the reference to Englishwomen.

"I don't quite understand," he remarked in a low tone. "How do you happen to know so much about 'em?"

Mr. Dainopoulos laughed again and handed the fare to the driver. He stepped out, held a bunch of keys to the light of the carriage lamp, and selected one.   Then he beckoned to Mr. Spokesly to alight.

"I'll tell you, Mister," he said, as he stooped, inserted the key, turned it, and pushed open the gate.   "Because I married one myself."

CHAPTER V

MR. SPOKESLY, in a state of considerable astonishment, sat by a balconied upper window and tried to get his recent experiences into some sort of focus. That last remark of Mr. Dainopoulos, that he had married one himself, had dislocated his guest's faculties, so that Mr. Spokesly was unable to note clearly by what means he had arrived at his present position, a balconied window on his right and in front of him a woman lying on a sofa. A woman whose brown hair, extraordinarily long and fine, was a glossy pile pressed into the pillow, and whose thin hand he had just relinquished.

"Well," he said, as Mr. Dainopoulos came forward with a lamp, his swart and damaged features giving him the air of a ferocious genie about to perform some nefarious experiment. "Well, I must say, I'm surprised."

Mrs. Dainopoulos continued to gaze straight out into the darkness over the Gulf.

"Of course," agreed her husband, seating himself and reaching for a large briar pipe. "Of course. And I'll bet you'd be still more surprised if you only knew—eh, Alice?" He screwed up one eye and looked prodigiously sly at his wife with the other, his palms slowly rubbing up some tobacco. Mrs. Dainopoulos did not remove her eyes from the darkness beyond the shore. She only murmured in a curt voice:

"Never mind that now, Boris."

"But it ain't anything to be ashamed of, you know," he returned earnestly, packing his pipe in a way that made Mr. Spokesly want to snatch it from him and do it properly.

"I know, but it wouldn't interest Mr. Spokesly, I'm quite certain," she muttered, and she suddenly looked at their visitor and smiled. It reassured that gentleman, as it was intended to do, that he was in no way responsible for this minute difference of viewpoint between husband and wife. Mr. Spokesly smiled, too.

"Don't mind me," he remarked, lighting a cigarette and offering the match to Mr. Dainopoulos. After sucking valiantly for a while and achieving a small red glow in one corner of the bowl, the latter rose and regarded his wife and his guest attentively for a moment.

"I'll tell you what I'll do," he said at length, and looked at his pipe, which was already out. "I'll go in and see Malleotis for a while. He'll be back by now. And you two can have a little talk before we have supper."

"Well, don't be all night. You know, when you and Mr. Malleotis get talking business——"

The woman on the couch paused, regarding her husband as he bent his head over her. Mr. Dainopoulos suddenly put his pipe in his pocket and put his hands on either side of the pillow. Mr. Spokesly could see nothing save the man's broad, humped shoulders. There was a moment of silence. Mr. Spokesly, very much embarrassed, looked out of the window. When he turned his head again Mr. Dainopoulos was putting on a large tweed cap and walking out of the door.

"I suppose," Mr. Spokesly remarked, and fixed his eyes upon the extremely decorative Scotch travelling rug which covered the woman's limbs, "I suppose he doesn't go off every evening and leave you here." He spoke jocosely. Mrs. Dainopoulos looked out into the darkness. There was a faint colour in her cheeks, as though the sudden revelation of the passion she could evoke had filled her with exquisite shame. Or perhaps pride. Her clear, delicate English face, the mouth barely closed, the short straight nose slightly raised, the brown hair spread in a slight disorder upon the pillow, were surely indicating pride. Some inkling of this possibility came to Mr. Spokesly, and he sat regarding her, while he waited for her to speak, and wondering how a woman like her had come to marry one of these here dagoes. Peculiar creatures, women, Mr. Spokesly thought; knowing nothing whatever about them, it may be mentioned. And when Mrs. Dainopoulos turned to look at him, soon after she began to speak, the prevailing fancy at the back of his mind was "She thinks I don't know anything about the ladies! Fancy that!"

"His business takes him out a good deal," she said in a low voice, "but he wouldn't go if he could help it. To-night is unusual."

"The pleasure is mine," said Mr. Spokesly.

"Not altogether," she smiled, and her speech became perceptibly more racy and rapid. "Don't flatter yourself. Mr. Dainopoulos was thinking of me."

"I dare say he does a good deal of that."

The woman on the sofa laced her fingers lightly and regarded her guest afresh.

"You are saucy," she murmured with a faint smile. Mr. Spokesly smiled more broadly. He was saucy, but he was certainly at home now with his companion. There was in her last speech, in the accent and inflection, something incommunicably indigenous, something no alien ever has or ever will compass.

"No need to ask what part of England you come from," he ventured.

"No?" she queried. "There seems nothing you don't know."

"Oh, excuse me, Mrs. Dainopoulos, that ain't fair. I can't sit here and twiddle my thumbs all the evening, can I? *That* wouldn't be giving you any pleasure as far as I'm aware. The boss didn't reckon I was going to play a mandolin or sing, did he?"

"Well, since you're so clever, what's the answer?"

"Not so very many miles from Charing Cross," he hazarded.

"Wonderful!" she said, laying her head back and smiling. Mr. Spokesly admired the pretty throat. "You ought to be in the secret service. Perhaps you are," she added.

"Of course," he agreed. "They've sent me out to see where all the nice London girls have got to. But am I right?"

She nodded.

"Haverstock Hill," she said quietly.

"No! Do you know Mafeking Road? When I was a kid we lived at sixty-eight."

"Yes, I know it. Don't you live round there now?"

"No, not now. We live down Twickenham way now."

And Mr. Spokesly began to tell his own recent history, touching lightly upon the pathos of Eastern exile, the journey home to join up, and his conviction that after all he would be a fool to go soldiering while the ships had to be kept running. And he added as a kind of immaterial postscript:

"And then, o' course, while I was at home I got engaged."

Mrs. Dainopoulos stared at him and broke into a brief titter behind a handkerchief.

"*That's* a nice way to give out the information," she remarked. "Anybody'd think getting engaged was like buying a railway ticket or sending a postal order. Is she nice?"

"Well," said Mr. Spokesly, "*I* think so."

"Very enthusiastic!" commented the lady with considerable spirit. "Dark or fair?"

"Well," he repeated, "I should say dark myself."

"You don't intend to take any chances," Mrs. Dainopoulos retorted. "Haven't you a photo to show me?"

Mr. Spokesly felt his pockets, took out a wallet containing a number of unconvincing documents, some postage stamps and a five-piaster note.

"Matter of fact," he said, "I don't seem to have one with me. I got one on the ship, though," he went on. "Bring it ashore to-morrow."

"Sure you didn't tear it up by mistake or send it away in the laundry?" she demanded, watching him intently.

"Oh, all right, go on with the sarcasm," he protested, but enjoying it very much none the less. "Mr. Dainopoulos, you'll be telling me, has got your hair in a locket, I suppose."

Mr. Spokesly stopped abruptly. He saw an expression of extraordinary radiance on the girl's face as she lay there, her thin pale fingers holding the handkerchief by the corner. It suddenly occurred to Mr. Spokesly that this woman was loved. For the first time in his life he became aware of a woman's private emotional existence. He achieved a dim comprehension of the novel fact that a woman might have her own views of these great matters. He did not phrase it quite like this. He only sat looking at the girl on the sofa and remarking to himself that women were peculiar.

"Wouldn't you do that?" she demanded. The light in her eyes diminished to a steady warm regard.

And Mr. Spokesly began to assert himself once more. Women being so peculiar, there was no sense in being bullied into any of this here sentiment. He was a man of the world about to make a—what was it called? Marriage of convenience . . . something like that. Not that exactly, either. Ada was a darned fine girl. This invalid lady seemed to think he didn't know what love was.

"Who? Me?" he ejaculated. "Can't say as I see myself, I admit. Not in my line. Not in any Englishman's line, I don't think. And speaking for myself, Mrs. Dainopoulos, I reckon I'm past that sort of thing, you know. Can't teach an old dog new tricks, can you? I look at it this way: so long as there's enough to keep the pot boiling, it's easy enough to fall in love with anybody, you see, and when you're married . . . soon get used to it. Ada and me, we're *sensible*."

"You've got it all arranged, then," said Mrs. Dainopoulos, smiling faintly and looking out into the darkness once more.

"What's the use o' bein' anything else?" inquired Mr. Spokesly, resuming something of the perfect officer pose, hard-bitten, practical, and matter-of-fact. "All that business o' dyin' o' love, you know, I reckon's so much moonshine. All right in a novel, o' course, but not in real life. *You* don't reckon there's anything in it, really, I mean?" he asked doubtfully.

"I think everything's in it," she sighed. "I think it must be horrible, being married, without it. Haven't you felt you couldn't do without her? That you'd die if you didn't get her; work, and do somebody else in the eye for her? Haven't you?"

"That lets me out," he said soberly, lighting a fresh cigarette. "I'm not guilty."

There was a brief silence. Mr. Spokesly was puzzled. He could not fit this experience in with one of the two cardinal points in an Englishman's creed, the belief that no English girl can really love a foreigner. The other, of course, is that no foreign girl is really virtuous.

"That's a nice thing to say!" she retorted, trembling a little with her emotions. "If that's the new way they have at home——"

"Oh, I don't know," he began and he looked at her. "I'm afraid you're getting all upset. I'm sorry, really, I didn't think you'd have been so serious about it. As if it mattered to you!"

"I'm thinking of *her*," she said with a little hysterical sob. "You mustn't——"

Mr. Spokesly was in a quandary again. If he put Ada's adoration in its true perspective, he would not think very highly of himself. He took no real pleasure in speaking of himself as a promised man even to a married woman. Yet how was he to get this particular married woman in delicate health and extremely robust emotions to see him as a human being and not a monster of cold-blooded caution? And there was another problem. What of this new and astonishing revelation—new and astonishing to him, at any rate—that love, to a woman, is not a mere decoction of bliss administered by a powerful and benevolent male, but a highly complicated universe of subjective illusions in which the lover is only dimly seen as a necessary but disturbing phantom of gross and agonizing ineptitudes? The wonder, however, is not that Mr. Spokesly was slow to discover this, but that he did not live and die, as many men do, without even suspecting it. He nodded his head slightly as he replied:

"You're right in a way," he muttered. "She thinks I'm—well, she thinks I'm brave to go to sea in war-time!" The extreme incongruity of such an hallucination made him giggle.

"She would! You are!" said the woman on the couch,

almost irritably. "What do you want to laugh for? Don't you see what you miss?" she added in illogical annoyance.

"That the way you feel about Mr. Dainopoulos?" Mr. Spokesly asked. The woman turned her face so that the lamplight illumined her coiled hair and for a moment she did not reply. Then she said, her face still in the shadow:

"You'd only laugh if I told you."

"No," declared Mr. Spokesly. "Honest I won't. Laugh at meself—yes. But you—that's different."

"But you don't believe in love at first sight, I can see very well."

"I only said I hadn't anything like that happen to me," he replied slowly, pondering. "But I s'pose it has to be something like that in a case like yours."

"I don't understand you."

"Well, you being English, you see, and Mr. Dainopoulos a foreigner."

"As an excuse, I suppose? Father made the same remark, but I never thanked him."

Mr. Spokesly looked at her soberly. Her eyes were bright and resolute, and the lamplight threw into salience the curve of her jaw and chin. A fugitive thought flitted about his mind for a moment and vanished again—whether her father was inconsolable at his daughter's departure.

"You got married at home then?"

"Yes, after Mr. Dainopoulos saved my life."

"Did he?"

"Of course. That's how we met. Didn't you ever hear of the *Queen Mab* accident? It was in the papers."

"Can't say as I did. I was out East so long, you see. Wait a bit, though——" Mr. Spokesly pondered. "I fancy I remember reading something about it in the home papers; an excursion steamer in collision with a cargo boat, wasn't it?" The girl nodded.

"Down the river. I was in it. My sister—she was drowned. We were going to Southend."

"I see. And Mr. Dainopoulos, he was with you and——"

"No. I'd never seen him then. You see, we were all

standing by the paddle-box when the other ship cut into us, my sister Gladys and two boys we'd been keeping company with. It was something awful, everybody screaming and the boat going up in the air. I mean the other end was going down. At last we couldn't stand, so we sat on the paddle-box. . Then all of a sudden the boat slid over to one side and we went in.''

Mr. Spokesly made a sound expressive of intense sympathy and interest.

''And next thing I knew was somebody was holding me up and he said, 'Don't move! Don't move!' But I couldn't! Something must have hit me when I fell in. I didn't know where then—the water was awfully cold. And then a boat came, and they lifted me in. And then he swam off again to find the others. I don't faint as a rule, but I did then. There were so many, and the screams—oh, it was shocking!

''But the worst was when we got on land again. It was near Woolwich and they turned a chapel or something into a hospital for us. And all the relations of the people on the *Queen Mab* came down, and Mr. Dainopoulos, who'd taken his landlady's daughter for the excursion, was sitting there in a blanket when the landlady and her husband came in. They hadn't found her. You know bodies don't come up sometimes, especially when a ship turns over. And they caught hold of him, calling out 'Where is our girl? What have you done with our girl?' They *screamed* at him!''

''Was he engaged to her?'' asked Mr. Spokesly.

''Just the same as I was with Georgie Litwell who was drowned. Keeping company.''

''And what happened then?''

''Why, we fell in love. That's what I was going to tell you so long as you promised not to laugh. He was in a whole-sale tobacco merchant's in Mark Lane then and he took lodgings near us at Haverstock Hill. Those other people behaved as though he'd held their daughter's head under. Really they did. How could he help it? He saved six besides me. It wasn't his fault the boat sank.''

''No, of course not. I see now.''

"And then, you know, Mother made a fuss because he was foreign. Mother's a Berkshire woman, and she said she'd never thought she'd live to see a child of hers marry a man from goodness knows where. She didn't half go on, I can tell you. And Father had his own way of making me perfectly happy. He'd ask me, how many in the harem already? And I couldn't do a thing, lying on my back helpless. And at last, with the doctor saying I needed a sea-voyage to get my strength back, I thinks to myself, I'll take one; and with the accident insurance I had had the sense to carry ever since I'd started going to business, and what Boris had in the bank, we went. Or came, rather. We've been here ever since and nobody's heard either of us regret it, either."

And as she lay there looking out into the darkness of the Gulf with shining resolute eyes, it was plain that this romantic destiny of hers was a treasured possession. It dominated her life. She had found in it the indispensable inspiration for happiness, an ethical yet potent anodyne for the forfeiture of many homely joys. It was for her the equivalent of a social triumph or acceptance among peeresses of the realm. It is to be suspected that she had ever in her mind a vision of the wonder and awe she had evoked in the souls of the suburban girls among whom she had spent her life, and that this vision supported her and formed the base of a magnificent edifice. And it was an integral part of this edifice that love should be a romantical affair, a flame, noted by all and fed by the adoration of a husband who was harsh to the world, but to her a monster of infatuated fidelity.

Something of this impinged upon Mr. Spokesly's consciousness and he regarded her for a moment with profound respect.

"I should say," he muttered, returning to his cigarette, "you haven't done so badly for yourself."

She gave him an extraordinarily quick look, like a flash of sheet lightning from a calm evening sky, which left him puzzled. He was not aware, at that time, that no woman will ever admit she has bettered herself by marrying a given man. She must retain for ever that shining figure of him she might have loved, a sort of domestic knight-errant in golden armour, who keeps occasional vigils at her side while the weary actuality slumbers in gross oblivion. Mrs. Dainopoulos knew that Mr. Spokesly saw nothing of this. She knew him for what he was, a being entirely incapable of compassing the secrets of a woman's heart. She knew he imagined that love was all, that women were at the mercy of their love for men, and that chivalrous ideas, rusted and clumsily manipulated, were still to be found in his mind. And she saw the fragility and delicate thinness of his love affair with Ada Rivers. Anything could break it, anything could destroy it, she reflected. Those fancies . . . of course he said he was engaged; but an engagement, as Mrs. Dainopoulos knew, having lived in a London suburb, was nothing. Yes, anything might make him forget Ada. And as she repeated the word "anything" to herself in a kind of ecstasy, Mrs. Dainopoulos turned her head quickly and listened. There was a sound of someone being admitted.

"So you've met your fate, anyway," she observed to Mr. Spokesly, yet still listening to the distant sound.

"Yes," he said with a smile, "I reckon you can cross me off as caught. What's that? Come back, I s'pose. Time for me to be off, anyway. I'm sure. . . ."

Mrs. Dainopoulos held up her hand. She was still listening with her head slightly inclined, her eyes fixed upon Mr. Spokesly, as though absently pondering the perilous chances of his emotional existence. Cross him off as caught! She smiled again in that lambent heat-lightning way of hers. A woman who spends her life in a reclining seclusion becomes very much of a clairvoyant, an electric condenser of emotions. Mr. Spokesly was agreeably flattered by the intent interest of his companion's gaze. Quite a nice little tête-à-tête he'd had. It gave him a thrill to sit in intimate exchange of love experiences with an attractive married woman, even if she was an invalid. He felt a bit of a dog. He would write to Ada and tell her. Or would he? Did he want Ada to know anything about this visit to a mysterious house in Macedonia, a house so clandestine and bizarre he could scarcely convince himself that it was the abode of virtue? Did he? Ada was a long way off, in beleaguered England. He suddenly wondered what Ada had to do with this at all. With an ease that rather disturbed him he told himself that you could never tell what might happen nowadays. No use worrying about the future. Why, he might never get home. He dropped the ash from his cigarette into the tray on the table. Someone was coming with a quick decisive step up the stairs. He smiled at Mrs. Dainopoulos, not quite sure why she was holding up her hand. She was thinking "cross him off as caught," and smiling, when the someone arrived at the door and knocked.

"Why didn't you get married before you left England?" she asked quickly, and added in louder tone, "Come in!"

In sharp contrast to the rapid movements without, the door opened with extreme cautiousness, and at first nothing could be seen save the hand on the knob. Mr. Spokesly had been thrown into some disorder of mind by that last question. Why hadn't he, anyway? It was something he had never decided. Why had they not done what thousands had done in England, which was simply to marry on the spot and sail a week, or perhaps a few days, later? Why had he not taken the hazards of war? He had more, far more, than many of those girls and boys at home. It was at this point, facing for the first time the unconscious evasions of life, that he found himself facing something else, a girl with a startled and indignant light in her eyes. He uncrossed his legs and began to rise as Mrs. Dainopoulos said, "Come in, Evanthia. It is all right."

She came in, letting the door swing to as she moved with a long rapacious stride towards the sofa. It was obvious she was preoccupied with some affair of intense importance to herself. Once Mr. Spokesly's presence had been indicated she became again absorbed in her errand. Her amber-coloured eyes, under exquisitely distinct brows, were opaque with anger, and she held one hand out with the fingers dramatically clenched, as though about to release a thunderbolt of wrath. The gesture was as antique as it was involuntary. One heard drums muttering and the gathering of fierce Ægean winds as she came on, and leaning forward, flung out both hands in a passionate revelation of sorrow. Mr. Spokesly sat down again, embarrassed and fascinated. He could not take his eyes from her. She was something new in his experience; a woman with passion and the power to express it. Such women are almost non-existent in England, where sentiment is regarded as legal tender for passion. He regarded her with a kind of stupefaction, as though he had never set his eyes on a woman before. One might say with approximate truth that he had not. His ways had lain among the artificial products of his age. In trepidation he realized, as he sat there watching the movements of this girl, that he would not know what to do with a woman like that. He sat there and listened.

"Gone?" repeated Mrs. Dainopoulos.

"Yes, they are all gone. The French sent soldiers. And they would not let me go to speak to him."

"But where will they go?"

The girl, whose eyes were bent upon the carpet at her feet, shrugged her shoulders violently.

"Who knows that? To Sofia; or to Constantinople. Oh, I would have gone, too. These pigs, pigs, pigs of French! Not a word! And he is gone!" She dragged a chair from the table, and sat down suddenly, thrusting her chin over her arm and staring at the floor. There was a moment's silence, while Mr. Spokesly sat in doubt and Mrs. Dainopoulos looked out over the Gulf.

"Gone!" muttered the girl again sullenly.

"Don't do that, dear. It is very bad for you when you get in such rages!" Mrs. Dainopoulos spoke in a soft cool tone, like a recumbent sybil whose knowledge of rage and sorrow was vast. The girl's foot swung to and fro more and more rapidly, the red Turkish slipper slapping the floor, "You will hear from him after a little."

"Ah, if they let him write. But these French! With their beards and hats like cooking pots! They see everything.

Of course he will write, but that is no good. He cannot send anything."

An expression of disappointment crossed the other woman's face as she patted the girl's shoulder.

"Wait a little," she said. "You can't tell yet."

"I would have given a thousand drachma to have got to the train," said the girl moodily. "And I would give a million to get to Constantinople. This place stifles me. I hate it . . . hate it."

She stood up suddenly, raising her hands to her magnificent coil of dark hair, and revealing the poise and vigour of her body. "Ah!" she moaned, bending over her friend and caressing her. "I am a bad girl, forgetting how ill you are. Evanthia is a bad, bad girl, with her troubles—and you have a visitor——" She turned her head for a moment and Mr. Spokesly was caught unawares in the brilliance of a dazzling yet enigmatic glance from the amber eyes.

"A friend of my husband's," said Mrs. Dainopoulos. "He is English, you know, like me. From London. We have been talking of London."

"Ah, yes!" The lingering syllables were a caress, yet there was no more comprehension in them than in the inarticulate sounds of an animal. The girl bent her dark head over the blonde masses on the pillow. "Forgive your bad girl, Alice."

"Oh, all right," said Mrs. Dainopoulos, emerging with an embarrassed English smile. "Only you must be good now and go back to bed. There's Boris coming in."

"I am going!" said the girl and started. And then she remembered Mr. Spokesly sitting there in dumb stupefaction, his gaze following her, and she turned to make him a bow with a strange, charming gesture of an out-flung hand towards him. The next moment she dragged the door open and passed out.

He looked up to see Mrs. Dainopoulos regarding him thoughtfully, and he made a sudden step forward in life as he realized the ineffectiveness of any words in his vocabulary to express his emotions at that moment. He made no attempt to corrupt the moment, however, which was perhaps another step forward. He sat silent, looking at the glowing end of his cigarette, endeavouring to recapture the facile equilibrium of mind which had been his as he followed Mr. Dainopoulos through the gateway an hour or so before. But that was impossible, for it was gone, though he did not know it, for ever. He was trying to remember the name Mrs. Dainopoulos had called her. Evanthia! And once at the beginning, Miss Solaris. Something like that. Evanthia Solaris. He said to himself that it was a pretty name, and was conscious at the same time of the inadequacy of such a word. There was something beyond prettiness in it; something of a spring morning in the Cyclades, when the other islands come up out of the mist like hummocks of amethyst and the cicadas shrill in the long grass under the almond trees. There was in it an adumbration of youth beyond his experience, a hint of the pulsing and bizarre vitality of alien races, a vitality fretted into white wrath by her will and her desire, as the serene breath of the morning is suddenly lashed into a tempest by the howling fury of an Ægean white squall. She was gone, yet the room was still charged with her magnetic presence, so that Mr. Dainopoulos came in quietly, put down his tweed cap, and seated himself beside his wife, and Mr. Spokesly scarcely noticed his arrival.

As he became aware of outside phenomena once more—and he was rather frightened to discover how his thoughts had flown out into the unknown darkness in search of the girl— he saw that Mr. Dainopoulos was preoccupied and anxious. They were speaking in a low tone and in a foreign tongue, Mr. Spokesly noted. He recalled a story he had read in a magazine some little time before—a story of an Englishman who had a most miraculous command of foreign languages, who overheard a conversation which revealed a plot to destroy the British Army. The plot was revealed by the simple process of torturing a beautiful girl of neutral origin who was to be forced to marry a brutal enemy colonel. It did not occur to Mr. Spokesly to reflect that beautiful girls are usually eager to marry colonels of any denomination, or that colonels do not usually blend love and espionage. But he did notice the extreme improbability of an Englishman being a linguist. It made the tale seem unreal and artificial. Especially when the story added that he was a naval officer of good family who afterwards married the beautiful neutral and settled in a castle in Dalmatia. Fanciful! Mr. Spokesly knew enough of naval officers to doubt the *dénouement*. He himself, for that matter, would rather live in a bungalow in Twickenham than in Dalmatia. As for foreign girls—he rubbed his chin, puzzled over his own blurred sensations. Mr. Dainopoulos was speaking again. The woman lay back, looking up at the high ceiling, an expression of calm and careful consideration on her face, which was illuminated sharply, like an intaglio, by the lamp. And Mr. Spokesly experienced a shock to discover that they were not speaking of the girl at all. They seemed to have forgotten her existence. They looked at him and so brought him into the conversation.

"I'll have to be getting back," he remarked, rising once more.

Mr. Dainopoulos went to the door and spoke in a low harsh tone into the darkness.

"I'll get you a boat," he said. "There's no boats allowed after dark, but I have a friend on the French Pier. He'll put you on board. Another night, you must come and eat supper. I have had plenty business to-night. I have to go out again later, too. You understand what I tell my wife? Well, the consuls have had to go home. The German and Austrian and Bulgar Consuls went away to-night. I do a good bit of business, you understand, with all these people, and I got to go and see a friend of mine about it. So—will you have coffee——? I'll get you a boat first, and you can come to-morrow night, eh?"

A girl of fifteen with a downcast disdainful countenance came in with a tray and set it on the table. One eyelash flickered towards Mr. Spokesly as she turned and made her way out. He looked at her entranced, noting her slovenly dress, the holes in her stocking, and the ugly slippers that slip-slopped as she moved her small feet. He noted these uncouth garnitures within which she moved with the restless yet indolent rhythm of a captive queen. His mind, as he drank the strong coffee and the tiny glass of cognac, was in a state of unusual exaltation. Never before had he faced an immediate future so fraught with glittering yet un-recognizable possibilities. Mr. Dainopoulos might be a rascal, yet he possessed the power to call up familiar spirits. As he sat there leaning towards the table, his hand abstract-edly on the bottle of cognac, thinking deeply of his multi-farious concerns, his dexterous dealings in and out among men who slew one another daily, he resembled some saturnine yet benevolent magician about to release a formidable genie who would fill the room with fuliginous vapour. Mr. Spokesly felt his scalp twitching with anticipation. He stepped across to say good-bye to Mrs. Dainopoulos.

"I never expected this," he said simply. "I've had a very pleasant time."

"Come to supper to-morrow," she said, smiling, "Always glad to see anybody from the Old Country."

"Sorry your lady friend couldn't stay," he muttered. "Like to see more of her. Well . . . I'll say good-night."

He smiled as he went down the staircase behind the pre-occupied Mr. Dainopoulos. He smiled because he could see, by virtue of his exalted mood, that the smug phrases which had always been adequate for his emotions, sounded foolish and feeble. Like to see more of her! Did he? It made him dizzy to think of, though, for all that. It made the simple business of returning to that house an adventure of the soul. Nor did the phrase "lady friend" describe her. He was comfortably vague as to the actual constituents of a lady. A lady was perhaps described as a woman with whom it was impossible to be wholly at ease. Yes, he whispered to him-self, but for a different reason. He felt defeated in his attempts to stabilize his impressions. He had no compari-sons. It was like comparing a bottle of wine with a bottle of milk. Even Ada . . . He moved so abruptly as he followed close on the heels of Mr. Dainopoulos that the latter looked at him in inquiry, and thought a remark was necessary.

"We can fix our little business any time before you go away," he murmured.

But Mr. Spokesly was not thinking of the little business just then. He found himself suddenly confronting the conviction in his mind that his Ada had been little more than a shining reflector of his own image. Ada, in beleaguered England, seemed very far away and her personality lost whatever distinction and magnetism it may have had while he was with her. He saw with perfect clarity a new truth beyond that first one—that Mrs. Dainopoulos had been aware of all this while she had plied her gentle smiling questions. Had she meant anything, then? How could one plumb the mind of a woman? There was something almost sinister in the notion that she had known all along how he was situated, how he felt, and let him sit there while a girl like an indignant enchantress came in and worked some sort of spell upon him. He began to wonder if the girl was real; whether he had not dreamed she was there. He was aghast at the insensibility of Mr. Dainopoulos who was leading the way across the street, his head bent and his damaged features set in a meditative scowl. In what way could one account for it? A woman like that! A woman already with a power over himself that frightened him. Ada! He thought of Ada almost as a refuge from this new emotion assaulting his heart. There was safety with Ada. He knew, within reasonable limits, the range of which she was capable, the tone and timbre of her soul. Here, he comprehended with surprising readiness, he would be called on to do something more than talk conventionally of love. It was all very well, he could see, to jog along from year to year, having a little fun here and there, and getting engaged and even married; but it was no more than the normal function of a human organism. Beyond that he could see something ruthless, powerful, and destructive. He experienced an extraordinary feeling of elation as he walked beside Mr. Dainopoulos towards the street car. He was perplexed because he would have liked to tell Ada the cause of this elation. He had a fugitive but marvellously clear view of Ada's position in the matter. She was away in the future, in a distant and calm region to which he had not yet gained admission. There was something he had to go through before he could get Ada. And while they jangled slowly along the quay, and Mr. Dainopoulos mumbled in his ear the difficulties imposed upon himself by the departure of the consuls, Mr. Spokesly caught a glimpse of what men mean by Fate. Though he knew it not, the departure of the consuls was an event of prime importance to himself. It was an event destined to precipitate the grand adventure of his life. Ada, in beleaguered England, would find her mechanically perfect existence modified by the departure of the consuls. Something he had to go through. He stared out at the shaded lights of the cafés and failed to notice that he no longer desired the tarnished joys of the sea-faring boulevardier. Here was a new motive. The facile and ephemeral affairs of his life were forgotten in their sheer nothingness. He drew a deep breath, wondering what lay in store for him.

They left the car and passed through the gates of the dock, along roadways almost incredibly muddy, to where transports worked in the cautious twilight of blue electrics and picket-boats moved up and down gently where they were made fast to the steps, their red and green side-lights giving the quiet stealthy hustle of the quays an air of brisk alertness. Tall negroes, in blue-gray uniforms and red fezzes, moved in slow lines loaded with sections of narrow-gauge track and balks of timber, or pushed trucks of covered material. At a desk in a wooden office sat a French *ajutant*, a blinding tungsten globe illuminating the short black hairs rucked up over his stiff braided collar and reflecting from an ivory-bald spot on his head as he spoke into a telephone. Mr. Dainopoulos slid sideways into the room and sat down on a bench by the door. The officer's eye flickered towards his visitor and he lifted a hand slightly to indicate recognition. Mr. Spokesly stepped in and sat down. On the wall was a drawing cut from the *Vie Parisienne*, a nude, with exaggerated limbs and an enormous picture-hat, riding on a motorcycle. The shriek, as of

a soul in torment, of a French locomotive, brought a scowl
to the officer's face as he conversed with his friends at the
Cercle Militaire. Ringing off with a fat chuckle he demanded
in rapid French how his old one was making it. The old one,
who was Mr. Dainopoulos, made no definite complaint, but
commented on the fact that a man could not sit in Floka's
and take a little drink with a friend without a certain person,
with a luxuriant beard, taking especial note of it. The *ajutant* threw himself back in his chair, tipped it, his heels grinding the boards, and grunted. That, he mumbled, was only
to be expected of Père Lefrote. Well, what was it now?
Mr. Dainopoulos indicated his companion, an officer from the
English ship arrived to-day, now anchored in the *rade*.
"What ship?" muttered the officer, looking Mr. Spokesly
over as though he were some unsavoury mongrel. From
Alexandria, said Mr. Dainopoulos, skilfully evading such an
impossible word as *Tanganyika*. "Ah-ha!" crowed the
officer, transferring his cold regard to his old one. So the old
one was on that game again. By the sacred blue, he was a
great old cock. And the officer, getting up, expressed his
conviction very fast that if the truth were only revealed, the
old one could do a neat business in *poulets de luxe* as well.
What? The truculent officer, halting at the door, his thumb
and finger busy with his moustache, looked back over his
shoulder at his old one. No, said the latter, he merely repeated what he had said so many times. He knew none of
those creatures, though he admitted three had arrived on the
transport *Jumièges* that morning. Was that so? Where
were they, then? At the Omphale or the Tour Blanche?
Come now! Mr. Dainopoulos lit a cigarette and as he trod
carefully on the smoking match murmured his conviction that
the ladies, whom a friend of his had seen land at Venizelos
Steps, entered automobiles, and might not be found at the
Omphale for some time. The officer drummed at the door
and nodded. True, but the old one knew of some ravishing
creature surely who would respond to the delicate attentions
of a lonely exile. A *marraine*, in fact. But the old one had
no such clients. He was a man of business purely. And if

it could be arranged his friend here would like to be put on board.

The officer, a frustrated and disappointed sensualist, whose imagination was tantalized but never fed by the fact that he was in the fabled Orient, the abode of lovely Circassians and other houris, nodded agreement. He owed Mr. Daino-poulos a few hundred francs and would have been at a loss even if that gentleman had suddenly produced a beautiful and expensive woman for his amusement. He was ever dreaming of a tremendous *affaire*, but he was too close-fisted a Norman from Darnetal to spend much on a sweetheart.

"True," he remarked and then called out into the darkness. "Yes," he said, turning his head into the light, "the *chaloupe* is going off now. Let your friend tell the patron the ship he wants." And he returned to this desk, yawned, and took up a copy of *Excelsior*. What a life, eh, my old one!

Mr. Spokesly pointed out the black bulk of the *Tanganyika*, and as the launch slid along the grating, stepped up and reached his room. The night-watchman said, "Chief steward he no back yet." Mr. Spokesly turned in. He switched out his light and lay for a while thinking with more precision and penetration than even the London School of Mnemonics would have ventured to guarantee. He had some difficulty in identifying himself with the man who had gone ashore with Archy Bates that evening. And he slid away into the deep sleep of the healthy seafarer with a novel notion forming at the back of his mind. Suppose he was ashore in Saloniki, what would happen then? If by some turn of the wheel he found himself there? He might be sick, for instance, and go to the hospital and be left behind. There was no dream, but he saw it—a storm and great toil and anxiety, and in the midst of it a girl awaiting the outcome of his exertions with enigmatic amber eyes.

CHAPTER VI

MR. DAINOPOULOS afterwards developed into an excellent diplomatist, his principal virtue being a knack of gauging personal values and extracting usefulness from apparently dry husks. He withdrew from the imaginative sensualist who sat during the night in a highly varnished pine shack brooding upon the exasperating proximity of inaccessible seraglios. A useful instrument in many schemes, he did not merit a whole evening. Like most sensualists of the grosser kind he was a bore, and Mr. Dainopoulos had other clients. He picked his way out of the incredible mire of the docks, and crossed over to the cleaner side of the road which extended from Venizelos Street past the Custom House, and which was being extensively remodelled by the army of occupation. Even as Mr. Dainopoulos crossed he could see a number of industrious beings mounted on newly erected telegraph poles, their movements illuminated by small bright lights so that they resembled a row of burning martyrs elevated by some Macedonian tyrant, their cries and contortions as they reached down into the darkness for material and tools recalling the agonies of shrivelling victims. The hotel was in blank darkness. The squirming, writhing exfoliations which constituted the Berlin architect's conception of loveliness showed not a glint of light. One could not believe that it had inhabitants, or that they were alive. Nevertheless, Mr. Dainopoulos halted before the massive double doors and rang the bell, a tall, high-shouldered shade demanding admission to a familiar vault. It was some time after he had relapsed into a motionless silence and an observer might have imagined him to have forgotten his errand, when one of the leaves of the door opened a few inches, and he raised his head. At the sound of his voice the door opened a little more so that he could slide his body sideways through the aperture. Then the door closed behind him and the hotel resumed its appearance of a monstrous Renaissance tomb.

Inside, the night-porter, a person in a slovenly undress of dirty shirt, riding-breeches open like funnels at the knee, and Turkish slippers, yawned and motioned his visitor to a chair while he slowly ascended the stairs, which were lit by a single invisible lamp on the landing. Mr. Dainopoulos remained sunk in thought. It was, in a way, a perfectly honest and rational proposition he had to make, but he found himself involved in some doubt as to the way the person above, an Englishman, would take it. He knew something of the English, being married to one of that race, and he sometimes reflected upon the unexpected workings of their minds. They were oppressively practical and drove wonderful bargains; and then suddenly they would flare into inexplicable passion over something which he for the life of him could not comprehend. If this person upstairs did that, what would it be? Mr. Dainopoulos shook his head. He could not say. He would have to take a chance. He might be tolerated, or sworn at, or laughed at, or arrested, or thrown down the stairs. All these things happened to honest merchandisers, he was well aware. He sometimes watched these English under lowered lids and marvelled. Personally he preferred German or American men. He felt nearer to them, less conscious of a certain incomprehensible reticence of soul which is peculiar to the English, a sort of polite and poignant regret that he should see fit to cumber the earth, which had happened, by a singular and unexplained destiny, to be their heritage. Association with them, under such circumstances as he encountered, was provocative of considerable thought. To men like him, the confused product of a hundred diverging stocks, from Illyrian to Copt, the phenomenon of these blond and disdainful beings, who came always in ships and were apologetic even in their invasions, bore the mark of something supernatural, since the contemplation of them in their own land filled a normal Latin with inarticulate contempt. Mr.

Dainopoulos had no pride. He would have found it an embarrassing impediment in his business. But he did devote an occasional moment of leisure to wondering how men could so impose their eccentric habit of thought upon the nations, and why he, for example, should be directed to obtain his personal ideals from a distant island in the northern seas.

The servant appeared on the landing, and Mr. Dainopoulos immediately went up.

The Berlin architect, no doubt in anticipation of invading armies, had exhausted his ingenuity in the façade and the reception rooms, and the chambers above were left in a state of disturbing starkness. Mr. Dainopoulos was led along corridors that chilled the heart with their bare rectangular perspectives, and was halted at length before a door behind which the voices of men could be heard in conversation. And in reply to a knock a slightly querulous voice intoned, "Come in, come in!" as though in infinite but weary patience with elementary intelligences. Mr. Dainopoulos stepped in.

Three men occupied the room. A naval lieutenant sat on the bed smoking a cigarette, a young man who did not raise his eyes to glance at the intruder. The owner of the room was a major, who was seated at a small escritoire near the window, and whose belt and cap hung over a chair. He was a man of thirty-odd, as clean as though he had been scoured and scraped in boiling water, the small absurd moustache as decorative as a nail-brush, and with a look of capable insolence in his blue-gray eyes. A small safe at his side was open and he remained stooping over this as he looked up and saw Mr. Dainopoulos standing by the door. The other man was in civilian tweeds, astride of a chair with his arms on the back, smoking a large curved meerschaum pipe. A clean-shaven circular-faced man of doubtful age, he was the only one of the three who regarded their visitor in a humane manner. He nodded slightly in response to the low bow made by Mr. Dainopoulos on his entry. The latter, however, knew better than to presume on this. He paused until the major invited him to approach, and the major did not do this. He simply waited, leaning over his safe, for Mr. Daino-

poulos to explain his intrusion, his existence on earth, and his
intentions as to the future, and anything else which might be
regarded as extenuating his conduct. When Mr. Dainopoulos remarked that he had called on a little matter of business,
the major bent his head again and went on investigating the
papers in the safe, as though Mr. Dainopoulos had suddenly
and completely evaporated.

"Well," he observed at length, straightening up and laying
some papers on his desk, "why do you call on a little matter
of business in the middle of the night?" He brought his left
arm up in a peculiar whirl to the level of his eyes and looked
at his wrist watch. "Eleven-twenty," he added in a tone of
detached contempt, and shot a severe look at his visitor.

Mr. Dainopoulos remained standing by the door and maintained his attitude of calm urgency. He explained that the
departure of the consuls had led him to remodel his arrangements. All three looked at him with attention when he made
this statement. The naval lieutenant, whose work it was to
examine and pass all neutral vessels, knew Mr. Dainopoulos
very well. To his regret he had never found that gentleman
doing anything at all shady, but he had never abandoned his
conviction that he would catch him some day. The civilian,
who was a censor and decoder of neutral correspondence, was
familiar with the Dainopoulos *dossier* in his office and had
read with surprise the chatty letters to girls in London which
came from the man's wife. He, however, was not in a position to reveal his knowledge, and looked at Mr. Dainopoulos
with good-tempered curiosity. The major, who knew his
visitor better than either of the others, having purchased
large quantities of stores from him at a handsome profit
to the vendor, looked as if he had been insulted when the
consuls were mentioned. As well he might, since those
astute gentlemen had done their best to keep all possible
material out of his hands, had blandly checkmated the armies
of occupation at every turn, even preaching a holy war against
them among the owners of Turkish baths in the Via Egnatia.
They had financed Hellenic Turks who laid injunctions on
rights-of-way, issued writs against movement of goods, and

sought to inflame French against English and Italian against both. The consuls had been the curse of every executive at Headquarters, for their resources and nerve seemed unlimited. They worked together like a team of experienced crooks on a steamship, and never for a moment were the invaders permitted to forget that the local government was neutral. The major was happier than he had been for a long while, though he lacked the emotional demonstrativeness proper to such a mood. All three of these men, by their reports, had aided in the grand *coup* which had culminated that evening in the expulsion of the consuls across the frontier. But their first thought, when Mr. Dainopoulos mentioned consuls, was that by some ghastly mischance the consuls had got back into Saloniki and the whole weary business was to begin again.

"Eh?" said the major, snarling up his upper lip so that his moustache looked more like a nail-brush than ever, and looking as if he were about to spring up and fasten his teeth in his visitor's neck. "What's that?"

Thus having evoked a suitable interest in his affairs, Mr. Dainopoulos drew a small notebook from his pocket and began to enumerate the list of goods the sudden departure of the consuls had left on his hands. In the midst of it, the major nodded to a chair and said, "Sit down over here, please." Mr. Dainopoulos came forward, sat down, and proceeded. The naval lieutenant reached over to the dressing table, took up a Turkish dagger and began turning it over in his hands, examining the edge with an intense stare. The censor drew steadily at his pipe and looked Mr. Dainopoulos up and down. He was a novelist, and of the three may be said to have had some practice in the gauging of character. He was aware, in spite of a life spent exclusively in southern England and among one small exclusive caste of English people, that this Levantine might have a view of his own. He was interesting. Where had he picked up that English wife? A slight shudder passed over him in spite of himself at the thought of an English woman in a Levantine's arms. No doubt, however, she was a housemaid or something of that sort. Must be making a lot of money. The censor felt a surge of indignation over this. His own family's resources had been quadrupled by the war; but that of course was the reward of patriotic endeavour. He found it intolerable that a neutral should make money out of bloodshed. Mr. Dainopoulos proceeded as calmly and collectedly as though he were a salesman in Birmingham or Liverpool. He certainly was unaware of inspiring horror and contempt. He even mentioned a thousand yards of Indian cotton drill which he had in his warehouse and which he had purchased for a song from a German firm in Alexandria a few days before the English had sequestered the business. The only point on which he was reticent was the fact that he had already been paid in gold for most of it by the consular agents; a most satisfactory arrangement for him, but unfortunate for them in the present juncture, since they had no receipt and the goods were to be held against their order. There was something exasperating in the spectacle of this man sitting there, with all the marks of clandestine knavery about him, merely offering *bona fide* goods for sale. He was a Greek in Greece, transacting business which, although he did not yet know it, was of vital importance to them, for a whole string of vessels bound for Saloniki had been sunk inside of two days, from the Start to Karaburun. They were at a loss for a week or so, and a week or so in war is not to be ignored. And here was an unprepossessing person offering them, at a comparatively reasonable rate, a remarkable consignment of material. Apart from their own needs in Macedonia they had recently sent a few thousand men to an island in the Ægean to prepare a base, and the ships bearing their stores were unreported. Sunk, of course. They sat in various poses thinking of all this, and Mr. Dainopoulos closed his notebook and took out a cigarette.

It should be said for him that if he had known their actual position his price would have been slightly higher, just as later on English merchants' prices became so high that men spat at the sound of their names. But he was not a profiteer in the modern sense. He knew nothing of advertising, for example. He thought 100 per cent. an adequate reimbursement for the risks of trade.

He was asked when he could effect delivery. He said in a week or ten days, some of it being on board a steamer on its way now from Alexandria.

"What steamer is that?" demanded the lieutenant.

"The *Kalkis*, four hundred tons," he replied. "I have had her a year now."

"What speed?"

"Oh, four. Perhaps four and a half. A very old ship. No good except for my business to the Islands."

"Don't know about that, my friend," muttered the major. "You may have to give up your business to the Islands. We commandeer our own ships; I don't see how you are going to get out of it."

"That would suit me," said Mr. Dainopoulos promptly. "She costs me fifteen thousand francs a month insurance. And coal is four hundred francs a ton in Port Said. I make very little out of her."

This was scarcely the literal truth, though Mr. Dainopoulos might be pardoned for depreciating his profits at a moment when a purchaser appeared. As a matter of fact he had made already out of that small ship about seven times her original purchase price and he had a neat scheme in hand which would make her a very good investment indeed.

"We have some business in the Islands, too, you see," the major remarked abstractedly. "I think you had better come to my office say about ten-thirty to-morrow. You know the place. Next to the Ottoman Bank, eh? G. O. S. Room Fourteen. Ask for Major Begg."

Mr. Dainopoulos, who would probably have done a thousand francs' worth of business before the major had had his bath, expressed his willingness to appear.

"Will you have a drink?" said the major in a harsh, browbeating tone which was believed by himself and many others of his class to evoke the very soul of bluff hospitality. Mr. Dainopoulos, however, had a strange feeling of having been good-humouredly kicked in the face. He declined the refreshment, not because he felt insulted, but because he knew the only drink these men had was whiskey and the smell and taste of the stuff made him sick.

"All right," said the major, regarding an abstainer with disfavour. He liked a man to take a drink. "To-morrow at ten-thirty. You might close the door. Thanks."

As he closed the door behind him, as requested, Mr. Daino-poulos reflected that he would have time to lay the matter before a French colonel he knew before reaching Room Fourteen. But he believed the best price was to be had from the British. He had found out that much in the course of his career—they did not haggle.

The three men he had left did not speak for a moment, waiting for him to get out of earshot.

"Looks like Providence," observed the lieutenant, making a lunge with the dagger at a knot in the bedstead.

The major pulled up his trouser leg and scratched a hairy calf. "These infernal fleas!" he muttered. "Yes, as you say, Providence. An angel very much in disguise."

"What about that ship, the *Kalkis?*" asked the censor.

"Oh, we shall probably charter her," said the major bitterly. "Take all the risk and pay him a princely sum for sitting tight here and doing nothing. We ought to buy, but we won't."

He sat silent for a moment. He was thinking of those men in Phyros, waiting for their stores, eating sparingly of their emergency rations, sampling the local cheese and bread and keeping a bright look-out for transports which were lying on their sides in eighty fathoms. Something would have to be done at once about them. This Dainopoulos had—here the major glanced at his shorthand notes—four thousand feet of timber and the Phyros crowd were frantic for timber for a jetty. Just think of it! A fertile island which these Greeks had had for a couple of thousand years, and no jetty yet! What could one do with people like that? Hopeless. Then there was flour. He simply had to have some flour soon. Dainopoulos said he had fifteen hundred barrels when the *Kalkis* came in.

There was in all this hard thinking no complete view of the war or of the world. If they could collar stores from some other front or from one of their allies, it was all one to them. Even the course of events had no interest for them beyond their own base. This was an inevitable result of the intensive pressure of responsibility on executives. They were not callous. They were simply busy. Their own lives were still bounded by the social barriers of England. They never spoke of private affairs except to some man of their own class who had been to one of the great public schools. For them the war was a war to perpetuate this social hierarchy, to place it once more upon an impregnable base. They wished to win, they but could see no difference between democracy and defeat. Even the novelist was a novelist within the radius of his social sphere, and remained within it in a city of Macedonia. He felt it incumbent upon him to remain also a gentleman, even at the expense of valuable collisions with alien temperaments. "He's a Greek, and I loathe them," summarizes, in the major's words, their collective sentiment. And their allies, it is to be feared, suffered under this highly specialized form of criticism. Nothing that happened was adequate to demolish this formidable *Kultur*. In victory and in defeat it was indestructible. Only the genius of the race, working in the very strongholds of that *Kultur*, can split it open and release new forces and aspirations. But of this even the novelist, who trafficked in happy endings, had no suspicion. He wrote a short story later, a story in which an English girl who had been carried off by a rascally Greek was rescued by an English officer who took her home to England and married her.

To the lieutenant the departure of the consuls and the impending formation of a provisional government were affairs of qualified good. A provisional government would immediately shriek for the return of all sequestrated property. It would demand the status of allies, and all their ships would start a complicated system of espionage and smuggling. It would be, in his opinion, a series of perfect days. Nobody was honest nowadays. Not a week ago he had caught naval stores going over the side of a ship into a local boat, and the guilty party was wearing three medals, for valour and distinguished service. He sometimes wished they would put him on a ship again. It gave one a chance to do something besides play detective anyway. The major spoke again.

"What about a captain for the *Kalkis*? We shall have to have one of our own men, Mathews."

"Afraid that's not possible," said the lieutenant. "We haven't too many men, you know. Better send him out with a convoy going to Alex. I might have had one of those chaps who were rescued the other day off that transport, but they've all gone home overland. And they won't stay, you know. All want to get home."

"Can one blame them?" asked the censor. "I read letters in which these seamen say they have not seen their families for seven or eight months."

"Dear me!" said the major drily. His own family were Indian Civil Service. "What you might call the hardships of war. Possibly we may find someone without family ties, Mathews."

The lieutenant smiled and ran his thumb along the blade of the Turkish dagger.

"Possibly," he replied. He smiled because the major was rather conspicuous at home for his affairs with married women.

"By the way," said the censor, following some obscure association of ideas, "I met Morpeth this evening and he was telling me they expected some new arrivals from Paris at the Omphale."

"Yes, I heard that," said the major, who was not at all interested. "It will be a riot. Probably three or four. And about thirty or forty Greek, French, Italian, and Serbian lieutenants, standing round six deep, making them squiffy on Floka's Monopole. No, thanks. Stale pastry, anyhow."

The lieutenant continued to smile.

"They'd better be doing that than slapping each other's faces and exchanging cards at the Cercle Militaire," he murmured.

"They do that anyhow—afterwards," said the major, thrusting his papers into the safe and lighting a cigarette. He shoved the door to with his foot, twirled the knob, and stood up.

"What about some golf to-morrow afternoon?" he demanded. "Didn't you say you had a friend coming ashore, Mathews?"

"Yes, from the *Proteus*. He'll be here about three, I think. Very decent chap, too."

"Right. We'll go out in the new car. See you in the morning."

Mr. Dainopoulos found the trolley cars had stopped running and began to walk home past the cafés of the front. On the other side of the road the stern rails of a score of small coasting craft moved up and down gently in the slight swell, and from here and there amid the confused dunnage on deck a figure moved in sleep, or a silhouette of a man bending over a lantern showed up for a moment. At intervals strains of American jazz music came from the haunts of pleasure, and one could get a glimpse now and then of a dreary dance-floor with half a dozen soldiers and sailors slathering clumsily to and fro, embracing women that gave one the horrors merely to look at, women like half-starved harpies or cylinders of oily fat, the sweat running down through the calcareous deposits on their faces and their squat chunky feet slewed sideways in bronze and coppery shoes. Mr. Dainopoulos hurried past these abodes. Mr. Bates, Archy Bates, a great business friend of his, was somewhere inside one of them, fulfilling his destiny as a patron of Aphrodite and Dionysos; but Mr. Dainopoulos had finished business for the day and he wanted to get home. This was not to be without meeting Archy. The cat-like smile on his unfortunate features, his hat on the back of his head, and his hands in his pockets, Mr. Bates emerged from the *Odéon Bar* just as a carriage appeared in the distance. Mr. Bates did not conceal his gratification. Would his friend come back and have a drink?

"Not to-night," said Mr. Dainopoulos quietly. "Me, I'm going home now. Excuse me, Mister."

"Now, now!" protested Archy, clinging with the adhesiveness of the pickled philanthropist. "Now, now! Lissen. Come-a-me to White Tower. Eh? Laddie? You-n-me, eh? Li'l' fren' o' mine Whi' Tower. She gotta fren', y' know. Here y'are."

The driver, seeing a possible fare, stopped, and Archy, still adhering, dragged Mr. Dainopoulos in after him.

"Stivan," said Mr. Dainopoulos to the driver, whom he knew, "go to the White Tower and when this gentleman has got out, drive me home quick, understand? Leave him behind. And go back to him if he wants you. Now!"

The driver at once set off up the road again and Mr. Bates, who, like Shakespeare, had small Latin and less Greek, sat smiling in the darkness, trying to formulate in his mind and articulate with his tongue something that just eluded him. To meet his old fren' like this—it was a—'strornery thing how he couldn't shay just how he felt. He smiled.

Mr. Dainopoulos sat without smiling. He was not a drinking man at any time, and the professional soak was a mystery to him. Mr. Bates was as much a mystery as the major. His actions had the disconcerting lack of rational sequence that one discerns in pampered carnivora. Absent-minded sensuality is a baffling phenomenon. Mr. Dainopoulos had something of the clear sharp logic of the Latin, and the vinous benevolence of Mr. Bates aroused in him a species of alert incredulity. He sat in silence, listening to the gurgle of his companion's incoherence. This was a phase of his daily existence which he never mentioned to his wife; his dealings with the more dissipated of her countrymen. To his relief the carriage stopped at the entrance of the Tower Gardens. He took Mr. Bates's arm to assist him to alight, but Mr. Bates had forgotten the White Tower. He was trying to sing and not succeeding very well. He sat erect, his hat pushed back until the brim formed a dark halo about his smile, beating time with one hand.

"Here you are, Mister Bates," said Mr. Dainopoulos, try-

ing to move him.   Mr. Bates resisted gently, drew back his
chin a little more and attacked a lower G:

> "*Mo-na, Mona, my own love !*
> *Art—thou not mine*
> *Through the long years to—be-e-e !*"

The sound of that small and strangely clear voice, after the
odorous gibbering speech, almost appalled Mr. Dainopoulos.
He spoke rapidly to the driver, instructing him to wait and he
would be paid in due time, and started off into the darkness.

Mr. Bates finished his song to his own satisfaction and
having smiled into the darkness for a while, began to wonder
where he was.   " 'Strornery thing, but he was almost shertain
ol' fren' of his had been there.   Mush 'ave been a mishtake."
He got out so suddenly the driver was scared.   Mr. Bates
took a bill out of his pocket, held it up uncertainly for a moment, and when the driver had clutched it, marched in an
intricate manner into the gardens.   His smile became more
cat-like than ever as the sound of syncopated music reached
his ear and he passed a woman strolling under the trees.   He
hummed his song again.   The evening, for him, was only just
beginning.

Mr. Dainopoulos hurried forward and soon left the region
of hard arc-lights behind.   His house was not far from here.
He wished to get home.   He regretted sometimes that his
business took him so much away from the house, for he retained sufficient simplicity to imagine that the laws of nature do not apply to love, that you can increase the volume
without diminishing the intensity.   But he consoled himself
with the thought that in a few years he would be able to devote himself entirely to his wife.   His dream was not very
clear in its outlines as yet, because the war now raging was
far-reaching in its effects.   It would be unwise to make plans
which the political changes might render impossible of accom-
plishment.   For the present he was satisfied to place his
reserves at a safe distance in diversified but thoroughly sound
securities, so that unless the civilized world turned completely

upside down and all men repudiated their obligations, he would be able to control his resources. There was not much doubt about that in his mind. He knew that business would go on, was going on, even while men moved in massed millions to destroy each other. While the line swayed and crumpled and broke, or surged forward under the incredibly sustained roar of ten thousand cannon, English and French and German business men were perfecting their plans for doing business with each other as soon as it was over. The ethical side of the question scarcely arose in his mind, since he had grown accustomed to wars and the money to be made out of them. To him the struggle in France and on the Slavic frontier was far off and shadowy, as was the grim game at sea. He was not to be blamed for measuring events by the scale in use by those of his race; and if there was somewhat more ferocity and sustained butchery in this war than in others, it was only another significant symptom of Anglo-Saxon temperament, because business, he knew quite well, was going on.

He knocked at the door in the wall which had so impressed Mr. Spokesly earlier in the evening, and was admitted after a parley by a middle-aged servant-woman.

"Madama gone to bed?" he asked, picking up a large cat that was rubbing herself against his leg, and putting her out into the garden.

"No, she's not gone to bed. She said she would wait for you to come home."

"All right. You can go to bed then," he retorted.

The woman shot the bolts and picked up the cheap pink glass lamp without answering. Mr. Dainopoulos made his way upstairs. There was no light in the room looking out over the sea. In their chamber beyond, a night-light, very small and rose-coloured, was burning on a small table below a picture of the Virgin, as though it were a shrine. It took the place of one, for his wife made the most of his rather dilapidated devoutness, and often left a candle burning there. There was an ulterior motive in her action which she had never formulated exactly even to herself. This was the appeal which a strange and sensuous religion made to her

romantic instinct. She would always be Church of England
herself; but the impression made by candles and an ikon upon
her girl-friends in Haverstock Hill in North London was
always before her. She could hear them breathe the word
"ikon," and then draw in their breath in an ecstasy of awe.
And the thought of it gave her pleasure.

But she was not in the chamber and he returned to the
other room in search of her.

She was lying as before, her eyes closed and her hands
clasped lightly over the tartan rug. A screen had been
opened and stationed between her and the window. This
was the hour to which his thoughts went forward occasionally
during the day of chaffering on the front, or in his blue-
distempered office with its shabby chestnut fittings in the
Cité Saul. To the western cynic there was a rich humour in
the sheer fortuitousness of their meeting in the midst of a
drowning multitude. To him it was not humorous at all.
To him it was significant of a profound fatality. To him it
confirmed his inherited faith in omens and the finger of God.
She was a common enough type of woman in most things,
yet she embodied for him a singular ideal of human achievement. He knew of nothing in the world comparable with
her, and the knowledge that she was his was at times almost
unbelievable. Whether she loved him was a question he
never faced. He believed it, and doubted, and believed
again. He knew by instinct that it was not a matter of importance as was the fact of possession. He extracted a rare
and subtle pleasure from the fragrant ambiguity of her smile.
After all, though it may be doubted if he had ever entertained
the thought, he was fortunate in his circumstances. He had
no need to be jealous or watchful. She lay there quietly,
thinking of course of him, while he was on his affairs in the
port.

He paused now and saw that she was asleep, and he set
the little night-light on the table and sat down near her,
watching her with an expression of grave enthusiasm on his
damaged features. He was not familiar with the stock witti-
cisms concerning the hollowness of marriage and the in-

evitable disgust which follows possession. Indeed, for all his rascality and guile in business he was a rather unsophisticated fellow. He possessed that infinite patience which is sometimes more effective in retaining love than even courage or folly. Another factor in his favour was his lack of facility for friendship. This worked both ways, for friendship is the secret antagonist of both business and love. He sat there, shading his eyes with his curved palm, watching his wife, thinking of past, present, and future in that confused and gentle abstraction which we call happiness, when she suddenly opened her eyes and looked at him for one brief instant with a blank and vacant gaze. Then she smiled and he bent over her.

" Back, Boris? " she murmured chidingly.

" My business, darling. I had to see a man."

" Always business. I thought you'd never come."

" First I had to take that gentleman to the French Pier, for a boat. And then I went to the Olympos Hotel. I think very good business."

" Don't talk about business now."

" But, my sweetheart, it is all for you. By-and-by you will see."

" See what, silly?" she asked, rumpling his hair.

" See what? You ask a funny question. I cannot tell you, not yet. But in my mind, I see it."

And he did, too. He saw, in his mind, a superb and curving shore of yellow sand encircling a sea of flawless azure. He saw a long line of white villas, white with biscuit-coloured balconies and green jalousies, rising amid gardens of laurel and palm; he saw white yachts rocking at anchor, and illuminated houseboats in the shadow of a great breakwater. He saw the spangled lights of a fairy city, a city filled with fabrics and jewels which he would buy for her. He saw all this, and in his mind the world had fought itself to a standstill and the cautious investor had come into his own. He saw the warweary battalions returning to their toil, slaving to pay off the cost of their adventure. This was the way of the world as he knew it. It was no use blaming him: he merely took ad-

vantage of human need and folly, as we all do. He had been
through wars before and knew the inevitable reactions, and
the almost incredible cheapness of money that followed. He
was by instinct one of those who, like camp-followers on a
grand scale, prosper amid the animosities of simpler folk; persons who found fortunes upon great wars, as did the Jews in
London after 1815 and the bourgeois bankers of Paris after
the Revolution. And it surprised him how little his wife
knew, how little she questioned the world in which she lived.
Of course it was charming, and he was fascinated just because
she had that amazing racial blindness to facts and lived in a
fanciful world of her own. The English were all like that, it
seemed to him.

He put his arms about her.

"In my mind I see it. You wait. Everything you can
think of, all very fine."

"Here in Saloniki?"

"No!"

"In England?"

Mr. Dainopoulos laughed a little and shook his head. He
was quite sure England wouldn't be any place for him after
this war. In his own private opinion, there wouldn't be any
England within ten years from now, which shows how logical
and wide-awake Latins can make errors of judgment. In
any case, there were too many Jews there.

"Because I don't want to go to America," she remarked,
still rumpling his hair.

"America! What makes you think of America? You
must be losing your mind, Alice." He almost shivered. He
was just as well able to make money in America as anywhere
else, but what use would it be to him in such a place? It is
extremely difficult for the Anglo-Saxon to realize it, but men
like Mr. Dainopoulos find occidental institutions a spiritual
desolation. He recalled the time when he boarded in Newark, New Jersey, and worked in a felt-hat factory. The
house was of wood without even a floor of stone, and he
could not sleep because of the vermin. And the food! He
experienced afresh the nausea of those meals among the

roomers, the bulging haunches of the negroid waitress colliding with his shoulders as she worked round and served the rows and rows of oval dishes dripping with soggy, impossible provender. And the roomers: English, German, and American, with their horrible whiskey and their everlasting gibberish of "wop" and "dago," their hints and blustering invitations to join mysterious fraternities which no one seemed to understand or explain. Mr. Dainopoulos must not be censured for withdrawing from all this. He made no claims upon western civilization, and its lack of logic and continuity led him to prefer something less virtuous, perhaps, but also less of a strain upon normal human nature.

"You say you don't want to go to America. And I'll say it, too. I've been there, and that was enough for me. I should die there, with the food they give you. It's a fine country, with fine trees in the streets," he added, thinking of an imperial horse-chestnut tree which had thrust a branch bearing pale candles of bloom against his window out there, "and the big men are good men to do business. But not for me. Dirty wood houses and soot coming down all the time on the bed. Like ashes from the engines."

"Like London," said Alice, smiling.

But Mr. Dainopoulos had been living on a somewhat higher scale in London and he had not noticed the dirt so much. Moreover, he could always get the food he wanted in London.

"Well, where?" insisted Alice, humouring him.

"There's plenty places," he said soberly, rather faint as he compared their present surroundings with that dream-villa by the blue sea. "Too soon yet to be sure we get there. I got a lot of business to finish up first. And we're all right here for a while. You're not lonesome, darling?"

"Oh, no! You saw Evanthia here to-night?"

"Yes, I saw her, but she didn't tell me anything."

"He's gone away, with the consuls."

Mr. Dainopoulos gave a low whistle.

"I never thought about that. What'll she do now? That's bad for her, though."

"She wants to follow him but I don't think she can. I believe she heard he'll go to Constantinople. She said she'd do anything to get there."

"Well, if she wants to go to Constantinople, she might be able to," he said, pondering. "I heard to-day a ship might be going down to the Islands. There's always a chance. I'll see. But if she's got any sense she'll go back to her mother. That feller Lietherthal is good company but he'll go back to Munich by-and-by."

"She doesn't love him, I am almost sure."

"Evanthia, she don't love anybody except herself. I told you that."

"She loves me," said Alice.

"Well, p'raps she does, but you know what I mean."

"That gentleman this evening, Mr. Spokesly, he was interested in her."

"He's got a young lady in London," said Mr. Dainopoulos.

"Has he?" she murmured absently. "Do you think he'll come to-morrow night?"

"Yes, I think so. I bet you're goin' to have Evanthia in, too."

"Well, perhaps he'll fall in love with her," she whispered delightedly.

"What, and him with a young lady in London!"

"I don't think he's very fond of his young lady in London."

"Well, how do you know that? Women. . . ."

"Never mind. It's easy to tell if a man is in love," she answered, watching him. He held her tightly for a moment.

"Not so easy to tell about a woman," he said into her hair. "Is it, my little wife, my little wife?"

"Why, don't you know yet?" she bantered, giving him that secret, fragrant, ambiguous smile.

"My little wife!" he repeated in a tense whisper. And as he said it, he felt in his heart he would never know.

CHAPTER VII

IT WAS evening and the *Tanganyika*, a tall unwieldy bulk, for she had only a few hundred tons in her, lay at anchor waiting for her commander, who was ashore getting the ship's papers. She was about to sail for Alexandria, carrying back, through an area infested with enemy submersibles, some of the cargo already discharged and reloaded in the southern port. This apparently roundabout method of achieving results had in it neither malice nor inefficiency. Those who have had anything to do with military matters will understand the state of affairs, and the seemingly insane evolutions of units proceeding blindly upon orders from omnipotent commanders. The latter had ever before them the shifting conditions of a dozen theatres of war, and to them it was nothing that a crate of spark-plugs, for example, sorely needed in Persia, should be carried to and fro over the waters of the Ægean, or that locomotives captured from an Austrian transport and suitable for the Macedonian railroads should be rusting in the open air in Egypt. These men, scoured clean and pink as though with sand and boiling water every morning, in their shining harness and great gold-peaked hats, moved swiftly in high-powered motor cars from one consultation to another, the rows of medal ribbons glowing on their breasts like iridescent plumage. They lived in a world apart. For them it was inevitable that a whole fleet of ships should be no more than a microscopic point in some great curve named Supply. Behind them was a formidable element called Politics, a power which appeared to them to come out of Bedlam and which would suddenly change its course and make the labour of months of no avail. Their eyes were steadily fixed upon certain military dispositions, and they sent forth, from their lofty stations, standing orders which enclosed each subordinate commander in an isolated compartment, beyond which he could not possibly wander, but within which he could exercise a practically god-like power. This system, admirable because it relieved each executive from any concern with the final upshot of the struggle, ultimately reached the *Tanganyika*. Her captain, receiving his instructions from the Naval Transport office, found himself in sole charge of life and property upon her, while for subsequent sailing orders he was referred to the commanding officer of a sloop now moving slowly towards the boom. Captain Meredith in no wise objected to this. What struck him with ironical emphasis was the ineffectiveness of military traditions when applied to a ship with a civilian crew. He might issue orders, but who was to foreshadow the effect on the minds of the Orientals who steered and stoked and oiled below? What might he expect in a sudden disaster from those yellow enigmas padding to and fro or sitting on their hams drinking rice-water and staring at the shores of Macedonia with unfathomable eyes? He had been asked if in his opinion the crew were loyal, and he had wondered how any one could find that out. Loyalty, when you came to place it under analysis, presented a somewhat baffling problem. It was like trying to find out whether men were religious. The assumption, of course, was that all men had in them, deep down, something of ultimate probity. But of what use was that in such a sudden emergency as confronted one at sea these days? Captain Meredith refrained from dwelling too long upon probabilities as he returned to the *Tanganyika*. He hoped he would get through all right again. He had heard hints of a cargo for Basra, in the Persian Gulf; and until they could get him a white crowd he would rather not take any more risks in the Ægean. The longer the war went on the less important seemed abstractions like loyalty or patriotism, and the more shiningly important the need for unimaginative and quick-witted efficiency. There lay the trouble. The naval or military commander had behind him the prestige and power of service discipline and he was supported in his ruthless judgments by the rank and file. The naval officer spoke his orders in a quiet, refined voice, and massive muscular blue-jackets, drilled for years, sprang smartly to carry them out. Here, Captain Meredith reflected, it was not quite like that. Seamen in merchant ships were largely individualists. Had they, for example, been forced by law to go to sea immediately after being sunk, they would almost inevitably have rebelled and sulked ashore. Being free agents, they were filled with fury, and mobbed shipowners to send them out again. This was the good side. The bad side was the difficulty in getting them to obey orders. Moreover, as was made plain during his recent interview with the officers in the Transport Department, his own class, the commanders, had something to learn about doing as they were bid. They had shown him a Weekly Order, just in from Malta, demonstrating the urgent necessity of all captains carrying out their instructions. The huge *Afganistan*, triple screws and with four thousand souls on board, had been sunk and many lost, while her escort was awaiting her two hundred miles to the south. It was pointed out to Captain Meredith that the *Afganistan* was lost simply because her commander had disobeyed explicit orders given at Port Said. Well! It was not pleasant, but had to be borne. This was, he supposed, being faithful unto death. He climbed on board, waved good-bye to the lieutenant in the launch, and ordered the anchor up.

Mr. Spokesly was waiting at the gangway for that very purpose and went forward at once. Captain Meredith, on reaching his room, rang the bell. The second steward appeared at the door, a long lubberly lout with yellow hair plastered athwart a dolichocephalous cranium and afflicted with extraordinarily unlovely features.

"Where is the chief steward?" the captain demanded.

"In 'is room, sir. I was to sye, sir, as 'e ain't feelin' very well this afternoon, sir, if you'll excuse 'im."

"Drunk, I suppose," said the commander quietly.

"Ow, it's not for me to sye, sir," the creature whinnied, moving enormous feet encased in service shoes pilfered from cargo. "Was it tea you was wantin', sir?"

"Bring it," said Captain Meredith, regarding him with extreme disfavour, and the man disappeared.

Not much chance there, thought the captain, as he noted the awkward knuckly hands, with nails bitten to the quick, which arranged the tray before him and made a number of the indescribable motions peculiar to stewards. Hands! How marvellously they indicated character! He was reminded afresh of his own brother-in-law, a surgeon, of whose death in action he had learned during the week. Wonderful hands he had had, long with broad shallow points, indicative of a very fine skill with the knife. Now he was dead; and this creature here would no doubt survive and prosper when it was all over. The captain had been thinking a good deal during the past few days. An old friend of his, a schoolmaster in happier times, had suddenly descended upon him, a bronzed person in khaki with a major's crowns on his shoulder-straps. Had a few days' leave from the Struma front. He was not elated at his rise in rank, it transpired, for it had simply been a process of rapid elimination. All the senior officers had been killed; and here he was, an old gray badger of an elderly lieutenant promoted to major. There was a lull on the Struma, he said, his tired, refined voice concealing the irony. Very delightful to have a few days' peace on a ship with a friend. Now he was back on the Struma; and perhaps next time Captain Meredith got news there would be another gap in that little staff. He stepped out on the bridge. The anchor was coming up.

Mr. Spokesly was thinking, too, in spite of the immediate distraction of heaving-up. It had been a week of extraordinary experiences for him. As he leaned over the rail and looked down into the waters of the Gulf, and noted the immense jelly-fish, like fabled amethysts, moving gently forward to the faint rhythmic pulsing of their delicate fringes, he began to doubt afresh his identity with the rather banal person who had left England a couple of short months before. He found himself here now, outwardly the same, yet within there was a readjustment of forces and values that at times almost scared him. For he had reached a position from

which it was impossible to gauge the future.   Nothing would
ever be the same again.   He was frankly astonished at his
own spiritual resources.   He had not known that he was
capable of emotions so far removed from a smug commonplace.   Love, as he had conceived it, for example, had been
an affair of many oppressive restrictions, an affair of ultimate
respectability and middle-aged affection.   Oh, dear, no!   It
appeared to be a different thing entirely.   He discovered
that once one was thoroughly saturated with it, one stepped
out of all those ideas as out of a suit of worn and uncomfortable clothing.   Indeed, one had no need of ideas at all.   One
proceeded through a series of transmigrations.   One arrived
at conclusions by a species of intuition.   Life ceased to be an
irritating infliction and became a grand panorama.

And yet in the present situation what did it all amount to?
With its well-known but inexplicable rapidity, rumour had
already gone round the ship hinting at a trip to the Persian
Gulf.   If that were so, Mr. Spokesly, by all the laws of probability, would never be in Saloniki again.   Yet he was quite
confident that he would be in Saloniki again.   He had no
clear notion of what he proposed to do when he reached
Alexandria, but he was determined to manage it somehow.
He had a feeling that he was matched against fate and that he
would win.   He did not yet comprehend the full significance
of what he called fate.   He was unaware that it is just when
the gods appear to be striving against us that they need the
most careful watching lest they lure us to destroy ourselves.
He was preoccupied with the immediate past; which he did
not suspect is the opiate the gods use when they are preparing
our destinies.   And while he was sure enough in his private
mind that he would get back to Saloniki somehow, the slow
movement of the *Tanganyika* as she came up on her anchor
gave the episode an appearance of irrevocable completeness.
He was departing.   Somewhere among those trees beyond
the White Tower, trees that shared with everything else in
Saloniki an appearance of shabby and meretricious glamour,
like a tarnished and neglected throne, was Evanthia Solaris.
And the ship was moving.   The anchor was coming up and

the ship was going slow ahead. Mr. Spokesly looked down at the water that was gushing through the hawse-pipe and washing away the caked mud from the links and shackles. As far as he could see he was going back to Alexandria, back by devious ways to London, and Evanthia Solaris, with her amber eyes, her high-piled glossy black hair and swift, menacing movements, would be no more than an alluring memory. And as the anchor appeared and the windlass stopped heaving while the men hosed the mud from the flukes, Mr. Spokesly began to realize, with his new-found perception, that what he took to be confidence was only desire. He was imagining himself back there in Saloniki; a man without ties or obligations. He saw an imaginary Spokesly seizing Evanthia and riding off into the night with her, riding into the interior, regardless of French sentries with their stolid faces and extremely long bayonets. As he recapitulated the actual conditions he saw he had only been dreaming of going back there. He had drawn all the money he could and he owed Archy Bates a ten-pound note. Stowed away under his clothes in his cabin he had nearly an oke, which is about three pounds, of a dark brown substance which Mr. Dainopoulos had mentioned was worth eighty pounds in Egypt if it were adroitly transferred to the gentleman who had expressed his willingness to do business with the friends of Mr. Bates. Here lay the beginnings of that desire, it seemed. That eighty pounds might put Mr. Spokesly in a position to go where he liked. It might; but the chances were that Mr. Spokesly would fail to get away from himself after all. It is not so easy to be an outlaw as it appears, when one has been one of the respectable middle classes for so long. The seaman is as carefully indexed as a convict, and has very little more chance in ordinary times of getting away. Mr. Spokesly knew that and had no such notion in his head. What he did meditate was some indirect retirement from the scene, when a pocketful of loose cash would enable him to effect a desirable manœuvre in a dignified manner, and he would have no need to forfeit his own opinion of himself. The temperament of the crook may sometimes be innate, but in most cases it is the

result of a long apprenticeship. Mr. Spokesly wanted
money, he wanted a command, he even wanted romance;
but he did not want to be wicked. He could no more get
away from Haverstock Hill, North West London, than
could Mrs. Dainopoulos with all her romantical equipment.
Therein lay the essential difference between himself and Mr.
Dainopoulos, who also desired respectability, but who had
in reserve a native facility for swift and secret chicanery.
Mr. Dainopoulos slipped in and out of the law as easily as a
lizard through the slats of a railing. Mr. Spokesly could not
do that, he discovered to his own surprise and perhaps regret.
Unknown to himself, the austere integrity of distant ancestors
and the hard traditions of an ancient calling combined to
limit his sphere of action. The reason why many of us remain merely useful and poverty-stricken nonentities is that
we can serve no other purpose in the world. We lack the
flare for spectacular exploits; and even the war, which was to
cleanse and revitalize the world, has left us very much as we
were, the victims of integrity.

When he had seen the anchor made fast and the compressors screwed tight, Mr. Spokesly went aft to get his tea.
He was to go on watch at eight. This was the Captain's
idea, he reflected. They were supposed to pick up a new
third mate in Alexandria. In the meanwhile the Captain
was taking a watch. It was very unsatisfactory, but
what was one to do? The Old Man had been very
quiet about the shore-going in Saloniki. Hardly left the
ship himself. Had that friend of his, a major, living
in the spare cabin. Whiskies and sodas going upstairs
too, the second steward had mentioned. Too big to
notice what his own officers were doing, no doubt. If he
knew what his chief officer was doing! By Jove! Mr.
Spokesly was suddenly inflated, as he sat eating his tea, with
extraordinary pride. He had recalled the moment when he
had walked into the concert-hall of the White Tower Gardens
with Evanthia Solaris. The proudest moment of his life.
Every officer in the room had stared. Every woman had
glared at the slim *svelte* form with the white velvet toque set

off by a single spray of osprey. As well they might, since
they had never seen her before. They had seen the toque,
however, in Stein's Oriental Store, and had wondered who
had bought it. And as they had moved through the dense
throng of little tables surrounded by officers and cocottes,
amid a clamour of glasses and laughter and scraping chairs,
with music on the distant stage, Mr. Spokesly experienced
a new pleasure. They sat down and ordered beer. Upstairs a number of Russian officers, in their beautiful soft
green uniforms, were holding a girl over the edge of a box and
enjoying her screams. Someone threw a cream cake at the
girl who was singing on the stage and it burst on her bosom,
and everyone shrieked with laughter. The girl went into
a paroxysm of rage and snarled incomprehensibly at them
before flinging out of sight, and they all bawled with merriment. It was rich. Suddenly the Russian officers pushed
the girl over the edge of the box and she dangled by her wrists.
The audience howled as she kicked and screamed. The
uproar became intolerable. Officers of all nations rose to
their feet and bawled with excitement. One of them put a
chair on a table and reached up until he could remove the
dangling girl's shoe. It was filled with champagne and
passed round. The girl was drawn up and disappeared into
the box. The manager appeared on the stage to implore
silence and order. Someone directed a soda-siphon at him
and he retired, drenched. Finally a large placard was displayed which informed the audience that "*À cause du tapage
le spectacle est fini,*" and the curtain descended. They went
out into the gardens, Evanthia holding his arm and taking
short prinking little steps. Why had she wanted to go to
such a place? He was obliged to admit she hardly seemed
aware of the existence of the people around her. She sat
there sipping her beer, smiling divinely when she caught
his eye, yet with an air of invincible abstraction, as though
under some enchantment. Mr. Spokesly was puzzled, as he
would always be puzzled about women. Even his robust
estimate of his own qualification as a male was not sufficient
to explain the sudden mysterious change in Evanthia Solaris.

Was she afraid, she who gave one the impression of being afraid of nothing? But Mr. Spokesly was not qualified to comprehend a woman's moods. His destiny, his function, precluded it. He never completely grasped the fact that women, being realists, see love as it really is, and are shocked back into a world of ideal emotions where they can experiment without imperilling their sense of daintiness and vestal dedication to a god. And Evanthia Solaris was experimenting now. Her *liaison* with the gay and debonair creature who had journeyed out of Saloniki that night with the departing consuls had been an inspiration to her to speculate upon the ultimate possibilities of emotional development. Just now she was quiet, as a spinning top is quiet, her thoughts, her conjectures, merely revolving at high speed. With the quickness of instinct she had admitted this friend of Mrs. Dainopoulos to a charming and delicate comradeship committing her to nothing. That he should love, of course, went without saying. She was debating, however, and revolving in her shrewd and capable brain, how to use him. And it gave her that air of diffident shyness blended with saucy courage which made him feel, now he was soberly eating his tea on board the *Tanganyika*, outward bound, that she was a sorceress who had thrown an enchantment about him. And he wanted, impossible as he knew it to be, to go back there and resign himself again to the enchantment, closing his eyes, and leaving the *dénouement* to chance. No doubt the novelty of such a course appealed to him, for he came of a race whose history is one long war against enchantments and the poisonous fumes of chance. He went on stolidly eating his tea, substantial British provender, pickled pig's feet, beet-and-onion salad, stewed prunes, damson jam, and tea as harsh as an east wind. He loitered over the second cup, while the second steward passed behind him with a napkin, eager for him to finish, for that gentleman intended to gorge, while Archy Bates was indisposed, on pig's feet and pickled walnuts. Mr. Spokesly loitered because he knew, when he was once again in his own cabin, that he would be facing a problem which makes all men, except artists and scoundrels, uneasy. The problem was Ada. He did not want to think about Ada, a girl who was in an unassailable position as far as he was concerned. He wanted her to stay where she was, in beleaguered England, until he was ready to go back, until he had regained command of himself. He rose up suddenly and went along to his cabin. His idea was that Ada should wait for him, wait while he went through this extraordinary experience. His mind even went forward and planned the episode. He would get the money in Alexandria, get out of the ship somehow, return to Saloniki . . . and when the war was over he would of course return to England and find Ada waiting for him. It was an admirable scheme and more frequently carried out than Mr. Spokesly was aware. Yet he was secretly ashamed. He had also a vague, illogical notion that, after all, he was not contemplating any real infidelity to Ada since he fully intended to return to her. He was very confused in his mind. He was not accustomed to such crises. He took up the little green pamphlets of the London School of Mnemonics. An aphorism caught his eye. *Be sure your chin will find you out.* The idea was expanded in an essay on forcefulness of character. The theory propounded was that we have all of us a minute germ of character force which by exercise and correct training can be developed into a formidable engine for the acquisition of power, position, and wealth. Another aphorism ran: *Train the muscles of your mind.* Just as the use of dumb-bells brought out rippling rolls of muscle under a satin skin, so the use of the Mnemonic method of Intensive Excogitation rounded out the sinews of the mind and gave a glistening polish to the conversation. Above all, it augmented one's cerebral vitality. One became a forceful personality and exerted a magnetic influence over women. . . .

Mr. Spokesly's feet hurt him slightly. He went along to the pantry and ordered a bucket of hot water, and proceeded to go the rounds of the ship to see that all ports and doors were screened. His feet hurt him. And it seemed to him that his mind hurt him in very much the same way. He was in a mood which people like the London School of Mnemonics dread and deprecate more than anything else, a mood which renders suddenly valueless millions of dollars' worth of advertising, which empties theatres and leaves the purveyors of commodities with warehouses crammed with moribund stock. He was suspicious. He had suddenly perceived in a dim way the complete and humorous fallacy of trying to become somebody else through the mails. It did not present itself to him in this form. He was not clever enough to get anything so clear as that. The London School of Mnemonics prospered exclusively upon people who lacked the power of coherent thought. But he had become suspicious. He had lost faith, not in himself, but in the resources of ultra-modern advertising. He was beginning to wonder what Mr. Dainopoulos would say to the theory of Intensive Excogitation. Mr. Spokesly did not realize it, of course, but the mere fact that he was losing faith in the London School of Mnemonics was evidence of his progress in life. So much Evanthia Solaris had already done for him. She had induced in him a certain contempt and cantankerous suspicion of life. He saw himself with appalling clearness as the mate of a transport, quarrelling with dirty, insolent engineers who could not be induced to blind the scuttles of their cabins properly. And as he came back from the forecastle he heard Captain Meredith's quiet voice. The captain wanted the fall of the big steel boom made more secure. This boom was kept up against the mast, since it was too long to lay down. Mr. Spokesly blew his whistle. The bosun and a couple of seamen came out and began bending the heavy fall about the bollards near the standing rigging. Then they hauled on the guys which brought the boom hard up against the mast, and it appeared from the silence of the commander that he was satisfied. That, thought Mr. Spokesly, was what you had to put up with. He himself had sent a man up to the crosstrees hours ago to make fast the head of the boom. The man had not mentioned the fact that the dead-eye was loose up there, for the reason that he was a young chap and did not notice it. While the guys held the boom up he had slipped the pin into place and climbed down. And this was what one had to put up with. Impossible to give satisfaction. Day after day. Nag, nag, nag. Mr. Spokesly went back to his cabin and found Archy Bates sitting on the settee.

Archy was in that mood which follows heavy drinking by the initiated. Archy was always ready for each mood as it came and made the most of it. With a confidence that resembled to an extraordinary degree the faith of an inspired fanatic, he gave himself over to the service of the god for the time being. Coming back from ashore he had fallen out of the boat into the water and then fallen off the gangway into the boat again; yet his faith in his star never faltered. When the boat drifted from the grating he had assumed a stern expression, and raising his arms proceeded to walk across the water. When Archy was in that benign mood incidental to his return from a souse, there was nothing in the world to prevent him walking on water or ascending into the air, should he deem it a dignified thing to do. There was something rather awful, to one who believed in the laws of nature, in the inebriated accuracy of Archy's movements along intricate alleyways, through doors and up ladders. Through it all he held in reserve the fixed cat-grin which implied a bemused omniscience, a dreadful knowledge of secret human standards.

But that mood was gone and he sat here on Mr. Spokesly's settee, smoking a cigarette, completely normal and master of himself. It was a grotesque feature of his convalescence, this austere assumption of efficiency. He was very much upset at the way the second steward had made a mess of things that afternoon. Just as soon as he took his eye off him, things went wrong. It was most discouraging. And he would like to recommend him for promotion, too. By the way, had Mr. Spokesly heard the company was going to buy some ships? This was an example of the way Archy "heard" of things. No one could tell how he got hold of the most secret information while stewed. Mr. Spokesly was not alert. He made no comment, not realizing how nearly that stray remark might touch him.

It was a fac', Archy hiccoughed. Going to buy a lot of

ships. So he'd heard. He paused, trying to recapture the thought. Yes, now no sooner does the Old Man order supper than the silly josser loses his head. Ring, ring, ring, the Old Man did. Now that he had recaptured it the thought seemed less important than he had imagined. Mr. Spokesly, his friend, with whom he was going to do some nice little business, didn't seem in very good spirits. Archy bent his mind to the matter. It was just as well they weren't going back to Saloniki, he remarked reflectively.

"How do you know? And why just as well?" asked Mr. Spokesly, wishing Archy would go away. He wanted to be alone.

"Didn't you know?" said Archy, wondering. "The Old Man said so. The second steward overheard something about it when he took a tray up when the N. T. O. was here this morning. We're going to Calcutta. Oh, yes. And a good job, too."

"Why?" said Mr. Spokesly.

Mr. Bates winked, and smiled his cat-grin.

"Fact is, Mister," he remarked in a low tone, "I went a little farther than I intended. Nice little widow she is, and it simply wouldn't do for me to be seen round there any more. She gave me this as a keepsake." And Archy drew a ring with an enormous emerald set in pearls from his vest-pocket. He put it on his little finger and turned it about.

"What!" ejaculated Mr. Spokesly. "Gave you that? Why, it's worth a couple of hundred pounds."

"Three hundred," corrected Archy. "Easy! Ah, my boy, you don't know what it is to have the ladies fancy you. Straight, Mister, they're a nuisance."

Mr. Spokesly looked at Archy Bates and wondered just how much of this was true. The value of the ring staggered him, as well it might, since Archy, who always pretended to be drunker than he really was, had discovered it in the uphol-stery of an ottoman on which he was sprawled, his left hand closing over it and moving it softly into his pocket while the right arm had encircled the waist of the widow. He assumed she was a widow, of course, since he saw nothing of her husband. And he had honestly forgotten it until after he had come aboard. He really had some difficulty in not believing himself that she had given it to him. He took it off and handed it to Mr. Spokesly, who looked puzzled.

"Keep it for me," Archy said. "I'm very careless. I might lose it. Give it to me in Alexandria."

"Oh, I'll do that, all right." Mr. Spokesly took it. "I'll put it away."

"You got it all right?" said Archy, meaning the dark brown substance concealed in among the clothes in Mr. Spokesly's drawers.

"Yes," said that gentleman shortly.

"How much . . . ? That all? Why, I got four okes. Not coming back here, you see. I'll keep half for Calcutta. You can get a thousand rupees an ounce there. Nearly— let's see—nearly five hundred pounds an oke. Think of it!"

Mr. Spokesly thought of it and wondered what sort of fight the London School of Mnemonics would put up against that sort of thing. Archy's kind of success was very hard to dismiss as pure luck. He scored every time. He made money, he enjoyed life, and widows were "stuck on him," and gave him costly souvenirs. What efficiency could match this? After the war Archy would be in a position to do as he had occasionally mentioned—buy a nice little tavern and enjoy himself thoroughly. His wife had often wanted him to do it. He sat there on the settee, blinking and smiling in his feline way, and actually seemed to exude prosperity. It was nothing to him that Captain Meredith had no use for him. He had no use for Captain Meredith, so that cancelled out. Captain Meredith could pay him off any time he liked. Archy could write letters to the Company as well as Captain Meredith, come to that. Just for a moment Mr. Spokesly had the wild notion that Archy was beyond the reach of any one on earth, that he was too clever to be caught.

"Well," he said as the boy appeared with the bucket of hot water. "I go on at eight, Archy."

Archy got up, yawned, and stretched.

"I feel a bit tired. I believe I'll have a sleep. Rather

strenuous evenin' last night, not half. You ought to have been with me, Mister. Some little piece. Wanted me to stay. . . . Well, I'll say good-night."

There it was again, thought Mr. Spokesly. Archy could lie on his settee all day, recovering from his cups, and now he could turn in and have a comfortable sleep. Mr. Spokesly removed his socks and lowered his feet into the generous warmth. That was better. After all, a man had to depend on himself. Schools of Mnemonics couldn't do much when there were people like Archy and Dainopoulos in the world. He remembered the ring, and took it out of the drawer to look at it. The heart of the emerald shot lambent flames at him like the cool green shadows beneath a waterfall. He saw it on the slim, supple hand of Evanthia. A gust of strange feeling shook him suddenly. He became aware, with inexplicable poignancy, of the mystical correlation between jewels and love, as though precious stones were only the petrified passions of past days. And how could one reconcile the beauty of these things, and the fact that they seemed ever to be found in the possession of ignoble men? More than a year's salary, and Archy could throw it to him to keep for him. And a woman had given it to him. Mr. Spokesly was beginning to be a little uncertain of his own knowledge of women. They seemed incalculable. It seemed impossible to chart the course of any of them for any length of time. He winced as he wondered what Ada would say if she knew what he was up to. He had no need to wonder. He knew perfectly well that she would forgive and sympathize and let it be forgotten. That was the way with English girls. He realized with a great uplifting of the heart that this was part of the Englishman's goodly heritage. He thought of himself, coming home at last to Ada, and how she would stroke his hair and murmur "silly old boy," and he would be at peace. Peace! In the meanwhile there was the war. It did not look so very good for the time being. The Germans seemed an uncommonly tough proposition. Mr. Spokesly wondered why all those military men, who wrote testimonials for the London School of Mnemonics, couldn't show their amazingly improved mentality by giving the enemy a licking. All very well to write, "Six months ago I was a sergeant: now I am a major-general, and I consider it is entirely due to your System." After all, what we needed was somebody who could keep the Fritzies away from the Channel ports. He sighed. He would have to dry his feet and go up on the bridge. As he stood up to open a drawer to find a fresh pair of socks he slipped the ring into his trousers pocket and forgot it.

As he went out into the alleyway to go forward, the last faint streaks of light were vanishing from the sullen sky over the mountains of Thessaly and a heavy blanket of clouds had come up from the eastward, so that the night was ideally dark for running through these perilous waters. Ahead of the *Tanganyika* could be seen a faint light, carefully screened so that only an observer high up and astern of her could see it at all. This was the pilot light on the sloop, and Captain Meredith mentioned in a low voice the necessity of keeping it in view, as otherwise they might run each other down, it was so dark. There were two other transports behind, one on each quarter, who would also need watching. They had just received a general wireless call that a submarine-course had been observed N. by N.-N.-E. from Skyros, which would bring her into their zone about one in the morning. Escort would signal change of course by a red light shown in three periods of two seconds each. And, the captain added, he himself would be lying on his settee just inside the door.

He vanished in the intense darkness and Mr. Spokesly found himself high up, alone in that darkness, and in charge of the ship. She vibrated strongly, being almost in ballast, and rolled perhaps three degrees either way in a leisurely rhythm. Along her sides he could see a sheer bottle-green glow from fore-foot to where it was lost in the white cascade churned up by the emerging propeller. Beyond this one could only catch a sort of rushing obscurity, for the sea was smooth and unbroken by the long invisible swell. The clouds now covered the whole sky so that one could see nothing on the forecastle-head.

Mr. Spokesly paced to and fro, watching the faint and occasionally vanishing light on the escort. He ran over in his mind the ship's company and ruminated on their various employments. The gunner would be asleep alongside of his gun; for of what use was it to stand by if one had no target? The crew were all asleep, save the helmsman and the two lookouts on the forecastle. The chief was no doubt seated in his cabin smoking and thinking of his wife and children in Maryport. Mr. Chippenham, who came on at midnight, was asleep. And there would be Archy, turned in without a care in the world. Mr. Spokesly's hand came in contact with the ring in his pocket. He must not forget to stow it away safely when he went below again. It would look funny if he lost it. He remembered he owed Archy a ten-pound note. Must pay that in Alexandria, too. Things might happen in Alexandria, he reflected with pleasure. There was that talk of the company getting more ships—there might be something in it. The Old Man was so infernally close-lipped about everything. Fancy the chief officer of a ship having to get that sort of news from a steward, just because the captain didn't trust anybody! He threw his arms up on the dodger and stared into the darkness. The silence was broken suddenly by the rhythmic clatter of a shovel-blade against iron—the call of the fireman to the coal-passers for more coal. They shouldn't make that noise, Mr. Spokesly thought with a frown. Though, come to that, the screw was making noise enough anyhow. Every now and again, as the vibrations of the vessel failed to synchronize, a low muttering rumble came up from the deck members culminating in hoarse rattles of pipe-guards and loose cowls, and running aft in a long booming whine. Mr. Spokesly strained his eyes to catch the pilot light again. Even with the binoculars he could not distinguish the sloop's hull. One comfort, they were not zigzagging. It would only increase the risk of collision on a night like this. Another thought occurred to Mr. Spokesly as he looked away from the glasses for a moment. He felt that if he himself were in a submarine out there he would be much more anxious to avoid a ship than to find her. The chances of being run down were too many. He did not realize that the *Tanganyika,* seen from sea level, was a solid black bulk, jangling and booming her way through the sea and leaving an immense pathway of phosphorescence behind her. He had no time to realize it. He had no time to adjust himself to any philosophical possibilities before it came with a crashing roar that left him, for an instant, unconscious. The deck and the bulwark below him heaved up and burst into crooked screaming flames as the beams and plates were torn asunder. He stood with his hands gripping the top of the dodger, staring hard into the murk, and then he comprehended. He flinched sideways as a horrible sound smote his ears, a whine rising to a muffled shriek, as the loosened fall of the big boom tore through the blocks, and the boom itself, a fifty-foot steel girder, was coming down. As he reached the port-engine telegraph, tugging at it mechanically, the great mass struck the wheelhouse with a noise of rending wood, breaking glass, and a faint cry that ceased at once.

Mr. Spokesly stood for perhaps three seconds holding the telegraph handle, and he heard a second explosion, a hollow concussion amidships that sent a great column of water into the air so that the *Tanganyika* seemed to have shipped a heavy sea. He could scarcely appreciate the importance of this. He turned with an effort towards the wheel-house and captain's quarters. There was a sound of steam escaping somewhere down below. The boom had crushed through the bridge rails and lay across his path as he stepped over. And there was a dreadful silence up there. Men were running and calling down below, but here was silence. The steering gear was demolished, and behind that . . . He felt sick. He took a step down the ladder and looked again, and this time he fell forward on his face. The ship had gone down by the stern.

"This won't do," he muttered, scrambling up. "Who's in command?" He blew his whistle. "Hi! Tong Pee!" he called to the helmsman. Tong Pee, crushed to a pulp under the binnacle, made no reply. He had never been a communicative person, Tong Pee, and now he had no choice. The sudden complete comprehension of what had happened behind Tong Pee sent Mr. Spokesly down the ladder in a panic. "This is no good," he said anxiously to himself. "No good at all." And he blew his whistle again in a rage.

But the men on the boat-deck were in no mood to pay attention to whistles. The ship was going down. Her after deck was under water, for the second torpedo had hit the engine room and all aft was flooded. The forward hold was light and was keeping her bows up so that she was gradually assuming a vertical position. And the men on the boat-deck were crying "Wah! Wah!" and "Hoi! Hoi!" and stampeding past in a stream towards the boats. They came up staggering with piles of bedding, with corded boxes and crates full of white rats. They came up festooned with mandolins and canaries in cages, with English dictionaries and back-numbers of the *Police Gazette*. They tore each other from the boats and stowed their treasures with long wailing cries of "Hoi! Hoi!" They slipped and slithered away aft in heaps and fought among each other for invisible personal effects. One of them suddenly showed a flashlight in the darkness and the others leapt upon him to take it, and it ricochetted away into the scupper and went out. If one of them by infinite toil got into the boat the others tore him away with howls of anguish. And the deck became steeper. The boats, already swung out, sagged away from the davits and fouled the falls. The sound of scuttering feet and frantic throats was lost in a number of extraordinary sounds from below, like skyscrapers collapsing into a waterfall, as the boilers carried away from their stools and crashed into the engines, which gave way also, and the whole mass, swirling in steam like the interior of a molten planet, plunged through the bulkheads into the empty holds. And then the boats began to fall clear and some of the struggling beings about them dropped away into the void. Mr. Spokesly, hanging to the rail beneath the bridge, found himself sobbing as though his chest would burst. He took off his coat and threw it at the men who were twined in a knot by the nearest davit. The *Tanganyika* was now at a very steep angle.

Mr. Spokesly took off his boots. It flashed through his mind that he was in command. "Oh!" he thought, "I can't leave her!" And then the thought of the others, down there, in their cabins, and the loneliness of it up here with these yellow maniacs, pierced his heart. "I must go," he sobbed. And indeed he had to, for the *Tanganyika* was going down. He could hardly keep his balance. Hot steam was blowing up in great gray gusts from the fiddley-grating. He was near the water now. It might be too late. He jumped.

For a moment as the chill of the water struck him, for he had been in a bath of sweat as he stood there sobbing, he thought he had been killed. He was a good swimmer, for they had made a point of it in his old training-ship. He struck out away, away from the ship as fast as he could. He realized more keenly, now, how dangerous it was to remain near. Twelve, thirteen, fourteen, fifteen strokes. He turned over, treading water and shaking the moisture from his eyes. He was horrified to find how close he was. The ship's bows were towering over him and wavering to and fro. And as he turned to get farther out, he felt himself raised up on a vast billow of smooth water that was rolling in over the *Tanganyika*. He was carried forward and whirled over and over. With something that was almost obstinacy he made up his mind to do the best for himself, kept his mouth shut for one thing, and avoided wearing himself out with useless efforts. And he suddenly brought up against something that nearly knocked the breath out of his body and scraped all the skin off his face. He spread his arms and grasped. He thought hard and quick. The bow! He held on. It was not going down, but up, he was sure. And then, to his surprise, for he really had no authentic belief that he would survive this unusual affair, he found himself out of the water hugging a long iron ridge that trembled just awash.

He began to think again. The mass of metal to which he was clinging was vibrating as though from a series of heavy submarine blows. Huge groans and sharp cracks communicated themselves to his body. He had no faith in the ship remaining long like this. In all probability the forward hatch would get stove in or the peak would fail and then, with the whole ship flooded, she would go down. Away off he heard a heavy detonation. There was a sparkle of red fire and a crack as the sloop fired a three-pounder into the darkness. He caught sight of a faint light which gave him her position. Boom! More depth-charges. Very active now, he thought with unreasoning bitterness, now it was all over. He saw the blur of the sloop moving fast towards him. He threw his leg over the stem, sat up, and putting two fingers of each hand in his mouth, blew a piercing whistle. The next moment he was almost blinded as a searchlight swept across the water and remained fixed upon him. It was appalling, that intense white glare showing up his frightful loneliness out there on the calm heedless sea. The beam wavered and vanished. And at the same moment some premonition made Mr. Spokesly prepare to move off. The *Tanganyika* was going down. Deep bellowings in her interior gave warning. He decided not to wait, and slipped into the water. And before he had reached the boat whose oars he heard working rapidly just ahead of him, there was a final swirl and hiccough on the water, and the *Tanganyika* was gone.

When he woke it was some twenty hours later, for the surgeon had bound up his face and put stitches into a number of lacerations in his body, and had given him cocaine to make him sleep. The sloop was anchoring down by the flour mills, and looking out through his port-hole Mr. Spokesly could see the gardens of the White Tower of Saloniki.

CHAPTER VIII

MR. SPOKESLY sat at a little distance from the large table in the Transport Office and listened to the gentleman with four rings of gold lace on his sleeve. It was a lofty and desolate place in the yellow stucco building opposite the dock entrance. The transport officer was a naval captain; with a beard, a brisk decisive manner, and a very foul briar pipe. He was explaining that they needed a third mate for a ship going to Basra and Mr. Spokesly would just do for the job if he would waive his right to a passage home and go to Port Said instead. It was at this point that Mr. Spokesly, rather shaky still from his immersion and extensively decorated with pieces of plaster, took a hand.

"No," he said and kept his gaze on the floor.

"Why not?" demanded the captain, very much astonished.

"No reason's far as I know. But I'm not going third mate of anything, anywhere, any more. That's that."

"Well, of course, we can't *force* you to go, you know."

"I know you can't."

"But we shall really have to draw the attention of the owners to the fact that you refused to go."

"That's all right. But I'm not going. I'll go home if you don't mind. Or if I can get a job here I take it my articles finished with the *Tanganyika*."

"No doubt, no doubt. But what could you get here?"

"I don't know what I could do. But I'd shine shoes on the steps out there before I went third mate. . . ."

"There's no need to go back to the question if you refuse to volunteer."

Mr. Spokesly stood up. He was in a rage. Or rather he

119

was resuming the rage which had assailed him when the *Tanganyika* was going down and which had been suspended while he made good his claim on life. The smug way in which this bearded stranger disposed of him was intolerable. Mr. Spokesly knew this man would never dream of sending one of his own caste to a third mate's job on a Persian Gulf coaster with the hot season coming on. He knew that he himself, being a merchant seaman, was regarded by all these brass-bound people as an inferior, a shell-back, a lob-scouser, and no dire need would ever make them accept him as one of themselves. And he had a glimpse, in his rage, of another truth, for one often sees these things in flashes of anger. He just caught sight of the fact that these people, with their closely guarded privileges and esoteric codes, were fighting much more for their class than for England, that an England democratized and ravished of her class system would be to them a worse place than an England defeated by a class-conscious enemy. But the immediate grievance was personal. He stood up.

"Volunteer," he repeated. "Excuse me, Mister, I came home from out east and took a second mate's job, there being nothing better about. I went mate when the other man died. I've had a master's ticket this ten years. Now you want me to go third mate. Where shall I end up? In the forecastle? Volunteer! I can tell you, I'm beginning to regret I ever left Hong Kong."

"I see. Of course we can't help that, you know. You'd better go and see the paymaster commander. Perhaps he can put you on a ship."

Mr. Spokesly took the cap, a size too large for him, which he had got on credit at Stein's Oriental Store, and went out. He was feeling very bitter. No man feels he is doing himself justice in clothes that are too large for him. Mr. Spokesly wanted to go away and hide until he could get rid of his enormous golf-cap and the coat which hung on him, as he himself put it, like a bosun's shirt on a capstan-bar. He went downstairs into the street. The sun had forced its way through vast banks of blue-black and gray-white clouds and

brought out unsuspected tones in the roadway ankle-deep in
bright yellow mud, in the green uniform of a Russian soldier
who was carrying a polished copper kettle, and in the black-
green waters of the Gulf crested with silver plumes. Without analyzing the causes of the change, Mr. Spokesly felt
more cheerful. He would go to the paymaster commander,
who was in the Olympos Palace Hotel, and get the price of
a drink anyway. He put his hands in his pockets and
whistled. His hand had closed over the ring. He thought
of Archy, the shiningly successful one, the paladin of pilferers,
the financial genius, down among the crawfish and awaiting
those things he saw on a stall just over there, eight-armed
horrors with enormous bald heads and bulging eyes and
hooked beaks. And as he came to the corner of the Place
de la Liberté, he encountered a gentleman in the uniform of
a lieutenant of reserve. He was an elderly person, with the
subdued air of those men who have somehow attained to a
command without ever making any mistakes or achieving
any remarkable successes. His uniform was badly cut, his
trousers bagged at the knees, and a large blue anchor was
tattooed on his left hand. But to Mr. Spokesly he was an
angel. He was not surprised when this person made some
trivial remark to open the conversation. And it soon appeared that he, too, was nursing a grievance.

"What? You off the *Tanganyika?* Why, you only went
out yesterday. No, the day before. Dear, dear! And what
are they going to do with you?"

"Want me to go up the Persian Gulf third watch-keeper of
a six-hundred-ton coaster," said Mr. Spokesly, feeling the
ring in his pocket and scowling.

"Ah! Just fancy that."

"And I been mate this six years, mind you."

"Just so. How about a drink? Floka's, you know, just
up here. I quite understand," this elderly angel added,
raising his hand. "This is all on me, if you don't mind."

"But I can't really, Mister. Not from a stranger," protested Mr. Spokesly.

"Well, call it a loan, then, until you can see the paymaster.

Here, take these two notes. There now! You owe me a sovereign, eh? Here we are."

Mr. Spokesly would have had some trouble in admitting it, but the fact remains that as they sat down at one of Floka's little tables and his new friend asked him if he could do with a gin and bitters, he could scarcely answer because he was on the verge of tears. After the icy courtesy of the navy, for the officers of the sloop had not permitted him to forget for a moment that he was only a seaman, this warm human kindliness was almost too much. It really would have been a good thing for him if he had been able to have what is called a good cry. But he had been brought up to believe that such emotion was foolish, whereas it is often the highest wisdom.

"What is your job here?" he asked after the drinks had arrived.

"Well, as a matter of fact, I'm in a state of suspended animation," answered the other, who had been a commander in tramp steamers for some years. And he began to tell his story. He had joined up in the usual way, and after knocking about in a shore job in the Bristol Channel, some brilliant creature hit on the idea of sending him out to Saloniki to act as harbour master. They needed one, too, he observed in parentheses; an experienced man to straighten things out. Very good. He arrived.

"And what do I find but I am to take my orders from a sub-lieutenant R. N. who's about the age of my second boy who was killed at Mons, a cocky young fellow who knows just as much about running a harbour master's office as I do about painting pictures! Well, I went to the captain of the Base and I told him as plain as I could, I simply didn't see my way to do it. I couldn't, Mister! I went in to see this young lordship one day on some business, and he kept me waiting half an hour while he was telephoning about a girl he'd met. I told the Captain of the Base I really would have to go home. You know the saying: Standing rigging makes poor running gear. And now," he concluded with a quiet smile, "I believe I've refused duty or something. I do wish I could get a ship again. This waiting about is awful. But my owners have had so many losses, I can't expect a command for a long time even if I could get out of this." And he touched the lace on his sleeve. "These navy people are all right in their own line of trade, I suppose, but they don't seem to understand our troubles at all. They say the most curious things."

"How do you mean?"

"Why," said the old fellow in a whisper, "we had a lot of ships in dock last week or so, so many that the anchors got fouled. One ship would drop her anchor across another's cable, you see. Well, one captain sent in a report he could not get his anchors up and in consequence he'd be delayed getting out. What I wanted to do, what I was going to do, was to move the other ships and give him room. If necessary, some of them could go out and round the breakwater, you understand. But my young lordship, this sub-lieutenant, says, 'Can't he slip his anchors?' in that tone of voice that they use trying to make you feel as though you were an errand boy. Just fancy that! 'Can't he slip his anchors?' 'I dare say he can slip them all right,' I said, 'but wouldn't he find them useful in Genoa?' Which was where he was going. You read a lot in the papers about what wonderful chaps they are, but . . . I don't know."

They sat there, those two, getting themselves pleasantly communicative on gin and bitters, swapping stories of the incompetence of others and their own obscure virtues, until Mr. Spokesly realized he would have to see the paymaster and discover what was to happen to him.

"Well," he said, "I must go. I suppose I'll see you again."

"I'm at the Olympos. I'll show you where to go. You'd better get a room there, too, if you can. I think I'll get along now and see what my young lordship is up to. Slipping some more anchors, I expect. See you later."

And he moved off, in his slovenly fitting uniform and large broad-toed shoes. Mr. Spokesly watched him. There, he thought, went a man who'd had a command for years. And treated like a dog! He would be like that himself in twelve or fifteen years' time. These official people only thought of themselves. The only thing to do was to take a leaf out of their book and look after Number One. He went into the hotel.

He came out again in about a quarter of an hour. "So that's the way we're treated," he muttered, walking away. "Anybody would think I'd committed a crime, not going down with everybody else." This was rather hard on a harassed paymaster who could do nothing for Mr. Spokesly save advance him two hundred francs, as per regulations regarding distressed ships' officers, and promise him a compassionate passage home at some future date, unless Mr. Spokesly's owners authorized something more generous. With the two hundred francs in his pocket he walked away with the general idea of getting a suit of clothes. And then— perhaps it was the backward glance he took as he stood at the upper end of the noisy, dirty little Place de la Liberté and saw the sunlight dancing on the green-black water and on the polished brass funnels of the launches; perhaps it was the glimpse he caught of the far peaks of Thessaly that gave him an uplifting of the heart. His mood changed. He saw the thing suddenly not as a grievance but as an adventure, in which he would have to decide for himself. These naval people were only cogs in wheels. If they wanted him they could come for him. He recalled again the important fact that with the loss of the *Tanganyika* he became exactly what he had so greatly desired—a free agent, so long as he did not press his claim for passage home. There was nothing in his way now except this life-long habit of going to somebody for orders. Men had made great fortunes, he had heard, by being cast adrift in a foreign port in some such fashion. And others, he reflected cynically, had come down in the world to be weak-kneed bummers and drink-cadgers. There it was again. It rested with the man himself. What was it the little green books of the London School of Mnemonics had said? Mr. Spokesly laughed shortly as he thought of them lying at the bottom of the sea. A good place for them. Lot of rubbish, if the truth were known. Fat lot of use they were now, for instance. That chap Dainopoulos was worth a ton of scientific flub-dub about training one's memory. Why not go and see Dainopoulos now? See if his talk about a job would amount to anything. And Mrs. Dainopoulos. And Evanthia Solaris. He drew a deep breath and looked out across the dancing sea. A battalion began to march along the quay, drums and fifes thudding and squeaking behind them, a long line of khaki figures with overcoats curled in a thick band across their bodies, hung all over with an extraordinary assortment of utensils. Going up to the front, he reflected, to be shot or dismembered or racked with dysentery. They got the glory, too. They were "the boys at the front," and they filled the public eye. They and the navy. They had pensions provided and so on. Mr. Spokesly was not a trustworthy authority on the business and emoluments of soldiering. He held always the civilian's point of view. He had been brought up among a class of people who kept silent on the subject if a member of their family enlisted. Even the war, which abolished the necessity for shame, did not eradicate the fundamental animosity of these middle-class folk towards the military. Mr. Spokesly himself had an old aunt, who lived on her husband's insurance money at Hendon, who still alluded to "the red-coats," though scarlet had been abolished. It was, like their terror of dear bread, in their blood. They were individualists, these bourgeois from whom Mr. Spokesly came. They were the folk whose relatives were established in distant colonies where they had raised families of tall sons who had come back into the fight so changed in character that the people of England did not know them. They were the folk who "went out" to the East and into Africa as traders and factors, and who carried Haverstock Hill with them up the Nile and the Hoang Ho. Unimaginative and devoid of conscious art, they furnished, without knowing or caring much about the matter, the raw material of romance. They did outrageously romantic things under the pretence of providing for their families or getting orders for their firm. And it was this generic inherited character, working to the surface during the reaction from his recent exertions and emotional stress, that meant more to Mr. Spokesly than either the war or the London

School of Mnemonics. The basis of romantic adventure is character, and a man's real character is sometimes overlaid with curious artificial ornaments. Mr. Spokesly had been very much in error both as to his own character and his destiny. He had no more need of memory training than Mr. Dainopoulos. In the future his care would be to forget rather than remember. His recent experiences had taught him much. What was to come would teach him still more.

He found Mr. Dainopoulos in his extremely diminutive office in a cross-street near the Post Office. Mr. Dainopoulos was ostensibly a money-changer. In front of his premises was a glass case with an assortment of currency. A few sovereigns in a saucer caught the eye, and might have inspired the casual passenger with polite wonder how they had found their way there when honest men in England had forgotten how they looked. And at the back of his premises Mr. Dainopoulos had a safe nearly as large as the office. Between these two emblems of financial affairs were a table and two chairs. On the walls were musty insurance calendars and obsolete steamship sailing lists, for Mr. Dainopoulos had done a brisk agency in the past with emigrants, stimulating the cupidity of Balkan peasants with lively handbills describing the streets of New York and Chicago as being paved with gold. At the present moment, when Mr. Spokesly came in, the other chair was occupied by a long thin person folded loosely together and smoking a cigarette in a holder nearly a foot long. He had one of those physiognomies that baffle analysis by the simple expedient of never under any circumstances meeting one's eye. The pinched cranium, the cold, pale blue eyes, the hooked nose coming down over a toothless mouth to meet an up-turning pointed chin, might lead one to think him old, yet he was no more than forty-five in fact. His long sallow hands were hairless and garnished with several seal-rings, and on one skinny wrist hung a slave bangle. He had his chair tipped back against the wall, one leg dangling, the other hooked by the heel into the cross-bar, while over the raised sharp knee-joint he had draped his forearm. He was talking with great animation, his jaws moving rapidly like the jaws of a ventriloquist's dummy, which he altogether resembled, and his toothless gums gave out a hissing lisp. Mr. Dainopoulos jumped up.

"My dear friend!" he exclaimed, with that faint Latin crow on the upper register which is so disconcerting to the northerner. He took in the situation rapidly. It was unusual for him to be ignorant of anything for long. He very often knew of disasters before the Intelligence Department, having means that they lacked for gathering news from obscure sources. He needed no schools of mnemonics to teach him the inevitable deductions from Mr. Spokesly's queer cap and baggy coat, while the long strips of plaster made him utter inarticulate sounds of sympathy.

"Let me introduce you. This is Captain Rannie. He's skipper of my little ship the *Kalkis*. Captain, I want you to know this gentleman. His ship's just been sunk."

Even at the moment when he offered a limp hand Captain Rannie did not raise his eyes above Mr. Spokesly's side pockets, and he lost no time in resuming the conversation. Mr. Spokesly found that this was one of Captain Rannie's most notable peculiarities. He had the air of a silent, reserved man, and he gave one a strong impression of being silent and reserved since he never divulged anything about himself. Yet he was always in the midst of an interminable monologue. When you met him he was talking rapidly in a low, ill-tempered lisping voice, he continued whether you had business with him or not, and he was still at it when you bade him good day. He talked extremely well, with a sort of heavy varnish of culture instead of fine polish, and he took occasional deep breaths in order to sound his periods correctly. The subjects of his discourse were two: his own virtues and the sins of everybody else on earth. Perhaps this was why he was never finished, since both subjects were inexhaustible. No one had ever given him a fair deal and he had given up expecting it. There were many things about himself to which he never alluded, but he gave the impression that in strict justice he ought to allude to them and very unfavourably, since he had been so badly treated by the other parties. He was never heard to mention the war, for example, or his own participation in the fray. He talked, indeed, as a very garrulous being from another planet might, after a few intensive lessons on human frailty. At the present moment he was giving it as his fixed opinion, and supporting it with an overwhelming mass of fresh evidence, that everybody—the agent in Port Said, the crew including the mate and the engineer, the warship who had peremptorily demanded his name and port of origin, and the captain of the port who had assigned him a bad berth nearly three miles from the dock —was in a conspiracy to make his life a hell on earth. After he had shaken hands with Mr. Spokesly his arm dropped slackly across his knee once more, leaving the cigarette-stained fingers to make expressive motions emphasizing the ghastliness of the tale he unfolded. And never once did he raise his eyes to either of his auditors. It almost seemed as though he could not bear to look in the faces of those beings from whom it was impossible to obtain justice.

"I ask you, what is a man to do? What can he do, as commander of the vessel, when his own officers decline, absolutely pointblank decline, to give him ordinary decent respect? Let alone carrying out explicit orders. It's enough to make a man throw up the whole thing in disgust. If I've told my chief officer once I've told him fifty times, I will not have a cuspidor on the bridge for the man at the wheel. My helmsman must have the common decency to refrain from spitting while on duty. What is the result? He laughs in my face. Simply takes not the slightest notice. The same with everything else. Do I give orders to have the captain's tea served at four sharp? What does he do but stops the steward on his way down, drinks the tea, spits in the cup, and tells the man to take it to the captain. And when I ordered him to his room he threatened me. Actually threatened the commander of the ship. I of course logged him for insolent, unbearable, and insubordinate behaviour, and when I read the entry to him according to regulations, he tore the book to pieces and not only threw them at me but offered me bodily violence. I was attacked! And the engineer is, if anything, worse. Stood looking in the port and laughed at the chief officer's ruffianly behaviour. Do you suppose for a single moment I can tolerate this sort of thing?"

"Well, well, Captain, I tell you what . . ." began Mr. Dainopoulos.

"And another thing," continued Captain Rannie, without looking up, "the man's no good in a pinch. Several times on the voyage I've had literally to tell him his work. No sense of his position. Sits on the fore hatch and has long conversations with the crew. I make no charges, mind, none whatever, but I am as certain that man carries my conversation forward as I am of my own existence. When eight bells ring at my orders, he is frequently nowhere to be seen, and if I send the man at the wheel to find him and bring him up, as I have had to do more than once, he keeps the man with him in his room playing cards, leaving me at the wheel. That's gratitude. That's the sort of thing I have to put up with from this man. Do you suppose for a moment that I can allow it to go on for ever?"

"Well, Captain," said Mr. Dainopoulos again, "I can see we shall have to . . ."

"In Port Said," cut in Captain Rannie, "I scarcely saw the man. Positively I might have had no chief officer! But for me the ship would have been looted over and over again. More than once, when I was going ashore on ship's business, I found he had sent the boat away on some perfectly trivial errand of his own, to buy him some cigarettes or to fetch his laundry. And when I made an absolutely justifiable protest and issued explicit orders that the boat was not to leave the ship's side except at the express orders of the commander, what happens? Nothing but insults and foul innuendoes. This sort of treatment might appeal to some ship masters. You can't tell, there's no accounting for tastes. Personally, I simply will not have it. I have been patient long enough. I make every allowance for defective education and ignorance of the ordinary decencies of life. I hope I realize everybody cannot be the same. But this is going too far."

"Yes, yes," said Mr. Dainopoulos hurriedly. "I quite agree with you, Captain. We'll make a change right away. Now if you'll . . ."

"Putting aside all personal feeling," continued Captain Rannie, and indeed he had gone right on while his employer was speaking, "putting all that to one side, I feel it my duty as master of the vessel. The man is not fit to be a ship's officer."

"I'll get you a seat, Mister," said Dainopoulos to Mr. Spokesly, and he hurried out and over to a small café, returning with a chair.

"No satisfaction in going on like this, as any one can see not blinded by prejudice. No one would believe, no one, what I have to put up with. Not a soul on the ship who shows the faintest glimmer of gratitude." And Captain Rannie was suddenly silent.

"That's what we'll do," said Mr. Dainopoulos in a loud, sympathetic voice, "and I'll see if I can't get you a better anchorage. This afternoon I expect I'll have a lighter for you. How will that do, Captain?"

"I expect nothing, and I'll not be disappointed," replied the captain. "My experience leads me to expect things when I get them. If anything has happened on board since I left, don't blame me. I give you full warning. The man is not to be trusted. I have difficulty in keeping my hands off him. I only refrain as a matter of dignity. I would not soil my hands with such—such riff-raff. I hope I am not misunderstood. There's a limit to human endurance, that's all."

"I know how it is, Captain. Don't you worry. Only, you know as well as I do he was the only man I could get at the time."

"I make no charges," said Captain Rannie, suddenly rising to some six feet two, to Mr. Spokesly's intense astonishment. "I hope I am above that sort of thing. But, I must really say, things could be managed better if more attention was paid to the express wishes of the master of the vessel." And without looking up or indicating in any way that he was conscious of their presence, Captain Rannie walked away and disappeared into the Place de la Liberté.

Mr. Dainopoulos looked after him for a moment with an expression of perplexity on his marred features and then sat down.

"What's the matter with him?" inquired Mr. Spokesly, very much interested. "Is he touched at all?"

"No, he's all right. Only he grumble grumble too much," said Mr. Dainopoulos scratching his chin philosophically.

"I should think he does if he's always like that. What is his job worth?"

"Seven hundred drachma a month I pay him, and he says it's not enough."

"That so? Hm!" Mr. Spokesly was thinking. "That's about thirty pound a month. And I suppose he finds the ship." Mr. Dainopoulos nodded.

"Fifteen hundred drachma a month for that, and he says he lose money on the job."

Mr. Spokesly was looking down at the floor, flicking the ash from a cigarette, and he did not see the sudden wide-open stare Dainopoulos fixed upon him, as though beholding him in a new aspect.

"Why, think of it. Here you are, without a ship!" he exclaimed.

"No doubt about that," muttered Mr. Spokesly.

"Well, why not make a trip for me? This ship she's not very *beeg*, but she's going down to the Islands for the Government, you understand."

"For the Government? A transport?"

"One trip. After that I'll have something else much better for you. Yes, much better."

"What, go mate with this Captain Rannie?"

"One trip," said Mr. Dainopoulos, holding up his forefinger. "I can fix you for four hundred drachma a month."

"You said something, first time I came ashore, about a skipper's job," said Mr. Spokesly.

"That's just what I mean. Something better, see? This skipper," he added, leaning forward and lowering his voice, "he no good! But he got a paper from me, you understand, for a year, so I can't do nothin'."

"What about me?" said Mr. Spokesly, rather to his own surprise. "Do I get a paper, too?"

"Only one trip,'" countered Mr. Dainopoulos. "You go one trip and I'll fix you for a *beeg* ship."

"Well, I can't do any better, and going home may be a wash-out," mused Mr. Spokesly. "I'll get some clothes."

"You go to a friend o' mine and he'll get you everything. Here's the number. Jean Tjimiski Street. You better get uniform, see, and wear all the time. Better than plain clothes. Plenty trouble goin' aboard ship without uniform. And then you come to my house."

"I was going to the Olympos," began Mr. Spokesly.

"Too dear! Olympos no good," hastily began Mr. Dainopoulos who was not at all anxious to have an employee of his drawn into conversation by the people who lived at the Olympos. "You come to my house. I will speak to the officer who buy the stores from me and he will be glad if captain and mate both English, you understand. That all right?" And he patted Mr. Spokesly on the shoulder.

"You mean, come and stay with you?"

"Certainly. Why not? My wife, she likes you very much. And Miss Solaris, eh?"

"Well, I don't notice she likes me so very much. She tolerates me. I don't understand that girl, Mister."

Mr. Dainopoulos looked very serious at this. He shook his head. He lit a cigarette, blew the smoke away, and put his face close to Mr. Spokesly's.

"Never mind her, Mister. Keep away from her. She's a fine girl but she's got funny ideas. And she's crazy about that feller what's gone away. She thinks he's a king and she's a queen. You understand what I mean? She ain't here at all, you see? She's got notions she's goin' to find him and he'll take her back to Austria or somewhere. I can't tell you all about it. I laugh when she tells us all her fool notions. She thinks you can get her on your ship and take her back to her . . . yes!" Mr. Dainopoulos was humorously hideous as he reiterated this astounding notion on the part of Evanthia Solaris. "And when I says to her, 'Aw, he's gone away now; won't be back for six months, maybe,' she call me a liar. 'He'll come back,' she say to me. 'I want him! Ha, ha!'"

"Well," said Mr. Spokesly, looking meditatively at the immense safe. "She's right after all, and you're wrong. I'm here, ain't I?"

"And that's why I tell you, look out. These women, they ain't like Englishwomen, Mister."

"How?"

But Mr. Dainopoulos couldn't explain how. It is not easy to explain how. Perhaps, if Mr. Dainopoulos had been less absorbed in making money and had dabbled in the fine arts, he might have hit upon some adequate comparison. He might have said, for example, that the difference was like the difference between the rose, with its perfume and its comprehensible thorns, and the poppy, or the hemlock or the deadly nightshade, blooms of fatal lure and incalculable perils. Mr. Dainopoulos knew the difference but he did not know the English for it. He must have sensed in some way the latent danger for a man like Mr. Spokesly, a man with much unconscious romanticism in his nature, for he shook his head vigorously and said several times, "You look out. She'll fix you to do something crazy. You're engaged, or I'd say, keep away from her. But since you're engaged, well, look out, that's all. By and by she'll forget all her fool notions and get married."

"Well," said Mr. Spokesly. "I got to get out of these clothes before I see anybody. I'll take a walk up to see your friend the tailor. See you later." And he walked towards Venizelos Street.

He was profoundly disturbed at this unexpected revelation of the attitude of Evanthia Solaris. If that girl had designed to cast a spell upon him, she could have chosen no more potent elixir than this sublimated essence of quixotism. She wanted him to get her back to the gay and impudent young person who had almost tweaked the noses and pulled the beards of the serious French officers who had seen him safely locked in the train bound north through the lines. Without being competent to analyze his complex emotions, Mr. Spokesly was in no doubt of their reality. He would do it. It appealed to his particularly English ideal of chivalry, which is embodied in the immortal phrase "making a woman happy." He would do it. He would astonish her by his sudden solicitude for her happiness. And it must be admitted that, whatever else he failed to do, Mr. Spokesly succeeded in astonishing her. Evanthia Solaris was perfectly equipped to achieve her own happiness, equipped with the weapons and instincts of the jungle; and the spectacle of an Englishman at his ancient and honourable pastime of making a woman happy, while it never caused her to relax her vigilance, certainly inspired her with novel emotions.

Mr. Spokesly was so lost in his reflections, most of them confusingly agreeable, that he started when a familiar mellow voice asked him where he was going. His friend the Lieutenant of Reserve was standing at the corner of the Place. It was evident that the billet of deputy-assistant harbour master carried no crushingly onerous duties. The old lieutenant looked as though he had had a number of little drinks since Mr. Spokesly had left him. He stood leaning on a cane looking on benevolently at the busy scene.

"Floka's is right here," he said. "S'pose we have a couple? Beautiful morning, isn't it? Well, and how did you get on?"

Mr. Spokesly had time to think. He recalled his own motto of keeping one's eyes open and one's mouth shut. His angle of vision had changed since the morning hour. He no longer felt sore with the navy or miserably alone in the world. He had got a promise of a command—a promise he had never before approached in his life. And a woman had said she wanted him. He regarded his elderly companion with composure as they stepped over and sat down at a little table.

"Not so bad," he said, drawing out his two hundred francs and handing over twenty-five. "Much obliged. No, can't

say when I'm goin' home.   Paymaster said he'd let me know.
How's things?   Any more anchors to slip?"

The answer was a fat chuckle.

"Oh, my young lordship's not there this morning," said the
lieutenant. "Playing golf!" He drank his gin and bitters
thirstily, which is a bad sign. "Golf! I'd golf him, if I had
my way. Lucky there's nothing much doing just now. As
it is I've had a heavy morning, getting things straightened
out. I think I'll have another and then we might try a bit o'
lunch. So you'll be on your own for a few days. I wish I
could get home. I'm going to see the Captain of the Base
to-morrow. If that's no good, I'll write to the Admiralty."

They had another and the lieutenant gave an outline of the
letter he proposed to write to the Admiralty. He also gave
Mr. Spokesly his views of the naval situation, attributing the
nation's reverses entirely to mismanagement of the harbours.
They were not very clear views, and their value was vitiated
by a peculiarly irrelevant argument that consular agents
ought to be recruited from the ranks of retired shipmasters.

"'Tired shipmasters," he repeated, with unconscious irony,
after the tenth drink that morning. "Practical men. Size
up situation. But what's the use? Gov'ment won't lissen
t'reason." He put down his glass and paid the reckoning.
Although he was not conscious of it, the lieutenant was a
happy man. He owned his own semi-detached villa over
at Chingford, near London, and the villa adjoining. His
children were all grown up. Years ago he had put his
money into shipping and it had failed to pay a divi-
dend of more than three per cent. Now he was getting
nearly thirty per cent. His health was good, for even the
interminable little drinks at Floka's had no great effect upon
him. He was doing very well out of the war. A life of careful and cautious command was being crowned by a season of
gentle conviviality. He had achieved a position of respectable eminence without ever having had an idea in his head.
For him neither the arts, the sciences, nor philosophy existed.
His patriotism was a rootless organism floating in a calm sea
of sentiment. An intermittent melancholy assailed him at

the times when he thought of his son killed at Mons. A wild young fellow. Got into a very expensive set in that insurance office, where he worked. Brought up to be a gentleman, so one couldn't very well grumble. Upset his mother something terrible. And now he was gone and would never be any expense to anybody again. And his old father was left to jog along as best he could. Ah, well! His other boy, now, in an aircraft factory, was doing well. Wonderful how he'd taken to these here motors. Probably get a very good billet after the war was over. Saving money, too. Ah, well! It was an ill wind that blew nobody any good. He tried to fix his attention, which had wandered a little, on what Mr. Spokesly was saying. That gentleman was preoccupied with his own immediate future and was trying to get away without hurting any feelings. Keeping his eyes open and his mouth shut involved dropping all unnecessary "top-hamper" as he himself phrased it. He rose.

"I got to go and get some clothes," he explained. "I simply can't go round like this, you know. Suppose I look in at the hotel this evening, eh?"

"Do!" said the lieutenant with dreamy cordiality. "Very thing. Tell the waiter, will you? I think I'll have another before I go round to lunch."

It was just about this time that a keen-faced naval man, engaged in mending the shaft of a groggy driver with some plasticine and a strip of insulating tape, made a remark to a young sub-lieutenant with features of almost girlish delicacy, who was assisting.

"One of your people," he said crisply, "is continually pestering me. Middle-aged. Lieutenant Reserve. Smells abominably of cough-drops. Wants to go home. Is he any use?"

"Not in the least," said the young sub-lieutenant with equal crispness. "He might be if he didn't get half-stewed every day. The cough-drops are to conceal . . ."

"Oh, obviously!" said the Captain of the Base. "I knew that, thank you. But look here. Just give him a hint, will you, that there's too much to do just now in my office to have him coming in two or three times a week with a long yarn."

"What shall I do with him?" asked the sub-lieutenant deferentially.

The captain took a stance and swung the club.

"Don't care what you do with him," he said, taking a deep breath. "Lock him up, send him out in a transport, make him run round and round the White Tower, so long as he doesn't come to my office."

"Right-o, sir. He shall run round and round the White Tower for the duration of the war. He'll do less harm there than anywhere else."

CHAPTER IX

WHEN Mr. Spokesly had left his friend to have one more, he experienced that comfortable feeling of having left someone behind which is one of the most tangible and gratifying results of getting on both in the world and in life. The incident crystallized for him, so to speak, the gaseous and indefinable emotions which had been passing through his mind since he had been fished out of the water. Avoiding the callous brutality of the expressed sentiment, he derived a silent and subtle satisfaction from the workings of a fate which had singled him out to survive a ship's company of men as deserving as he, but who were now none the less out of the running. Mr. McGinnis, who had obligingly died a startling but convenient death, had merely gone before. He would be waiting, no doubt, on the Dark Shore, his pink jaws going continually, ready to navigate them to their long home. Mr. Spokesly had not had a great deal to do with death heretofore, and he was much struck with the extreme ease with which one can grow accustomed to the horror of an elderly shipmaster being ordered about "like a dog," as the saying is. In a way, he could scarcely refrain from regarding his friend the lieutenant in the same light as his late shipmates. He was clear enough on this point now: that the way to success is not through a nursing-home for grievances. No one who had met Captain Rannie, for example, could regard a grievance as a worthy or valuable possession. And Mr. Spokesly, to whom had been denied access to the great founts of wisdom, had to progress by noting his fellowmen and their reactions upon his own feelings. He hastened away up Venizelos Street, full of vigour and hope, as though it lay upon him to achieve something of the

138

work foregone by those so suddenly finished with life, who were now moving about, a bewildered and somewhat undisciplined little band of incongruous shades, lost and forgotten as the colossal armies of the slain went past. And he became aware, quite suddenly, in the midst of the bright noisy street, of life being an instinctive, momentary, impersonal affair after all. As he put it, like a lot of insects, and somebody steps on us, and we're squashed, and all the others go swarming on over us. And with that mysteriously heartening notion, Mr. Spokesly had a vividly imagined glimpse of those same armies marching through the shadows, millions of them, of all nations, silently moving towards an eternity of passionless intelligence. It would make no difference then, he thought. All we got to do, is make the best bargain we can for ourselves. Carry on! Like insects. . . .

They looked like that. They swarmed in the narrow street, almost crawling over one another with brilliant and distinctive markings and in their hard dark eyes an expression of maniacal acquisitiveness. Their glances were almost like antennæ, waving to and fro in the bright, stench-laden air, communicating to the alert and secular intelligences within the warning of an approaching danger or victim. Like insects, too, they hived in dark holes, which they called shops, in the backs of which one could see their eyes glittering, lying in wait. And down the steep street came other insects, warrior ants astride of horses caparisoned in blue and silver, and green and gold, with shining metallic wing-cases and fierce head ornaments. They, too, moved on with the air of automata, without emotions or any consciousness of good or evil. They came on down, as they had come along that ancient Via Egnatia, beneath the great arch twenty centuries ago, just as hard-eyed janizaries had come in later times, settling in their swarms upon the city. Down the steep ancient street they came, settling heavily into their saddles with a clash of metal and wheeze of leather as their horses took the descent; and watching them with shining eyes from a doorway was Evanthia Solaris, an exquisite apparition in pale saffron with an enormous black hat. She was raised a step or two above the sidewalk, and Mr. Spokesly could see that slender gracile figure from the buff-coloured shoes and stockings of sheer yellow silk to the broad brim of black straw shading the pale dark face aglow with excitement. One would have imagined that she was watching the soldiers of her country riding out to defend her, or riding in to rescue her. She leaned forward a little, her lips parted in a smile, and an officer, noticing her in her doorway, sat straighter, raised his sword and smiled in reply. Her response was ravishing. She blew a kiss, and Mr. Spokesly marvelled at her enthusiasm. As well he might, for Evanthia was rehearsing a part. Patriotism to her was a fine brave gesture and she was practising it. It appealed to her dramatic instinct. Just as she would suddenly smother Mrs. Dainopoulos with impulsive caresses, so she cheered a lot of stolid soldiers who were nothing to her and in whose sentiments she had no share. Always Evanthia was certain of some sphere in the world where people act like this, and where they luxuriate in rare and beautiful emotions. She played at this as a western child plays hostess to her dolls. To her, for a brief blinding moment, it was real, and she loved the officer with the saluting sword. And Mr. Spokesly, rather scared, if the truth be told, and acutely conscious of his anomalous attire, slipped into a shop and dickered with a long-nosed Jew for a pair of Turkish slippers, while over his shoulder he saw the girl, now the soldiers were gone, step daintily into the road and go on down, with her delicate prinking walk, an exquisite moth among hard-eyed ferocious-looking insects.

And so he found himself at last in a small room, behind a window full of formidable uniforms, containing a dreamy-eyed Greek tailor and an overworked American sewing machine. A number of suits hung in rows on one side and on the wall was a steel engraving showing Parisian Men's Fashions of a dozen years before. As he owed for a consignment of velvet khaki which Mr. Dainopoulos had picked up somewhere and sold him at a noble profit, Mr. Theotokis was disposed to do his best for Mr. Spokesly. So he took his measure and ascertained by painful cross-examination what a chief officer's uniform was like. Yes, like that, with one, two, three rows of lace, one quarter wide. H'm! And in answer to the demand for a suit ready to wear, he sized Mr. Spokesly up and nodded reflectively. He had something. He rummaged behind the festoons of coats and drew out a fine pin-check suit such as sporting characters affect in the country. He held it up and regarded it with misgiving. It appeared from the book to be made to the order of one Jack Harrowby, Transport *Tanganyika*. Mr. Spokesly started. Harrowby was one of the wireless operators, a youth about his own build and distinctly sporting in temperament. He remembered Harrowby, all right. Why had he not fetched his suit? Mr. Theotokis shrugged his shoulders almost to his ears and spread his hands. No money. Wanted to pay next trip. Another phenomenal shrug. Mr. Theotokis was desolated to disappoint Jack Harrowby, but no money, no suit. Mr. Spokesly recalled something Archy Bates had said about Harrowby drawing a lot of money, having started a tremendous love affair in town. Evidently he was going to cut a dash in his pin-checks. Perhaps he looked forward to the races at Alexandria. And now . . . Mr. Spokesly pursed his lips firmly, took off the anomalous coat he was wearing, and slipped his arms into Jack Harrowby's coat. It was an extremely good fit. Jack Harrowby's trousers needed turning up and a touch of the iron, and they would do. A tremendous love affair he had had on, Mr. Spokesly recalled. Girl in a post-card shop, it was said. Perhaps it was the suit which had been ordered by Jack Harrowby to make love in. Mr. Spokesly had not been attracted by that short buxom little creature in the post-card shop; but now he felt he would like the sensation of going round to see her, in Jack Harrowby's suit. It was the sort of thing that chimed in with his mood of modest satisfaction. It would not be doing Jack Harrowby any harm. That wise youth, who had gone ahead and made the most of his opportunities, was now done with pin-check suits and girls in post-card shops.

A hundred francs at first, it came down to eighty on invoking the name of Dainopoulos, so Mr. Spokesly took it
with him and promised to call next day.

There was something dashing about a finish like that, he
reflected, as he sat down on the bed in a room in the Olympos
Hotel. A word to the paymaster had secured him that privilege. He regretted he had not noted more particularly the
sporting Jack Harrowby, but it did not do to have much
traffic with those fellows, they were so cheeky. He untied
his parcel and looked again at the late Harrowby's selection
in suitings. He had bought a hat on the way down, too, a
gray felt, respectably stylish. Now he would be able to
resume his place in the world. He would not feel like a fireman out of a job when he went to see these naval gentry.
As he folded up his wrinkled and salt-stained trousers he remembered the ring and took it out. That was a rather
peculiar turn, the way he happened to have it. Just a fluke,
putting it in his pocket in his hurry. Mr. Spokesly took his
lip in his teeth as he tried to get the hang, as he called it, of all
these intricate turns in his destiny. He recalled the unusual
and puzzling exaltation he had experienced that evening when
he went ashore with Archy, and he began to wonder whether
after all it would be good for a man to know too accurately
what the future held for him. His hands, so to speak, were
full now. Life was tremendously interesting, once one got
away from routine and discipline and all these conventional
ideas. He was, practically, a free agent now. It was up to
himself to go ahead carefully and make no silly mistakes.
No harm in walking round to that post-card shop near the
Ottoman Bank, however. He remembered seeing Jack
Harrowby hanging over the counter once, as he went by. A
dark little piece with a powdered nose.

Mr. Spokesly could not have explained this ridiculous
curiosity about a girl he did not know, but it was a simple
enough by-product of his new state of mind. There is nothing unusual in a man, suddenly awakened to full consciousness
by some one woman, becoming interested in all women. So
far from a man being unable to love more than one woman, it

may be doubted whether at first he can do anything else. The tender solicitudes and almost religious exclusiveness are later phases of the passion. Mr. Spokesly even looked forward to a sentimental intimacy with Mrs. Dainopoulos. It made him feel a bit of a dog, as did this affair of Jack Harrowby's flame. As he went along the Front he wondered if she would go out to lunch with him. And then he saw that the post-card shop was shut up and a sentry stood in front with his rifle on his shoulder. Mr. Spokesly walked on and turned up the next street. The sight of that closed shop and the sentry gave him a chill all down his spine. What had happened? He made his way to the establishment of Mr. Dainopoulos. That gentleman at once exclaimed at the improved appearance of his friend, but without quitting his accounts which littered the desk and overflowed on to the shelves along the sides. He offered a chair and a cigarette. Mr. Spokesly watched him with respect. He had sense enough to see that Mr. Dainopoulos was only doing business in the old-fashioned way, as it was done in England and in New England, too, before shipowners became too exalted to talk to their own shipmasters or to go down to meet their own ships. There might be something in this business for him even after the war. If it grew there would be an overlooker needed. He let his mind go forward. Perhaps the *Tanganyika's* sudden eclipse was really a blessing in disguise. An ill wind blowing prosperity in his direction. It would be unjust to say of him that he did not regret the loss of those lives. He did, as sincerely as anybody else. But he was alive and they were dead, and if there is one thing men learn promptly it is the difference between the quick and the dead. So he let his mind go forward. And when Captain Rannie suddenly came in, Mr. Spokesly almost failed to recognize him. Not that Captain Rannie particularly desired recognition. He sat down and continued a monologue on the decay of morals in the merchant service. Went back to the ship, and what did he find? Nothing done. Mate and engineer playing cards in the cabin. Cook drunk. And so on. From bad to worse.

"But where's the harm in a game of cards, Captain?" asked Mr. Spokesly, slightly amused.

This question upset Captain Rannie very much. He was unused to questions from strangers. It interrupted the flow of his thought. He looked down at his feet and took out a cigarette.

"Ah!" he said, as though an astonishingly fresh argument was about to be born. "Ah! That's the point, that's the point. No harm at all. It's the principle that's at stake— I expressly stated my dislike of the cabin being used as a gambling-den and these officers of mine expressly disregard my repeated instructions. And it's coming to a point," he added darkly as Mr. Dainopoulos hurried across the street to speak to an acquaintance, "when either they get out or I do."

It was obvious that Captain Rannie lived in a world of his own, a world in which he was the impotent, dethroned, and outraged deity. Now he was prepared to abdicate into the bargain. He hinted at ultimatums, distinct understanding, and other paraphernalia of sovereignty, for all the world as though he were a European power. By all this he meant nothing more than to impress Mr. Spokesly with the solemn responsibility of being chief officer under him. But Mr. Spokesly was regarding him with attention and he was not impressed. He was looking for the elusive yet indubitable mark of character which is so necessary in a commander, a gesture often closely imitated, which carries out to men the conviction that he bears within himself a secret repository of confidence and virtue, to be drawn upon in moments of conflict with the forces of nature and the turbulent spirits of men. And he did not find it. Mr. Spokesly had had no opportunity of discovering this repository in himself. Indeed, many men achieve great deeds and die gloriously without ever having been conscious of the sacred force. But he knew it and felt it when he came near it, whatever cantankerous habits of grievance he may have cultivated. And it was necessary for him now to judge men for themselves. Imitations would not do. As though aware of the scrutiny and the motive, Captain Rannie proceeded with even more eloquence, and more like a ventriloquist's dummy than ever, to outline what in his opinion was the whole duty of an officer. The long scrawny wrist with the slave-bangle, the cigarette held loosely between yellow fingers, waved as though deciding the fate of principalities. He spoke in full resounding periods, he made dramatic pauses, and invoked the eternal principles of justice and decency and honour. And Mr. Spokesly didn't believe a word of it. He was anxious for the mate to lose his job because he wanted it himself. But he was secretly in sympathy with him. And having failed to find what he was looking for, the genius of command, he began to wonder what there was inside this man at all. It couldn't be simply all this tosh he was emitting. He must have some springs of love and hate in him, some secret virtue or vice which kept him going. Mr. Spokesly was interested. Men were not so simple, so negative, now he himself was out on his own, to decide for himself, to be master of his own fate.

"Are you married, Captain?" he asked, in a brief pause, with a flash of intuition. Captain Rannie dropped the match he was holding, changed his legs and began moving his neck violently in his collar while he swallowed. Several times he opened his mouth to speak and nothing happened. He looked hard at Mr. Spokesly's boots.

"I make it a rule," he said at length, "and I expect all my officers to bear it in mind, to have no dealings in personalities. I ask no questions about a man's private life and I expect none. I hope this is understood from the first. There's one thing I simply will not tolerate and that is prying into my private affairs."

"Well, hang it, I only asked a perfectly natural question. No offence, Captain."

"Precisely. None offered, none taken. It's the principle I insist on."

"I suppose you've been out here some little time," ventured Mr. Spokesly.

"That is a matter that concerns me and nobody else," said Captain Rannie. "That's one thing I find very much in vogue nowadays. Ceaseless curiosity about irrelevant matters. Do I ask you how long you've been out here? I certainly do not. I consider it's nothing to do with me. And yet I am considered unreasonable simply because I demand common decent respect for my own private affairs."

"The Captain he no like to talk about his affairs," said Mr. Dainopoulos, who was listening. "Don't you worry. You'll find him all right, Mister. To-morrow you start on the *Kalkis*. That all right, Captain?"

Captain Rannie seemed under the stress of some terrific emotion. He swallowed, his foot tapped the floor, the slave-bangle shot up out of sight; and he regarded a point about three feet up the wall with a malignant glare.

"I'm sure I'd never dream of interfering in such a matter," he said. "What you do I must stand by. You make the bed, I have to lie on it. That's what a shipmaster's for. He's a doormat, for everybody to wipe their feet on. No matter what happens, he has to take the blame. *I've* no objection in the world. I expect nothing, and that's all I get."

Mr. Dainopoulos evidently knew his captain, for he said: "All right. That's fixed. Now, when we've had something to eat we'll go see the Transport Officer. He's the man."

"I hope you don't want *me* to go with you," said Captain Rannie, looking down at the floor as though he saw the bottomless pit just on the point of opening under their feet. "I've only seen the man once and then he failed to show the very slightest glimmer of comprehension of what I had to put up with. Might as well talk to a stone wall. Absolutely. I'm sure *I* don't want to see your Transport Officer."

"I was going to ask you," said Mr. Spokesly, "if you don't mind, a question. You seem to be in the know all round here."

"What is it?" said Mr. Dainopoulos, regarding Mr. Spokesly with sudden interest. He even left his pen in the air while he listened.

Mr. Spokesly mentioned the incident of the suit of clothes left behind by the indigent Jack Harrowby and the memories

of the post-card shop evoked by the interview with Mr. Theotokis.

Mr. Dainopoulos let his pen descend to the document he
was auditing and nodded in comprehension.

"Yes, all finished, eh? Wal, what you think?" he went on
nonchalantly. "She little damn fool. She tell plenty stories
to anybody who get sweet on her, you unnerstand? She
hear *Tanganyika* go south, time so and so. She talk"—here
Mr. Dainopoulos made a gesture with his thumb and fingers
indicating violent blabbing—"ba-ba-ba-ba! Now she's in
jail. *Tanganyika*, wal, you know all about *Tanganyika*,
Mister. You unnerstand; these peoples, French, English,
they play, you know, golf and tennees, and seem half asleep."
He shook his head. "No! Not asleep. Very bad business
that. Me; I go all the time like this." And he drew a
perfectly straight line with his pen along the edge of his desk.
"That crooked business no good."

Captain Rannie was suddenly overtaken by a violent fit
of coughing, and buried his nut-cracker features in a large
plum-coloured silk handkerchief. His head was bowed, his
shoulders heaved horribly, and from him came a sound like an
asthmatic horse whinnying. He might have been laughing
save that laughter was unknown to him beyond a short sharp
yawp, a "Ha!" involving a lift of the diaphragm and an
intake of breath. And since none had ever seen him laugh
they would not suspect merriment in this dreadful cacophony,
this laryngeal uproar, which had so suddenly assailed him.
Mr. Dainopoulos looked at his captain very sternly and then
renewed the proposal to eat. Captain Rannie rose, joint by
joint, and stuffed his plum-coloured handkerchief into his
breast pocket.

"No," he said, and Mr. Spokesly wondered if the man ever
agreed to anything except under protest. "No, I'm a two-
meal-a-day man myself. I find I am less bilious on two
meals a day. And anyhow, after that, I couldn't possibly
eat anything."

And he coughed himself out of the door.

Mr. Dainopoulos stared after him, his features destitute

of any emotion at all. Captain Rannie halted, turned half round, and it almost seemed as though for once in his life he was going to raise his eyes and look somebody square in the face. But he paused at the second button of his owner's waistcoat and nodded several times, his toothless mouth open, a perfect ventriloquist's dummy.

"I'll have indigestion for a fortnight," he said. "Absolutely." And he started off again, the plum-coloured handkerchief to his face, his shoulders heaving, making a noise like a foundered horse.

"What's the matter with him?" Mr. Spokesly felt justified in asking.

"He's an old bum!" said Mr. Dainopoulos with a gloomy air, but made no further allusion to the bronchial troubles of his captain. The fact was, as Mr. Spokesly became aware in time, that Mr. Dainopoulos, in the course of his many negotiations, was obliged to entrust some of the business to his employees. And a stroke of business entirely correct to him did not make that impression upon Captain Rannie, who was under the illusion that he himself was the soul of honour. So he was, in theory. When Captain Rannie did a mean and dishonourable action, it bore to him the aspect of an act of singular rectitude. And he promptly forgot all about it. He wiped it out of his mind as off a slate. It was gone; had never existed, in fact. For the exploits of others, however, he not only never left off thinking about them, but he could not be induced to refrain from discussing them, for ever and ever. Anyone who had ever had any dealings with him would find him an embarrassing witness at the Day of Judgment, if we are correct in assuming that witnesses will be called. Mr. Dainopoulos could not afford to quarrel with him, but he sometimes wished he had a more amiable disposition, and could get on better with his crew. And he felt for him also the puzzled contempt which men of affairs feel for the sensualist. An elderly man who, as Mr. Dainopoulos had heard, had a wife somewhere and a married daughter somewhere else, and who was continually engaged in some shabby unmentionable intrigue, made one feel a little un-

comfortable and slightly ashamed of one's species. Captain
Rannie's view of his own conduct was not available, for he
never by any chance recognized the existence of such affairs
in his intercourse with other men. His sentiments about
women were unknown save what might be gathered from
his short sharp yawp—"Ha!"—whenever they were mentioned, the laugh of a noble nature embittered by base in-
gratitude. So he visualized himself. No one had ever betrayed the slightest gratitude for anything he had ever
done. So he would be revenged on the whole pack of them—
Ha!

It was Mr. Spokesly's chance question, whether the Captain was a visitor at the house, which let him fully into the
mind and temper of his new employer.

"He's not that sort of man," said Mr. Dainopoulos, shovel-
ling beans into his mouth with a knife. "My wife, she
wouldn't like him, I guess. He's got something of his own,
y'unnerstand. Like your friend Mr. Bates, only he don't
drink. He take the pipe a leetle. You savvy?"

Mr. Spokesly remembered this conversation later on, when
events had suddenly carried him beyond the range of Mr.
Dainopoulos and his intense respectability. He remembered
it because he realized that Mr. Dainopoulos at that time, and
behind his mask of bourgeois probity, which had been so
enigmatically received by Captain Rannie, was devising a
daring and astute stroke of business based on his exact
knowledge of the Ægean and his relations with the late consuls of enemy powers. And Captain Rannie, of course, had
been aware of this. But at the moment Mr. Spokesly easily
abandoned the morals of his new commander and listened
to what might be called the wisdom of the Near East. He
thought there was no harm in asking Mr. Dainopoulos what
he thought of the emerald ring. That gentleman evidently
thought a great deal of it. He offered to buy it, spot cash,
for a thousand drachma, about one sixth of its actual value.
He merely shrugged his shoulders when he heard the tale of
a woman giving it to Archy. According to his own experience
that sort of woman did not give such things away to any-

body. He thoroughly understood precious stones, as he understood drugs, carpets, currency, bric-à-brac, dry goods, wet goods, and the law of average. He noted a minute flaw in the stone, and finally handed it back hurriedly, telling Mr. Spokesly to give it away to some lady.

"Or throw it into the sea," he added, drinking a glass of wine in a gulp.

"What for?" demanded Mr. Spokesly, mystified by this sudden fancy.

"Bad luck," said Mr. Dainopoulos laconically. "It belong to a drowned man, you unnerstand! Better give it away."

"I'll give it to Miss Solaris."

Mr. Dainopoulos eyed Mr. Spokesly over his shoulder as he sat with his elbows on the table holding up his glass. Mr. Spokesly put the ring in his pocket.

"She'll take it, all right," said his friend at length, and drank.

"What makes you so sure?" asked Mr. Spokesly.

Mr. Dainopoulos was not prepared to answer that question in English. He found that English, as he knew it, was an extraordinarily wooden and cumbersome vehicle in which to convey those lightning flashes and glares and sparkles of thought in which most Latin intelligences communicate with each other. You could say very little in English, Mr. Dainopoulos thought. He could have got off some extremely good things about Evanthia Solaris in the original Greek, but Mr. Spokesly would not have understood him. If he were to take a long chance, however, by saying that the vulture up in the sky sees the dead mouse in the ravine, he was not at all sure of the result.

"Aw," he said in apology for his difficulty, "the ladies, they like the pretty rings."

"I can see you don't like her," said Mr. Spokesly, smiling a little.

"My friend," said Mr. Dainopoulos, and he turned his black, bloodshot eyes, with their baggy pouches of skin forming purplish crescents below them, on his companion.

"My friend, I'm married. Women, I got no use for them, you unnerstand? You no unnerstand. By and by, you know what I mean. My wife, all the time she sick, all the time. She like Miss Solaris. All right. For my wife anything in the world. But me, I got my business. By and by, ah!"

"What about by and by?" asked Mr. Spokesly, curious in spite of himself. He began to think Mr. Dainopoulos was a rather interesting human being, a remarkable concession from an Englishman.

Mr. Dainopoulos did not reply immediately. He had a vision splendid in his mind, but it was hazy and vague in details. His somewhat oriental conception of happiness was tempered by an austere idealism inspired by his wife. He could never have achieved his ambition, let us say, in Haverstock Hill, London N., or Newark, N. J. He demanded a background of natural features as a setting for his grandiose plans for the future. No westerner could understand his dreams, for example, of a black automobile with solid silver fittings and upholstery of orange corded silk, in which his wife could take the air along a magnificent corniche road flanked by lemon-coloured rocks and an azure sea. Other refinements, such as silken window-blinds, striped green and white, keeping the blinding sparkle of that sea from invading the cool recesses of voluptuous chambers, came to him from time to time. But he could not talk about it. He did not even speak to his wife of his dream. He believed she knew without his telling her. She knew nothing about it, imagining that he was merely concocting some little surprise such as buying a cottage in the country down in Warwickshire, where she believed her people came from in the days of William the Fourth. Buying cottages was not her husband's idea of solidifying a position, however. For him, living in a hovel while making money was justified by frugality and convenience, but retiring to a cottage would be a confession of defeat.

So he did not enlighten Mr. Spokesly. He paused awhile and then remarked that he hoped to get finished with business some day. No one could possibly take exception to this.

They did not see the officer who had been so anxious for Mr. Spokesly to visit the Persian Gulf during the coming summer. That gentleman had gone to see a dentist, it appeared, and a young writer informed them that it would be all right so long as the captain of the vessel was British.

"Yes, he's British all right—Captain Rannie—he's got a passport," said Mr. Dainopoulos. And when he was asked when he would be ready to load, he said as soon as the Captain gave him a berth.

"He put us three mile away, and it takes a tug an hour and a half to get to the ship," he remarked, "with coal like what it is now."

"Well, of course we can't put everybody at the pier, you know," said the young writer genially, quite forgetting that Mr. Dainopoulos had deftly inserted an item in the *charte partie* which gave him a generous allowance for lighterage. "All right," said he, as though making a decent concession. "You know they tell me they want this stuff in a hurry, eh?"

The young writer did not know but he pretended he did, and said he would attend to it. So they bade him good day and took their way back to the Bureau de Change. Mr. Dainopoulos had left it in charge of a young Jew, a youth so desperately poor and so fanatically honest that he seemed a living caricature of all moral codes. Neither his poverty nor his probity seemed remarkable enough to keep him in employment, doubtless because, like millions of other people in southeastern Europe, he had neither craft of mind nor hand. Mr. Dainopoulos got him small situations from time to time, and in between these he hung about, running errands, and keeping shop, a pale, dwarfed, ragged creature, with emaciated features and brilliant pathetic eyes. He was wearing a pair of woman's boots, much too large for him, burst at the sides and with heels dreadfully run over, so that he kept twitching himself erect. Mr. Dainopoulos waved a hand towards this young paragon.

"See if you can find him a job on the *Kalkis*," he said. "Very honest young feller." They spoke rapidly to each other and Mr. Dainopoulos gave an amused grunt.

"He say he don't want to go in a ship. Scared she go down," he remarked.

The boy looked down the street with an expression of suppressed grief on his face. He rolled his eyes towards his benefactor, imploring mercy. Mr. Dainopoulos spoke to him again.

"He'll go," he said to Mr. Spokesly. "Fix him to help the cook. And if you want anybody to take a letter, he's a very honest young feller."

The very honest young feller shrank away to one side, evidently feeling no irresistible vocation for the sea. Indeed, he resembled one condemned to die. He and his kind swarm in the ports of the Levant, the Semitic parasites of sea-borne commerce, yet rarely setting foot upon a ship. He drooped, as though his limbs had liquefied and he was about to collapse. Mr. Dainopoulos, however, to whom ethnic distinctions of such refinement were of no interest, ignored him and permitted him to revel in his agony at a near-by café table.

"You come to my house to-night," he said to Mr. Spokesly. "I got one or two little things to fix."

"Me too," said his new chief officer, who suddenly felt he needed urgently to meet his own kind again. Mr. Dainopoulos was all right of course, but Mr. Spokesly still retained the illusion that Anglo-Saxon superiority was accepted by the world like gravity and the other laws of nature. It would not do to make himself too cheap, he reflected. He had an unpleasant feeling that his late captain on the *Tanganyika* would have stared if he had seen his chief officer hobnobbing with a money-changer and a Jewish youth of almost inconceivable honesty and destitution. Mr. Spokesly's wit, however, was nimble enough now to see that Captain Meredith himself had not always been a quiet, refined, and competent commander; and moreover, Captain Meredith might quite conceivably have seen and taken a chance like this himself, had he been in the way of it. But just now what was wanted was a chat and a drink with a friend. He would go down to the hotel and find the lieutenant.

But this was not to be. As he entered the foyer of the

hotel, a major and a round-faced person in civilian clothes regarded him with exaggerated attention. Their protracted examination of him made him feel somewhat self-conscious, and to ease the situation he spoke to them.

"I'm looking for a friend of mine," he said, "a lieutenant in the Harbour Office. I don't know his name."

"Don't know his name!" said the major, boring into Mr. Spokesly with his cold ironical stare.

"I only met him this morning," he explained. "Me coming ashore from the *Tanganyika*, you see."

"Oh, yes." This in a more human tone.

"And him being the only man I know, pretty near, I was looking for him."

"I see. Well, old chap, he's generally about pickled this time of day, if he's the man I think you mean. Up at the Cercle Militaire—d'you know it?—or the White Tower Bar. Better take a look along."

"Thanks," said Mr. Spokesly with a slight smile.

"Don't mention it. By the way, are you being sent home?"

"I'm going on a local ship down to the Islands," he replied.

"Not the *Kalkis*?"

Mr. Spokesly nodded, and said he was going mate.

"Well, look here. I'm Officer of Supply, you know. You might look me up—you know where it is—and we'll have a word about the cargo. Yes, in the morning."

The major and his friend the censor, who was also a novelist, gazed after Mr. Spokesly as he went out.

"I believe that fellow Dainopoulos is on the level after all," said the major, drawing hard at his cigarette. "I know his skipper is a Britisher, and this chap's all right, I should say. Well, he's making enough out of it to give us a fair deal."

"Most of these local people are on our side, I think," said the other.

"If we pay them more than the other side," added the major drily. And then they went up to get ready for their dinner.

Mr. Spokesly called a carriage and started along the *quai*. He wondered what they wanted of him about the cargo! Was it possible Captain Rannie was not regarded with complete confidence at headquarters? He recalled the extraordinary reception the Captain had given to his owner when Mr. Dainopoulos described the undeviating rectitude of his course. Mr. Spokesly was not simple enough to suppose that the *Kalkis* was as innocent as she looked in the distance. He knew that the delicate and precarious position of the Allies in Saloniki rendered it necessary to wink at a good deal of adventurous trading in which the local Levantine merchants were past-masters. It could not be helped. But he was puzzled to account for Captain Rannie. How had he come to be in the employ of Mr. Dainopoulos? And what was the lure which held him to a sort of snarling fidelity? Perhaps he also had a tremendous love affair, like Jack Harrowby. Mr. Dainopoulos had hinted at shabby intrigues. Even Mr. Dainopoulos, however, was not quite on safe ground here. Captain Rannie had his own way of enjoying himself, and an essential part of that enjoyment was its secrecy. He couldn't bear anybody to know anything about him. He was averse, in fact, to admitting that he ever did enjoy himself. It was too much like letting his opponents score against him. And so people like Mr. Dainopoulos, familiar with evil, imagined the captain to be much more wicked than he ever ventured to be. The drug whose aid he invoked made him look not only aged but sinful as a compensation for the glimpses into the paradise of perpetual youth which it afforded him while he was lying amid huge puffy pillows, in a house near the Bazaar. It gave him genuine pleasure to escape every familiar human eye, and arrive by devious ways at a secret door in a foul alley, which gave on to the back of the house where a quiet, elderly woman and her thirteen-year-old daughter received him and wafted him gently away into elysium. He was a sensualist no doubt, yet it would puzzle a jury of angels to find him more guilty than many men of more amiable repute. When he sank into one of his torpors, the quiet woman holding his pulse, he felt he was getting

even with the wife and daughter who had made him so unhappy in past days. Captain Rannie never did anything
without what he called "full warrant." He considered he
had full warrant for killing himself with drugs if he wished.
He merely refrained out of consideration for the world.
Away back in the womb of Time, some forgotten but eternal
principle of justice had decreed to him the right to do as he
pleased, provided, always provided, he did his duty in his
public station. This is a common enough doctrine in Europe
and a difficult one to abrogate. Mr. Spokesly, driving along
the *quai* toward the White Tower, would have been the last
to deny what Captain Rannie called "a common elementary
right." He was invoking it himself. What he was trying
to do all this while was to achieve an outlet for his own personality. This was really behind even his intrigue with the
London School of Mnemonics. He was convinced he had
something in him which the pressures and conventions of the
world had never permitted to emerge. It must be borne in
mind that the grand ideal of sacrifice which swept over us
like a giant wave of emotion at the beginning of the war
behaved like all waves. It receded eventually, and those of
us whose natures were durable rather than soluble emerged
and began to take in the situation while we dried ourselves
as quickly as possible. We wondered if there might not be
some valuable wreckage washing ashore soon. We got into
the universal life-saving uniform, of course, and assumed
conventional attitudes of looking out to sea and acting as
chorus to the grand principal performers; but the habits and
instincts of generations were too strong for us. We kept one
eye on the beaches for wreckage. Patriotism became an
intricate game of bluffing ourselves. We had returned with
naïve simplicity to the habits of our Danish and Saxon and
Norman ancestors. Like the Jews in London who joined
lustily in the chorus of "Onward, Christian Soldiers," we
missed the joke in our furious eagerness to seize the opportunity. But there were many, and Mr. Spokesly was one,
whose acquisitive genius was not adequately developed to
deal with all the chances of loot that came by, and who were

preoccupied with the fascinating problem of establishing their egos on a higher plane. Merely becoming engaged had been an advance, for Mr. Spokesly, because men like him can move neither upward nor downward without the aid of women. Once removed from the influence of Ada by a series of events which he could not control, he was the pre-destined prey of the next woman ahead. Those who view this career with contempt should reflect upon the happiness and longevity of many who pursue it. Mr. Spokesly was no sensualist in the strict meaning of the word. He simply experienced a difficulty in having any spiritual life apart from women. He could do with a minimum of inspiration, but such as he needed had to come from them. All his thoughts clustered about them. Just as he experienced a feeling of exaltation when he found himself in their company, so he could never see another man similarly engaged without re-garding him as a being of singular fortune. Always, more-over, he conceived the woman he did not know as a creature of extraordinary gifts. Evanthia Solaris seemed to have eluded classification because, without possessing any gifts at all beyond a certain magnetism bewilderingly composed of feminine timidity and tigerish courage, she had inspired in him a strange belief that she would bring him good fortune. This was the kind of woman she was. She went much farther back into the history of the world than Ada Rivers. Ada was simply a modern authorized version of Lady Rowena or Rebecca of York. She accepted man, though what she really wanted was a knight. Evanthia had no use for knights, save perhaps those of Aristophanes. She, too, ac-cepted men; but they had to transform themselves quickly and efficiently into the votaries of a magnetic goddess. Sighs and vows of allegiance were as nothing at all to her. She had a divinely dynamic energy which set men going the way she wanted. The gay young devil who had been sent packing with the consuls and who was now sitting in his hotel in Pera was wondering at his luck in escaping from her and scheming how to get back to her at the same time. Yet so astute had she been that even now he did not suspect that she was scheming, too, that she was in an agony at times for the loss of him, and talked to Mrs. Dainopoulos of killing herself. She was scheming as she came walking among the grass-plats at the base of the Tower and saw Mr. Spokesly descend from a carriage and take a seat facing the sea. She came along, as she so often did in her later period, at a vital moment. She came, in her suit of pale saffron with the great crown of black straw withdrawing her face into a magically distant gloom, and holding a delicate little wrap on her arm against the night, for the sun was going down behind the distant hills and touching the waters of the Gulf with ruddy fire. She saw him sitting there, and smiled. He was watching a ship going out, a ship making for the narrow strait between the headland and the marshes of the Vardar, and thinking of his life as it was opening before him. He took out a cigarette and his fingers searched a vest-pocket for matches. They closed on the emerald ring and he held the cigarette for a while unlit, thinking of Evanthia, and wondered how he could make the gift. And as he sat there she seemed to materialize out of the shimmering radiance of the evening air, prinking and bending forward with an enchanting smile to catch his eye. And before he could draw a breath, sat down beside him.

"What you do here?" she asked in her sweet, twittering voice. "You wait for somebody, eh?"

"Yes," he answered, rousing, "for you."

"Ah—h!" her eyes snapped under the big brim. "How do I know you only tell me that because I am here?"

Her hand, gloved in lemon kid, was near his knee and he took it meditatively, pulling back the wrist of it until she drew away and removed it herself, smiling.

"Eh?" she demanded, not quite sure if he had caught her drift, so deliberate was his mood. He took the ring out of his pocket and grasped her hand while he slid the gem over a finger. She let it rest there for a moment, studying the situation. No one was near them just then. And then she looked up right into his face leaning a little towards him. Her voice caught a little as she spoke. It was ravishing, a ring like that. For a flicker of an eyelash she was off her guard.

and he caught a smoulder of extraordinary passion in her half-closed eyes.

"You like me," she twittered softly.

The sun had gone, the gray water was ruffled by a little wind, the wind of evening, and as the guns boomed on the warships in the roadstead the ensigns came down.

"You like me," she said again, bending over a little more, for his eyes were watching the ships and she could not bear it. Suddenly he put his arm across her shoulders and held her. And then he used a strange and terrible expression.

"I'd go to hell for you," he said.

She leaned back with a sigh of utter content.

CHAPTER X

HE LOOKED down from his window in the morning into a garden of tangled and neglected vegetation sparkling with dew. Over the trees beyond the road lay the Gulf, a sheet of azure and misty gray. He looked at it and endeavoured to bring his thoughts into some sort of practical order while he shaved and dressed. The adventure of the previous evening, however, was so fresh and disturbing that he could do nothing save return to it again and again. At intervals he would pause and stand looking out, thinking of Evanthia in a mood of extraordinary delight.

She must be, he reflected, one of the most wonderful creatures in the world. He had not believed it possible that any woman could so transmute the hours for him into spheres of golden radiance. The evening had passed like a dream. Indeed, he was in the position of a man whose dreams not only come true but surpass themselves. His dreams had been only shabby travesties of the reality. He recalled the subtle fragrance of her hair, the flash of her amber eyes, the sensuous delicacy and softness of her limbs and bosom, the melodious timbre of her voice. And he paused longer than usual as he reflected with sudden amazement that she was his for the taking. The taking! How deliciously mysterious she had been as she made it clear he must take her away, far away, where nobody knew who she was, where they could be happy for ever together! How she had played upon the strong chords of his heart as she spoke of her despair, her loneliness, her conviction that she was destined for ill fortune! She injected a strange strain of tragic intensity into the voluptuous abandon of her voice. She evoked emotions tinged with a kind of savage and primitive religious mania as she lay in his arms in the scented darkness of that garden and whispered in her sweet twittering tones her romantic desires. And the thought that she was even now lying asleep in another room, the morning sun filtering through green shutters and filling the chamber with the lambent glittering beam-shot twilight of a submarine grotto, was like strong wine in his veins. She depended on him, and he was almost afraid of the violence of the emotion she stirred in him. She had touched, with the unerring instinct of a clever woman, his imagination, his masculine pride and the profound sentimentalism of his race towards her sex. She revealed to him a phase in her character so inexpressibly lovely and alluring that he was in a trance. She inspired in him visions of a future where he would always love and she be fair. Indeed, Mr. Spokesly's romantic illusions were founded on fact. Evanthia Solaris was possessed of a beauty and character almost indestructible. She was preëminently fitted to survive the innumerable casualties of modern life. She was a type that Ada Rivers, for example, would not believe in at all, for girls like Ada Rivers are either Christian or Hebrew, whereas Evanthia Solaris was neither, but possessed the calculating sagacity of a pagan oracle. Such a catastrophe as the departure of the consuls had enraged her for a time, and then she had subsided deep into her usual mysterious mood. So his illusions were founded on fact. She could give him everything he dreamed of, leaving him with imperishable memories, and passing on with unimpaired vitality to adventures beyond his horizon. There was nothing illogical in this. Being an adventuress is not so very different from being an adventurer. One goes into it because one has the temperament and the desire for adventure. And Evanthia was by heredity an adventuress. Her father belonged to that little-known and completely misunderstood fraternity— the *comitadji* of the Balkans. It is not yet comprehended by the western nations that to a large section of these southeastern people civilization is a disagreeable inconvenience. They regard the dwellers in towns with contempt, descending upon them in sudden raids when the snows melt, and returning to their mountain fortresses laden with booty and sometimes with hostages. They maintain within political frontiers empires of their own, defying laws and defeating with ease the police-bands who are sent to apprehend them. They have no virtues save courage and occasionally fidelity and no ideals save the acquisition of spoil. They invariably draw to themselves the high-spirited youths of the towns; and the girls, offered the choice of drudging poverty or the protection of a farmer of taxes, are sometimes discovered to have gone away during the excitement of a midnight foray. So had Evanthia's mother, a lazy, lion-hearted baggage of Petritch whose parents had breathed more easily when they were free at last from her incessant demands and gusts of rage. But the man who had carried her off into the mountains was nearing the end of his predatory career, and very soon (for he had no enemies, having killed them all) he was able to purchase a franchise from the Government and turn tax-farmer himself. He was so successful that he became a rich man, and the family, fighting every inch of the way, took a villa in Pera. It was there Evanthia was educated in the manner peculiar to that part of the world. When she was eighteen she could make fine lace, cook, fight, and speak six languages without being able to write or read any at all. The villa in which they lived was for ever in an uproar, for all three gave battle on the smallest pretext. They lived precisely as the beasts in the jungle live—diversifying their periods of torpor with bursts of frantic vituperation and syncopating enjoyment. Neither European nor Asiatic, they maintained an uneasy balance on the shores of the Bosphorus between the two, until Evanthia's mother, a vigorous, handsome brunette trembling with half-understood longings and frustrated ambitions in spite of her life of animal indolence, suddenly ran away and took her daughter with her. She had fallen in love with a Greek whom she had met in Constantinople, a man of forceful personality, enormous moustaches, and no education, who was selling the tobacco crop from his estate in Macedonia. Evanthia's father, now a man of nearly sixty, did not follow them. He suffered a paroxysm of rage, broke some furniture, and made furious preparations for a pursuit, when one of the servants, a tall, cool Circassian girl with pale brown eyes and an extraordinarily lovely figure, broke in upon his frenzy and told him an elaborate story of how his wife had really gone to France, where she had previously sent a sum of money, and how she herself had been implored to go with them but had refused to desert her master. It was quite untrue, and took its origin from the French novels she had stolen from her mistress and read in bed; but it hit the mark with the man whose only domestic virtue was fidelity. And the Circassian creature made him an admirable companion, ruling the villa with a rod of iron, inaugurating an era of peace which the old gentleman had never experienced in his life.

Evanthia had to adjust herself to new and startling conditions. The swart Hellene stood no nonsense from his handsome mistress. He beat her every day, on the principle that if she had not done anything she was going to do something. When Evanthia began her tantrums he tried to beat her, too, but she showed so ugly a dexterity with a knife that he desisted and decided to starve her out. He cheerfully gave her money to run away to Saloniki, laughing harshly when she announced her intention of working for a living as a seamstress. She arrived in Saloniki to hear stirring news. She was about to enter a carriage to drive to the house of a friend of the Hellene, a gentleman named Dainopoulos, when a young man with glorious blond hair and little golden moustache, his blue eyes wide open and very anxious, almost pushed her away and got in, giving the driver an address. This was the beginning of her adventures. The young man explained the extreme urgency of his business, offered to do anything in his power if she would let him have the carriage at once. She got in with him, and he told her his news breathlessly: War. It seemed a formidable thing to him. To her, life was war. She had no knowledge of what war meant to him in his country. To her London, Berlin, Paris were replicas of Constantinople, cosmopolitan rookeries where one could meet interesting men. Saloniki immediately became a charming place for Evanthia Solaris. The young man was the vice-consul. His father was a wealthy ship-chandler at Stettin, and he himself had been everywhere. It was he who first confirmed her vague gropings after what one might call, for want of a better word, gentility. She was shrewd enough to suspect that the crude and disorderly squabbling in the Pera villa, or the grotesque bullying on the tobacco plantation, were not the highest manifestations of human culture. As has been hinted, she was sure there were people in the world who lived lives of virtuous ease, as opposed to what she had been accustomed. Their existence was confirmed by her new friend. He was the first man she had liked. Later she became infatuated with him. In between these two periods she learned to love someone in the world besides herself.

It would not do to say that she, in her barbaric simplicity, assumed that all Englishwomen lay on their backs and had angelic tempers. But she did arrive at a characteristically ecstatic conclusion about Mrs. Dainopoulos. That lady was so obviously, so romantically genteel that Evanthia sometimes wanted to barter her own superb vitality for some such destiny. She never considered for a moment, until she met Mr. Spokesly, the chances of being adored as Mr. Dainopoulos adored his wife. She knew Mr. Dainopoulos would never dream of adoring a woman like herself. She regarded him with dislike because he betrayed no curiosity about herself and because he obviously knew too much to be hoodwinked by her arts. He even ignored her rather amusing swagger when she paraded her new acquisition, a handsome vice-consul. She knew he would not have tolerated her at all had not his wife expressed a desire to have her remain. Mrs. Dainopoulos had no intention of countenancing evil; but she had been humane enough to see, when Evanthia told her story, how impossible it was for a girl with such a childhood to have the remotest conception of Western ideals. Mrs. Dainopoulos, in fact, belonged to the numerous class of people in England who manage "to make allowances," as they call it, for others. And possibly, too, Evanthia, with her bizarre history and magical personality, possibly even

her naïve assumption that she was destined to be mistress
of men, appealed to the Englishwoman's flair for romance.
Evanthia, contrasted with Haverstock Hill, was wonderful.
And to Evanthia, the victim of sudden little spurts of girlish
posing, pathetic strivings after an imaginary western self,
the invalid woman was a sympathetic angel. She never
laughed when Evanthia pretended an absurd lofty patriotism
or inaugurated a season of ridiculous religious observances,
dressing in white and holding a crucifix to her breast. She
did not deride Evanthia's remarkable travesty of English
dress, or Evanthia's embarrassing concoctions in the kitchen.
These gusts of enthusiasm died out, and the real Evanthia
emerged again, a velvet-soft being of sex and sinuous delicacy, of no country and no creed, at home in the world, a
thing of indestructible loveliness and problematic utility.

And now, while Mr. Spokesly stood at his window gently
rubbing his chin and looking down into the dew-drenched
garden, Evanthia was lying in another room, smoking a
cigarette and meditating. She had a very astute and clearly
defined plan in her mind, and she lay thinking how it could
be carried out. Unhampered by so many of our modern
educational distractions and complexes, her mental processes
would have exacted the admiration of the London School of
Mnemonics. The apparent impossibility of leaving Saloniki
and reaching Constantinople meant nothing at all to her. It
had always been an almost impossible task to go anywhere if
one were a woman. Women, in her experience, were like
expensive automobiles. They were always owned by somebody, who drove them about and sometimes ill-treated them
and even rode them to destruction, and who lost them if they
were not carefully guarded. Moreover, the parallel, in her
experience, went farther, because she observed that nobody
ever thought less of them because they were costly to run.
Evanthia was now like an ownerless machine of which no one
perceived the value or knew how to start. She had been
getting accustomed to the notion that independence had its
pleasures and defects. She lay thinking with quiet efficiency,
until her cigarette was burned down, and then suddenly

sprang out of bed. With extraordinary speed and quietness, she rolled up her great masses of black hair, slipped into a yellow kimono and Turkish slippers, and went downstairs. The contrast between her pose, with nothing save the slow curl of smoke coming from the deep pillow to show she was alive, and the sharp vitality of her movements in the kitchen, was characteristic. She could not help doing things in a theatrical way. Mr. Dainopoulos was much nearer the mark than even he knew, when he said in his caustic way that Evanthia imagined herself a queen. There were times when she thought she was an empress walking down ivory staircases strewn with slaughtered slaves. She had a way of striding to the door when she was angry and turning suddenly upon him, her head lowered, her amber eyes full of a lambent, vengeful glare. Mr. Dainopoulos would remain as impassive as a dummy under this exhibition of temperament, but his attitude was artistically correct. She might be exasperated with him, but she really regarded him as a dummy. He represented the cowed and terror-stricken vassal shrinking from the imperial anger. And now she moved in a majestic way here and there in the great stone kitchen, making black coffee and spooning out some preserved green figs into a plated dish. This she arranged on a tray. In imagination she was a great lady, a grand-duchess perhaps, taking refreshment to a secret lover. She loved to figure herself in these fantastic rôles, the rôles she had seen so often at the cinemas. The exaggerated gestures and graphic emotions came naturally to a girl at once theatrical and illiterate. She walked away with the tray in her hand, ascending the stairs as though rehearsing an entrance, and stood stock still outside Mr. Spokesly's door, listening.

Mr. Spokesly was listening, too. He had heard the slip-slop of the loose slippers, the tinkle of spoon against china, and then a faint tap. He went over to the door and pulled it open.

"You!" he said, with a thrill. He could not have said a word more just then. She smiled and held a finger to pursed lips to enjoin silence. He stood looking at her, hypnotized.

"Drink coffee with me?" she whispered sweetly, holding up the tray. And then she moved on along the passage, looking back over her shoulder at him with that smile which is as old as the world, the first finished masterpiece of unconscious art.

She led the way to a darkened room, set the tray down, and pushed the green shutters away, revealing a wooden balcony with chairs and a green iron table. Below, in the hush of early morning, lay the road, and beyond the trees and houses that followed the shore they could see the Gulf, now streaked and splotched with green and gray and rose. The early morning, charged with the undissipated emotions of the night, is a far more beautiful hour than the evening. To Evanthia, however, who had always dwelt amid scenes of extravagant natural beauty, this exquisite sunrise, viewed as it were in violet shadow, the invisible sun tingeing the snow of the distant peaks with delicate shell-pink and ivory-white, the vessels in the roadstead almost translucent pearl in the mist, the shore line a bar of solid black until it rose ominously in the sullen headland of Karaburun—all this was nothing. To Mr. Spokesly it was a great deal. It became to him a memory alluring and unforgettable. It was a frame for a picture which he bore with him through the years, a picture of himself on a balcony, listening to a girl in a yellow kimono while she whispered and whispered and then sat back in her chair and raised her cup to drink, looking at him over the rim of it with her brilliant amber eyes.

"I don't know as it can be done," he muttered, shaking his head slightly, gulping the coffee and setting the cup on the table. "Not so easy, I'm afraid."

"*You* can do it," she whispered imperiously.

"S'pose you get caught?" he replied cautiously. She waved a hand and shrugged.

"*N'importe. C'est la guerre.* That don't matter. You can do it, eh?"

Mr. Spokesly rubbed his chin.

"I don't say I can and I don't say I can't. *He* might be able to get you down there as a passenger."

She shook her head vigorously, and leaned over the table, touching it with her long filbert nails.

"No!" she said. "He says 'no good.' Nobody allowed to go Phyros, nobody to Alexandria. Nobody. You understand?"

He looked at her as she leaned against the table and then his gaze dropped to where the yellow wrap had opened so that he could see her bosom, and he felt a dizziness as he looked away. It was characteristic of Evanthia that she made no sudden gesture of modesty. She leaned there, her white throat and breast lifting evenly as she breathed, awaiting his answer.

"Yes, I understand," he answered, looking out to where the *Kalkis* was emerging from the distant haze. "But what I don't see is why you want to do it."

"I want to go wis you," she whispered sharply, and he looked at her again to find her gazing at him sternly, her finger on her lips.

And Mr. Spokesly suddenly had an inspiration. Here he was again, mewing like a kitten for somebody to come and open the door, instead of taking hold and mastering the situation. He took a deep breath, and lit a cigarette. He must play up to this. No good fooling about. In for a penny, in for a pound. Could it be managed? He decided it could. It was evident Mr. Dainopoulos knew something about it but had no intention of taking an active part in the adventure. Mr. Spokesly realized he himself had no notion where the *Kalkis* was going after discharging in Phyros. It seemed Evanthia did, or had some notion of it. Yes, it could be managed. His hand closed over hers as it lay on the table.

"I'll fix everything," he said. "You be ready and I'll do the rest."

Her face grew radiant. She became herself again—a woman who had got what she wanted. She rose and stroked his hair gently as she bent over him.

"Now I get some breakfast, *mon cher*," she twittered sweetly. "You stop here. I call you." And with a soft,

sibilant flip-flop of her heelless slippers, which showed her own
pink heels and delicate ankles, she disappeared.

And Mr. Spokesly, who had come home from distant
places to join the forces, who had become engaged in an
exemplary way to a girl who was now wondering, away in
beleaguered England, why Reggie didn't write, tilted his
chair a little and allowed his mind to go forward. When he
asked himself what would be the upshot of this adventure,
he was compelled to admit that he didn't know. What
startled and invigorated him was that he didn't care. He saw
himself, as they say, on deck in fine weather, a full moon pouring her glorious radiance down upon them, and Evanthia beside him in a deck chair under the awning. He saw himself
in some distant harbour, after much toil and anxiety, sitting
at cafés with bands playing and Evanthia in that corn-
coloured dress with an enormous black hat. And then his
thoughts went so far forward that they lost coherence and he
grew dizzy again. His chair was tilted back against the opened
jalousie and he stared with unseeing eyes across the glittering water. It was the dream he had had before, on the
Tanganyika, only a little clearer, a little nearer. They were
dead, while he was alive. There you had it. Perhaps in a
little while he, too, would be dead—a bomb, a shell, a bullet—
and the dreams would be for others while he joined that great
army of silent shades. Why had he never seen the simplicity
of it before? This was the mood for adventure. You forgot
the others and went right on, getting the things that are yours
for the taking, never counting the cost, finding your dreams
come true. . . .

Then you went back to beleaguered England, and Ada
would be there, waiting.

And then, as he sat there, he came slowly back to the
present and saw that the *Kalkis* was moving. He saw steam
jetting from the forecastle and that told him they were heaving up the anchor. An obsolete old ship, he reflected, with
the exhaust from the windlass blinding everybody and making it difficult to see the bridge. The *Kalkis* began to move.
Now she had way on and was turning towards him. Com-

ing in to a new berth, Mr. Spokesly noted. He rose, and Mr. Dainopoulos appeared at the door leading to the balcony.

"You all right, eh?" he inquired, and seeing the empty cups made a peculiar grimace. He pointed to the *Kalkis*.

"You got a new berth?" said Mr. Spokesly.

"Yeh. Over here," said Mr. Dainopoulos. "It's the best we can get just now. No room inside. Now," he went on, "You got to go on board, see, and have a look round. There's two hundred ton to be loaded quick, but I think her winches, they ain't very good. You let me know. The captain, he talk plenty about *new* winches. Where do I get new winches, eh? I ask you, where do I get 'em, out here?"

This time, when called, Mr. Spokesly was ready.

"We'll get her loaded," he said. "If it's all light general we can do it, winches or no winches. Is the other mate finished?"

"Just about. He don't get any more pay, anyhow."

Evanthia suddenly came out of the shadow of the room and looked at them in a theatrical way, as though she were about to begin a big scene and was waiting for her cue from the rear.

"Breakfast," said Mr. Dainopoulos, upon whom this sort of histrionics was lost, and they went down to a room on the ground floor, a room that was full of moving green shadows and pale green beams as the dense foliage of the garden swayed in the breeze. It was like sitting in a recess at the bottom of the sea. The slim girl with the contemptuously taciturn expression was laying the table.

"My wife, she don't come down," said Mr. Dainopoulos, devouring lamb stew. They might have been in the breakfast room of a home in Haverstock Hill. Only the figure of Evanthia hissing incomprehensible commands into the ears of the sullen young girl, who stared at Mr. Spokesly and moved unwillingly into the kitchen, recalled the adventure behind this little scene. On the walls were enlarged photographs of the father and mother of Mr. Dainopoulos, life-size coloured prints in gold frames that were enclosed in an outer glass case on account of flies. The furniture had come, at his wife's order, from Tottenham Court Road, and was a glossy walnut with dark green plush. A giant dresser of black Anatolian oak which stood against one wall bore on its broad shelves a couple of blue and green and yellow Armenian vases and a great shining copper tray like an ancient shield. Across this shield the green sunlight wavered and shook so that even Mr. Dainopoulos allowed his eye to rest on it. He wanted to get rid of that dresser and buy one of those white kitchen cabinets he saw in advertisements. He did not know furniture, strange to say, or he would have asked an extremely high price for his dresser. He sat looking at the light playing on the copper shield, which sent it flying back in a fairy flicker athwart the ceiling, which was dark brown and riven with huge cracks, and doing a little posing on his account.

"My wife she don't come down," he said. It reminded him of something he had been going to tell Mr. Spokesly that first night and his wife had stopped him. Why did she always do that? Always there was something about the English he couldn't follow. He went on with his lamb stew, noisily enjoying it, and pretending he did not see Evanthia's rehearsal of one of her favourite poses, a great madama dispensing hospitality to her guests in the morning room of her *château*.

"I met a major yesterday," said Mr. Spokesly, "in the Olympos. He said he wanted me to go and see him about the cargo."

"Eh!" Mr. Dainopoulos stared, knife and fork raised.

"Oh, I fancy he just wants to give us a few hints about the discharging in Phyros."

"He can do that," said Mr. Dainopoulos, letting his hands fall to the table. "He can do that. Yes," he went on, seeing the possibilities of the thing, "you go along and tell him you'll attend to it all yourself, see? You fix him. The captain, he don't like government peoples."

"I'll go this morning, after I've got some gear."

"It ain't a very long voyage to Phyros," said his employer.

"Where do we go, from Phyros?" asked Mr. Spokesly.

"To Piræus for orders," said the other quickly. Mr. Spokesly could not help glancing at Evanthia, who regarded him steadily.

"I see," he said. Piræus was the port of Athens. Athens, just then, was a peculiar place, like Saloniki. So that was it.

"Captain Rannie said he didn't know," he observed. Mr. Dainopoulos grunted.

"Perhaps he didn't know, when you ask him. I think I got a charter, but I ain't sure. I take a chance, that's all."

After they had finished and as he was waiting for Mr. Dainopoulos, he saw Evanthia in the garden, an apron over her pink cotton dress, smoking a cigarette.

"So it's Athens you want," he said, smiling. She put her finger to her lips.

"By and by, you will see," she said and led him away down among the trees. She pulled his head down with a gesture he grew to know well, and whispered rapidly in his ear. And then pushed him away and hurried off to look for eggs in the chicken-house. He joined Mr. Dainopoulos in a thoughtful mood, more than ever convinced that women were, as he put it, queer. He was so preoccupied that he did not notice the lack of originality in this conclusion.

Mr. Dainopoulos was thoughtful, too, as they made their way into the city and he opened his office. He was in a difficulty because he did not know how far Mr. Spokesly, being an Englishman, could be trusted with the facts. He was perfectly well aware of the difference between doing a little business in hashish, which destroyed the soldiers in Egypt body and soul, and an enterprise such as he had in mind. What would be Mr. Spokesly's attitude after his interview with the major, and after getting away to sea? He had said he was taking a chance of a cargo. This was scarcely true; but he was taking a chance in sending Mr. Spokesly out ignorant of what was in store for him. But he decided to do it. He decided to make that drug-rotted old captain of his earn his salt. He would let Captain Rannie tell Mr. Spokesly after they were at sea. Scraping his chin with his fingernail as he stood in front of his big safe, Mr. Dainopoulos felt sure that, out at sea, there would be no trouble. Then he opened his safe. He would make sure. The major had his own personal influence, no doubt; and it would be a powerful one if he exercised it. Mr. Dainopoulos could imagine him engaging Mr. Spokesly's interest tremendously with the story of those men waiting for their stores in Phyros. He took out a cash-box, and closing the safe went back to his desk.

"Listen here, Mister," he said, and suddenly broke off to wave away the young Jew, who was gazing in upon them with eyes enlarged and charged with pathos. "Listen here," he went on when the youth had vanished like a wraith. "I want to fix you so you'll be all right if anything happens, you understand. I don't know. Perhaps the Government take the *Kalkis* when she get to Piræus—plenty trouble now in Piræus—and you gotta come back here. So I pay you six months now. You give me a receipt for six months' pay."

"What for?" demanded Mr. Spokesly, astonished.

"You understand, easy to cover risks with underwriter, yes. But s'pose I buy another ship and I got no captain. See?"

Something told Mr. Spokesly, though he did not understand at all, that money was money. The man was straight anyhow, he thought, taking the pen. He'd watch that old Rannie didn't try any monkey tricks. Very decent of him. He signed. He took the money in large, blue and purple denominations, crisp, crackling, delicious.

"And you don't forget," said Mr. Dainopoulos, turning towards the safe again. "By and by I'll have some more business, big business, and you'll get a big piece o' money if you work in with me. When you come back, eh? Out here, plenty business but nobody honest, to manage." He paused, looking down at the floor, hampered by his deficient English to explain what he meant. He was rather moved, too, because he saw, right there in his own continuing city, opportunities for business undreamed of by the tall blond officers in their shining brown harness down at headquarters. He saw buildings going up which would be sold for a song, a floating dock which might be acquired for a purely nominal sum when the war was over. He saw jetties and rolling-stock and launches which would be sold at hurried auctions for knock-down prices, a score at a time. But one must have some-body one can trust, a partner or a manager. Mr. Daino-poulos wanted no partners. His temperament was to feel his way along alone, making sudden rushes at his objective or sitting down to wait. A partner was of no use to him. But he figured that someone like Mr. Spokesly would be of great assistance in his business as he planned it later.

He put his cash-box away, slammed his safe shut, and began to open his shop for his ostensible business of money-changing.

"Now you get out to the ship as soon as you got your gear," he said, "and that young feller 'll go with you in the boat."

Mr. Spokesly was startled to see how close the *Kalkis* was in shore, opposite the house. Without a glass he could see the balcony and the window within which Mrs. Dainopoulos lay watching the sunlight on the sea. As he came nearer to the ship, however, sitting in the row boat with the trembling young Hebrew beside him, he became preoccupied with her lines. And indeed to a seafaring man the *Kalkis* was a problem. She resembled nothing so much as the broken-down blood animal whom one discovers hauling a cab. Mr. Spokesly could see she had been a yacht. Her once tall masts were cut to stumps and a smooth-rivetted funnel at the same graceful rake was full of degrading dinges. A singularly shapely hull carried amidships a grotesque abortion in the form of a super-imposed upper bridge, and the teak deck forward was broken by a square hatchway. All the scuttles along her sides, once gleaming brass and crystal, were blind with dead-lights and painted over. Another hatch had been made where the owner's skylight had been and a friction-winch screamed and scuttered on the once spotless poop. As Mr. Spokesly once phrased it later, it was like meeting some girl, whose family you knew, on the streets. A lighter lay alongside loaded with sacks and cases, and the friction-winch shrieked and jerked the sling into the air as a gang of frowzy Greeks hooked them on.

They came round her bows to reach the gangway and Mr. Spokesly gave way to a feeling of bitterness for a moment as he looked up at the gracile sprit stem from which some utilitarian had sawed the bowsprit and carefully tacked over the stump a battered piece of sheet-copper. It affected him like the mutilation of a beautiful human body. What tales she could tell! Now he saw the mark of her original name showing up in rows of puttied screw-holes on the flare of the bow. *Carmencita.* She must have been a saucy little craft, her snowy gangway picked out with white ropes and polished brass stanchions. And now only a dirty ladder hung there.

Leaving the little Jew to get up as best he could, Mr. Spokesly climbed on deck and strode forward. He was curious to see what sort of mate it could be who came into port with a ship like this. His professional pride was nause-ated. He kicked a bucket half full of potato peelings out of the doorway and entered the deck-house.

Garlic, stale wine, and cold suet were combined with a more sinister perfume that Mr. Spokesly knew was rats. He looked around upon a scene which made him wonder. It made him think of some forecastles he had lived in when he was a seaman, forecastles on Sunday morning after a Saturday night ashore on the Barbary Coast or in Newcastle, New South Wales. It was the saloon, apparently, and the break-fast had not been cleared away. A large yellow cat was gnawing at a slab of fish he had dragged from the table, bringing most of the cloth, with the cruet, after him. On the settee behind the table lay a man in trousers and singlet, snoring. He was wearing red silk socks full of holes, and a fly crawled along his full red lips below a large black mous-tache. In a pantry on one side a young man with a black moustache and in a blue apron, spotted with food, was smok-ing a cigarette and wiping some dishes with an almost in-credibly dirty cloth.

"Where's the cap'en?" demanded Mr. Spokesly in a voice

so harsh and aggressive he hardly recognized it himself. The young man came out wiping his hands on his hips and shrugging his shoulders.

"Where's the mate?"

The young man pointed at the figure on the settee. Mr. Spokesly went round the table and gave the recumbent gentleman a shake. Uttering a choking snort, the late chief officer opened his eyes, sat up, and looked round in a way that proved conclusively he had no clear notion of his locality. Eventually he discovered that the shakings came from a total stranger and he focussed a full stare from his black eyes upon Mr. Spokesly.

"I'm the new mate," said the latter. "Where's my cabin?"

"Ai!" said the other, staring, both hands on the dirty tablecloth. "Ai! You gotta nerve. What you doin' here, eh?"

"All right," said Mr. Spokesly, "I'll see to you in a minute. Here, you! Where's the mate's cabin, savvy? Room, cabin, bunk."

The young man, wiping his hands again on his hips, went over to an opening which led down a stairway and beckoned. Mr. Spokesly followed.

What he found was very much of a piece with the saloon. One side of the ship was occupied by a large room marked "Captain." On the other side were two cabins, the forward one of which he was given to understand was his. To call it a pigsty would not convey any conception of the dire disorder of it. The delicate hardwood panelling of the yacht had been painted over with a thick layer of greenish-white paint; and this was coated, at each end of the bunk, with a black deposit of human origin where the oiled head and neglected feet of the late incumbent had rubbed. The walnut table was marked with circles where hot cups had been set down, and the edges were charred by cigarette-ends left to burn. The basin was cracked and half full of black water. Mr. Spokesly gave one glance at the toilet shelf and then turned away hastily to the young man, who was watching him in some curiosity.

"You speak English?" he was asked curtly.

"Oh yass, I spick Ingleesh. Plenty Ingleesh."

"Right. Get this place clean. You savvy? Clean all out. Quick, presto. Savvy?"

"Yass, I savvy."

"Go on then."

"I finish saloon. . . ."

"You let the saloon alone. Clean this place out *now*."

There was a footfall on the staircase and the late chief officer, Cæsare Spiteri by name, came slowly down, holding by the hand-rail fixed over the door of the alleyway. There was a dull smoulder in his large bloodshot black eyes which seemed to bode trouble. He came forward, elaborately oblivious of Mr. Spokesly, his shoulders hunched, his large hand caressing his moustache. He spoke rapidly in Greek to the nervous steward, who began to edge away.

"Hi!" called Mr. Spokesly. "Do what I tell you. See here," he added to Mr. Spiteri, "you finished last night, I understand. You get your gear out of this and get away ashore."

"Yah! Who are you?" snarled Mr. Spiteri in a quiet tone which made the steward more nervous than ever.

"I'm mate of this ship, and if you don't get out in five minutes . . ."

He had no chance to finish. Mr. Spiteri made a circular sweep with one of his stockinged feet, which knocked Mr. Spokesly off his own, and he fell backwards on the settee. The effect upon him was surprising. Reflecting upon it later, when he got away to sea, Mr. Spokesly was surprised at himself. He certainly saw red. The filthy condition of the ship, the degradation of the yacht *Carmencita* to the baseness of the *Kalkis*, and his own spiritual exaltation, reacted to fill him with an extraordinary vitality of anger. Mr. Spiteri was not in the pink of condition either. He had been drinking heavily the previous evening and his head ached. He went down at the first tremendous impact of Mr. Spokesly's fleshy and muscular body, and Mr. Spokesly came down on top of him. He immediately sank his large white teeth in

Mr. Spokesly's left hand. Mr. Spokesly grunted. "Leggo, you bastard, leggo!" And at short range mashed the Spiteri ear, neck, and jaw hard and fast. Mr. Spiteri let go, but his antagonist was oblivious until he saw the man's face whiten and sag loosely under his blows, while from his own head, where the plaster had come off in the struggle, blood began to drip over them both.

Mr. Spokesly got up, breathing hard, and pointed into the room.

"Get busy," he said to the steward, "and clean all up. Shift this out of the way," and he touched the redoubtable Spiteri with his foot. Quite unwittingly, for he had been in a passion for the moment, Mr. Spokesly had struck hard on one of the vital places of a man's body, just behind the ear, and Mr. Spiteri, for the first time in his life, had fainted.

Out on deck, the new mate realized what he had let himself in for, and clicked his tongue as he thought, a trick he had never been able to abandon since he had left school. Tck! Tck! He saw his young Jew friend making expressive motions with his hands to the boatman who was waiting for his money. Mr. Spokesly had an idea. He whistled to the boatman.

"You wait," he called and held up his hand. Then he beckoned to the youth.

"What's your name?" he demanded. The youth laid his hand on his breast and made a deep obeisance.

"Yes, yes!" shouted the exasperated chief officer. "What's your name? Moses, Isaac, Abraham, eh? Never mind, come on." He led the way into the saloon and waved his hands. The cat rushed out of the door, followed by a kick.

"Now you clean up, understand?"

To his unalloyed delight the youth did understand. The latter's nervous prostration had been due chiefly to the fact that he was entirely ignorant of what was expected of him. He took off his deplorable coat and grasped a bucket.

Mr. Spokesly went downstairs again.

Mr. Spiteri was resting on one elbow watching the steward

take his simple personal effects from the drawers under the bunk and stow them in an old suitcase.

"Get up on deck," ordered Mr. Spokesly. "I wouldn't have a swab like you in the forecastle. Don't wonder the Old Man complained."

Mr. Spiteri rose half way, coughed and spat, rose to his feet, and wavered uncertainly towards the stairs.

"Come on, stuff 'em in! That'll do. Now take it up and pitch it into the boat."

The steward hurried up with the bulging and half-closed suitcase and Mr. Spokesly followed with his predecessor's boots.

"Down you go," he said, dropping the boots into the boat and following them up with the suitcase. "That's it," as he saw Mr. Spiteri step from the ladder and topple against the thwarts. "Now we'll see who's in charge of this ship."

He walked to the bridge-rail, put two fingers in his mouth and blew a shrill blast. Presently out of the little forecastle emerged a stout man in a canvas apron and sporting a large well-nourished moustache. Mr. Spokesly's heart sank.

"Come here!" he shouted, beckoning.

"What's the matter, Mister?" said the aproned one, climbing up the abominable ladder with its stairs of iron rods. Mr. Spokesly's heart rose again.

"You English?" he asked.

"Sure, I'm a French Canadian," retorted the other. "What's the matter? Are you the new mate?"

"Yes," said Mr. Spokesly. "I'm the new mate. Are you the bosun?"

"Sure I am," said the other indignantly. "What did you think I was? The cook?"

"Now, now, cut it out," warned the new mate. "I've had all I can stand just for the present. How many men have you got?"

"Three. How many did you think I got? Thirty?"

"Bosun, if you want it, you can have it, but I tell you straight you got to help me get this ship clean."

"Sure I will. What did you think I was doin'?"

"Send a man along with a bucket of soft soap and water," said Mr. Spokesly hastily. "I'll go round with you later."

"Where's that other mate?" asked the bosun, rather mystified.

"Over the side," said Mr. Spokesly, pointing.

"You seen the captinne yet?" the bosun pursued.

"Plenty, plenty. Send a man along."

Mr. Spokesly turned and to his intense astonishment found Captain Rannie in the saloon.

"Why, where were you all the time?" he asked.

"In my cabin," said Captain Rannie, staring at the floor nervously. "I must say you make noise enough when you join a ship."

"Well, Captain, I'll argue all you want later. Where's the medicine chest?"

"In my cabin."

"Then you'll have to give me the run of it to stop this bleeding. Got any friars' balsam?"

"I—I—I'll see. I'll see." Captain Rannie objected to be approached directly. He was already beginning to wonder, after listening to the very emphatic remarks of his new chief officer through the bulkhead of his cabin, if he had not made a mistake in demanding a change. Very unsettling, a change. He went downstairs again and unlocked his door. It had three locks, Mr. Spokesly observed in some surprise. After opening the door, Captain Rannie stepped through and quickly drew a heavy blue curtain across.

"I'll bring it out to you," he said from within.

Mr. Spokesly dragged the curtain back and stepped in himself. He was indignant at this extraordinary treatment. He was astounded, however, to see Captain Rannie shrink away towards the settee, holding up his arms.

"Don't you dare to touch me!" he shrieked in a very low key. "Don't you . . ."

Mr. Spokesly suddenly caught sight of himself in the glass across the room. He was not a very reassuring spectacle. His face was dirty and blood-smeared, and his collar was torn away from his throat. He closed the door.

"Captain," he said, "we'd better have an understanding right at the start. I'm going to be mate o' this ship for six months."

"You think you are," whispered the captain, slowly approaching a cabinet on the wall. "You only think you are."

"Well, I been paid for it anyway," said Mr. Spokesly, examining his wounded hand. "So we'll take it for granted. Now if you back me up, I'll back you up. Why didn't you come out and help me when that stiff started to make trouble?"

Captain Rannie absolutely ignored this question. He was in a corner, and like some animals in similar plight, he might almost be said to have feigned death. He stood stock still looking into his medicine chest, his back to Mr. Spokesly, his high shoulders raised higher. He was in a corner, for he had been betrayed already into the demonstration of nervous fear. It was the knowledge of his horror of the slightest physical contact with others that Mr. Spiteri had been unable to resist.

"He's nearly bit my thumb through," went on Mr. Spokesly, walking over to the wash-bowl. The ship shook as the winch hurled the slings into the air. Down below a worn pump was knocking its heart out in a succession of hacking coughs.

Captain Rannie, the flask of friars' balsam in his hand, turned slowly from the cabinet and moved cautiously to the table. He set it down, went back, and drew out a roll of bandage. He was beginning to recover his normal state of mind. Everything so far had taken the form in his view of violating the privacy of the commander. Everything! Here was this man, not five minutes on the ship, actually forcing his way into the captain's room. Captain Rannie had never heard of such a thing in his life. It loomed before him with the grimness of an irrevocable disaster. He had always had that last resource in his encounters with Spiteri— he could go into his room, lock all three locks, draw the heavy blue curtain, and remain in a mysterious seclusion for as long

as he liked.   Now—he almost shuddered with anguish—
here was this new chief officer—a perfect stranger—didn't
know him from Adam—washing his wounds absolutely in
the sacred wash-bowl, standing in not over clean shoes on the
very piece of matting on which he himself, the master of the
vessel, stood while shaving and making stern faces at himself
in the glass as he rehearsed imaginary scenes with the rabble
outside.   In a few moments Mr. Spokesly's eyes, grown
accustomed to the sombre twilight of the blue curtains of the
scuttles, would be wandering round the cabin, noting things
Captain Rannie showed to no one.   No one.   He grew fierce
as he thought of his outraged privacy.   He must get this
man out of the room quickly.   He slopped friars' balsam on
some cotton wool, and fixing his pale, exasperated gaze upon
Mr. Spokesly's thumb, began to bind it up.   Mr. Spokesly
felt an urgent need for a smoke.   He reached out and drew a
cigarette from a box on the table and Captain Rannie's
head bent lower as he flushed with a renewed sense of out-
rage.   Nothing sacred!   Without the slightest hint of a request.

"We may have a passenger, I hear," said the oblivious Mr.
Spokesly as he managed to get the cigarette alight.

"Oh, dear me, no!" retorted Captain Rannie, with a sort of
despairing chuckle.   "Quite impossible, quite.   I shouldn't
dream of allowing anything of the sort."

"Not if the boss wanted it?"

"Oh, no doubt, in that case, the master of the vessel would
be the last to hear of it."   He returned to the cabinet to cut
some plaster.   Captain Rannie had not a bedside manner.
His method of affixing the plaster made his patient grunt.
Gazing over the upraised arm of the captain, Mr. Spokesly
suddenly fixed his eyes with attention on the pictures round
the bunk.   They were pictures of people who were, so to say,
the antithesis of his new commander, pugilists and wrestlers
and dancers, men and women of exaggerated physical development.   Some of them were so stark in their emphasis
on the muscles that they resembled anatomical diagrams.
There were photographs, too, of sculptures—sharp, white, and

beautiful against black velvet backgrounds; boys wrestling, girls dancing, a naked youth striving with a leopard. And on a hook near the door was a set of those elastic cords and pulleys whereby athletic prowess is developed. Mr. Spokesly suddenly lost his belligerent mood. He had encountered something he did not quite understand. He turned as the captain finished and his eye fell on shelves packed with books. And outside the winch groaned and squeaked, down below the pump thumped and bucketed.

"I'll go," said Mr. Spokesly. "I must find the bosun. . . ." And he went out, eager to go at the job and get rid of this dreadful grime on the unhappy old ship. As he went the captain stood in front of the medicine chest swallowing something, a dull red flush on his peaked and wrinkled face. Suddenly he darted to the door and slammed it, locking it and hurling the curtain across. And then he sat down in a wicker chair and covered his eyes with his hand. He was trembling violently.

For he was a man who was at war with the world. He was so preoccupied with this tremendous conflict that the disturbance in Europe scarcely sounded in his ears. He was a man without faith and without desire of hope. In the years behind him lay the wreckage of honour, when he had gone out east to the China Coast and never gone back. Revenge, he had called it, and called it still, for unascertained and undefined injuries. Since then he had had freedom. He had hugged the thought of the woman, who had imagined herself so clever at blinding him, working in poverty to keep herself and her brat. Her brat, ha—ha! Away out there in China, a thousand miles up an immense river, in the home river-port of his country ship, he said ha—ha! and fell to improving himself. Driven to devise a mode of existence both unsocial and unintellectual, he had stumbled upon strange things in human life. He accumulated vast stocks of scandal about humanity, and delved into repositories of knowledge which most men avoid and forget. Those and the pipe, which led him into another life altogether, the life of irresponsible dreams, wherein a man's mind, released from the body yet retaining the desires of the body, ranges forth into twilights of oblivion, clutching here and there at strange seductive shapes and thrilling to voices not heard before. Captain Rannie, out there, was much happier than many men who hold their souls in leash and render their accounts exactly. He sailed up and down his great river, a mystery to the Chinamen of the crew, a joke among the Europeans. It did not become apparent to him or anybody else that anything was happening to him. Nothing was happening to him save that the lacquer and varnish and ornament of his conventional upbringing in England were nearly all gone, and underneath there was nothing save himself, a timid, sensitive, sensual, quarrelsome creature with a disposition that seemed to rational people to have gone rancid with the heat. They bore with him because he was used to the work, and he was a warm man in silver dollars, too, they said. But the country-ships began to go home. The colossal freights out of England could not be resisted. Captain Rannie was ordered to take his ship home. Home! He funked horribly but he funked losing his job still more, and he took her home as far as Port Said, with a cargo of tobacco from Sumatra. But farther he would not go. He made himself ill, an easy trick with a well-stocked medicine chest, and no one suspected a man would be striving to avoid reaching England. It was generally just the other way round. He went to the hospital until the ship was gone and then became convalescent, moping about Port Said in his yellow pongee suits and enormous panama hat, smoking innumerable cigarettes and discovering among other things a new world of gigantic phantoms.

It was not difficult, he found, to discover the dealers in drugs and he set out, as a buyer of tobacco. But although his first trip to Saloniki and back to Alexandria was successful and enormously profitable, he became aware that he was being uncomfortably shadowed, and he left again in an Italian steamer. It was here he encountered Mr. Dainopoulos, bound home from a business trip to Egypt; where he had been buying up cheap the stocks of ship-chandlers who had been caught by the sudden withdrawal of troops from the

Dardanelles for service in the north. Mr. Dainopoulos had bought a small ship and now needed a commander.

So far, one might say, Captain Rannie had simply lived the life of many of his condition, Englishmen who had grown soft and flaccid during their long exiles and who now crept furtively along in the shadow of war, neither very honest nor very crooked, ignoble and negligible. But as he sat there now behind his locked door and heavy curtain, shading his eyes with his hand, he faced the immediate future with dread. The sight of Mr. Spokesly, bandaged and plastered, hurrying out to get on with the work, made him see with painful clearness where he himself had fallen and how problematic was the task ahead. He would not tackle a job like this again, he told himself. Never again. He would get away out East again with what he had already made and resume the old, safe, easy river-life, receiving his stacks of "reading matter" from London, reading until his brain was soft and soggy with foolish dreams. It was the best life he knew and he longed to get back to it. After this voyage. How he hated all this! When he came back into the world of urgent men after one of his long periods of stupor, he was horrified at the necessity of living at all, and sometimes contemplated suicide. Now he was afraid, not so much of any punishment which might befall him as of the destruction of his way of life, the harsh secular interferences, the spying out of his useless secrets and his long-hid dishonour. It was his very life now, this carefully contrived oblivion in which he lay like an insect in a cocoon. It was beyond his power to desire a return to England. The very thought made him tremble. One of the secrets he guarded with such hysterical care was his loathing of women. Men though thim a rake, a *viveur--ha-ha!* That was what he wanted them to think. He could not bear any intimacy at all. This new chief officer—that was the disturbing element in his reverie—must be given to understand there could be no intimacy, none whatever.

He listened to the sounds of scrubbing outside, vigorous thumps and kicks as the mops went to and fro. There were voices, too, the ingenuous bawlings of that bosun, offensively active. An unwarrantable intrusion! Quite unnecessary, all this waste of soap and soda. Captain Rannie began to revive: the white tabloid he had swallowed as the door closed behind Mr. Spokesly was getting its work in. He felt better. He would go ashore and explain to Mr. Dainopoulos that this sort of thing could not go on. He examined himself in the glass with stern attention. His gray hair, parted just off the middle, was touched with a brush. Good. He was ready. He lit a cigarette. He unlocked the door and went out.

Up on deck Captain Rannie was immediately aware of a novel state of affairs. It was so long since he had experienced the sensation he could scarcely identify it. There was some-one in charge. The old accommodation-ladder, untouched since the time of Spiteri's advent, was down and the teak steps hastily scrubbed. Made fast to the grating was his boat, washed and with a red and yellow flag on the stern-seat. Mr. Spokesly in a pair of the bosun's rubber boots and with his coat off, came up, blowing a whistle. A young Norwegian came clattering up the ladder from the fore-deck.

"Go and wash your face," said Mr. Spokesly. "And take the cap'en ashore."

Captain Rannie, as he sat with the tiller in his hand and watched the young Norwegian pulling with all his might, felt extraordinarily proud. That was the way to handle these people. He had been right after all. Be firm. New blood, a tight hand. Some respect now for the master of the vessel. And no intimacy. "Take the captain ashore." Brief, curt, attentive. That, he held, was the thing. To dwell apart, within a shining envelope of secular discipline, unquestioned, unhampered, and unloved—that in Captain Rannie's mind was the priceless privilege of command.

CHAPTER XI

MRS. DAINOPOULOS, who was born Alice Thompson, lay on her Tottenham Court Road sofa with a Scotch plaid rug over her, looking out across the sunlit Gulf whenever she raised her eyes from her book. It is not extraordinary that she should have been fond of reading. Suffering actual pain only occasionally, she would have found time hang most heavily but for this divine opiate, whereby the gentle and gracious figures of sentimental fiction were gathered about her and lived out their brief lives in that deserted theatre of the ancient gods, between the silent ravines of the Chalcidice and the distant summits of Thessaly.

For without having in any degree an original imagination she had a very lively one. The people in books were quite as real to her as the people around her. Just as she followed the characters in a book while reading, so she only knew actual human beings while they were in the room with her. As she read her books, so she read people, with intense interest as how it would end and always longing for sequels. There was no doubt in her mind, of course, that you could not have a story without love, and this reacted naturally enough upon her judgments of people. She herself, she firmly believed, could not exist without love. Nobody could. It was a world of delicate and impalpable happiness where people always understood each other without speech, responding to a touch of a hand, a note of music, the sunlight on the snow-capped mountains, or the song of a bird. Released from the indurating business of daily chores and the calculations of housekeeping, and placidly secure in a miser's infatuation, she lived an almost effortless emotional existence. She had gone through many stages, of course, like most exiles, from petulance to indifference; but by this time, as she looked up from her book and watched the *Kalkis* swinging in the current and disappearing from time to time in billows of white steam from her winches, Mrs. Dainopoulos was almost fiercely sentimental. Beneath a manner compounded of suburban vulgarity and English reserve, she concealed an ardent and romantic temperament. People, in her imagination, behaved exactly as did the characters in the books she had been reading. She was the author, as it were, of innumerable unwritten romances, enthusiastic imitations of those Mr. Dainopoulos obediently ordered in boxes from London. She adored those books which, the publisher's advertisement said, made you forget; and she never took any notice at all of the advertisement, often on the opposing page, of the London School of Mnemonics which sought to sell books that made you remember. Yet forget-me-nots were her favourite flowers. To her, as to Goethe, art is called art because it is not nature. The phantasmagoria of Balkan life, the tides of that extraordinary and sinister sea which beat almost up against her windows, left her untroubled. For her there was no romance without love, and of course marriage. For Evanthia she cherished a clear, boyish admiration blended with a rather terrified interest in her volcanic emotional outbreaks. The difference between the two women can be compared to the written story and the ferocious transformation of that story known as a film-version. Mrs. Dainopoulos quite comprehended that Evanthia could do things impossible for an English girl. Even in her seclusion Mrs. Dainopoulos had learned that the Cité Saul was not Haverstock Hill. But she saw no reason why Evanthia should not "find happiness," as she phrased it, fading out with a baby in her arms, so to speak. She did not realize that girls like Evanthia never fade out. They are not that kind. They progress as Evanthia progressed, borne on the crests of aboriginal impulses, riding easily amid storms and currents which would wreck the tidy coasting craft of domestic life. They are in short destined to command, and nothing can sate their appetite for spiritual conflict.

But Mrs. Dainopoulos did not know this. She lay there

looking out at the ineffable beauty of the Gulf, a novel of Harold Bell Wright open on her lap, dreaming of Evanthia and Mr. Spokesly. How nice if they really and truly liked each other! And perhaps, when the war was over, they could all go to England together and see the Tower and Westminster Abbey! This was the way her thoughts ran. She never spoke this way, however. Her speech was curt and matter-of-fact, for she was very shy of revealing herself even to her husband. Her sharp, small intelligence never led her into the mistake of interfering with other people. Instead she imagined them as characters in a story and thought how nice it would be if they only would behave that way.

And then suddenly in upon this idyllic scene burst Evanthia, excited and breathless.

"Oh!" she exclaimed. "What shall I do?"

"Why, whatever is the matter, Evanthia? Your eyes shine like stars. Do tell me."

Evanthia came striding in like an angry prima-donna, her hand stretched in front of her as though about to loose a thunderbolt or a stiletto. She flung herself down—a trick of hers, for she never seemed to hurt herself—on the rug beside the bed and leaned her head against her friend's hand. It was another trick of hers to exclaim: "What shall I do? *Mon Dieu! que ferai-je?*" when she was in no doubt about what she was going to do. She was going after her lover. She was going on board the *Kalkis* before she sailed, on some pretense, and she was going to the Piræus in her, whence she could get to Athens in a brisk walk if necessary, and when she got there God would look after her. She had convinced herself, by stray hints picked up from the domestics of the departed consuls, that her lover would go to Athens. There was as much truth in this as in the possibility of the *Kalkis* going to Piræus. It was conjecture, but Evanthia wanted to believe it. She had never been in a ship, and she could have no conception of the myriad changes of fortune which might befall a ship in a few weeks. She might lie for months in Phyros. With Evanthia, however, this carried no weight. God would take care of her. It was rather disconcerting to reflect that God did. Evanthia, all her life, never thought of anybody but herself, and all things worked together to bring her happiness and to cast her lines in pleasant places. Just at this time she was concentrating upon an adventure of which the chief act was getting on board that little ship out there. Everything, even to the clothes she was to wear, was prepared. She had gone about it with a leisurely, silent, implacable efficiency. And now she relieved her feelings in a burst of hysterical affection for her dear friend who had been so kind to her and whom she must leave. She could do this because of the extreme simplicity of her personality. She was afflicted with none of the complex psychology which makes the Western woman's life a farrago of intricate inhibitions. Love was an evanescent glamour which came and passed like a cigarette, a strain of music, a wave of furious anger. Evanthia remembered the hours, forgetting the persons. But for that gay and spirited young man with the little blond moustache and laughing blue eyes, whom she believed was now in Athens flirting with the girls, her feeling was different. He had won from her a sort of allegiance. She thought him the maddest, wittiest, and most splendid youth in the world. She did not despise Mr. Spokesly because he was not at all like Fridthiof. She could not conceive in that stark and simple imagination of hers two youths like Fridthiof. His very name was a bizarre caress to her Southern ears. How gay he was! How clever, how vital, how amusingly irreligious, how careless whether he hurt her or not. It was a fantastic feature of her attitude towards him that she liked to think of herself as possessed by him yet at liberty to go where she wished. She was experimenting crudely with emotions, trying them and flinging them away. She had at the back of her mind the vague notion that if she could only get back to Fridthiof he would take her away into Central Europe, to Prague and Vienna and Munich, dream cities where she could savour the life she saw in the moving pictures—great houses, huge motor-cars, gems, and gallimaufry. She dreamed of the silken sheets and the milk-baths of

sultanas, servants in dazzling liveries, and courtyards with
fountains and string music in the shadows behind the palms.
Perhaps. Without history or geography to guide her, she
imagined Central Europe as a sort of glorified *Jardin de la
Tour Blanche*, where money grew upon trees or flowered on
boudoir-mantels, and where superb troops in shining helmets
and cuirasses marched down interminable avenues of handsome buildings. There was no continuity in her mind between money and labour. Men always gave her money.
Even Mr. Dainopoulos gave her money, a little at a time.
The poor worked and had no money. There would always be
money for the asking. When the war moved up into the
mountains again, as it always did after a while (for she remembered dimly how the armies went crashing southward
into Saloniki in the war of 1912 and later fought among themselves and came crashing back again, passing through the
valley like a herd of mastodons), there would be more money
than ever, and the rich merchants would send away again to
France and Italy for silks and velvets and *bijouterie*. Ever
since she could remember money had been growing more and
more plentiful. The Englishman who had given her that
splendid emerald ring and who had said he would go to hell
for her, had plenty of money, although not long before he had
had to jump into the water and swim to the shore with only
his shirt and trousers. She might have to swim herself.
Well, what of that? More than once she had done the
distance from the bathing house to the Allatini jetty and
back. Looking through lazy, slitted eyelids she knew she
could swim to the *Kalkis* with ease. Such matters gave her
no anxiety. Evanthia's problems were those of an explorer.
She was making her way cautiously into a new world, a world
beyond those French bayonets. She hated the French because they invariably assumed that she was a *demi-mondaine*
and treated her as bearded family men treat daughters of
joy. Perhaps she hated them also because Fridthiof had
exhausted his amusing sarcasm upon them as his hereditary
enemies; but this is not certain because the Balkan people
do not conceive nationality save as a tribal clannishness.

Evanthia's notions of patriotism were gathered from films shown in Constantinople of imperial-looking persons sitting on horses while immense masses of troops marched by and presented arms. It was fascinating but perplexing, this tumultuous, shining, wealthy outside world, and Evanthia was ready to abandon everything she knew, including Mrs. Dainopoulos, for a look at it. Blood did not matter out there, Fridthiof had told her. *Demokracy* made it possible for any woman to become a princess. So she gathered from his highly satirical and misleading accounts of European customs beyond French bayonets. A suspicion suddenly assailed her as she lay on the rug stroking her friend's hand.

"This Englishman, is he faithful, *honnête ?*"

Mrs. Dainopoulos allowed the leaves of her book to slip slowly from her fingers. She smiled.

"Englishmen are always faithful," she said, with a little thrill of pride. Evanthia let this pass without comment. Fridthiof had once told her the English had sold every friend they ever had and betrayed every small nation in the world, with the result that they now sat on top of the world. He also expressed admiration for their inconceivable national duplicity in fooling the world. And Evanthia, if she reflected at all, imagined Mrs. Dainopoulos was of the same opinion since she had married a Levantine. Mr. Spokesly, however, had said he would go to hell for her, which was no doubt an example of the national duplicity.

"Humph!" she said at length and sat there looking at the sky over the trees.

"He's engaged, *fiancé*, you know, to a girl in England, but I don't think he loves her very much. I think he is beginning to like a friend of mine, Evanthia. Did you go to the cinema last night?"

"Oh, yes, yes. It was beautiful. I love the American pictures, cowboys. They shot the police dead. And in the end the girl had a baby."

"But wasn't she married first, dear?" asked the sick lady, laughing.

"Oh, yes. It was beautiful," answered Evanthia dreamily.

"Very, very beautiful.   They ride and shoot all the time, in America."

"And have babies," added Mrs. Dainopoulos.

"No!" said Evanthia with startling lucidity.   "Fridthiof has been there."

"I thought you had forgotten him, dear. You know I think he was not a good influence for you."

Evanthia murmured, "Ah, yes," and smiled.

"I don't think he always told you the truth.   I am afraid he made things up to tell you."

"I think he is gone to Athens."

"Why?"

"I speak to the old Anna Karoglou who sweep in the Consulate.   She hear the Consul's wife say she has a sister in Athens."

Mrs. Dainopoulos was not prepared to accept this as conclusive evidence, though she knew these illiterate people had their own mysterious news agencies.

"Well," she said, "*you* can't go to Athens just now, can you?"

"The Englishman will get me a passport," answered Evanthia.   "He said he would get one."

"Did he though?   That's very kind of him."

"Yes, he will do anything for me, anything."

"Have you sent word to your mother?   I feel responsible for you, Evanthia dear."

"Oh, I come back," said the girl airily, "I come back."

"I don't believe you will," said Mrs. Dainopoulos gravely. "I don't believe you will."

"Yes, yes.   Come back to my dear friend."

She did too, later on, very much damaged.   She arrived in a crowded train of horse-cars, her clothes in a crushed old basket and a refugee ticket fastened to her blouse with a huge brass safety pin.   She did not dwell on her adventures.   So many women were going through very much the same thing. And Mr. Dainopoulos by that time was too rich and too busy getting richer to bother about a stray like her, and he did not ask.   To the end it remained an impalpable grievance with her that she made no impression upon her dear friend's husband.

She jumped up now, and, kissing Mrs. Dainopoulos, hastened away to see to the evening meal. Downstairs, standing in the doorway of the dining room, she caught the young girl putting some candied plums in her mouth and broke into a swirl of vituperation. Mr. Spokesly, coming in behind his employer at that moment, thought it was remarkably like a cat spitting. The servant suddenly slipped past Evanthia, eyes downcast and smouldering, and scampered out of sight. Mr. Spokesly looked after the lithe little form with the slender cotton stockings and little cup-like breasts under the one-piece cotton dress. He had an idea that that girl would like to knife both Evanthia and himself.

He followed Evanthia out into the garden.

"It's all right," he said. "I got everything on board. But no passport. Nothing doing."

"No?"

He shook his head in confirmation. Most emphatically there had been nothing doing. They were all in a decidedly ugly mood, with that darned girl of Jack Harrowby's in gaol for telling about the times of sailing. They knew well enough the girl had been a fool, an innocent go-between; but they weren't having any more of it. The young lady with friends in Athens would have to exist without them until the war was over. Let her apply to the Provisional Government and then, if all was satisfactory, they would forward the application to the War Office, who would look into it. Sometime next year would be a good date to expect a reply— probably in the negative. That was all he could get out of them. He looked glumly at Evanthia, who stared back at him thinking rapidly. She had not expected a passport. To her a passport was an infernal contrivance for landing you in prison unless you paid and paid and paid an interminable succession of officials. When she had exclaimed to Mrs. Dainopoulos, "Oh, what shall I do? *Que ferai-je ?*" she had been really thinking aloud. What should she do if the Englishman failed to get a passport? Even that was a pose because she had decided what to do. She drew Mr. Spokesly farther away from the house and turned to him with an expression of smiling composure on her face. He stared as though fascinated. She was going to spring something on him, he was sure. In the intervals between sleep and his herculean labours to get the *Kalkis* ship-shape and Bristol fashion he sometimes wondered whether she had not taken him literally when he had said he would go to hell for her. Another thing: it appeared he had to do this for nothing. He was to get her back to her lover and receive a purely nominal reward. He took hold of her shoulders and kissed her hair. He was certainly taking a chance in trying to get her a passport. He had had to be truculent. He was only trying to do a decent turn to a neutral. Mr. Dainopoulos would have applied himself only he felt he was in a delicate position, having chartered his ship to the Government, and so did not want to embarrass them. And so on. A new Mr. Spokesly. Perhaps his visit to the Post Office for letters had something to do both with his truculence and his present air of fascinated interest in Evanthia's face. For there had been no letters. There you were, you see. Out of sight, out of mind. The new Mr. Spokesly was a shade more rugged than the other, a shade harder in the line from ear to chin, a shade more solid on his pins. Evanthia pulled his head over to her ear.

"What time ship go away?" she asked hurriedly.

"To-morrow," he muttered, remembering Jack Harrowby's indiscretion. "To-morrow, but you mustn't tell anybody."

"Pst! Who should I tell, stupidity! To-night you go on the ship, eh?"

"They won't let a lady go through . . ." he began and she pulled his ear.

"Tck! You go on the ship. By and by, late, late, I come, too."

"No. Look here, dear, the picket launches 'll see a boat as soon . . ."

She held up her finger warningly.

"I wait. You come. Watch! In the window a little light. Pprrp!"

She flicked her fingers at him and ran away.

Mr. Spokesly looked after her and sighed with relief and anxiety at the same time. He knew it was a ticklish game to play. If she started coming out in a boat from the shore here, as sure as death those naval pickets who were for ever rushing about would dart up and want to know all about it. And get both him and his employer into trouble. It was up to her now. He had bought an officer's tin trunk and it had been three parts full of her clothes when he went aboard with it. He doubted if she could make it. Well, he had arranged to spend the night on board because Captain Rannie was off on some peculiar jamboree of his own, and he would keep a look-out for the little light. And then Mr. Spokesly saw a light in his mind. He smiled. His imagination was not a facile piece of machinery. He saw things steadily and sometimes saw them whole, but he did not see them at all if they were any distance ahead. He had now caught sight of what lay ahead. He smiled again, and went in to supper.

Mr. Dainopoulos, who was always well aware of things very far away ahead, was much occupied in his mind, but he kept up a good flow of conversation to cover his anxiety. He had been approached that day by the authorities with a proposal. The new Provisional Government was like most governments of the kind, frock-coated, silk-hatted, kid-gloved politicians with extensive vocabularies and limited business experience. The agriculturists of the hinterland were in dire need of implements, machinery, and fertilizers. What was needed was a responsible person or syndicate who would act as purchasing agent, financing the operation against the harvest. The Government proposed to authorize an issue of half a million drachma to a duly constituted syndicate. It was an alluring prospect. His friend Malleotis was in it, too, and thought it a good thing. Mr. Dainopoulos, while he talked to Mr. Spokesly, was developing the plan of campaign in his head. He was, so to speak, flexing his mental sinews. His extremely financial brain was working, and the more he considered it the more lucrative the thing appeared to be. Mal-

leotis had insisted on a two-year agreement as there might be
losses on the coming harvest.   Long-headed man, Malleotis.
Yes, yes, hm.   .   .   .

Here is presented in moderate contrast the divergent
temperaments of Boris Dainopoulos, a man of business, and
Mr. Reginald Spokesly, a man of a type much more common
than many people imagine.   Mr. Spokesly had no business
ability whatever.   It simply was not in him.   His *métier*,
when he was fully awake, was simply watch-keeping, which is
a blend of vigilance, intelligence, and a flair for being about
at the critical moment.   Out of this is born the faculty and
the knack of commanding men, which is a very different
thing from bossing men in business.   And so, while his
employer was already immersed in a new and fascinating deal
which might make him much richer than he had ever hoped
in so short a time, Mr. Spokesly had forgotten that money
existed save as change for the pocket, and was devoting the
whole spiritual energy to the contemplation of an affair of the
heart.   And this is a problem in which ethics plays no part at
all.   The moralist has ever a tendency to applaud the man
diligent in business.   But the business man is dependent
upon the emotionalist and the sensualist, too, for the success
of his designs.   As has been pointed out by an authority the
world is a stage and the men and women players.   Had he
lived in later times he might have remarked that the world
is not quite so simple as that.   There are business men and
ticket-speculators nowadays, for example.

Another thing which preoccupied Mr. Dainopoulos was his
responsibility towards Mr. Spokesly.   He didn't want anything to happen to him.   His wife was always talking about
him.   Of course that baggage Evanthia was after him, but
Mr. Dainopoulos was not worrying about her.   He was
anxious that Mr. Spokesly should not get into trouble over
this trip.   There might be something about the latter part
of the voyage that the chief mate wouldn't like at all.   If
anything miscarried he might not be able to prove he did not
know what was going on.   Mr. Dainopoulos mentioned it in
the garden afterwards.

"Don't you interfere with the captain, Mister," he remarked, over a cigarette.

"Eh!" said Mr. Spokesly, wondering very much. "How can I interfere with a man like him? He sets the course, and I run it off. No business o' mine what he's doing."

This was so exactly in accordance with Mr. Dainopoulos's views and so exactly what Mr. Spokesly ought to say supposing he knew everything, that the former looked hard at the mate and uttered a cackling snarl of astonished satisfaction.

"Why, that's just it. You let him settle everything."

"Except the work about the deck."

"Ah-h!" Mr. Dainopoulos was not lying awake at night worrying about the condition of the deck of the *Kalkis*. But he said nothing more than his guttural "Ah!"

"And the accommodation has got to be kept clean while I'm there," babbled Mr. Spokesly.

"Why, certainly, certainly," assented Mr. Dainopoulos.

"I ought to tell you I tried to get a passport for Miss Solaris," said Mr. Spokesly in a low tone. "They wouldn't hear of it."

"I told her three or four times it was no good," said Mr. Dainopoulos irritably. "What does she think she is?"

"Well, she's got the idea she wants to go to Athens and . . ."

"She won't go to Athens."

"You mean the ship don't go to Piræus?"

"I mean she won't go to Athens."

"Well, I done the best I could for her. She could have my cabin, and I'd sleep in the chart-room."

"How can she get on board?" asked Mr. Dainopoulos. "Does she think I'm goin' to get myself into a lotta trouble for her? Why, let me say to you, Mister, I do plenty business with these peoples, but I could not get a passport now for Mrs. Dainopoulos. No! How can I get one for a girl who nobody knows nothing about? Such foolishness!"

"Just what I told her and she laughed at me and told me she'd manage it."

"She may do that. She can get one of these officers to fix

it, very likely. You know how they are, these French officers. Anything for a pretty young lady."

"She wouldn't do that," said Mr. Spokesly with a troubled air. "She's a friend of Mrs. Dainopoulos, remember."

"I remember all right. But plenty of women do that sort of business all the time in war. Every war the same. Something, I dunno what you call it, gets 'em. They go crazy, a little. They like the uniforms and the tom-te-tom-tom-tom of the music. You know what I mean. I tell her she oughta get a job in Stein's. But she don't like anybody to tell her anything. She ain't nothin' to me. Her mother . . . ! Humph!" And Mr. Dainopoulos flicked his thumbs outward.

"What I told her was, if she did get aboard, she'd have a trip down to the Islands and back. But she don't understand."

"She don't understand nothin' only buyin' clothes an' thinkin' she's one of these here grand duchesses in Russia," snapped Mr. Dainopoulos. "Don't you take any notice of her nonsense stuff."

"Well, I'm supposed to be disinterested in this," said Mr. Spokesly with a slight smile. "I mean, I will say she's been straight about it."

"About what?" said Mr. Dainopoulos, somewhat mystified.

"That sweetheart she had, who went away."

"Oh, him! He's gone."

"She reckons he's in Athens."

"She reckons anything she hears and she can believe anything she wants. It don't hurt nobody."

"That's right, but what do you think?"

"Nothin'. What's it got to do with me? I'd be a fine sorta fool to mix up with her business, me doing business with the English Army, eh? Whatta you think I am?"

"She's neutral, I suppose."

"Yes, but *he* ain't. He was assistant vice-consul and he used to go aboard the ships and talk his English. He was in London years. Talks English better than you do. And he was sendin' reports all the time 'n the Consul's bag." Mr. Dainopoulos gave a curt chuckle. "Nothin' to do with me. They thought he was a Y. M. C. A. feller. Made them laugh. And they used to tell him where they been and where they was goin'. . . . Yes, he was all over the place. She's crazy about him, I know. But he's forgot all about her long ago. You no need to worry about him."

Mr. Spokesly was not worrying about him. One does not worry about rivals who are in all probability three or four hundred miles beyond the battle line. But he was pained at Mr. Dainopoulos's estimate of Evanthia. He felt sorry for a man who was unable to appreciate the flavour, the bouquet, so to speak, of so delicious a personality. When Mr. Dainopoulos said warningly, over his shoulder, his scarred and unlovely features slewed into a grin, "You watch. She'll fool you," he did not deny it. What he wondered at was the failure of his employer to appreciate the extreme pleasure of being fooled by a woman like Evanthia. For Mr. Spokesly had of late discovered that a man can, in some curious subconscious way, keep his head in a swoon. Like the person under an anæsthetic, who is aware of his own pulsing, swaying descent into a hurried yet timeless oblivion, whose brain keeps an amused record of the absurd efforts of alien intelligences to communicate with him as he drops past the spinning worlds into darkness, and who is aware, too, of his own entire helplessness, a man can with advantage sometimes let himself be fooled. For Mr. Spokesly, who had always prided himself on his wide-awake attitude towards women, it was a bracing and novel experience to let Evanthia fool him. It was really a form of making a woman happy since some women are incapable of happiness unless they are fooling men. But he was unable to get Mr. Dainopoulos to see this aspect of the affair. Mr. Dainopoulos was not the man to let anybody fool him unless it might be his wife. It may be doubted that even she managed it. He was very largely what we call Latin, and the Latins are strangely devoid of illusions about women. She mystified him at times, as when she checked him in his desire to tell people that away back he had an

English relative. He was very proud of it and he could not understand his wife's reluctance to hear him mention it. It certainly gave him no clue to their characters; but like many men of diversified descent he had occasional fits of wanting to be thought English. He had been very indignant with that fresh young Fridthiof Lietherthal, who had laughed at his deep-toned statement, "I have British blood in my veins," and remarked airily, "Well, try to live it down, old man, that's all." Very indignant. Thought he was everybody, that young feller. And *he* had a Swedish mother! And said he envied the Englishman his colossal *ego*, whatever that might be. A smart-aleck, they would call him in America.

He walked down the road with Mr. Spokesly, who was going to take the car along and then go aboard. He said:

"I'll be on board the ship to-morrow morning early. Anything you want, let me know and I'll have it sent over in the afternoon before you sail. This will be a good trip for you, and when you come back, by that time I'll have a good job for you."

Mr. Spokesly decided to take a carriage. As he bowled along he turned over in his mind the chances of seeing Evanthia Solaris again. He had no faith in her ability to make an effectual departure from Saloniki. Yet he would not have taken a heavy wager against it. She had an air of having something in reserve. He smiled as he thought what an education such a woman was. How she kept one continually on the stretch matching her moods, her whims, her sudden flashes of savage anger and glowing softness. And he thought of the immediate future, moving through dangerous seas with her depending upon him. If only she could do it! This was a dream, surely. He laughed. The least introspective of men, he sometimes held inarticulate conversations. He had often imagined himself the arbiter of some beautiful woman's fate, some fine piece of goods. There was nothing wicked in this, simply a desire for romance. He was a twentieth-century Englishman in the grand transition period between Victorianism and Victory, when we still held the conventional notions of chivalry and its rewards. It should not be forgotten that when a knight actually did win a fair lady he had some voice in her disposal; and it was a vestige of this instinct which appeared in Mr. Spokesly as speculations concerning Evanthia's future.

He decided to go in and look up his elderly friend in the Olympos. He found him standing in the entrance, holding a black, silver-headed cane to his mouth and whistling very softly.

"Why, here you are! You *are* a stranger! What do you say if we have a couple? Not here. I know a place a little way along. How have you been doing now?"

Mr. Spokesly said he had been busy on a new job and hadn't had much time for going out.

"On that little Greek boat, isn't it? I must say you've got a great old cock for a commander."

"What do you know about him?"

"Oh, I just happen to know the story and it may not be true after all. But they do say he had a Chink wife and practically lived like a Chink up-river. And you know what that means for an Englishman. However, that's neither here nor there. This is the place."

He pushed open a couple of swing doors and they entered a large, barn-like room filled with tables and chairs. At the back a small stage was erected and beside it stood a piano. The flags of the Allies, wrongly drawn, and a portrait of Venizelos looking like a Presbyterian minister in shell-rim glasses, were the only decorations of the dirty walls. A number of men in uniform were lounging about, drinking beer and smoking cigarettes. The elderly lieutenant led the way to a table near the piano. Immediately a waiter, who looked like a New York gun-man, signalled to two women who were seated in different parts of the room, and went forward to take the order. This was for beer, and while they drank, one of the women, a fat middle-aged person without neck or ankles, after the manner of middle-aged Greek women, clambered on to the stage. The other, a girl with black spiral curls on each side of her face, curls like the springs on

screen doors, and with a short skirt that showed quite ab-
normally thin legs, sat down at the piano and drove with an
incredible lack of skill through the accompaniment of a song.
It seemed to be a race between the two of them. The fat
woman was already stepping down from the stage as she
gabbled the final bars of her supposedly risky French song.
An intoxicated ambulance driver hammered on the table with
his glass and then roared with laughter. The two women
came swiftly to the table and sat down by the lieutenant and
Mr. Spokesly.

"This is my little friend," said the lieutenant, chucking the
fat middle-aged creature under a number of chins. The
sinister waiter appeared, swept away the beer-glasses, and
stood poised for instant flight. The fat woman muttered
something in reply to the lieutenant's request to name her
poison and the waiter almost instantly produced two bottles
of Greek champagne, a notable blend of bad cider and worse
ginger-ale.

"Let me pay," suggested Mr. Spokesly, but his friend put
up his hand, smiling.

"I always treat my little friend," he said, and patted her
short, pointed fingers.

"Feefty francs," said the waiter, and his eyes glared into
the lieutenant's wallet with almost insane ferocity.

Mr. Spokesly was glad he had not been permitted to pay
for the two bottles with their shoddy tinfoil and lying labels.
The eyes of the women never left the polished pigskin note-
case while it was in sight. It was almost provocative of
physical pain, the dreadful look on their faces in the presence
of money. Their features were contorted to a set, silent snarl
and their eyes had the black globular lustre of a rat's. The
girl with the ringlets snuggled near Mr. Spokesly and began to
project one of those appalling intimacies which are based on
the insignificance of personality. To him, at that moment
almost entirely dominated by a vivid and delicious character,
the bizarre efforts of this unwashed painted *gamine* to assume
the pose of sweetheart was almost terrifying, and he avoided
her rolling eyes and predatory claws with a sense of profound

shame. His elderly friend, however, was thoroughly enjoying himself. He had reached that period of life, perhaps the best of all for a seafaring man, when he is happily married and comfortably situated, and he can now give his mind to those sentimental fancies which he had to pass up earlier in life owing to economic stress. A seaman's mind is an involved affair in which thoughts and emotions and desires are stowed entirely without reference to academic order. So the old lieutenant, who had had a son killed at Mons and who truly loved his wife, and who was looking forward to loving his grandchildren, was now having a little time off from his elderly duties, and enjoying the unaccustomed pleasure of being a bit of a dog. This was his little friend, this oleaginous vampire who received a percentage of the price of the drinks ordered and all she could wheedle out of drunken customers. There is nothing incomprehensible in this. One is permitted to marvel at these modern Circes, however, who turn men into swine by transforming themselves.

"If you don't mind," said Mr. Spokesly after trying the champagne, "I think I'll have some more beer."

His friend smiled happily and pinched the cheek of his little friend who was now on his knee with a fat arm over his shoulder.

"This is something like, eh!" A young man was playing the piano noisily.

"How's things at the office?" said Mr. Spokesly.

The old fellow chuckled.

"Oh, what do you think is the latest? My young lordship told me in future I was to run round and round the White Tower from nine to five. For the duration of the war, he says. What do you think of that? That's what we get for joining up. Serving our country. Why, it's a joke. What is it, dear?" He listened attentively to his little friend's whisper. "She wants to know if you are going to stand treat to your little friend," he said to Mr. Spokesly.

Mr. Spokesly's little friend, with her emaciated limbs, lemon-coloured French boots, and infuriating ringlets, was smiling in what was supposed to be irresistible coyness. The waiter was already sweeping away the bottle and glasses, which were full and which would be carefully decanted, rebottled and served up to the old lieutenant the following evening.

"Oh, all right. But I can't stay long. I have to get aboard, you know."

"He can't go till you get there," argued his friend.

"Ah, but I've a special reason for wanting to be on board to-night."

"Well, here's luck to the voyage."

"Good luck," said the women, touching the edge of the glasses with their lips and setting them down again.

"Feefty francs," said the waiter, glaring over a black moustache at the fistful of money Mr. Spokesly drew from a trouser pocket.

The pianist crashed out some tremendous chords. The old lieutenant's little friend whispered in his ear.

"What's that, dear? Oh! She wants to know if you'll stand the musician something, seeing you haven't been here before. It's usual."

Mr. Spokesly, without changing his expression, put down a ten-franc note extra.

"You give me a leetle tip?" said the waiter, watching the money going back into his victim's pocket. But he had postponed his own private piracy too long.

"I'll give you a bunt on the nose if you don't get away," muttered Mr. Spokesly. And he added to his friend: "I must go. May not see you again, eh?"

"Very likely not, very likely not. You see, I may be transferred to the Red Sea Patrol."

"Well, so long. Good luck."

He breathed more freely when he got outside. Sixty francs for a quart of carbonated bilge and a racket like nothing on earth.

He was mortified at seeing an Englishman posing as a fool like that, but he was honest enough to admit to himself that he had been that Englishman over and over again.

"Why do we do it?" he wondered as he was borne swiftly

over the water by the launch. And the married men, he reflected, were always the worst.

"Where's your ship?" growled the petty officer, sidling along the engine house and taking one of Mr. Spokesly's cigarettes.

"*Kalkis*, little Greek boat just ahead," said Mr. Spokesly, slipping a couple of shillings into a waiting palm. "And look here, can you wait a second when I get aboard? My skipper wants to go ashore."

"Tell him to double up then."

Captain Rannie was standing on the grating at the head of the gangway, charged with a well-rehearsed monologue on the extreme lack of consideration experienced by some shipmasters. Mr. Spokesly ran up and cut him short.

"Hurry up, sir. Boat's waiting," and before he was aware of it Captain Rannie, with one of his shins barked in getting aboard, was halfway across the gulf.

"Now," said Mr. Spokesly to himself, looking towards the houses. "I wonder what's going to happen."

CHAPTER XII

A T FIRST it seemed as if nothing would ever happen again. There were no electric lights on the *Kalkis*, although she had a very fine dynamo in her engine-room, because one of her engineers in time past had cut away all the wiring and sold it. The donkey-boiler fire was banked and the donkeyman gone ashore. She swung at anchor in absolute silence. The launch was half a mile away. Over the Vardar valley was a glare as of distant conflagrations, and along the front shore the sparkling entrances of the palaces of pleasure from which Mr. Spokesly had just come.

He went down and unlocked the door of his cabin. It was much cleaner than it had been for years, but smelled of new paint. He opened the scuttles, hooked back the door, and lit the brass gimbal-lamp. His tin trunk was stowed under the bed-place. Clean fresh canvas was on the floor and a rag mat by the bunk. A piece of lilac-tinted toilet soap, which is almost indispensable in an English guest room. A clean towel, which he had bought himself at Stein's. The next room was a bathroom, but it was not yet in an entirely satisfactory condition. It had been used to keep chickens in at some time and had also served as a store for the steward. And fresh water had to be carried from the pump, as all the plumbing had been cut away and sold.

Well, it would do. Mr. Spokesly opened the trunk and began to lay the contents in different drawers. He did it clumsily, as a matter of course, so that things of silk and cotton were crumpled and twisted, and he regarded his results dubiously. He decided he would be a failure as a lady's maid, and lighting a cigarette ascended to the deck. A fine thing, he reflected, if she never came and he had all those fal-lals and frills to carry about the ocean!

207

There seemed to be no one on board. And it suddenly occurred to him that this might be an actual fact. He looked into the galley and found no one there. He walked forward to the bridge-deck rail and blew his whistle. Presently up from below, and framed in the doorway of the scuttle, appeared an alarming phenomenon. Its hair stood in conflicting directions, a large moustache cut across between two round black eyes and a red mouth full of yellow teeth, one cheek was covered thickly with lather, and the other, already shaved, was smeared with blood.

"What's the matter?" said the bosun.

"Where's the watchman?" asked Mr. Spokesly.

"He's down here talking to me."

"What are you doing, shaving?"

"Of course I am. What did you think I was doing? Cutting my throat?"

"Looks damn like it," muttered Mr. Spokesly, and sauntered away aft to look at the shore. The indignant apparition in the forecastle scuttle gradually sank from view like the phantoms in old-fashioned grand opera, and was replaced by a lumbering creature in a blue jersey, with curling blond hair, and carrying a bucket of soap-suds. Mr. Spokesly heard him, presently, banging about in the galley.

There was a seat aft near the hand-steering gear, one of those old-fashioned affairs with curiously moulded cast-iron ends and elaborate teak slats, and he sat down there with the telescope to his eye watching the dark mass of trees and roofs where Mr. Dainopoulos lived. Except for a street lamp shining among the trees and an occasional blue spit from a trolley-car, he could discern nothing. Even the room where Mrs. Dainopoulos usually lay was not lighted. It was just about this time that Mr. Spokesly reached the lowest point of his confidence. The magnetism of Evanthia's personality, a magnetism which made him feel, in her presence, that she was capable of achieving anything she desired, and which is sometimes confused with the faculty of command, was wearing away in the chill, dark emptiness of the night. There was a quality of sharp and impersonal skepticism in the air and in those glittering shore-lights beyond the black and polished surface of the Gulf. There was now no wind; the evening current and breeze had faded away, and both the water and the air were hanging motionless until the early morning, when they would set eastward again, to bring the ships' bows pointing towards the shore. And it was slack water in the minds of men floating on that dark and sinister harbour. There were other men sitting and looking towards the shore, men whose nerves had been worn raw by the sheer immensity of the mechanism in which they were entangled. They were the last unconsidered acolytes in a hierarchy of hopeless men. They had no news to cheer them, for the ships sank a thousand miles away. They endured because they were men, and the noisy lies that came to them over the aërials only made them look sour. Great journalists in London, their eyes almost popping from their heads at the state of things on the sea and at the Front, thumped the merchant mariner on the back in bluff and hearty editorials, calling him a glorious shell-back and earning his silent contempt. The stark emphasis placed upon his illiteracy and uncouthness did more harm than good. The great journalists accepted the Navy and the Army on equal footing, but they felt it necessary to placate the seaman with patronage. They were too indolent to find out what manner of men they were who were going to sea. And while the politicians fumbled, and the Navy and Army squabbled with each other and with their allies, and the organized sentiment of the world grew hysterical about Tommy and Jack, the seaman went on being blown up at sea or rotting at anchor. And of the two the former was invariably preferred. Mr. Spokesly, setting down the telescope to light another cigarette, was following this train of thought, and he was surprised to come on the conviction that an active enemy who tries to kill you can be more welcome and estimable than a government without either heart or brains who leaves you to sink in despair. Indeed, he began to carry on a little train of thought of his own, this habit having had more chance to grow since the London School of Mnemonics had gone to the bottom with the

Tanganyika and a good many other things. He said to himself: that's it. It isn't the work or the danger, it's the monotony and feeling nobody gives a damn. Look at me. Now I'm on my own, so to speak, gone out and started something myself, I feel twice as chipper as I did when I was on that darned *Tanganyika* and they didn't seem to know where to send her or what to do with her when she got there. I wonder how many ships we got, sailing about like her, and gettin' sunk, and nobody any better off. They say there's ships carryin' sand to Egypt and lumber to Russia. That's where it is. You trust a man to boss the job and he can make a million for himself if he likes; you don't mind. But if he muffs it, you want to kill him even if he is a lord or a politician. I must say we got a bunch of beauties on the job now. Good Lord!

It might be imagined that having found so fertile and refreshing a theme, Mr. Spokesly would have abandoned everything else to pursue it to the exceedingly bitter end. But he no longer felt that cankering animosity towards authority. He saw that authority can be made exceedingly profitable to those who display dexterity and resilience in dealing with it. Mr. Spokesly had associated long enough with Mr. Dainopoulos, for example, to conceive a genuine admiration for that gentleman's astute use of his position in the midst of diverse and conflicting authorities. Mr. Dainopoulos might be said to be loaning the Government the tackle to pull down the branches laden with fruit, and then charging a high price for the privilege of putting that fruit into his own pocket. Even the shipowners of England could teach him nothing about profits. Indeed, later on, when the war was over, and he himself was expeditiously disposing of his interests in ships, for he had known wars before and the slumps that followed them, it was to those same shipowners that he sold some of his most deplorable wrecks at the top of the market, rather mystified at their blind eagerness to close with him at any price. He was heard to say, on the Bourse at Alexandria, on that always cool loggia where so many deals are consummated over coffee and *granita*, "This will not last.

You take my advice. Sell that ship of yours to the English."
And his dark-skinned companion, who had been doing very
well in the tobacco trade from the Piræus and Saloniki, would
very likely sell, at a price that made him wonder if the English
had discovered a river of money somewhere. And both of
them would continue to sit there, fezzed and frock-coated,
playing with their rosaries, and discussing cautiously the
outlook for Nilotic securities in the event of the English
withdrawing. . . .

But that came later. Mr. Spokesly would have been even
more impressed if he had been aware of the ultimate destination of the freight he had been stowing so industriously into
the *Kalkis*, or of the total emoluments accruing to Mr. Dainopoulos from that freight from first to last. The old adage
about turning your money over was not often so admirably
illustrated. Archy's absurd speculations and traffic in
villainous drugs seemed microscopic compared with the
profits to be made by a good business man. Which is perhaps one of the most embarrassing criticisms of war in the
modern sense, that it places a formidable premium upon
the sutlers and usurers, so that they now sit in high places,
while the youths of invincible courage are either rotting under
wooden crosses in France or looking for shabby situations
across the sea. But Mr. Spokesly, sitting there with his telescope, which revealed nothing, was not criticizing the business
men. He was admiring them, and wishing the military and
political and naval men could be half as clever at their game as
the business man was at his. It was a confusing and kaleido-
scopic problem, this of money. As soon as you got a lot of it,
he reflected, the value of it went down until you had only a
little and then the value of it went a little lower. And then,
when you were occupied in some way which prevented your
making very much, the value crept slowly up again. That is,
unless you were a business man, when of course you turned
your money over and scored both ways.

Keeping company with these general fancies in Mr.
Spokesly's mind was a speculation concerning his own part in
Evanthia's adventure. He looked at his watch. Ten o'clock.

By looking hard through the telescope he could make out a faint radiance from the upper window of the Dainopoulos house.   No doubt it was closed and they were sitting there as usual with one of the Malleotis family to keep them company. Then what was he supposed to do?   In the novels he had read, the hero with projecting jaw and remarkable accuracy with firearms was never in any doubt about what he was to do.

It was at this moment that he thought of the bosun.

He liked that person more than he would have admitted. Invariably toiling at something in his immense canvas apron, the bosun's globular eyes were charged with an expression of patient amazement at a troublesome world.   If Diogenes, who lived in these parts, had revisited his ancient haunts and encountered Joseph Plouff, he would have made the acquaintance of a peculiar type of honest man.   The bosun was honest, but he had been born without the divine gift of a bushel to conceal the blaze of his probity.   But in spite of his virtue Mr. Spokesly found him congenial.   In the midst of the little community of seamen, he was the only one who spoke even passable English.   He was the man-of-all-work, bosun, carpenter, lamp-trimmer, winchman, storekeeper, and sometimes acting second mate.   For the engineer, with his Egyptian donkeyman and two Maltee firemen, Plouff and his Scandinavian sailors had a fierce contempt.   For "the captinne," Plouff entertained an amusing reverence, as though Captain Rannie's mastery of monologue appealed to the voluble creature.   In his own heart, however, there was neither bitterness nor that despair of perfection which made Captain Rannie so uncomfortable a neighbour.   In his own view Plouff was an ideal bosun who was continually retrieving his employers from disaster, but he attributed this to the fortunate fact that "he had his eyes about him at the time" rather than to the hopeless incompetence of the rest of the world.   And it was characteristic of the captain that he should regard Plouff with intense dislike.   Plouff therefore had avoided him adroitly and sought comfort from the mate. Spiteri was not able to appreciate the bosun.   When Plouff explained how he had found several bolts of canvas secreted in the chain locker, Spiteri was not impressed because he had put them there himself, intending later to take them ashore and sell them. Also Plouff was eternally wanting to chip something, which did not suit Spiteri at all. If you once began chipping the rust and scale on the *Kalkis*, you might carry something away and what good would that do you? And Plouff, in his big apron, would be told to go to Halifax, which infuriated him, for he thought Halifax, Nova Scotia, was meant, and he had some mysterious feud with Nova-Scotiamen generally.

So Mr. Spokesly found him congenial, a garrulous monster of unintelligent probity, and it occurred to him suddenly to enlist the bosun in this enterprise. Apparently he was going ashore. Mr. Spokesly wondered how he was going to manage it. He blew his whistle, and the bosun, who had his head in the galley door talking to the watchman, withdrew it and called out:

"What's the matter?"

"Come here, Bos', I want you."

Plouff knew by the sound of the word "Bos'" that a friendly conversation was contemplated and he went aft stroking his pomatumed moustache and licking his chops in anticipation, for he loved to talk to his superiors.

"How are you going ashore?"

"Me?" said the bosun, amazed. "In a boat, of course. How'd you think I was goin'? In a flyin' machine?"

"Well, where's the boat?"

"Why, down there. Here's the painter," said Plouff, laying his hand on it, very much bewildered.

"But I thought they didn't let you use the ship's boats after sundown."

"Yes, they got all them rules, but there's always easy ways," said Plouff with gentle scorn.

"Where do you land?"

"Why, right here," and Plouff pointed to where Mr. Spokesly had been looking with the telescope.

"Is that so? But I've seen no jetty."

"No, there's no jetty. It runs alongside of the garden,

you see, and there's big doors where the old feller used to keep his boat."

"What old feller?"

"Why, do you mean to say you don't know? I thought everybody knew that place."

"Well, go on. Spit it out. *I* don't know all the joints in this town."

"Neither do I, but I know a good many of 'em. Well, you see that house with the corner like a turnip, Turkey style? That's the house. It used to belong to an old guy who lives way over there," and Joseph Plouff waved his arm eastward towards Chalcidice. "Big farm for tobacco he got. Old Turk he is, I s'pose. Well, he has this house here and he had it built with a boat-house so the boat can go right in and out o' sight. And there wasn't any other way in. He comes down the mountain, gets into his boat, and sails over to his house when he wants to have good time. And when the house was lit up all the gels in the town gets into their glad rags an' goes off in boats to have some fun. They rows up to the house, and the old feller sittin' on his balcony gives 'em a look-over and then he gives the word to let 'em in. Well, he must ha' made a mistake, same as we all do at times, for one night he had a row with one o' these gels an' she went for him. I reckon he was tryin' to get her to go home quietly and she thought he was tryin' to push her into the water instead of into her boat. So what does she do but poke his eyes out. You have to watch that with the gels here," said Plouff sagely, looking at Mr. Spokesly. "It's easy to do and they got the way of it. You push hard here," and he put his forefinger against the outer side of his eye-ball, "and the eye pops out like a cork out of a bottle. That was a fine mix-up, I guess. They tied her head to her feet and shoved her into the water, and then they had to get the old feller back to his farm over there. Fine mix-up there, too, I expect, what with his wives fightin' to get at him and him not bein' able to see which way to run. Now he lives out there, blind and rollin' in money since the war, and his wives keep him at home all the time. And the house was sold. You can get a drink there now. I was there last night. American bar with Greek drinks."

"And are you goin' there to-night?"

"Sure I am. What did you think I was shavin' for?"

"Well, listen to me, Bos'. I wish I'd known it was as easy as that. You see I've got a friend who wants to make the trip with us, but we can't get a passport."

"Why can't he come back with me?"

"It's a young lady, Bos'."

The bosun started back as though in horror at these words.

"Is that the way the wind blows?" said he. "Well, this is what you'd better do. . . ."

"Can we get a boat at that place?"

"We might, easy enough. She can come in by the garden and there's a boat in the old boat-house, if she had any help. Where's she goin' to sleep?"

"In my cabin."

"And all that work I done down there for a stranger?"

"No, you done it for me. And I done it for this lady friend o' mine. She's goin' to meet her sweetheart in Athens, you understand."

The bosun, whose eyes had gradually assumed an expression of having been poked out by the method he had spoken of, and replaced by an unskilful oculist, now gave an enormous smirk and drew himself into an attitude of extreme propriety.

"Oh-ho! But the captinne . . ."

"Never mind him just now. I have a reason for thinking he won't mind. In fact, I believe he knows all about it but pretends he don't, to save himself trouble. Skippers do that, you know, Bos'."

"You bet they do!" said Joseph Plouff with immense conviction. "And then come back at you if things go wrong. I been with hundreds o' skippers and they was all the same."

This of course was a preposterous misstatement and of no significance whatever, a common characteristic of people who are both voluble and irresponsible. Mr. Spokesly let it pass. The riding-light threw the bosun's features into strange contortions as he stood with his round muscular limbs wide apart and his arms, tattooed like the legs of a Polynesian queen, crossed on the bosom of his blue-and-white check shirt.

"Well, what are you going to do about it?" asked the chief officer calmly. "You talk a hell of a lot, Bos', but you haven't said much yet."

"Because you ain't give me a chance. You ask me all about that American bar where there ain't any American drinks and I had to tell you, didn't I? And I was goin' to sugges' something, only you wouldn't listen."

"What?"

"Go yourself. Come with me. You can get out into the street by the garden. It used to be a movin' picture place, but they stopped it because of the lights. And it's mostly French sailors go there. American bar, see? What the *matelots* call *hig' lif'*. I speak French, so I go there. Now you come along and see what we can do."

"And leave the ship?"

"The ship won't run away, I can promise you that. And the watchman's there in the galley, ain't he? I'll get my coat."

"And how do I know when she'll come, supposing she does come to this place you're talking about?"

"You want me to tell you that!" said the bosun in a faint voice, lifting his broad features to the heavens in protest. "I thought you knew," he added, looking down again at Mr. Spokesly.

"Sometime before daylight," muttered that gentleman, getting up. "I'll go with you, but mind, you got to stand by to row me back whenever I want you. Understand? No going off with your *matelots*. Nice thing, if anything should happen and me out o' the ship."

"All right, all right. You don't need to get sore with your own bosun," said Plouff. "I can tell you, you might have a worse one. Here's me, sits all the evening, playin' rummy and one eye on the ship from that American bar, and all you can do's get sore. What do you think I am, a bum? If it hadn't been for me havin' my eyes about me in Port Said, them A-rabs would ha' stove her in against the next ship twenty time. Me sittin' up half the night makin' fenders. Oh, yes!"

"Come on then. You're as bad as the Old Man when it comes to chewing the rag. Can you talk French like that?"

"As good as English. Faster. More of it. I know more French words than English."

"Lord help us." Mr. Spokesly poked the tiller-bar into the rudder and hung the latter over the stern of the boat, which Plouff had been hauling along to the gangway. "Now then. Got a lantern? Don't light it. Bear away."

Instructed by Plouff, Mr. Spokesly steered due east away from the ship and concealed by it from the eyes on watch on the warships. Then after half a mile he turned sharply about and Plouff slowed down until the boat just moved through the water and they were quite lost in the intense darkness. Plouff said:

"Now we got nothing to be scared of except searchlights. But it's only Wednesday night they work 'em."

"Why do you get only Frenchmen at this place?" asked Mr. Spokesly.

"Because it's near their hospital and rest-camp. The English are all down by the Bersina Gardens. So the Frenchies go to talk to the poilus. French sailors don't have much truck with English sailors, you can bet."

"Well, you wouldn't if you couldn't talk to them either," retorted Mr. Spokesly. "Now where do we go in?"

"Ship the rudder," said the bosun. "I'll fetch round myself."

They were now in the profound shadows of a short back-water formed by the corner of the old *café-chantant* and cinema garden which had been fashioned out of the romantic dwelling whose earlier history Plouff had recounted with such relish. The big doors of the water entrance had been re-moved and the shed itself partly boarded over. There was no one in sight, and only a small tin lamp on the wall, but there was an air of recent occupancy, of human proximity, of frequent appearances, about the place. A boat was thrust half under the planks, and the door at the back had a black patch where many hands had polished it in passing through. Beneath the door shone a crack of bright light. Plouff, shipping his oars, brought up softly alongside the other boat, and stepped ashore across the thwarts with the painter in his hand.

"Here we are," he chuckled. "Snug as a bug in a rug. Bring her in under. Make fast."

The door was opened about six inches and a face with an exceedingly drooping moustache peered out from beneath the slovenly looking cap of a French petty officer of marine.

"*Qu'est-ce que c'est ?*" he demanded.

"*Comment ça va, mon vieux !*" retorted Plouff, advancing. "*Mon lieutenant—bon garçon. Oh-h, mon vieux, il faut que je vous dis que nous avons une grande affaire. Où est la belle Antigone ?*"

"*Chez elle,*" muttered the other. "*Entrez. Bon soir, Monsieur Lieutenant.*"

Mr. Spokesly walked through into a lofty hallway. A door on the left led into the darkness of the garden, another on the right opened upon a large chamber, dimly lighted and bounded by a lattice-work terrace, and in front ascended one of those imposing staircases which the Latin inserts into the most insignificant edifices. The room on the right was simply a rough-and-ready café, with a small bar in the corner set up in an unfurnished residence. Upstairs was a select gambling hell for officers only. And practically French officers only. There was only one reason why English officers, for example, did not visit this place. They did not know of its existence. It was a club. Madame Antigone was the caretaker who also managed the canteen on the ground floor, and encouraged, by her formidable discretion, the maintenance of a small corner of France in an alien land. Not the France of popular fancy with *cocottes* and *cancan* dancing and much foolish *abandon*, but the France of the Cercle and the Casino, sober-minded devotees of roulette and connoisseurs of sound liquor.

Some of the latter was immediately forthcoming. Even
Mr. Spokesly, whose conception of a drink was that of most
English and Americans—a decoction of no ascertainable
flavour and with the kick of a vicious horse—even he appreciated to a small degree the body and generous vintage of the
wine brought to their table by a soldier in hospital dress. He
looked round as he drank. There were men of all ranks of the
land and sea forces, clean-shaven and boyish, ferociously
moustached and obscured by short, truculent beards. They
played dominoes or cards, smoked and sipped, or conversed
with the grave gestures which are the heritage of a thousand
emotional years. They were not demonstrative. Indeed,
the French Navy is so undemonstrative one might imagine it
recruited entirely from the Englishmen of modern fiction.
There is no doubt that the nature of their profession has left
its mark upon them. For them is no vision of conquest or
gigantic death-grapple with a modern foe, but rather the
careful guarding of a remote and insalubrious colonial empire.
It has made them attentive to fussy details, faithful to
fantastic conceptions of honour, partial to pensioned ease and
married life if one escapes the fevers of Cochin China and
Algeria. Among them Plouff was accepted as a weird vari-
ant of undeniable home stock, a creature who led a double
life as Englishman and Frenchman, *un monstre*, a grotesque
emblem of the great *Entente*. They stood about him as he
sat, his head far back on his shoulders, his large red mouth
open beneath the great moustache, telling them the story
of his lieutenant's incredible gallantry. They listened in
silence, glancing deferentially towards Mr. Spokesly from
time to time, as though he were acquiring a singular and
heroic virtue in their estimation for his audacity in fumbling
with a woman's destiny. But Mr. Spokesly himself felt
neither heroic nor audacious. He was uneasy. He interrupted the eloquence of his bosun as soon as he had finished
his drink. He had a picture in his mind of Evanthia waiting
somewhere, waiting for him with her amber eyes smouldering
and ready to break out into a torrent of reproaches for his
sluggish obedience. She had achieved that ascendancy over

him. He was conscious of a species of mingled terror and delight in her personality. He rose.

"What's the matter?" demanded Plouff, astonished.

Mr. Spokesly regarded him with considerable impatience.

"How can I stop here?" he inquired. "You ought to have more sense," and he walked away towards the garden.

Plouff looked round at his circle of listeners, as though calling them to witness the strenuous nature of service with the English, and followed. He found Mr. Spokesly pausing irresolutely by the foot of the stairs, confronting a large woman with strongly marked brows and a severe expression who was descending the stairs with the air of a proprietress.

"Ah, Madame Antigone," said Plouff in hurried French. "This gentleman is the lieutenant of my ship. He has an assignation with a young lady who lives in a house near by."

The woman regarded Plouff steadily and shook her head. She was turning away as though she took no interest whatever in the matter.

"This is not a house of assignation," she said gravely, merely recording a casual fact.

"Oh, most surely not!" ejaculated the eloquent Plouff. "Madame totally misunderstands the situation. All that was suggested was that possibly Madame would permit the young lady to enter the garden. We have a boat, and here am I to row. Madame, to-morrow we sail; it is the last night for us. You can understand, Madame?"

Whether Madame understood or not was locked in her own broad, handsome bosom. She advanced as though Joseph Plouff and Mr. Spokesly had no corporeal existence, shaking her head and muttering softly that it was impossible. For a second the defeated bosun stood looking after her. Impossible? The massive form of Madame Antigone swam forward into the café and passed out of view. So it was impossible. Plouff became aware of his chief officer's expression.

"What are we going to do now?" said Mr. Spokesly irritably, going towards the garden. "Lot of use you are with your Frenchy friends. Let's get out of this."

"How could I help it?" demanded Plouff, breaking into a trot to keep up with Mr. Spokesly's anxious stride. "What's the matter, anyway? You don't understand, Mister. This way, round here. This is the path. Look out, you might hit your head—very low here under the trees. No, not yet. Here's the—that's it. Where are you goin' now? To the house?" Plouff whispered, a little out of breath, for Mr. Spokesly had been striding along oblivious to everything. What was the matter with the man? What was it to him if the girl did miss her passage? Ah!—— Plouff, as they came out upon a soft-earth cart-track that led away into the darkness, had a sort of spasm in his brain. Of course! This was an *enlèvement*. Ha! What a wooden-headed booby he had been to miss an obvious thing like that. Ho-ho! Plouff had a wife somewhere in the world, and as he never under any circumstances remembered to send her any support, he was romantic in his ideas concerning *enlèvements*. And mysteriously enough, Plouff became instantaneously more devoted to the task in hand, in spite of Mr. Spokesly's disgust. That officer realized he was pressing ahead without any clear notion of his future actions.

"I wonder what Dainopoulos 'ud think if he saw me hanging round," he mused. "Nobody on the ship, too! Well, here goes." And he whispered to the attentive Plouff.

"Do you know where the cars are, Bos'?"

"Of course I do. What do you take me for?"

"Go on, then, go on. I'll know the house if I see it."

Plouff was getting excited.

"And she come down with you?" he demanded.

"I don't know yet, man. Wait."

And suddenly they emerged upon the street.

Mr. Spokesly paused in the shadow of the wall enclosing the house they had left. On either hand extended an obscure and empty street. From that retired vantage the suburbs of Saloniki were wrapped in a peace as complete as that of the harbour. A faint hum, as of a distant trolley-car, came along the wires overhead. Mr. Spokesly reflected quietly, noting the landmarks, getting his bearings. The

Dainopoulos house was a little farther on, he guessed. As he took a step forward, a door banged some distance off, and a dog gave a few ringing howls.

"Is it far?" asked Plouff in a tense whisper. Mr. Spokesly looked at him. He was very much excited, and looked foolish, with his round eyes and extraordinarily pretentious moustache.

"No, I don't think it is," said Mr. Spokesly. "I got an idea it's just along on the other side." And then, as they moved up the road and the view changed somewhat, opening out on a familiar clump of trees, he added, "Yes, it's just along here," and mended his pace.

And he advanced upon the place where he believed Evanthia to be waiting for him, in a mood of mingled fear and pleasure. Perhaps there was shame in it, too, for he almost felt himself blush when he thought of himself sitting there on the *Kalkis* waiting. And but for an accident—Plouff was the accident—he might have been waiting there still. He grew hot. He saw that his long habitude of regarding women as purchasable adjuncts to a secular convenience had corrupted his perception of character. Why had he not seen immediately that she would expect him to carry out the whole enterprise? Where had his wits been, when the amber eyes smouldered and broke into a lambent flame that seemed to play all round his heart? That was her way. She never supplicated, evoking a benign pity for her pathetic and regretted womanhood. Nor did she storm and rail, getting what she desired as the price of repose. She simply accepted the responsibility with a flickering revelation of her soul in one glance from those amber eyes. And left him to divine the purpose in her heart. He thought of all this in the few moments as he moved up to the house with the active and enthusiastic Plouff at his heels like a shadow. And he wondered if she would keep him waiting. That, at any rate, was not one of her faults.

There was no light in the front of the house. That was not promising. He crossed over and took an oblique view of the windows behind the trees of the garden. And she was there. He saw a shadow on the ceiling, a shadow that moved and halted, with leisurely deliberation. He walked to the gate and tried it. It was shut.

"Listen Bos'," he said, holding that person's shoulder in a firm grip. "You've got to give me a leg over. Then— listen now—go back and get the boat out, and lay off the end of the garden. Savvy?"

"Yes. Now, up you go," said Plouff. "What do you want to hold me like that for? Over?"

There was no need for the question or for a reply. Mr. Spokesly, assisted by an energetic heave from Plouff, flew over the gate and came down easily on the flags below. He heard Plouff depart hastily, and went round into the garden to discover what he might have to do. It was easy to push along the path and look up at the lighted window. She was there. He could see her arms above her head busy with her hair. While he stood there she took a large hat from her head and presently replaced it by a black toque with a single darting cock's feather athwart it. Once he saw her face, stern and rigid with anxiety over the choice of a hat. And he saw, when he flung a small piece of earth gently against the window, the arms stop dead in their movements and remain there while she listened. Again he flung a piece of earth, a soft fragment that burst silently as it struck the glass, and the light went out.

Mr. Spokesly bethought him of the gate over which he had come and he made his way back to see if it could be opened from within. It could, and he opened it. And then, just as he was preparing for a secret and stealthy departure, bracing his spirit for the adventure of an *enlèvement*, the door behind him opened and shut with some noise, and Evanthia Solaris, buttoning a glove, stood before him, a slender black phantom in the darkness.

He was dumfounded for a moment, until the full significance of her action was borne in upon him. She had surrendered her destiny to his hands after all. It was with him that she was willing to venture forth into unknown perils. What a girl! He experienced an accession of spiritual energy as he advanced hurriedly in the transparent obscurity of the garden. She did not move as he touched her save to continue buttoning a glove.

"Ready?" he whispered.

She gave him an enigmatic glance from behind the veil she was wearing and thrust her body slightly against his with a gesture at once delicate and eloquent of a subtle mood. She was aware that this man, come up out of the sea like some fabled monster of old, to do her bidding, was the victim of her extraordinary personality; yet she never forgot that his admiration, his love, his devotion, his skill, and his endurance were no more than her rightful claim. Incomparably equipped for a war with fate, she regarded men always as the legionaries of her enemy. And that gesture of hers, which thrilled him as a signal of surrender, was a token of her indomitable confidence and pride.

"For anything," she said, smiling behind her veil. "What have you done?"

"I've got a boat," he whispered. "It's all ready. Where are they?" He pointed to the house.

"Asleep," she said, pulling the gate open.

"Don't make so much noise," he begged. She stopped and turned on him.

"I can go out if I like," she said calmly. "You think I am a slave here?"

"Oh, no, no. You don't understand . . ." he began.

"I understand you think I am afraid of these people. Phtt! Where is the carriage?"

"It's only a little way. You can't get boats down at the landings. Just a little way."

"All right." She pulled the gate to and the latch clicked. And then she put her gloved hand lightly on his arm, trusting her fate to him, and they walked down the road in the darkness.

"Have you got everything?" he asked timidly.

She did not reply at once. She was looking steadily ahead, thinking in a rapt way of the future, which was full of immense possibilities, and which she was prepared to meet with a dynamic courage peculiarly her own. And at that moment, though her hand lay on the arm of this man who was to take her away, she was like a woman walking alone in the midst of perils and enemies, towards a shining destiny, her delicate body sheathed in the supple and impenetrable armour of an inherited fortitude. She smiled.

"Everything," she murmured in French. "Have I not thee?" And she added, so that his face cleared of doubt and he, too, smiled proudly: "Ah, yes. What do we need, if we have each other?" He strained her suddenly to him and she stood there looking up at him with her bright, fearless, amber eyes smiling. She said:

"The boat?"

They reached the corner and for an instant the dark unfamiliarity of the lane daunted her.

"Down here, dear," he said, holding her close. "I have a man I can trust in the boat. He's waiting."

They advanced silently, turning the corners of the lane and stooping beneath the boughs of the sycamores. Her faint adumbration of doubt inspired in him an emotion of fiery protectiveness. For a moment, while they were among the trees in the garden, they halted and stood close together. The door swung open, letting out a long shaft of yellow light for an instant, showing up in sharp silhouette a chair, a table, some garbage, and a startled cat. And closed again with a bang and a rattle that mingled with the steps of someone going off up the lane.

"What is this place?" she whispered, looking up into the sky for the outline of the roof. "Ah, yes!" she said, noting the bulging cupola on the tower. "I see."

"You know about this place?" he asked as they reached the low parapet at the bottom of the garden. She pressed his arm in assent. She did. Women always know those facts of local history. Evanthia recalled, looking out over the obscure and shadowy waters of the Gulf, the tale of that old votary of pleasure. Men were like that. Behind her infatuation for the gay young person supposed to be in Athens, she cherished a profound animosity towards men.

She stood there, a man's arm flung tensely about her, another man cautiously working the boat in beneath where she stood, the blood and tissues of her body nourished by the exertions of other men, meditating intently upon the swinish proclivities of men. She even trembled slightly at the thought of those proclivities, and the man beside her held her more closely and soothed her with a gentle caress because he imagined she was the victim of a woman's timidity.

"It's all right, dear," he murmured. "Now I'll get down." He stooped and cautiously lowered himself into the boat, which rose and fell in a gentle rhythm against the sea-wall. And for a moment Evanthia had a slight vertigo of terror. She found herself suddenly alone. That arm—it had sustained her. She looked down and descried Mr. Spokesly standing with his arms extended towards her.

"Quick, dear! Now!" His face showed a white plaque in the darkness; face and hands as though floating up and down below her disembodied, and the faint tense whisper coming up mysteriously. She felt the rough coping with her fingers and leaned over towards the face.

"Hold me!" she breathed, and swung herself over. She felt his hands grip firmly and closing her eyes, she leaned backward into the void, and let go.

"Now push off, Bos'," said Mr. Spokesly, holding her in his arms. "We're away." He set her down and took the tiller. "Easy now, Bos'," he added, breathing hard.

Plouff, his eyes protruding with decorous curiosity, pulled out and began to row cautiously into the darkness. It was done. She sat on a thwart, her gloved hands folded in her lap, demure, collected, intoxicating. It was done.

"All right now?" he whispered exultingly. She looked at him, an enigmatic smile on her veiled face, and touched his knee. His tone was triumphant. He imagined he was doing all this, and she continued to smile.

"Ah, yes!" she breathed. "Always all right, with you." He pressed her hand to his lips. She let him do this.

"The ship?" she said gently.

"Soon," he said. "We must be careful. Tired?"

"A little. Where is the ship?"

"That is her light. We go this way—keep out of sight."

"How long?"

"Soon, soon."

She became trustful as they turned and made for the ship. Plouff, stifling his desire to proclaim his incomparable efficiency, brought up imperceptibly against the grating and, stepping out, crept intelligently up the ladder to make sure of the watchman. That person was, as Plouff expected, drowsing comfortably over the galley fire. He tiptoed to the bulwarks and whispered:

"Come up. All clear!"

Mr. Spokesly drew Evanthia upon the gangway and guided her steps upward. Plouff stood at the top, his head thrust forward and his hand gripping the bulwark as though about to fling himself upon them. His globular eyes and glossy curling moustache made him look like some furtive and predatory animal. He slipped down the gangway, got into the boat, and pushed off. Plouff was off to have a night free from responsibility. His chief officer was on board. *Sacré!* His chief officer had *joli goût*. And he, Plouff, had his eyes about him. And his wits. There was something behind this. So, not a word!

And the two passengers, whom he had transported so neatly and without arousing either the watchman or the suspicious picket-boats, went into the cabin and, after closing the door, Mr. Spokesly lit the swinging lamp. Evanthia looked about her.

"A ship," she said absently, revolving the novel idea in her mind.

"You must go to bed," said he gravely. "And you must stay down in there until I tell you it is all clear. Do you understand?"

"Yes, I understand."

"I'll show you," he said, and he carefully piloted her down the companion. She leaned forward daintily to peer as he lit her lamp.

"It's the best I could do," he whispered.

"Beautiful. Tck!" she saw her clothes in the drawer he opened and patted his arm. She regarded him curiously, as though seeing him in a fresh light. "You are very good to me."

"Easy to be that," he muttered, holding her and breathing heavily. "Good-night!"

He closed the door and strode away to the companion, and he was about to mount when a thought struck him. She must keep her door locked, in case somebody came down. He walked back.

And as he put out his hand to open the door again to tell her this, he heard the key grind in the lock.

He paused, and then went away up, and very thoughtful, turned in.

CHAPTER XIII

FROM his conspicuous post on the forecastle Mr. Spokesly watched the elderly lieutenant—his old friend whom he had met at Floka's—descend the ladder into his launch. The ship was already moving, the anchor was awash, and the elderly lieutenant wavered somewhat as he put out his hands to grasp the rail running along the cabin of his launch. It was evening, and he was, Mr. Spokesly could see, adequately full. Indeed, he had been reinforced by more than one whiskey and soda before he had arrived with the captain's sailing orders. And Captain Rannie, who was watching him as though hoping he might by some fortunate turn of fate slip into the water and vanish for ever, had placed a bottle of whiskey and a syphon at his elbow in the cabin and permitted him to help himself. The old fellow had been very full of a triumph he had achieved over the authorities. He had been transferred to the Transport Office, where it was evident they needed an experienced ship's officer to keep a general eye upon things. All very well, these naval people, in their way—here he filled his glass again—but what did they know about *our* work? Nothing! The soda shot into the glass, cascading all over the table. He drank. Incredible, absolutely incredible what queer things these people thought up. Told him to run round and round the White Tower for the duration of the war! Him! An experienced officer! Nice thing that, now! He drank again and refilled his glass. But he had been transferred. . . .

Captain Rannie sat out this sort of thing for over half an hour and then went up on the bridge and pulled the whistle lanyard. The *Kalkis* uttered a yelp, followed by a gargling

cry ending in a portentous hiccough. Mr. Spokesly remarked:

"They are signalling to heave up, sir."

"Then heave up," Captain Rannie had snapped, and had
run down again. He found the elderly lieutenant smiling
and refilling his glass. He did not see the expression of
impatience on the captain's features as he entered.

"Anchor's coming up," the captain said in a distinct tone.
"Steward, take the glasses." He gathered up the papers,
muttering, and went down to his room. This sudden ces-
sation of hospitality penetrated the old lieutenant's consciousness. He rose up and went out to the gangway, and
it was there Mr. Spokesly saw him. It could not have been
better, the chief officer remarked to himself. The old souse
had turned up most providentially. The long-nosed quarrelsome creature who usually came out to the transports, and
who always found out everything that was going on, was sick
in the hospital out on the Monastir Road. The vessel gathered speed. They were away.

And Captain Rannie, who now appeared on the little
bridge in company with a yellow-haired man at the wheel,
was in a mood in which a much larger bridge would have been
a comfort to him. The binnacle interrupted his headlong
march from side to side, his head down, his hands in his
trouser pockets. He would swing round suddenly and
plunge across as though he had a broad thoroughfare ahead
of him. At the binnacle he had to turn a little and edge past
it before he could take three more strides and bring up against
the end. Mr. Spokesly, who was finishing up on the forecastle, noted his Commander's movements and asked himself
the cause of the agitation.

For Captain Rannie was agitated beyond his customary
disapproval of mankind. He had had a long conference with
his employer that morning before coming on board. They
might not see each other again for some time, it was understood. The interview had taken place in the little office in
the Rue Voulgaróktono, off the Place de la Liberté, and the
usual crowds had thronged the street while they talked. Mr.

Dainopoulos had gone on with his business, rising continually to change money, and once he went away for half an hour to look at some rugs. Captain Rannie had remained coiled up on his chair, smoking cigarette after cigarette, listening to his owner's remarks, his eyes wandering as though in search of some clue.

"You understand," Mr. Dainopoulos had said in the course of this conversation, "I'm doing this for my wife. My wife likes this young lady very much. Another thing, the young lady's mother, she's married again. Man with plenty of money. I do his business for him here."

Captain Rannie looked hard at a crack in the linoleum near his foot.

"I'm sure it doesn't make the slightest difference to me. I know nothing about it, nothing at all. My chief officer was going to say something to me this morning and I shut him up at once. I knew perfectly well from the very first there was something like this in the wind and I made up my mind to have nothing at all to do with it. As master of the vessel it's impossible . . . you can quite understand . . . eh?"

"That's all right," replied Mr. Dainopoulos, looking at his open palm. "No passport. Once you get outside, no matter. The young lady, she give me a paper. She loves my wife. She gives everything she may have to my wife."

"Which isn't much, according to what you told me before. You grumbled to me, and said in so many words she cost you a lot of money to keep for a companion to your wife."

Mr. Dainopoulos stared hard at his captain's sneering face.

"That was before her mother got married again. Miss Solaris, she tell me her mother want somebody to look after the farms, by and by."

"I don't want to hear anything about it," burst out Captain Rannie, turning round in his chair so that he could hear better.

"And she say, she say," went on Mr. Dainopoulos steadily, "her mother perhaps, you understand, some women have one, two, three, four husband, you see? Well, her mother want a good man of business. So Miss Solaris she sign a paper for me. She give everything to my wife."

"Everything! Which is nothing, I've no doubt."

"Ah-h! Not nothing. I sell his tobacco now, and it's not nothing, I can tell you. No! By and by, Miss Solaris, now her mother marry again, will be rich. But she's crazy about that feller I told you she had here."

"I don't remember anything about it. I make it a rule to have nothing to do with passengers. I expect no less," announced Captain Rannie, alert to hear every word.

"Well, if a woman wants a man, she gets him," observed Mr. Dainopoulos gravely.

"That's true, I admit," was the unexpected reply.

"And you know well enough she'll find young Lietherthal easy if she wants him. Me, I think she'll stay round with *him*." And Mr. Dainopoulos jerked his finger in the direction of the *Kalkis*.

Captain Rannie suddenly reversed himself on his chair and changed legs, uttering a sound like a snort.

"Yes," said Mr. Dainopoulos. "My wife she thinks maybe he marry her."

Captain Rannie moved his foot up and down and smiled unpleasantly.

"No hope of that," he muttered.

"Yes!" repeated Mr. Dainopoulos, jumping up to change a five-pound note into excellent Greek drachmas. "Yes! If she wants him to do it, it will be easy enough. You don't know her."

Captain Rannie was heard to say in a low, hurried tone that he didn't want to.

Mr. Dainopoulos grinned, which did not improve his appearance. He waved his fingers at his captain with a gesture indicating his jocular conviction that he did not believe it.

"If I was single . . ." he began, and ended with a loud "H—m!" and smiled again.

Captain Rannie flushed dark red with annoyance. It was

one of the scourges of his existence that he had to let men imagine he was a terrible fellow with women. *He!* And he loathed them. He would strangle every one of them if he had the power. Blood-sucking harpies! As he walked the bridge now, keeping a sharp eye upon the buoys of the nets which were coming into view, he recalled the shameful way his generosity had been played upon by those women of his own family. Daughters leagued with mother and aunt against him! But he had paid them out, hadn't he? Ha-ha! He savoured again, but with a faint flavour of decay, that often-imagined scene when they realized at last that he was gone and gone for good. That was the way to treat them. No nonsense. As for this passenger in the chief officer's cabin, he hadn't seen her, and he hoped she'd fall overboard in the night, and a good riddance. Good heavens! Hadn't the master of a ship enough responsibility on a trip like this without loading him down with a creature like that? In any case, she must remain in her cabin. Under no circumstances could he permit her on deck. To be meeting her on the stairs or promenading—the very thought made him feel faint.

Another thing Mr. Dainopoulos had said:

"A very good thing for him, too. He would make a lot of money—here." Captain Rannie didn't believe it. He had arrived at a complete and horrifying conviction that Europe was collapsing of its own weight, that the only hope for anybody was to do as he himself was doing—sending all his money to the Anglo Celestial Bank in Hong-Kong to be exchanged for silver dollars. That was the place—China. Down the far reaches of memory he saw the great River, smooth and shining, stretching away from the long quays of the port. No storms, no pitching or rolling, no rocks, no finding of one's position. And when he stepped ashore in spotless yellow pongee silk suit and great sun-helmet, he was somebody. Here, in Europe, he was nobody. Out there once more, with plenty of hashish, he could face the future.

He had said:

"She must land on arrival."

"You tell her," said Mr. Dainopoulos, "when you arrive. Put her ashore. He'll take her. You will find plenty of friends, on arrival."

Captain Rannie received this information without ecstasy. He did not go sailing about the world in search of friends. He was very worried. Mr. Dainopoulos favoured him with another grin.

"Why not take her ashore yourself?"

Captain Rannie shrank as if from a blow.

"You're the captain," added Mr. Dainopoulos.

Captain Rannie turned on his chair, his shoulder hunched, as though to ward off an impending calamity.

"Why, I thought you liked a little fun," said Mr. Dainopoulos, surprised.

"Don't speak of it," said Captain Rannie in a stifled voice. "I make a point of never interfering. Never allude. . . . Purely personal. . . ."

"Well," said his owner, in some perplexity, "please yourself. I daresay you understand what I mean. You'll have a good bit of time, you know, on arrival. You won't have coal, you know, to go very far. . . ."

He had made no reply to this, remaining hunched up on his chair, staring fixedly at the floor. Mr. Dainopoulos had stood up, looking at him for a while.

"You can do it?" he had asked softly. "Remember, the papers you carry will mean big money if you get through."

Still no answer.

"It is easy," went on Mr. Dainopoulos. "You do not change your course, that is all. Keep on. East-southeast."

Captain Rannie was perfectly well aware of all this, but he lacked the superficial fortitude to discuss it. He kept his head averted while his employer was speaking, his long wrist with the slave-bangle hanging over his knee. Change his course! That phrase had two meanings, by Jove! And his course was east to China, as soon as he could collect. He could do it. Talking about it to a man who was making fifty times, a hundred times, more than himself, was horrible to him.

He had got up suddenly and put on his hat, harassed lest this sort of thing should bring bad luck, for he was superstitious. At the back of his mind lay an uneasy fear lest that girl business should spoil everything. Who could foresee the dangers of having a woman on the ship? His ship! He, who could not bear to go near them at all, who treated even elderly creatures with brusque discourtesy! It would bring bad luck.

And now at last he was slipping through the nets, bound out upon a voyage of almost dismaying possibilities. It was a voyage of no more than thirty-six hours. Captain Rannie shivered and stood suddenly stock still by the binnacle as he thought of what was to transpire in those thirty-six hours. Could he do it? He was beginning to doubt if he could. He said to the helmsman:

"Keep her south and three points east," and went into the little chart room.

The Ægean Sea is a sea only in name. It could be more accurately described as a land-locked archipelago. Emerging from any of the gulfs of the mainland, gulfs which are nearly always narrow and reëntrant angles with walls of barren and desolate promontories, one can proceed no more than a few hours' steaming on any course without raising yet more promontories and the hulls of innumerable islands. Closed to the southward by the long bulk of Crete lying squarely east and west like a breakwater, it presents its own individual problems to the navigator, the politician, and the naval commander. The last named, indeed, was finding it anything but a joke. The very configuration of the coast-line, which rendered a sally from the Dardanelles a feat of extraordinary folly and temerity, made it a unique hiding place for the small craft who slipped out of Volo and emerged from the Trikari Channel after dark. Submarines, coming round from Pola, could run into rocky inlets in the evening and would find immense stocks of oil, in cans, cached under savage rocks up the ravines of almost uninhabited islets of ravishing beauty. Gentlemen in Athens, in a hurry to reach Constantinople, took aëroplanes; but there was another way, across the Ægean Sea, in small sailing ships which were frequently blown out of their course at night and would take refuge in Kaloni, whence it was easy to reach the mainland of Asia Minor. And this business—for it was a business—was so profitable, and the ships of war so few in proportion to the area, that it went on gaily enough "under our noses" as one person said in disgust. Not quite that; but the problem did not grow any simpler when there was yet another neutral government—with ships—at Saloniki, a government that might be almost hysterically sympathetic to the cause of freedom and justice but which might also be imposed upon by conscienceless and unscrupulous merchants already in collusion with other unscrupulous people in Constantinople. This was the situation when the *Kalkis* turned the great headland of Karaburun and headed south-southeast on the journey from which she never returned. Captain Rannie, staring at the chart on which he had pencilled the greater part of her course, southeast from Cape Kassandra, bearing away from the great three-pronged extremity of the Chalcidice peninsula, was aware that she would not return, but he found himself flinching from the inevitable moment, drawing nearer and nearer when he must face success or failure. When he asked himself, echoing Mr. Dainopoulos, could he do it? He was not sure that he could.

From this reverie he was roused by Mr. Spokesly appearing on the bridge. For a moment he was almost betrayed into a feeling of relief at the approach of a companion. He opened his mouth to speak and Mr. Spokesly, standing by the door, stopped to listen. But nothing came. Captain Rannie knew the secret power of always letting the other man do the talking on a ship. He said nothing. He crushed down the sudden craving to confide in Mr. Spokesly. He wanted—just for a moment—to call him in, shut the door, and whisper, with his hand on Mr. Spokesly's shoulder, "My boy, we are not going to Phyros at all. We are going to . . ."

No, he stopped in time. Why, he might stop the engines, blow the whistle, run the ship ashore! He stepped out beside Mr. Spokesly who was looking down at the compass, and wrote some figures on the slate that hung in view of the helmsman.

"That's the course."

"All right, sir."

"Call me at midnight if necessary. I'll relieve you at two o'clock. Time enough to change the course then."

"All right, sir."

Captain Rannie gave a rapid glance round at the diverging shores as they opened out into the Gulf, and turned away abruptly. Mr. Spokesly heard him descending, heard him unlock his door with a series of complicated clicks and rattles, heard him slam and relock it, and finally the vigorous jingle of curtain rings as he drew the curtain across.

Mr. Spokesly struck a match and lit the binnacle lamp, a tiny affair which shone inward upon the vibrating surface of the card. He did not attempt to walk up and down. His moods never demanded that of him. Perhaps it would be better to say his nature did not demand it. He was feeling much better than he had been all day. He had been nervous about Evanthia's safety in that room. Had had to make some bullying remarks to the steward about trying to get in where he had no business. To the puzzled creature's stammering explanations he had replied with more bullying: "Keep out. Don't come down here at all until I say you can." The steward had come to the conclusion that in addition to a crazy skipper whose room smelt of hashish and florida water, they now had a crazy mate who had something in his room he was ashamed of.

And yet Mr. Spokesly need have had no fear. Evanthia lay in her bunk all day. She knew perfectly well that she must remain within that room as one dead until the ship got outside. So she lay there, her eyes half closed, listening to the sounds of men and machinery, the sunlight screened by the yellow curtain tacked over the little round window, hour after hour all day, with a stoicism that had in it something oriental. It was about an hour past noon when there had come a smart thump on the door. She had got out and listened and the sharp whisper outside had reassured her.

And when she had slipped the bolt and opened the door a few inches, Mr. Spokesly had thrust a glass of wine and a tin box of biscuits upon the washstand and pulled the door shut. And she had got back into the bunk and lay munching, and smiling, and sometimes kissing the emerald ring on her finger, the ring which was sailing out once more into the darkness. And as the day wore on, she peeped out and saw the tug go away with its empty lighter, heard the ominous thutter and thump of a gasolene launch under her, and heard the arrival of strangers who entered the cabin overhead. And then the clink of a glass.

Her reflections, as she lay in that bunk, her eyes half closed, were of that primitive yet sagacious order which it seems impossible to transfer to any authentic record. Her contact with reality was so immediate and instinctive that to a modern and sophisticated masculine intellect like Mr. Spokesly, or Mr. Dainopoulos even, she appeared crafty and deep. As when she locked the door. She had not imagined Mr. Spokesly returning. The whole complex network of emotions which he had predicated in her, modesty, fear, panic, and coquetry, had not even entered her head. She had formidable weapons, and behind these she remained busy with her own affairs. So, too, when she had given everything she might possibly inherit to her benefactress, she saw instantly the immediate and future advantages of such a course. She could always come back, when the detestable French had gone away home, and live with her friend again. She knew that old Boris better than he knew himself. She knew that he would do anything for his wife. Also she knew him for one of those men who stood highest in her own esteem—men who made money. For men who did not make money, who were preoccupied mainly with women, or books, or even politics, she had no use. She did not like Mr. Dainopoulos personally because he saw through her chief weakness, which was a species of theatricality. She had a trick of imagining herself one of the heroines of the cinemas she had seen; and this, since she could not read and was unable to correct her sharp visual impressions by the great traditions of art, appeared to be no more than a feminine whim. It was more than that. It was herself she was expressing at these moments of mummery. She had those emotions which are most easily depicted by grandiose gestures and sudden animal movements. It was her language, the language in which she could think with ease and celerity, compared with which the coördinated sounds which were called words were no more to her than the metal tokens called money. So there was nothing extraordinary in her quick grasp of the situation which demanded a mouse-like seclusion for a while. She lay still, even when footsteps clattering down the ladder were obliterated by the spluttering whoop of the whistle. And then came a novel and all-embracing sense of change, a mysterious and minute vibration which becomes apparent to a person situated well forward in a vessel beginning to move under her own power. Ah! the *machine à vapeur*, the *vapore*, the fire, the agitation behind. For perhaps a single second her quick flame-like mind played about the incomprehensible enigmas of mechanism. She, for whom unknown men in distant countries were to scheme and toil, that they might send her yachts and automobiles, music-machines and costly fabrics, jewels and intricate contrivances for her comfort and pleasure, had the conceptions of a domestic animal concerning the origins of their virtues. For her the effortless flight of a high-powered car ascending a mountain road was as natural and spontaneous as the vulture hanging motionless above her or the leaf flying before her in an autumn wind. Her gracile mentality made no distinction in these things, and the problems of cost never tarnished the shining mirror of her content. Upon her had never intruded those mean and unlovely preoccupations which distract the victim of western civilization from the elementary joys and sorrows. She had always been fed and cared for and she had no shadow of doubt upon her mind that nourishment and care would ever cease. Her notion of evil was clear and sharp. It implied, not vague economic forces, but individual personalities whom she called enemies. Any one announcing himself as an enemy would be met in a primitive way. She would back into a corner, spitting and biting. If she had a weapon, and she always had, she would use it with cool precision. She lay in her bunk now without a care in the world because she possessed the power of animating men to bear those cares for her. She could inspire passion and she could evoke admiration and remorse.

She saw the sun going down, saw him disappear as into a glowing brazier among the mountains, and the coming of darkness. Evanthia hated darkness. One of the whims she indulged in later days was the craving for a shadowless blaze of light. She moved in her bed place and turning on her elbow stared at the door, listening. Someone came down the stairs. A door was unlocked, slammed, and locked again. She became rigid. Her eyes glowed. Who was that? She got up and sought for matches to light the lamp. But she had left it burning the night before and the oil was exhausted. And her watch had stopped. She put on her black dress and did her hair as well as she could before the dark reflection in the mirror. She had very little of that self-consciousness which reveals itself in a fanatical absorption in minute attentions to one's appearance. She was, so to speak, always cleared for action, for love or war. She twisted her dark tresses in a knot, thrust a great tortoise-shell comb into them, unlocked the door and went out.

It was thus she came up the stairs into the lighted saloon and encountered the steward, who was laying the table for supper. He was leaning over the table setting out knives and forks. He looked over his shoulder and saw a face of extraordinary loveliness and pallor, with dark purple rings under the amber eyes, coming up out of the gloom of the stairway. He dropped the things in his hands with a clatter and whirled round upon her, his jaw hanging, his hands clutching the table.

"Sh-h!" she said, coming up into the room and advancing upon him with her finger to her lips. "Who are you?" she added in Greek.

He was about to answer that he was the steward, in spite of the obvious injustice of such a query, when the outer door

leading to the deck was opened and the young man named
Amos appeared with a tray of dishes. He stepped into the
little pantry to set down his burden and then made a profound obeisance.

"Tch!" said the lady. "Who is this?"

"The pantryman, Madama."

"Tell him to fill my lamp with oil."

"Your lamp, Madama?" quavered the steward. "Is
Madama in the Captain's room? I have not been told."

Evanthia beckoned Amos and pointed down the stairs.
"The room on the right," she said. "Fill the lamp with oil
and light it. Make the bed. Go!"

She watched him descend.

"Now," she said to the steward, "is this the way you
attend to passengers? Bring me some meat. I am starving."

"Yes, yes! In a moment, Madama." He hurried to and
fro, twisting the end seat for her to take it, dashing into his
pantry and bringing out dishes, a cruet, a napkin. Evanthia
seated herself and began to devour a piece of bread. She
watched the steward as he moved to and fro.

"Where is the captain?" she asked.

"In his room, Madama. He has eaten and now he sleeps
till midnight."

"And the officer?"

"He is on the bridge, Madama."

"Who eats here?"

"The officer and the engineer."

"Is the Engineer English?"

"Maltese, Madama."

The man spoke in low, respectful tones, his eyes flickering
up and down as he sought to scan her features. This was
most marvellous, he was thinking. The new chief officer
brings a woman, a ravishing creature, on board in secret.
This explains the abuse of the morning. What would the
captain say? He must tell Plouff. He had mentioned to
Plouff the singular behaviour of the chief officer when he,
the steward, had attempted to enter that gentleman's cabin.

Plouff had laughed and pushed him out of the road. It was time to call Plouff to relieve the chief officer. He hurried to the galley to fetch the stew. He lifted the canvas flap which screened the lights from a seaward view and found Plouff seated in a corner talking to the cook.

"Hi, Jo," he whispered, "Madama on sheep! Madama on sheep! Yes."

"What's the matter with you?" demanded Plouff disdainfully. "What are you makin' that funny face for?"

"She come oop," went on the steward with much dramatic illustration. "I look, see Madama. You savvy? Very nice. Very beautiful."

"Has she come out?" asked Plouff with interest.

"Yaas. She come oop."

"I'll go up and tell the mate," said Plouff. "You savvy, Nicholas, plenty mon' if you look after her. Fix her up. The mate, you savvy?" and Mr. Plouff rubbed the sides of his two forefingers together, to indicate the tender relations existing between Mr. Spokesly and the lady.

"Oh, yaas, I savvy all right, Jo." The steward writhed in his impotence to express the completeness of his comprehension, and hurried away.

Mr. Spokesly listened in silence to the news.

"I'll go down," he said. "If you see a light of any sort, stamp on the deck."

"Well, I should think so. I ain't likely to stand on my head, am I?" said Plouff, peeping at the compass.

Mr. Spokesly went down without replying to this brilliant sally. He stood for a moment looking over the rail at the sullen end of the sunset, a smudge of dusky orange smeared with bands of black and bronze, and wondered what the night would bring for them all. The little ship was moving slowly through a calm sea that shone like polished black marble in the sombre light from the west. Ahead, the sky and sea merged indistinguishably in the darkness. No light showed on the ship. She moved, a shadow among shadows, with no more than a faint hissing rumble from her engines. Mr. Spokesly moved aft, inspired by a wish to see for himself if all the scuttles were screened. He found the engineer smoking near the engine hatch.

"All dark?" he said, pausing.

"Everything's all right here, Mister Mate," said the man, a quiet creature with an unexpected desire to give every satisfaction. Mr. Spokesly was puzzled to account for the captain's dislike of Mr. Cassar.

"Why don't you go and eat?" asked Mr. Spokesly.

"The steward, he tell me there's a lady in the cabin, Mister Mate, so I t'ink I'll wait till she feenish."

"You don't need to," was the steady answer.

"Yes, I wait till she feenish, all the same."

"Very well. Mind they keep the canvas over the hatch. It shows a long way across a smooth sea, you know."

"I watch 'em, Mister Mate."

And Mr. Spokesly went forward again. In spite of the gravity of their position, without guns or escort, he felt satisfied with himself. He passed once more by the rail before going in. In his present mood, he was mildly concerned that Evanthia should have found it necessary to "turn the key in his face." He didn't intend to do things that way. It would be pretty cheap taking an advantage like that. Was it likely he would run all this risk for her, if that was all he thought of her? He was painfully correct and logical in his thoughts. Well, she would learn he was not like that. He would treat her decently, and when they reached Piræus, he would carry out her wishes to the letter. He could not help worrying about the day or two they would remain in Phyros. She would have to keep out of sight. . . . He opened the cabin door and went in. He had a strange sensation of walking into some place and giving himself up, only to find that he had forgotten what he had done. A strange notion!

She looked up and regarded him with critical approval. She had finished eating and sat with her chin in her hands. The swinging lamp shed a flood of mellow light upon her, and her arms, bare to the elbow, gleamed like new ivory below the shadowy pallor of her face. And as he sat down at the other end of the table, facing her, he had another strange notion, or rather a fresh unfolding of the same, that at last they met on equal ground, face to face, measured in a mysterious and mystical antagonism. She lifted her chin, a movement of symbolical significance, and met his gaze with wide-open challenging amber eyes.

And when he went up on the bridge half an hour later, she expressed a charming and sudden desire to see the things he did there, and the mystery of the night.

"You'll be cold," he muttered, thinking of the night air. He led her carefully up the little ladder, and she shivered.

"Bos'," said Mr. Spokesly in a low tone. "Have you got an overcoat?"

"Of course I have. What do you think I am?" demanded the rather tired Plouff.

"You wouldn't if you had had to jump into the water as I did," said Mr. Spokesly patiently. "I want you to bring it up here for this lady."

"Of course I will. Why didn't you say so?"

"You can sit here," said the chief officer. There was a seat at each end of the bridge screened by a small teak house with glass windows, and he pushed Evanthia gently into the starboard one. "And now put this on," he added when Plouff appeared holding out an enormous mass of heavy blue cloth.

And into that dark corner she vanished, so obliterated by the coat that only by leaning close to her could Mr. Spokesly discern the gleam of her forehead and eyes. But when he had seen that she was comfortable, he took himself to the centre of the bridge and stood there looking out over the dodger and thinking of the question she had put to him in the cabin. By and by, she had retorted upon his avowal of independence, he would go back to his sweetheart, his fiancée, in England, and what would Evanthia do then? That was the question. He stared into the darkness and sought some kind of an answer to it. It cut to the very quick of his emotion for her—that extraordinary sentiment which can exist in a man's heart without impairing in any way his authentic fidelities. He wanted to make her see this, and he could not find words adequate to express the subtle perversity of the thought. He had a sudden fancy she was laughing at him and his clumsy attempts to justify his devotion. He turned and walked over to her and bent down. He could see the bright eyes over the immense collar of the coat.

"England is a long way away," he whispered. "I mean, very distant. Perhaps I shall never get back. And nobody writes to me. No letters. So, while I am here, you understand?"

He remained bent over her, his head lost in the darkness of the little recess, waiting for a reply which did not come. And he thought, going away to the binnacle again:

"She is right. Nobody can excuse themselves in a case like this. The only way is to say nothing at all."

He did not go near her for a long while. Then an idea came to him, so simple he wondered he had not thought of it before. He was not making the most of the situation. He glanced back at the helmsman. He was far back, behind the steering wheel, and the faint glow of the binnacle lamp was screened by a canvas hood. Mr. Spokesly bent over the girl again.

"You do not believe me?" he muttered. "You think I am not sincere? You think I would leave you?"

He leaned closer, watching her bright deriding eyes, and she nodded.

"Ah yes," she sighed. "By and by you would go."

"You think because other men do that . . . you think . . . ?"

She nodded emphatically.

". . . all men alike?" he finished lamely.

"They are!" she said quickly and laid her head against his shoulder for a moment with a faint chuckle of laughter.

"All right," he whispered gravely, "they are, as you say. But when we get ashore in Athens, we will get married. Now then. . . ."

His tone was low but triumphant. She could have no reply to that. It swept away all doubts in his own mind: and he thought her mind was like his own, a lumber room of old-fashioned, very dusty conventions and ideals. If he married her she must be convinced of his sincerity. It did not occur to him that women are not interested very much in the sincerity of a man, that he can be as unfaithful as he likes if he fulfills her conception of beauty and power and genius, that a woman like Evanthia might have a different notion of marriage from his own.

And she did not reply. He moved away from her, uplifted by the mood of the moment. There could be no reply to that save surrender, he thought proudly.

And Evanthia was astonished. She sat there in the darkness, bound upon a journey which would bring her, she believed, to the amiable and faithless creature who had touched her imagination and who embodied for her all the gaiety and elegance of Europe. And this other man, a man of a distant, truculent, and predatory race, a race engaged in the destruction of European civilization as a sacrifice to their own little tribal god (which was the way Lietherthal had explained it to her) was proposing to marry her. It bereft her of speech because she was busy coördinating in her swift, shrewd mind all the advantages of such a scheme. There was an allurement in it, too. Her imagination was caught by the sudden vision of herself as the chatelaine of a villa. Yes! Her eyes sparkled as she figured it. He came towards her again and, leaning over, buried his face in the clean fresh fragrance of her hair. She remembered that magical moment by the White Tower when he had transcended his destiny and muttered hoarsely that he would go to hell for her. She put the question to herself with terrible directness—could she hold him? Could she exercise the mysterious power of her sex upon him as upon men of her own race? She closed her eyes and sought blindly for an accession of strength in this crisis of her life. She put her arms up and felt his hand on her face. And then, giving way to an obscure and primitive impulse, she buried her teeth in his wrist. And for a long while they remained there, two undisciplined hearts, voyaging through a perilous darkness together.

CHAPTER XIV

MR. SPOKESLY, looking down from the bridge at the upturned and uncompromising face of Joseph Plouff, frowned.

"What does he say?" he repeated uneasily.

"He says keep the course."

"You gave him the note?"

"No, he didn't open the door. He just said, to keep the course. I said 'You mean, don't alter it, Captinne?' and he said, 'No.'"

Plouff handed up the note Mr. Spokesly had given him, and the puzzled chief officer took it and opened it, as though he had forgotten or was uncertain of its contents. But before he read it afresh, he took a look round. This told him nothing for he was entirely lost in a white fog that rolled and swirled in slow undulating billows athwart the ship's bows. For four hours he had been going through this and the captain had not made his appearance on the bridge. Each time had come up the same message, to keep the course. And at last Mr. Spokesly had written a little note. He had torn a page out of the scrap-log and written these words:

To Captain Rannie
Sir,
We have run our distance over this course. Please give bearer your orders. Weather very thick.
R. Spokesly. Mate.

And he hadn't even opened the door. It was this singular seclusion which caused Mr. Spokesly so much anxiety. Fog, and the captain not on deck! Plouff, whose presence was an undeniable comfort for some reason or other, pulled himself up the steep little ladder and stood staring lugubriously into the fog.

"Funny sort of old man, this," muttered the mate.

"He's always the same at sea," said Plouff, still staring.

"What? Leaves it to the mate?"

"Yes. Always."

"But . . ." Mr. Spokesly looked at the fog, at Plouff, at the binnacle, and then hastily fitted himself into the little wheel-house. He bent over the chart with a ruler and pair of dividers, spacing first a pencilled line drawn from Cape Kassandra to a point a few miles south of Cape Fripeti on the Island of Boze Baba, and then along the scale at the edge of the chart.

"See what's on the log, Bos', will you?" he called.

This was serious. Within a few minutes the course ought to be altered to due south. The usual four knots of the *Kalkis* had been exceeded owing to the smoothness of the sea, which accounted for their arrival at this position before six o'clock, when the captain would once more take charge. Another thing was that from now on they would be on the course of warships passing south from the great base at Mudros, the landlocked harbour of Lemnos. The bosun came up again and reported thirty miles from noon. Well, the log was about ten per cent. fast, so a note said in the night order book. It was five-thirty now, which gave them twenty-seven miles from noon or nearly five knots. That brought them due south of Fripeti.

Mr. Spokesly looked at Plouff, who was looking at the fog with an expression of extreme disillusion on his round face. And again at the chart. There was nothing more to be extracted from either Plouff or the chart. The pencilled line which indicated their course ended abruptly. Where, then, were they bound? Keep on the course, the captain said. Mr. Spokesly laid the parallel ruler against the line and produced it clear across the chart. He stood up with a sharp intake of breath and regarded the impassive Plouff, who looked down at the chart with respectful curiosity.

"Say, Bos'," he began. "This is a funny business."

"What's a funny business?" demanded Plouff, looking round, as though expecting to see something of an extremely comical nature being performed. The pause gave Mr. Spokesly time to reflect. He cleared his throat.

"The Old Man staying down there. He ought to . . . but then he says keep . . ."

"'Hold her on the course,' were his words," said Plouff obstinately, adding, "Hasn't she got a clear road?"

"Yes . . ." muttered the mate jerkily, "road's clear . . . humph!" he stared at the chart. "Oh, well! By George, I wish this damn fog would clear away."

"What's the matter with the fog?" said Plouff. "We're safe in the fog, ain't we? You can bet them *unterseeboats* 'll keep in under the islands this weather. Too much chance o' gettin' stove in," he added sympathetically. The mate did not reply for a moment. He was very uneasy. He studied the chart. Indeed, he could not get away from that pencilled line running right into the Gulf of Smyrna. And Phyros was south of Khios. He was tired and sleepy. Eight hours was a long while to stay on the bridge. He would be glad when they got in. *Got in where?* He stared again at the chart. And the Old Man locked in his room. Always did that, eh?

"Go away, Bos'," he said, suddenly. "You got to be about to-night, you know. We'll be anchoring. . . ."

He forgot what he was saying, staring hard at the chart. Plouff slipped down into the fog and clattered away forward.

But Mr. Spokesly was not unhappy. There was an unfamiliar yet desirable quality about this life. The sharp flavour of it made one forget both the ethical and economic aspects of one's existence. At the back of his mind was a boyish desire to show that girl what he was made of. And when they got to Athens he would—— Athens! The word sent him back to the chart. Keep on the course. He was sailing across a wide ocean and the old familiar landmarks were hull down behind the fog. There was something symbolic in that fog. It was as though he had indeed left the world of his youth behind, the world of warm English hearts, of cantankerous affections and dislikes, of fine consciences and delicate social distinctions, and was passing through a confusing and impalpable region of vaporous uncertainty to an unknown country. He was not unhappy. The future might be anything, from silken dalliance behind green jalousies in some oriental villa with a fountain making soft music, which is the food of love, to a sudden detonation, red spurts of savage flame, and a grave in a cold sea. He went out and looked at the compass. And at the fog. Now that Plouff was gone down he felt lonely. He stamped on the deck to call the steward. The captain would have to be called. If he did not come, he, the mate, would go down and inform him that the course would be changed without him. That would be the only way. He had never had a commander like this, nor a voyage like this, for that matter. He paused suddenly in his thoughts and looked down, pinching his lower lip between finger and thumb. He had an idea. To achieve anything, one had to be eternally prepared for just such unexpected predicaments. Here he was, with an invisible commander and an invisible horizon. And down in a cabin below him was Evanthia Solaris, a distinct and formidable problem. He was going to marry her. He saw his destiny, almost for the first time in his life, as a ball which he could take in his hand and throw. And the direction and distance depended entirely upon his own strength, his own skill, his own fortitude. He was going to marry her. And he saw another thing for the first time—that marriage was of no significance in itself for a man. What he is, brain and sinew, character and desire, is all that counts. He saw this because he had left the old life behind beyond the fog. Back there, marriage was a contrivance for the hamstringing and debasing of men, a mere device for the legal comfort and security of women who were too lazy or incompetent or too undesirable to secure it for themselves. Ahead he had a strange premonition that he was going to have a novel experience.

He was.

· He was aroused by the helmsman reaching out and striking

four soft blows on the little bronze bell hanging by the awning-spar over the binnacle. Six o'clock. And the young Jew, in a huge apron and a high astrakhan cap he had picked up somewhere, came slowly up the bridge ladder.

"Captain," said Mr. Spokesly, making a number of motions to signify knocking at a door and calling somebody out. "Savvy?"

The frightened creature, who was quite unable to comprehend the extraordinary phenomenon of the fog on the sea, and who regarded Mr. Spokesly, moreover, as a species of demi-god, raised his remarkable face as though in supplication, and backed down again. It was evident to him that his employer had consigned him to some distant place of torment from which he could never return. Yet even in his timid heart there was hope. Already he had given his allegiance to that beautiful and haughty creature whose cabin it was his trembling joy and pride to put in order. His ears were alert at all times to catch the sharp clapping sound of her hands when she needed him, and then he flew below. She would speak to him in his native tongue, which was Spanish, and ravish his soul with words he could understand, instead of the terrifying gutturals of those powerful Franks who walked to and fro on the top of the tower above them and gave incomprehensible commands.

"Fear not," she assured him. "When the ship reaches the port, thou shalt go with me as my servant. The lieutenant shall give thee money as wages when he is my husband."

"Merciful Madama, what port? Whither do we go? Is it beyond the clouds?"

"Ah," she retorted, leaning back on the cushions of the settee, and blowing cigarette-smoke from her beautiful lips. "I would like to know that myself. Beyond the clouds? You mean this fog. Yes, far beyond the clouds. Did you not hear anything at all in the Rue Voulgaróktono?"

"Nothing, Madama, except that once I heard Señor Dainopoulos tell Señor Malleotis that they, someone, had reached Aidin."

"Aiee?" ejaculated Evanthia, sitting up and fixing her

burning amber eyes on the frightened and hypnotized creature. "And didst thou hear nothing else? Aidin! Tchk!"

"I do not know, Madama," he quavered. "Unless there is a port called Bairakli."

Evanthia showed her teeth in a brilliant smile and patted the youth's arm.

"My servant you shall be," she chuckled. "No, there is no port called Bairakli, but it is near to a city you and I will find good. Shalt live at Bairakli, Amos! Tck—tck! What a fool I was. Oh! Caro! *Oh mein lieber Mann!*" And she sang sweetly a few notes of a song.

The young man stared at her in stupefaction.

"Go," she said, pushing him with a characteristic gesture, at once brusque and charming. "You need have no fear. Your fortune is made."

A few minutes past six Captain Rannie climbed the bridge ladder and examined the compass without addressing his chief officer, bending over it with an exaggerated solicitude. Apparently satisfied, he went into the chart room and immediately pushed the ruler from its significant position, pointing into the interior of Asia Minor. There was an indefinable nervous bounce about him which indicated a highly exalted state of mind. He seemed, Mr. Spokesly imagined, to be assuming truculence to cover timidity. He probably knew that his insistence on keeping the course had aroused conjecture, and the ruler, lying as it did on the chart, confirmed the idea. Yet he did not speak. Funking, Mr. Spokesly decided, obstinately remaining close to the dodger and staring straight ahead—towards Asia Minor. If the Old Man thought he was going to get away with it . . . he cleared his throat and remarked:

"About time to change the course for Phyros, sir?"

And to his surprise Mr. Spokesly, in the midst of his highly complex cogitations, found himself listening to a jaunty and characteristic monologue which touched upon—among other things—the one rule which Captain Rannie insisted was the *sine qua non* of a good officer, that he should accept the commander's orders without comments. Otherwise, how could discipline be maintained? As to the course, he, Captain Rannie, would attend to that immediately. And while he appreciated it, of course, there was no real need for Mr. Spokesly to remain on the bridge after he had been relieved.

Mr. Spokesly, still looking ahead, wanted to say sarcastically, "Is that so?" but he was tongue-tied, dumfounded. Here was a man, apparently of straw, who was jauntily inviting him to clear out and mind his own business. He pulled himself together.

"Unless we pick up a Mudros escort somewhere round here," he muttered, turning away.

Captain Rannie came out of the chart room from which his lean and cadaverous head had been projecting to deliver his homily on obeying orders, and looked all round at the white walls of fog. It was as though he were contemplating some novel but highly convenient dispensation of Providence which he was prepared to accept as one of the minor hardships of life. All consciousness of Mr. Spokesly's presence seemed to have vanished from his mind. He spoke to the helmsman, walked to port and looked down at the water, looked aft and aloft, and resumed his stroll.

And Mr. Spokesly, craftily placed at a disadvantage, turned suddenly and clattered down the ladder.

"Well," he thought to himself, pausing on the deck below and still holding to the hand-rail, "he can't keep it up for ever. And I can't do anything in this fog. He's going to pile her up."

But as he went into the saloon he could not help asking himself, "What for?" What gain had Captain Rannie or Mr. Dainopoulos in view when they ran a valuable cargo on the rocky shores of Lesbos or Anatolia? The word "ran" stuck in his mind. "Running a cargo" in wartime, eh? One didn't run cargoes on the rocks, in war-time. He stared so fixedly at Amos, who was laying the table, that in spite of Evanthia's assurance of future good fortune, the poor creature trembled and grew pale. Mr. Spokesly understood neither Greek nor Spanish, or he might have derived some enlightenment from a conversation with the young Jew. He frowned and went on down to his cabin. He wanted sympathy in his anxiety. And it was part of his Victorian and obsolete mental equipment to expect sympathy from a woman.

She was standing before the little mirror, setting the immense tortoise-shell comb into her hair at the desired angle, and she gave herself a final searching scrutiny, as she turned away, before flashing a dazzling smile at him.

"What is the matter?" she asked in her precise English, seeing the worried expression on his face. He sat down on the settee, and she seated herself close beside him, smiling with such ravishing abandon that he forgot the reason for his concern.

"If I can only get you ashore," he muttered, holding her to him and kissing her hair.

"Where?" she whispered, watching him with her bright amber eyes.

"That's just it," he said. "I don't know where."

She put her finger to her lips.

"I know," she said.

He put his hands on her shoulders and held her away a little, staring at her.

"You!" he breathed incredulously. "You?"

She nodded, her eyes kindling.

"Here," he said hoarsely. "You must be straight with me, dear. Tell me what you know. The captain, he's very funny to-day."

"Ismir!" she called into his ear in a ringing tone. "Beautiful, beautiful Ismir!"

"What's that you're talking about?" he demanded doubtfully. "I don't understand."

"No? Soon you will understand, when we reach Ismir."

"I've never heard of it," he declared. "But I can tell you, if the Old Man don't alter the course, we're going straight into Smyrna."

"Ah, yes," she sighed. "I remember now. You call it that. We call it Ismir, Turkish place. When I was little, little girl, we arrive there, my fazzer and my muzzer. Oh, beautiful! The grand hotels, the *bains*, the *plage*, the *quais*, the mountains, the *cafés-chantant*. *Aiee!* And Bairakli! I will show you. I was little, thirteen years old." She laughed, a soft throaty chuckle, on his shoulder, at some reminiscence. "Ismir! *Oh mein lieber Mann!* "

She intoxicated him with her bewildering moods, with her trick of recalling to his memory his early dreams of beautiful women, those bright shadows of unseen enchantresses which had tortured and stimulated his boyish thoughts. But he could not refrain from returning to the serious problem of how she knew so accurately the intentions of his commander.

"The captain tell you?" he asked expectantly. Her brow grew dark and a blankness like a film came over her eyes.

"I do not like your *capitaine*," she muttered. "He is like an old woman. Look at his face. And the silver ring on his wrist. Like an old vulture, his head between his shoulders. Look at him. He never lifts his eyes. Do not speak of him. But hear me now. When we reach Ismir, we will have a house, you and me, eh?"

He stared at her, entranced, yet preoccupied with the overwhelming difficulties of his situation.

"Oh, *mon cher*, you do not know how beautiful it is. The most beautiful city in the world."

"But how did you know? Why didn't you tell me? Did Mrs. Dainopoulos tell you?"

"Ssh! Madame Dainopoulos is an angel. She like you an' me very much. But Monsieur Dainopoulos, he say to me, if I want to see my friends in Pera, by and by there is a ship. You understand? An' then, here on the ship, I hear some-sing. Oh, tell me, *mon cher*, what time we arrive at Ismir?"

He was hardly listening to her, so busy were his thoughts with the vista opening out before him. He was vaguely conscious that he was passing through a crisis, that Fate had suddenly laid all her cards on the table and was watching him, with bright amber eyes, waiting for him to make out what those cards portended. Here, she seemed to say, is everything you have ever dreamed of, adventure, romance, and the long-imagined pleasures of love.

"To-night?" she persisted, lying back in his arms. And watching him, sensing his uncertainty, her gaze hardened, she sat up away from him, waiting for him to speak, as though she were fate indeed. Always she gave him that impression of hair-trigger readiness to fight, to rip and tear and give no quarter. As he looked at her now, turning over his dire predicament the while, he noticed the truculent solidity of her jaw, the indomitable courage and steadiness of her gaze.

"Wait," he muttered, putting up his hand and then holding it to his brow. "I must think. I don't know when we arrive. To-morrow, perhaps."

"Why do you look so sad?" she demanded. "*Mon Dieu!* To-morrow at Ismir. What happiness!"

"For you," he added in a low voice.

"And for you," she twittered in his ear and patting his hand. "I see the plan of Monsieur Dainopoulos now. We shall have good fortune."

There was a faint tap at the door.

"Supper, Madama," said the young Jew, making a low bow, and they went up.

Mr. Spokesly, sitting on the engineer's settee an hour later and discussing the matter cautiously with that person, was not so sure of the good fortune.

"What can we do?" he asked, and the engineer, who was of a peaceful disposition and perfectly satisfied so long as he got his pay, said:

"You can't do nothing in this fog. He's the captain."

"We may hit something," said Mr. Spokesly, who was talking more for comfort than for enlightenment.

"Why, yes, we may do that. Do it anywhere, come to that. Where do you think we are now, Mister Mate?"

"I don't know, I tell you. He says to me, 'I'll attend to the course,' and he may have put her round. But I've got a notion he's carrying out his orders. I see now why I got six months' pay. Did you?"

"No, I got a note on the captain, same as usual," said Mr. Cassar.

"What do you think they will do with us?" pursued Mr. Spokesly.

"I don't know, Mister Mate. There's always plenty o' work everywhere," was the equable reply.

"Is that all you think of?"

"I got a big family in Cospicua," said the engineer, standing up. "I can't afford to be out of a job. I think I'll go and eat, Mister Mate. Perhaps the fog will lift a bit and we can see what the course is."

They went out and climbed the ladder to the bridge-deck, and stood staring into the damp, palpable darkness. The absence of all artificial light, the silence, the tangible vapour concealing the surface of the sea, and possibly, too, the overhanging uncertainty of their destination, combined to fill them with a vague dull sense of impending peril. They were on the starboard side, abaft the lifeboat. They could not see the bridge clearly, and the forecastle was swallowed up in the blank opacity of the mist. It was a situation in which both care and recklessness were of equal futility. The imagination balked and turned back on itself before the contemplation of such limitless possibilities. And it was while they were standing there in taciturn apprehension that they suddenly sprang into an extraordinary animation of mind and body at the sound and vibration of a loud crash forward. The *Kalkis* heeled over to port from the pressure of some invisible weight and Mr. Spokesly started to run towards the bridge.

"They're shellin' her!" he bawled. "Stand by! Look out! What's that?"

He stood still for a moment, his hands raised to balance himself against the returning roll of the ship as she recovered. And in that moment, out of the fog, above him and over the rail, came an immense gray vertical wall of sharp steel rushing up to him and past into oblivion with a grinding splintering roar. There were cries, the dim glow of an opened door high up, the sough of pouring waters in the darkness, a shadowy phantom and a swirl of propellers, and she was gone.

And there was an absolute silence on the *Kalkis* more dreadful to Mr. Spokesly than the panic of the mob of Asiatics on the *Tanganyika*. He tried to think. Mr. Cassar had disappeared. They had been in collision with a man-of-war, he felt certain of that. There was no mistaking the high cleaving flare of those gray bows as they fled past. And she must have struck the *Kalkis* forward as well as amidships. A glancing blow. Yet there was silence. He strode forward and climbed the ladder to the bridge.

"Are you there, sir?" he called.

There was no answer. He went up to the man at the wheel, who was turning the spokes of the wheel rapidly.

"Where is the Captain?" he demanded harshly.

"He's over there," said the man confidentially, nodding towards the other side of the bridge. "What was that, sir? Explosions?"

"I don't know," said Mr. Spokesly angrily. "Ask the captain," and he went down again and descended the ladder to the fore-deck.

He fell over something here in the dark, something rough and with jagged edges. He felt it with his hands and discovered that it was one of the heavy cast-iron bollards which were mounted on either side of the forecastle head. Mr. Spokesly began to realize that he was confronting a problem which he would have to handle alone. He stepped over the mass of metal, which had been flung fifty feet, and immediately tripped upon a swaying, jagged surface that tore his clothes and cut his hands. He said to himself, "The deck is torn up. I must have a light." There was no sound from forward and he wondered miserably if any of them had been hurt. He climbed to the bridge again to get a hurricane lamp that he knew was in the chart room. While he was striking a match to light it he was once more aware of the fact that the engines were still going. So he hadn't stopped or anything. The captain's form was dimly discernible against the canvas dodger, extraordinarily huge and rotund. Mr. Spokesly's anger broke out in a harsh yell.

"Hi, Captain! Do you know your forecastle's carried away? Or perhaps you don't care."

"I won't be spoken to in that manner," came the lisping,

toothless voice from the darkness. "Go forward and report on the damage. I should think it wouldn't be necessary to tell an experienced officer his duty. . . ."

Mr. Spokesly, swinging the hurricane lamp in his hand, laid his other hand upon Captain Rannie's shoulder.

"Look you here, Captain. You won't be spoken to in that manner? You'll be spoken to as I want from now on. Do you get that? From now on. I'm going forward to report damage. And when I find out if the ship's sinking, I'll not trouble to tell you, you double-crossing old blatherskite you!" And he gave the captain a thrust that sent him flying into the pent-house at the end, where he remained invisible but audible, referring with vivacity to the fact that he had been "attacked."

"I'll attack you again when I come back," muttered his chief officer as he went down the ladder.

And the lamp showed him, in spite of the fog, what had happened. The fore-deck was a mass of ripped and twisted plates, splintered doors, and fragments of the interiors of cabins looked strangely small and tawdry out on the harsh deck. A settee-cushion, all burst and impaled upon a piece of angle iron, impeded him. "Won't be spoken to that fashion!" he muttered, holding up the lamp and peering into the murk. "Good Lord! The forecastle's carried away." He stumbled nearer. There was no ladder on this side any more. The high sharp prow had struck a glancing blow just abaft the anchor and sliced away the whole starboard side of the forecastle. Standing where the door of the bosun's room had been, Mr. Spokesly lowered his lamp and saw the black water rushing past between the torn deck-beams. And Mr. Spokesly had it borne in upon him that not only was Plouff vanished, but his cabin was gone. There was scarcely anything of it left save some splintered parts of the settee and the inner bulkhead, on which a gaudy calendar from a seaman's outfitter fluttered in the night breeze against the blue-white paint.

Mr. Spokesly's heart was daunted by the desolation of that brutally revealed interior. It daunted him because he could imagine, with painful particularity, the scene in that little cabin a few moments before. He had looked in at the door a day or two since, and seen Plouff, a large calabash pipe like a cornucopia in his mouth, propped up in his bed-place, reading a very large book with marbled covers which turned out to be the bound volume of a thirty-year-old magazine picked up for a few pence in some port. He could see him thus engaged a few moments ago. Mr. Spokesly gave a sort of half-sob, half-giggle. "My God, he isn't here at all! He's been carried away, cabin and bunk and everything. Smashed and drowned. Well!"

He felt he couldn't stop there any more. It was worse than finding Plouff's mangled body in the ruins. To have been wiped out like that without a chance to explain a single word to any one was tragic for Plouff. Mr. Spokesly gave a shout.

"Anybody down there?" There was no answer. He found himself wondering what the captain's comment would be upon Plouff's sudden departure for parts unknown. He tried to convince himself that there was no reason for supposing him to be dead. He saw him sitting up in his bunk in the sea, still clasping the large book and smoking the trumpet-shaped pipe, and indulging in a querulous explanation of his unusual behaviour. Which would not be his fault for once, Mr. Spokesly reflected. No doubt, however, Captain Rannie would log him for deserting the ship. Mr. Spokesly went aft and looked at the boat near which he had been standing when the collision happened. It was hanging by the after davit, a mere bunch of smashed sticks. Trailing in the water and making a soft swishing sound were the bow plates and bulwarks which had been peeled from the forepart of the *Kalkis* by the sharp prow of the stranger. And yet she seemed to have suffered nothing below the water-line. Mr. Spokesly, who knew Plouff kept the sounding rod in his cabin, wondered how he was going to sound the wells. He thought of the engineer, stepped over to the port side to reach the after ladder, and pulled himself up short to avoid falling over a huddled group gathered alongside the engine-room hatch.

"What's the matter?" he stammered, astonished. He saw

the steward, a coat hastily put on over his apron, Amos, whose glittering and protuberant eyes were less certain than ever of his future fortune, and Evanthia. She was not afraid. She was angry. She darted at Mr. Spokesly and broke into a torrent of invective against the two wretched beings who wanted to get into the boat and couldn't untie the ropes.

"Pigs, dogs, carrion!" she shrilled at them in Greek, and then to Mr. Spokesly she said,

"The ship. Is it finished?"

"No. Ship's all right. Why don't you go down?"

"*Mon Dieu!* Why? He asks why! Did you hear the noise? The bed is broken. The window, the lamp, *Brr-pp!*" She clapped her hands together. "Why? Go and see," and she turned away from him to rage once more at the two terrified creatures who had been unable to carry out her imperious orders. These had been to set her afloat in the lifeboat instantly; and willingly would they have done it, and gone in with her themselves; but alas, they had been unable to let the villainous boat drop into the water.

Mr. Spokesly was genuinely alarmed at this news. He left them precipitately and ran down the cabin stairs to find out if the ship was making water.

There was no need. The *Kalkis*, on rebounding from the terrific impact on her forecastle, had heeled over to starboard, the side of the ship had been buckled and crushed along the line of the deck, and the concussion had knocked the lamp out of its gimbals and it was rolling on the floor. He picked it up and relit it. He hurried out again to find the engineer. His training was urging him to get the wells sounded. Moreover, the filling of the forepeak through the smashed chain-locker had put the ship down by the head a little. She might be all right, but on the other hand. . . .

He found the engineer calmly hauling the line out of the forward sounding pipes.

"Is she making anything, Chief?" he asked anxiously.

"Just show a light please, Mister Mate. I got a flashlight here but it's gone out on me. Why, four inches. Nothing much *here*. We'll try the other side, eh?"

They scrambled over the hatch and hastily wiped the rod dry before lowering it into the pipe.

"Hm!" The engineer grunted as he brought the rod into view again. "*Three feet!* I reckon she's makin' some watter here through that bulkhead, Mister Mate. What say if I try the pumps on her, eh?"

"You do that, will you? I was afraid o' that, Chief. You know the bosun's gone?"

"Is that so? Gee! That's a big smash! The bosun? Tk—tk! I'll get the pump on her."

"Now!" said Mr. Spokesly to himself, "I'm going to see the Old Man." And he sprang up the ladders once more.

Captain Rannie was not to be seen, however. Mr. Spokesly went upon the bridge charged with belligerence. But Captain Rannie was an old hand. He had had an extraordinarily varied experience of exasperated subordinates and Mr. Spokesly's conscientious tantrums worried him not at all. Especially did he fail to appreciate the significance of his chief officer's anxiety at this moment since from his own point of view this smash in the fog, supposing they did not meet any inquisitive craft for an hour or two, and this was not at all likely—this smash was a piece of singular good fortune. The cruiser would report ramming a small vessel in the fog, and the people in Saloniki, knowing the position of the *Kalkis*, would conclude she was lost with all hands, when she failed to appear at Phyros. It was so perfectly in accordance with his desires that he decided to run down and get one of his own special cigarettes. Now that he was actually in the middle of carrying out the plans of the owner of the *Kalkis*, Captain Rannie suffered from none of the timidity and truculent nervousness which had assailed him the day before. He had more courage than Mr. Spokesly would ever admit because that gentleman was not aware that his captain was a bad navigator. To the bad navigator every voyage is a miracle.

So he came up jauntily, behind Mr. Spokesly, smoking a special cigarette, and ignoring his chief officer completely until the latter chose to speak. This was another trick he had learned in the course of his career of oblique enthusiasms and carefully cultivated antagonisms. He had once been savagely "attacked," as he called it, by a sailor simply because he waited for the man to speak before saying a word! He had found that men might growl at being treated "like dogs" but to rowel the human soul it was far better to act as though they did not exist at all. There was a blind primeval ferocity to be engendered by adumbrating, even for a few moments, their non-existence. And now, with everything in his favour, for he had heard the engineer's remarks on the condition of the bilges forward, he was resolved to "maintain his authority," as he phrased it, by "a perfectly justifiable silence."

But it was no use trying to convince Mr. Spokesly that he did not exist. That gentleman, in the course of the last few minutes, since the collision in fact, had experienced a great accession of vitality. He felt as though not only his own existence but the integrity of the ship as a living whole, her frame, her life, her freight, and the souls clinging to her in the blind white void of the fog, was concentrated in himself. He looked over the side and tried to see if the engineer had succeeded in getting the pump on that bilge. She was down by the head—no doubt of that. And yet there couldn't be any real fracture of that bulkhead, or the fore-hold would have filled by now. Lucky all the caps were well lashed on the ventilators. He looked over the side again. The fog seemed clearing a little. And the ship was moving faster. The beat of the engines was certainly more rapid. He stared at the ostentatiously turned back of his commander with a sort of exasperated admiration. He was evidently a much more accomplished scoundrel than Mr. Spokesly had imagined. Here he had extra speed up his sleeve. Why, it might be anything up to thirteen knots. Not that the *Kalkis* had boilers for that speed. Wow! He was a card!

"I suppose you know the bosun was carried overboard when that ship hit us," Mr. Spokesly remarked in a conversational tone as the captain approached in his stroll.

"And I've no doubt," said Captain Rannie with extreme

bitterness to the surrounding air, "that you blame me for not stopping and picking him up."

"You might have stopped, certainly," said his chief officer; "but the point is, if you'd been on your right course you wouldn't have hit anything."

"Oh, indeed! Oh, indeed!" said the captain.

"Yes, oh, indeed. You won't maintain you were on the right course, I suppose."

"I maintain nothing," snapped the captain. "I'll merely trouble you to ask the man at the wheel what course he was making when we were run into by one of those infernal, careless naval officers who think they know everything, like you. And after that I'll merely invite you to mind your own business."

"Mind my own business!" repeated Mr. Spokesly in a daze.

"And I'll mind mine," added the captain after a dramatic pause, and turning on his heel.

"You're like some bally old woman," began Mr. Spokesly, "with your nag, nag, nag. I don't wonder that Maltee mate used to go for you."

"Ask the man at the wheel what course he was steering," repeated the captain distinctly, coming back out of the gloom and wheeling away again.

"I'll be going for you myself before this trip is over," added the mate.

"And then kindly leave the bridge," concluded the captain, reappearing once more, as though emerging suddenly from the wings of a theatre and declaiming a speech in a play. Having declaimed it, however, he retreated with singular precipitancy.

"I must say, I've been with a few commanders in my time," Mr. Spokesly began in a general way. He heard his captain's voice out of the dark opining that he had no doubt every one of those commanders was glad enough to get rid of him. He could easily believe that.

"Perhaps they were," agreed Mr. Spokesly. "Perhaps they were. The point is, even supposing that was the case, they never made me want to throw them over the side."

The voice came out of the darkness again, commenting upon Mr. Spokesly's extreme forbearance.

"Don't drive me too far," he warned.

The voice said all Mr. Spokesly had to do was remove himself and come on the bridge when he was sent for. No driving was intended.

"Ah, you talk very well, captain. I'm only wondering whether you'll talk half so well at the Inquiry."

The voice asked, what inquiry? with a titter.

"There's always an inquiry, somewhere, sometime," said Mr. Spokesly, dully, wondering what he himself would have to say, for that matter. He heard the voice enunciate with a certain lisping exactitude, "Not yet."

"Oh, no, not yet. When the war's won, let's say," he replied. This seemed such a convenient substitute for "never," that he was not surprised to get no answer save a sound like "Tchah!"

"The fog's lifting," he remarked absently. It was. He could already see a number of stars above his head through the thinning vapour. "I'll leave you," he added, "must get some sleep. However," he went on, "we'll have another look at the bilges. I got a certificate to lose as well as you— if you've got one."

The captain remained in obscurity, and made no reply.

"I mean, if you haven't had it endorsed, or suspended, or any little thing like that."

There was no answer, and tiring of the sport, Mr. Spokesly picked up the hurricane lamp and went down again to sound the starboard bilge. He was getting very tired physically, now the reaction from the excitement of the collision had set in. He found the sounding-rod, neatly chalked, ready to lower. Very decent party, that engineer, he reflected. Rather disconcerting though in his almost perfect neutrality. The wife and the big family out at Cospicua, which is near Valletta, seemed to be a powerful resolvent of sentimental ideas. For such a man there was nothing of any permanence in the world to compare with a permanent billet. His loyalty was to his job rather than to abstract principles of nationality.

Well! The rod showed two feet eight inches. Mr. Spokesly breathed more easily. He had got his pumps going, then. He decided to go aft. Yes, the fog was clearing.

In the stress of the crisis through which he was passing, the mysterious and exacerbating strife going on between himself and the captain, Mr. Spokesly seemed to himself to be separated from Evanthia as by a transparent yet impassable barrier. The insignificance of such a creature in the face of a material disaster as had been impending appalled him. He saw with abrupt clarity how, if the ship had been mortally hit, and if there had been any manner of struggle to save their lives, she would not have sustained the part of fainting heroine rescued by lion-hearted men, or that of heroic comrade taking her place in the peril beside them. Nothing of the sort. She would have got into the boat and commanded the crew to row away with her at once. She did not know that Plouff was gone, and if he went down and told her, she would not care a flip of her fingers. That, he was surprised to realize, was part of her charm. She was so entirely pagan in her attitude towards men. She was one of those women who were born to be possessed by men, but the men who possess them can possess nothing else. They are the destroyers, not of morals, but of ideals. They render the imagination futile because they possess the powerful arts of the enchantresses, the daughters of Helios. They demand the chastity of an anchorite and the devotion of a knight of the Grail. While the virtuous and generous bend under the weight of their self-appointed travails, these pass by in swift palanquins of silk and fine gold, and are adored by the valiant and the wise.

And he was going to marry her.

He slept heavily on the engineer's settee. He had told that obliging person to give him a call at midnight—he wanted to see what the Old Man was up to. The Old Man, however, later gave Mr. Cassar explicit orders to let the mate sleep—he would remain on duty himself. The chief felt it incumbent upon him to oblige the captain, and Mr. Spokesly slept on, much disturbed none the less by grotesque and laboured forebodings of his subconscious being, so that he moved restlessly at times, as though some occult power within was striving to rouse him. Indeed, it was the spirit of duty struggling with wearied tissues. It was past three when the former was so far successful as to wrench his eyes open. He started up, stretched, looked at the engineer's clock, and muttered that he must have fallen asleep again. He put on his coat and cap, and taking a hurried glance at the engineer, who was sprawling on his back in his bunk with his mouth open and his fingers clutching the matted growth of black hair on his chest, he hurried out on deck.

The fog was gone, and a high, level canopy of thin clouds gave the night the character of an enormous and perfectly dark chamber. The *Kalkis* was moving so slowly, Mr. Spokesly could with difficulty keep tally of the beat of the engines. Yet she was moving. He could hear the sough of water, and there was a faint phosphorescence along the ship's side. And a change in the air, an indefinable modification of temperature and possibly smell, led him to examine the near horizon for the deeper blackness of a high shore. He listened intently, trying to detect the sound of waves on the rocks. He tried to figure out what the position would be now, if they had made the course he suspected. They ought to be under the southern shores of Lesbos by now. But if that were the case the cool breeze coming off shore would be on the port side. He listened, sniffed, and resigned himself passively for a moment to the impact of influences so subtle that to one unaccustomed to the sea they might be suspected of supernatural sources. He climbed to the bridge-deck and went over to where the smashed boat hung like a skeleton from the crumpled davit. And he was aware at once of the correctness of his suspicions. But it would not be Lesbos. It was the high land which juts northward and forms the western promontory of the long curving Gulf of Smyrna. He could see it as an intenser and colder projection of the darkness. And then his curiosity centred about the more complex problem of speed. They could not be doing more than a couple of knots. What was the old fraud's game? Waiting for a signal, perhaps. He had evidently got himself and his old ship inside any mines that had been laid between Chios and Lesbos. If there were any. Perhaps he was waiting for daylight.

This was the correct solution. Captain Rannie had crept as close in under Lesbos as he had dared according to the scanty hints he had gotten from Mr. Dainopoulos, who had been informed by a Greek sailor from a captured Bulgarian schooner that there was a safe passage inshore to the east of Cape Vurkos. The result, however, of clearing the southern coast of Lesbos in safety was to engender a slight recklessness in the captain. For his dangers were practically over. Even if he got run ashore later, they could get the cargo out of her. And he had made too much distance east before turning south, so that, in trying to raise a certain point on the western side, he had grown confused. The chart was not large enough. When Mr. Spokesly appeared once more on the bridge, Captain Rannie had rung "Slow" on the telegraph, and was endeavouring to locate some sort of light upon the immense wall of blackness that rose to starboard.

And it could not be asserted that he was sorry to see his chief officer. That gentleman could not do much now. Captain Rannie, with his binoculars to his eyes, was trembling with excitement. According to the chart he ought to see a red light on his port bow within an hour or two. There was a good reason for supposing that light was still kept burning even during the war. It could not be seen from the northward and was of prime importance to coasting vessels in the Gulf when making the turn eastward into the great inland estuary at the head of which lay the city. He was creeping along under the high western shore until he felt he could make the turn. It was shallow water away to the eastward, by the salt-works. It was nearly over. He would get the money, in gold, and wait quietly until the war was over, and take a passage back to China. He knew a valley, the Valley of Blue Primroses, a mere fold in a range of enormous mountains, where men dwelt amid scenes of beauty and ineffable peace, where he would live, too, far away from the people of his own race, and far from the detestable rabble of ships. He had never got on with seamen. Sooner or later, they always attacked him either with violence or invective. He would be revenged on the whole pack of them!

He heard his chief officer behind him and maintained his attitude of close attention. He was trembling. One, two, or perhaps three or four hours and he would know that all was well. He wished he could see better, though. During the fog there had been a curious sense of satisfaction in his heart because he knew that, whatever happened, his defective vision would make no difference. Oh, he could see all right. But those damned red lights. He was sure there was nothing, yet. That chief officer of his had gone into the chart room. Captain Rannie forgot himself so far as to titter. Imagine a simple-minded creature like that trying to put *him* out of countenance! Inquiry! A fine show *he* would make at the inquiry, with a woman in his cabin, and six months' pay in his pocket! Ho-ho! These smart young men! He hated them. There was only one kind of human being he hated more and that was a young woman. He was perfectly sincere. The Caucasian had come to him to appear like a puffy white fungus, loathsome to come in contact with. Without ever expressing himself, for there was no need, he had conceived a strong predilection for the Oriental. He loved the permanence of the type, the skins like yellow silk, the hair like polished ebony, the eyes, long and narrow, like black satin. He liked to have them on the ship, silent, incurious, efficient, devoid of ambition. He put the glasses in the little locker by the bridge-rail. There was no light to be seen.

He started towards the chart-room door and found himself confronted by his chief officer. He would have brushed past with his almost feminine petulance had not Mr. Spokesly once again seized his shoulder.

"She hasn't got steerage way," said the mate.

"What do you mean by steerage way?" he inquired sarcastically.

"Do you know where you are?" demanded Mr. Spokesly,

steadily, "or is it your intention to run her ashore? I'm only asking for information."

Captain Rannie forced himself into the chart room and putting on his glasses examined the chart afresh. Mr. Spokesly followed him in and shut the door.

"I won't have this," the captain began rapidly, laying his hand on the chart and staring down at it. "I won't have it, I tell you. You force yourself in upon me and I am obliged to speak plainly."

"I only want to tell you," said Mr. Spokesly, "that you are too far to the westward. The current is setting you this way," he tapped the chart where a large indentation bore away due south, "and by daylight you won't have sea room."

"I don't believe it!" exclaimed the captain, who meant that he did believe it. "I have taken the log every quarter of an hour."

"Well," said Mr. Spokesly, who was perfectly at ease in this sort of navigation, "the current won't show on the log, which is away out any way. I tell you again, she's going ashore. And it's deep water all round here, as you can see. It won't take a very heavy wallop to send her to the bottom with her bows opened out and the fore peak bulk-head leaking already. Put her about. If you don't," said the mate with his hand on the door and looking hard at his commander, "do you know what I'll do?"

He did not wait for an answer but went out and closed the door sharply. He picked up the telescope and examined the horizon on the port bow. He could discern without difficulty the lofty silhouette of a rocky promontory between the ship and the faint beginnings of the dawn. He turned to the helmsman.

"Hard over to port," he said quietly, and reaching out his hand he rang "Full ahead" on the telegraph. It answered with a brisk scratching jangle, and a rhythmic tremor passed through the vessel's frame, as though she, too, had suddenly realized her peril.

"You do what I say," he warned the man at the wheel, who did not reply. He only twirled the spokes energetically, and the little ship heeled over as she went round. Mr. Spokesly looked again at the approaching coast. There was plenty of room. He heard the door open and the captain come out.

"Easy now," Mr. Spokesly said. "Starboard. Easy does it. That's the style. Well, do you believe what I say now, Captain?"

"I'll report you—I'll have you arrested—I'll use my power——" he stuttered, stopping short by the binnacle and bending double in the impotence of his anger. "Remember, I can tell things about you," he added, pointing his finger at the mate, as though he were actually indicating a visible mark of guilt.

"Shut up," said Mr. Spokesly, staring hard through the telescope. "Hold her on that now, Quartermaster, till I give the word. There will be enough light soon."

Captain Rannie came up to his chief officer's shoulder and whispered:

"You're in this as deep as I am, remember."

"I'm not in it at all and don't you forget it," bawled Mr. Spokesly. The man at the wheel said suddenly in a querulous tone:

"I can't see to steer."

Captain Rannie had fallen back against the binnacle and the sleeve of his coat covered the round hole through which the compass could be seen.

"You threaten me?" he whimpered. "You threaten the master of the ship?"

"Threaten!" repeated Mr. Spokesly, looking eagerly through the binoculars. "Couple of points to starboard, you. I reckon she's all right now," he muttered to himself, "but we'll go half speed for a bit," and he pulled the handle. At the sound of the reply gong and the obsequious movement of the pointer on the dial Captain Rannie was galvanized into fresh life. It was as though the sound had reminded him of something.

"You've been against me ever since you came aboard," he announced. "I noticed it from the first. You had made up your mind to give me all the trouble you possibly could. I don't know how it is, I'm sure, but I always get the most insubordinate and useless officers on my ship. You go in these big lines and get exaggerated ideas of your own importance, and then come to me and try it on here. How can a commander get on with officers who defy him and incite the crew to mutiny? Don't deny it. What you're doing now is mutiny. It may take time, but I'll do it. I'll get you into all the trouble I possibly can for this. I—I—I'll log the whole thing. I'm sorry I ever shipped you. I might have known. I suspected something of the sort. A manner you had in the office. Impudent, insubordinate, self-sufficient. On the beach. Not a suit of clothes to your back. Had to borrow money—*I* heard all about it. And then bringing a woman on the ship. Told some sort of tale to the owner. All very fine. I might as well tell you now, since you've taken this attitude, that I knew we wouldn't get on. If it had been a regular voyage I wouldn't have had you. It's been nothing but trouble since you came. The other man was bad enough, but you . . ."

"Starboard, Quartermaster. Go ahead, Captain. That's one thing about you. Nothing matters so long as you can go on talking. Fire away if it eases your mind. But I'm taking this ship in. See the fairway? If you make anything out of this trip, and I dare say you'll make it all right, don't forget you owe it to me. You had me rattled a bit when you ran into that ship last night. I thought you knew what you were doing. And you were just scared. Sitting over there on that life-belt, blowing up that patent vest of yours. Thought I didn't notice it, eh? So busy blowing it up you couldn't answer me when I called you. Master of the ship! Yah!"

Captain Rannie was visible now, a high-shouldered figure with one hand in his pocket and the other resting on the corner of the chart house. During the night he had put on a thick woollen cap with a small knob, the size of a cherry, on the point of it, and it made him look like some fantastic creature out of an opera. It was as though he had materialized out of the darkness, an elderly imp foiled in his mischievous designs. He stood there, looking down at the deck, his

COMMAND

mouth working over his toothless gums, silently yet frantically marshalling the routed forces of his personality.

"All right!" he exclaimed. "You take her, I hold you responsible, mind that. I wash my hands of you. You incited my crew to mutiny. Defied my orders."

Mr. Spokesly turned suddenly and Captain Rannie rushed to the ladder and descended halfway, holding by the handrail and looking up at Mr. Spokesly's knees.

"Don't you attack me!" he shrilled. "Don't you dare . . ." He paused, breathing heavily.

Mr. Spokesly walked to the ladder.

"You'd better go down and pull yourself together," he said in a low tone. "You're only making yourself conspicuous. I can manage without you. And if you come up here again until I've taken her in, by heavens I'll throw you over the side."

He walked back quickly to the bridge-rail, and stared with anxious eyes into the stretch of fairway. He could not help feeling that something tremendous was happening to him. To say that to the captain of the ship! But he had to keep his attention on the course. Looking ahead, it was as though he had made the same error of which he had accused the Captain, of running into the land. On the port side the low shore in the half-light ran up apparently into the immense wall of blue mountains in the distance. A few more miles and he would see. He looked down at the torn strakes draggling in the water alongside, at the smashed boat, and the tangled wreckage on the foredeck. She was very much down by the head now, he noted. Yet they were making it. It would be any moment now when the land would open out away to the eastward and he would give the word to bear away.

And as the sun came up behind the great ranges of Asia and touched the dark blue above their summits with an electric radiance so that the sea and the shore, though dark, were yet strangely clear, he saw the white riffle of contending currents away to port, and got his sure bearings in the Gulf. And as he rang "Full speed ahead" he heard a step behind him and felt a quick pressure of his arm.

She was wearing the big blue overcoat, which was Plouff's last demonstration of his own peculiar and indefatigable usefulness, and her face glowed in the depths of the up-turned collar. The morning breeze blew her hair about as she peered eagerly towards the goal of her desire.

"See!" she cried happily, pointing, one finger showing at the end of the huge sleeve. "See the town?" She snatched the glasses and held them to her eyes. "Giaour Ismir!"

"You don't want to get into the boat after all," he said, putting his arm about her shoulders.

"Me? No! That fool said the ship would go down. Look! Oh, *quelle jolie ville !* "

"Where?" he said, taking the glasses.

"See!" She pointed into the dim gray stretch of the waters that lay like a lake in the bosom of immense mountains. He looked and saw what she meant, a spatter of white on the blue hillside, a tiny sparkle of lights and clusters of tall cypresses, black against the mists of the morning. And along the coast on their right lay a gray-green sea of foliage where the olive groves lined the shore. Range beyond range the mountains receded, barring the light of the sun and leaving the great city in a light as mysterious as the dawn of a new world. Far up the Gulf, beyond the last glitter of the long sea wall, he could see the valleys flooded with pale golden light from the hidden sun, with white houses looking down upon the waters from their green nests of cypresses and oaks.

"Why don't they come out?" he wondered half to himself. "Are they all asleep?"

"Oh, the poor ones, they must come out in a boat. They have no coal," she retorted. "Look! there is a little ship sailing out! Tck!"

He looked at it. Well, what could they do? He held her close. She must be interpreter for him, he said. Oh, of course. She would tell them what a hero he was, how he had brought them safely through innumerable dangers for her sake. They would live, see! Up there. He had no idea **how** happy they would be!

The little sailing boat was coming out, her sail like a fleck of cambric on the dark water.

He said there was no need to tell them he was a hero.

"They will know it," she said, "when they see the poor ship. Oh, yes, I will tell them everything. I will tell them you did this because you love me."

"Will they believe it?" he asked in a low tone, watching the city as they drew nearer.

"Believe?" she questioned without glancing at him. "It is nothing to them. What matter? I tell them something, that is all."

He did not reply to this, merely turning to give an order to the helmsman. The other seaman was coming along the deck, and he called him to take in the log and run up the ensign. It was nothing to them, he thought, repeating her words to himself. Nothing. They would make no fine distinctions between himself and the captain. Yes, she was right in that. He went into the chart room and got out the flags of the ship's name. She, the ship, was not to blame, he muttered. She had been faithful. "And so have I!" he cried out within himself. He could not make it clear even to himself, but as he bent the grimy little flags to the signal halyards and hoisted them to the crosstrees, and saw them straighten out like sheets of tin in the breeze, he had an uplifting of the heart. He rang "Stop" to the engine room, and went over to Evanthia.

"Go down," he said gently, "and tell the captain he must come up. We are going to drop the anchor. There is a boat coming alongside."

He stood watching the boat bearing down upon them. He tried to think clearly. Yes, the captain must come up. The complex animosities of the night must be put away. And though he was a little afraid of what lay before him in that great fair city rising from the sea, he had no regrets for the past. He felt, in spite of everything, he had been faithful.

CHAPTER XV

YOU can have no idea," said the flat and unemotional voice by Mr. Spokesly's shoulder, "simply no idea how miraculous the whole business seems to us. Astonished? No word for it. We were flabbergasted. For you saved the situation. You arrived in the nick, positively the nick, of time. I don't go beyond the facts when I say things were looking decidedly, well blue, for us. Oh, don't misunderstand me. No ill-treatment. Just the reverse, in fact. But you can understand we weren't bothering much about politeness when we couldn't get anything to eat. And that's what it amounts to."

"Yes, I suppose so," said Mr. Spokesly. "I must say, finding so many of you here, has surprised me."

"We had to stay. Couldn't get out," replied the other man, shooting a frayed cuff and flicking the ash delicately from his cigarette.

They were seated, as it were, at the centre of that vast crescent which the city forms upon the flanks of Mount Pagos. On either hand the great curves of the water-front sprang outward and melted into the confused colours of the distant shore. From their vantage point on the roof of the Sports Club, they could see in some detail the beauty of the buildings, the marble entrances, the cedar-wood balconies and the green jalousies of the waterside houses. They could see the boats sailing rapidly across the harbour from Cordelio in the afternoon breeze, and beyond, bathing the whole panorama in a strong blaze of colour, the sun, soon to set in the purple distances beyond the blue domes of the islands. To the right the shore curved in a semi-circular sweep to form the head of the great Gulf, while on their left the green waters, ruffled by

276

the breeze and given a magical lustre by the rays of the setting sun, stretched away into the distance.

And it was into this distance that Mr. Spokesly, his elbow on the stone balustrade of the roof of the Sports Club, was thoughtfully directing his gaze. Even with his physical eyes he could make out a faint dot, which he knew was the *Kalkis*. And while he listened to the remarks of his companion, his thoughts went back to the final catastrophe of the voyage. He had been leaning over watching the boat come alongside, his hand on the telegraph to put her astern, when the whole ship shook violently, there was a grinding of metal on metal and a sound as of a load of loose stones pouring harshly upon hollow iron floors. He stared round him even as he pulled the handle back to full astern, searching for some hint of the cause. And he realized he had been searching for something else, too. He had been voicelessly calling for Plouff and for the captain. As he sat calmly looking out across the water at the wreck—for he did not disguise from himself the fact that the *Kalkis* was a total loss—he was thinking of that moment when he had to decide what to do and had turned his head to call for help. And he knew now that if he had called, if he had run down and hammered on that man's door to come up and take charge, to resume the authority he had abdicated so short a time before, there would have been no answer.

That was the point around which his memories clustered now, although nobody save himself was aware of it. Indeed, there had been a distinctly admiring note in this gentleman's voice, flat and unemotional as it was by habit, when he had climbed up the ladder and set foot on the deck of the *Kalkis*. "You were very cool," he had said. He had not been cool. There had been a moment, just after he had pulled that telegraph-handle, and the ship, instead of slowly gaining sternway and moving off into the turbulence of her wake, had given another inexplicable shudder, and the bows sank into a sudden deathlike solidity when he rang "stop," as though that noise and that shudder and that almost imperceptible subsidence had been her death-throe, the last struggle of her

complicated and tatterdemalion career. That moment had
settled the *Kalkis* and it had nearly settled him, too. He had
turned right round and seen the man at the wheel methodi-
cally passing the spokes through his hands, his eye on the
ship's head, his ear alert for the word of command. Mr.
Spokesly had seen this, and for an instant he had had a shocking impulse to run to the far side of the bridge and go over,
into the water. A moment of invisible yet fathomless panic.
Looking back at it, he had a vague impression of a glimpse
into eternity—as though for that instant he had really died,
slipping into an unsuspected crevice between the past and
the future. . . . The man at the wheel was looking at
him. He heard a voice, the voice of the helmsman, saying,
"She don't steer," and the moment was past. He walked
firmly to the side and looked down at the boat, and heard
someone calling, "Where is your ladder?"

And the next thing he remembered was the remark of this
gentleman when he arrived on deck: "You were very cool."
He had said in reply: "There is something I wish to tell you.
I have sent for the captain and he has not come up. I must
go and fetch him." He remembered also the dry comment,
"Oh, so you are not the captain?" and the start for the cabin
as Evanthia came out, buttoning her gloves, dressed for
walking. He remembered that. The gentleman who had
told him he was very cool, and who sat beside him now on the
roof of the Sports Club, had been explaining that he came
as an interpreter and was English himself, when the door
opened and Evanthia appeared. He had stopped short and
let his jaw drop, and his hand slowly reached up to remove his
old straw hat. The others, who were in white uniforms with
red fezzes on their heads, stepped back involuntarily in stupefaction at such an unexpected vision. And he, dazed by his
recent experience, stood staring at her as though he were as
astonished as the rest. For she came up to him in that long
stride of hers that always made him feel it would be hopeless
to explain to her what was meant by fear, and slipped her
hand through his arm. "My husband," she said, smiling at
the men in fezzes, and she added, in their own tongue. "My

father was Solari Bey, who had the House of the Cedars near the cemetery in Pera."

It was she who had been "very cool." She was wearing her black dress and the toque with the high feather. Her eyes glowed mysteriously, and she stood beside him dominating them all. He heard the astonished interpreter mumbling: "Oh—ah! Really! Dear me! Most unexpected pleasure! Plucky of you, permit me to say. Oh—ah! . . ." and the men in fezzes making respectful noises in their throats as the conversation suddenly became unintelligible. He had stood silent, watching her while she spoke that bewildering jargon, the words rushing from her exquisite lips and catching fire from the flash of her eyes. There was a potent vitality in the tones of her voice that seemed to him must be irresistible to all men. She spoke and they listened with rapt attentive gaze. She commanded and they obeyed. They laughed, and bent their tall heads to listen afresh. She might have been some supernatural being, some marine goddess, come suddenly into her old dominions, and they her devout worshippers.

He heard the word "captain" and opened his mouth to speak to the interpreter.

"Is he English?" asked that gentleman. "She says he is a—well, I hardly know how to explain just what she means. . . . You had better tell this officer here. He speaks some English. Colonel Krapin? Ah, quite so. The colonel wishes me to say, he must see the captain. Perhaps, if you will allow us, we can sit down in the cabin, he says."

And when they had entered the cabin, and were seated about the table, the young Jew, who had been cowering in the pantry, was brought forth and ordered in crisp tones to descend and inform the captain.

"I knocked at the door," Evanthia told them quickly. "I said, a boat is coming. I heard him move. I heard him come to the door and then, he strike the door with all his force while I have my hand on it. The door shake, *boom !* The fool is afraid for anybody to go in. Ask the boy, the young Jew. He will tell you."

The colonel studied his sword, which he had laid on the table before him, and made a remark in a low tone. He had been somewhat embarrassed by the absence of the captain. Without a captain and without the papers which would apprise them all of the exact nature of the cargo, he was at a loss.

And the young Jew had come stumbling up the stairs, his hands outspread, and in quavering tones said something which had brought the officer to his feet and grasping his sword. He had remembered that moment.

"You know," said his companion with a slight smile, "really you know, when he came up and told us the captain was leaning against the door and wouldn't let him open it— said he could see the captain's shoulder, just for a moment I thought you had been let in. Poor old Krapin was in a funk. He was sure he was in a trap. You remember he wouldn't go down. Made *me* go."

"Yes," said Mr. Spokesly steadily, "I remember. I couldn't explain because I didn't know myself. He thought I was in the plot, I suppose."

"And now he thinks you . . ." he paused and flicked his cigarette again. "H—m! Down there in that dark passage, I was ready to think all sorts of funny things myself. I saw his shoulder. Extraordinary sensation running up and down my spine. I said, 'Captain, you are wanted.' No answer, of course. What is one to say in a situation of that kind? I ask you. For a moment I stood with my foot in the door and him leaning against it. It reminded me of my boyhood days in London when all sorts of people used to come round to sell things and try to keep you from shutting the door. For a moment I wondered if he thought I had come off in a boat to sell him something."

He gave a short laugh and looked down with reflective eyes upon the people walking in the street between the houses and the sea. His straw hat and linen suit were very old and frayed and his shoes were of canvas with rope soles. Yet he gave the impression of being very smartly attired. A gentleman. His bow tie burst forth from a frayed but spotless soft collar. A cotton handkerchief with a spotted blue border hung fashionably from his pocket. And his features had the fine tint and texture of a manila envelope.

"Absurd, of course. Yet in a case like that one doesn't know how to avoid the absurd. And finally, when I gave a smart shove, I said: 'Excuse me, Captain, I really must . . .' the shoulder disappeared and there was a most awful clatter and a thud. And then a silence. Frankly I was unable to open the door for a second, I was so upset. I half expected the thing to fly open and a crowd of people to rush out on me. That was the sensation I got from that rumpus. Imagine it!"

"Yes," said Mr. Spokesly, "I can believe you felt strange. But how was anybody to know?"

"And you still think it was an accident?" said his companion curiously.

"Yes, it was an accident," replied Mr. Spokesly steadily.

"H—m! Well, you knew him."

"I don't believe he had the pluck to do such a thing," went on Mr. Spokesly. "He hadn't the pluck of a louse, as we say. And you must remember he was all dressed for going ashore. He had all his money on him, all his papers. He very likely had his hat on. But for some reason or other, before he could do anything and speak to anybody, he had to take some sort of pill. Small, square white tablets. I've known him keep out of the way, go over the other side of the bridge and turn his back before speaking to me. I could see his hand go to his mouth as he came along the deck. I don't know for sure. Nobody will know for sure. But I know what I think myself."

"Yes? Some private trouble? That's the usual reason, isn't it?"

"He had a grudge against everybody. Thought everybody was against him. They were, but that was because he hadn't the sense to get on with them."

"Perhaps it was a woman," suggested his companion hopefully.

"Him! A woman? Do you think a woman would have anything to do with him?"

Mr. Spokesly's tone as he put this question was warm. It was a true reflection of his present state of mind. "My husband," Evanthia had said, and it was as her husband he had stepped ashore. And he was conscious of a glow of pride whenever he compared other men with himself. She was his. As for the captain, the very idea was grotesque. He stirred in his chair, moved his arm on the balustrade. He did not want to talk about the captain. The words, "Perhaps it was a woman," did not, he felt, apply exactly to any one save himself. He heard his companion reply doubtfully, as though there could be any doubt:

"Oh—well, you know, one has heard of such cases. Still, as you say, the circumstantial evidence is strong. Those tablets of his were all over the place, I remember."

"He had the medicine-chest in his room," said Mr. Spokesly.

"Yes. The Doctor showed me where he'd been mixing the stuff in a cup. And there was a mould for making them. So you think he had no intention of . . ."

"No intention of taking anything fatal himself," was the reply.

"Ah! Indeed! That opens up a very interesting departure," said the other.

"Not now," said Mr. Spokesly. "Not now."

"You'll excuse my own curiosity," said his friend, "but when I found him, you know, eh?"

"If he had found you," Mr. Spokesly remarked, looking towards the mountains to the eastward, "he would never have taken the trouble to mention it to a soul except officially. I didn't know him very well, but I should say he is better off where he is. I shall have to be getting along."

They rose and descended the broad staircases to the terrace facing the sea, a terrace filled with tables and chairs. Across the Gulf the lights of Cordelio began to sparkle against the intense dark blue of the land below the red blaze of the sunset. It was the hour when the Europeans of the city come out to enjoy the breeze from the Gulf, making their appearance through the great archway of the Passage Kraemer and sitting at little tables to drink coffee and lemonade tinctured with syrup. They were coming out now, parties of Austrians and Germans, with fattish spectacled husbands in uniforms with fezzes atop, and tall blonde women in toilettes that favoured bold colour schemes or sharp contrasts of black and white, with small sun-shades on long handles. There were Greeks and Roumanians and here and there a quiet couple of English would sink unobtrusively into chairs in a corner. And a band was tuning up somewhere out of sight.

Mr. Spokesly plunged straight down the steps of the terrace, past a group of Austrian girls who were taking their seats at a table, and who eyed him with lively curiosity, and started towards the custom house, his companion, whose name was Marsh, hurrying after him.

"By the way," said he. "I would like, some time, to introduce you to some of the crowd. They are really very decent. They have made things much easier for us than you might imagine. Of course, for the sake of my family and myself I have kept well in with them; but quite apart from the expediency of it, it has been a pleasure. You have been here nearly a week now," he went on, smiling a little, "and we have seen nothing of you."

Mr. Spokesly muttered something about being busy all day on the ship, getting the cargo out of her.

"Yes, but why not come round now? It is only just through the Passage, near Costi's. I can assure you they are a very interesting lot."

"Well, it's like this, Mr. Marsh. I'm under orders, you see. And I've got this launch now and I'm not so sure of the engine that I want to get stuck with it after dark. I'll tell you what. I'll come to-morrow, eh?"

And to this Mr. Marsh was obliged to agree. Mr. Spokesly dived into the custom house and made for the waterside, where a number of gasolene launches were tied up. It was one of these which, on account of the gasolene in the cargo of the *Kalkis*, he had been able to get for his own use. He had had long struggles with the engine, towing it out with him to the ship and working on it while the men loaded the barges.

Now it was in pretty good shape; he understood it well enough to anticipate most of the troubles. He got down into it now and took off his coat to start the engine.

It was not that he did not appreciate the offer of his friend. The crowd alluded to were well enough no doubt—clerks and subordinate officials who had gradually formed a sort of international coterie who met in a wing of one of the consulates. Indeed, one of them lived in a house not far from himself on the hillside at Bairakli. But he was in a mood just now which made him reluctant to mix with those highly sophisticated beings. He wanted to go home. As he steered his launch through the entrance of the tiny harbour and made straight across the Gulf towards the eastern end, he was thinking that for the first time in his life he had a home. And she had done it! With a cool indomitable will she had set about it. He knew he could never have achieved this felicity by himself. She had held out her hand for money and he had handed it over to her. If she had not watched he would not have had nearly so much, she told him, and he believed her. That was the key to his mood. He crouched in the stern of his boat and kept his eyes upon the house, a white spot against the steep brown slope of the mountain. That house, rented from a poverty-stricken Greek who had left most of the furniture, and an old woman, who had lived all her life in the village, as servant, represented for Mr. Spokesly his entire visible and comprehensible future. This was another key to his mood. It was as though he had suddenly cashed in on all his available resources of happiness, hypothecating them for the immediate and attainable yet romantic present. By some fluke of fortune he could see that he actually held within his grasp all that men toil and struggle for in this world, all that they desire in youth, all that they remember in age. But he had no certainty of the permanence of all this, and he lived in a kind of anxious ecstasy, watching Evanthia each day with eager hungry eyes, waiting with a sort of incredulous astonishment for the first shadow to cross the dark mirror of their lives.

As it must, he told himself. This could not last for ever.

And sometimes he found himself trying to imagine how it would end. To-night he was preoccupied with the discovery that each day, as the end approached, he was dreading it more and more. He had tried to explain this to her as they walked in the garden under the cypresses and looked across the dark waters of the Gulf, and she had smiled and said: "Ah, yes!" She was still a mystery to him, and that was another grief, since he did not yet suspect that the mystery of a woman is simply a screen with nothing behind it. She smiled in her alluring inscrutable way and he held her desperately to him, wondering in what form the fate of their separation would appear.

And when he saw that she had not come down to the jetty to meet him, as she had done on previous nights, he instantly accepted her absence as a signal of change. Yet at the back of his mind there burned a thin bright flame of intelligence that told him the truth. Evanthia had that supreme virtue of the courageous—her dissimulation was neither clumsy nor cruel. It was as much a part of her as was her skin, her hair, her amber eyes. He knew in his heart this was so and made of it a rack on which he tortured himself with thoughts of her fidelity. Each day the difference between this experience and the shallow clap-trap intrigues he had known became more marked to him. The thought of her out there, hidden away from other men, with her delicious graces of body and lucidity of mind, for him alone, was almost too poignant for him. As he came alongside the little staging, and made fast, he returned again to the foreboding thought of the day. There would come an end. And beyond the end of this he could see nothing but darkness, nothing save an aching void.

Nevertheless, as he came up from the jetty and stood for a moment in the road which followed the curve of the shore, and listened to the sounds of the village that nestled in the valley like a few grains of light in a great bowl of darkness, he was conscious of something which he could not successfully analyze or separate from his tumultuous emotions. He put it to himself, crudely enough, when he muttered: "I shall have to take a hand." He was discovering himself in the act of submitting once more to outside authority. Looking back over his life, he saw that as his hitherto invincible habit of mind. He saw himself turning round to call the captain. And now he was the captain. And Evanthia's enigmatic gaze was perhaps the expression of her curiosity. She was above all things in the world, stimulating. He found himself invigorated to an extraordinary degree by his intimacy with that resourceful, courageous, and lovable being, who would never speak of the future, waving it away with a flick of her adorable hand and looking at him for an instant with an intent, unfathomable stare. And as he started to climb the hillside, setting the loose stones rolling in the gullies and rousing a dog to give forth a series of deep ringing notes like a distant gong, he saw that the initiative rested with himself. He would have to take a hand. It would not do for him to imagine they could remain like this in almost idyllic felicity. The ship would be unloaded in a week or so and nothing would remain but to let the water into her after-hold and sink her, according to the commandant's orders, in the fair way. But he could not let himself sink back into a slothful obscurity. He had no interior resources beyond his almost desperate passion for this girl who seemed to accept him as an inevitable yet transient factor in her destiny, a girl who conveyed to him in subtle nuances a chaotic impression of sturdy fidelity and bizarre adventurousness. That was one of the secrets of her personality—the maintenance of their relations upon a plane above the filth and languor of the flesh, yet unsupported by the conventional props of tradition and honour. For she had so just a knowledge of the functions and possibilities of love in human life that he could never presume upon the absence of those props. It amazed him beyond his available powers of expression, that in giving him herself she gave more than he had ever imagined. She had given him an enormously expanded comprehension of character, an insight into the secrets of his own heart. And it was, perhaps, this new knowledge of what he himself might do, that was impelling him to "take a hand."

When he reached the gate set in the wall of the garden, he had decided to take a hand at once. He had a plan.

And it would have been a valuable experience for him, advancing him some distance in spiritual development, had he been able to see clearly and understandingly into her alert and shrewdly logical mind when he told her his plan. For she saw through it in a flash. It was romantic, it was risky, it was for himself. It might easily be for her ultimate good, yet she saw he was not thinking of that at all. And because he was romantic, because he visualized their departure as a flight into a fresh paradise, they two alone, she turned to him with one of her ineffably gracious gestures and loved him perhaps more sincerely than ever before. It was this romantic streak in the dull fabric of his personality which had attracted her, even if she had not perceived the emotional repose that same dullness afforded her. It was like being in a calm harbour at anchor compared with that other adventure, which had been a voyage through storms and whirlpools, a voyage that would inevitably end in shipwreck and stranding for her anyhow.

"I could do it," he was saying. "They don't know about it, but that boat is the fastest they've got in the harbour and, with luck, it would be easy to get away."

"To where?" she whispered, looking out into the fragrant gloom of the high-walled garden below them.

"Anywhere," he exclaimed. "Once outside, we'd be picked up. Or we could go to Phyros, and get home from there."

"Home?"

"Yes, home. England. I want you to come with me, stay with me, for good. I can't—I can't do without you. I've been thinking every day, every night. There's nobody else now."

She shot a glance at him. He was leaning forward in his chair, his eyes fixed on the floor thinking, in a warm tumult of desire, of the adventure. He saw the boat bounding through the fresh green wave-tops into the deeper blue of the Ægean, he steering, with his arm around her form which would be enfolded in that same big coat, making a dash for freedom.

And as she patted his arm gently, she knew he was not thinking of her save as a protagonist in a romantic episode. For to ask her to go to England was, from her point of view, the reverse of a dash for freedom. In her clear, cold, limited mentality, equipped only with casual and fragmentary tales told by the ignorant or the prejudiced products of mid-European culture, England was the home of debased ideals and gloomy prisons, of iron-hard creeds and a grasping cunning avarice. Her mercenaries were devoted to the conquest and destruction of all that made life beautiful and gay. Out of her cold wet fogs her legions came to despoil the fair places of the earth. And his fidelity, his avowed abandonment of the sentiments of the past, inspired her more with wonder and delight than a reciprocal passion. For she was under no illusions as to her own destiny. She, too, knew this would not last for ever. Her quick mind took in all the fantastic possibilities of his plan, and she perceived immediately the necessity of giving her consent. He must be kept in this mood of exalted happiness. Intuitively she knew that she herself fed on that mood, in which he rose superior to the normal level of his days. And in spite of her dismay at the mere thought of going out again upon the sea, leaving everything she understood and loved, leaving a land of whose spirit and atmosphere she was a part, she asked him when he wanted to go.

"Not yet," he replied, still gazing at the ground, and she looked at him with amazement. She could hardly repress an exclamation at his credulity. He actually believed she would go.

"And we will take all our money?" she suggested.

"Yes, of course," he agreed absently. It was part of his happiness to put everything in her hands. There was for him a supremely sensuous delight in the words, "It is all for you. Take it. Without you, it is of no use to me." He was unable to imagine a more complete surrender, nor could he believe that a woman would accept it save at the price of integrity. Evanthia was like that. Money was never her preoccupation, but she never forgot it. She had none of the futilities of book-education filling her mind like dusty and useless furniture, so that her consciousness of money was as clear and sharp as her consciousness of food or pain. And a sudden perception of his faith in her, his profound absorption in his own romantic illusions, struck her to a puzzled silence, which he took for assent and sympathy. She looked away from him and out across the sea. It was too easy.

"Evanthia," he whispered, and she turned her full, direct untroubled gaze upon him with a swift and characteristic movement of the chin.

"I love you," he muttered and touched her arm with his lips in a gesture of adoration. She looked at him with glowing amber eyes. Sometimes he almost terrified her with the violence of his passionate abnegation. She had never seen anything like it before. He became gloomy with love, she noted; and her quick wit transfused the thought into a presentiment. She would break the spell of his infatuation with a quick movement and lure him back to earth with a smile. She laughed now as he touched her.

"Tell me," he said, "you wish to come to England with me?"

"Ah, yes!" she sighed sweetly, nestling against him. "You an' me, in England."

"Some time next week I'll be ready," he said. "You must get plenty of food for the boat. And the money. Bring that."

She sat leaning against him, his arms about her, but at these words she stared past him into the darkness of the room thinking quickly. Next week!

"I am getting the engineer to make me a silencer, the boat makes so much noise," he explained.

"I understand," she murmured absently, slipping out of his arms. She must send into the town, she thought. Amos must go.

"To-morrow," he went on, "I go to the Club in the Austrian Consulate. Mr. Marsh asked me to go. I may be a little late. You won't mind?"

She turned upon him in the darkness where she was feeling

for the lamp, and gave him a blank stare. He never saw it; and if he had he would never have been able to understand that at that moment she could have killed him for his stupidity. He sat in silence wondering a little, and then the emotion had passed and she gave her delicious throaty chuckle.

"Ah, no, *mein Lieber*. I do not mind."

"Why do you sometimes call me your *Lieber?*" he asked playfully. "Is it a pet name?"

The lamp was alight and he saw her eyes smouldering as she raised them from the flame she was adjusting.

"Yes, *Lieber* means love," she said gravely.

"You are not sorry we did not go to Athens?" he asked, smiling.

"To Athens . . ." her face for a moment was blank, so completely had she forgotten the ruse she had employed in Saloniki. ". . . ah, I understand. Athens? No!" She turned the lamp up and began to set the table for supper.

This was the hour that appealed to him more than anything in their life. To see her moving about in a loose cotton frock, her bare feet thrust into Turkish slippers, to follow the line of her vigorous supple body beneath the thin material, and the expert rapidity of her hands as she prepared the simple meal of stew and young figs in syrup, red wine and coffee with candied dates, was sheer ecstasy for him. He would sit in the dusk of the window, sprawling in his chair, his head sunk on his breast, breathing heavily as he devoured every motion with his eyes. It never occurred to him to wonder what she was thinking about as she worked with her eyes cast down towards the white table or turning towards the door to call in musical plangent accents to the old woman in the kitchen below. She was an object of love and for him had no existence outside of his emotional necessities. He asked in lazy contentment if she regretted Athens. Her eyes, declined upon the table, were inscrutable as she reflected that the young Jew was even then in the city finding out for her whether any officers had arrived from Aidin.

"We'll have a house like this, in England," he remarked, smiling. "And you will forget all about Saloniki, eh?"

He would expect this, of course, she thought. It was the duty of a woman selected by a romantic to forget everything in the world except himself. She was thinking of Saloniki even as she smiled into his eyes and nodded. And Saloniki was thinking of her. It was at this hour that Mrs. Dainopoulos said to her husband:

"You are sure they reached port safe?"

Mr. Dainopoulos, who had heard, by his own intricate and clandestine methods, of the unconventional arrival of his ship in Giaour Ismir, and who was not bothering himself very much about either Evanthia or Mr. Spokesly since both had served his turn, remarked:

"Yes, all safe."

"You know, Boris, I should never forgive myself if anything happened to her. If he did not marry her as soon as they got on shore. I did it for the best. Encouraged it, I mean. I do believe he was trustworthy."

"Don't you worry, Alice," he said gruffly. "You'll see that girl again. What you like I get you? I done a beeg business to-day."

"What was that? How much?" she asked with assumed interest. She did not want to know, but she knew he liked her to ask.

"Oh, the British give me the paper for a big cargo I got for 'em. You count this, now: *Thirty—five—thousand— pound.* Eh? Ha—ha!" He leaned forward and covered her hands with kisses murmuring: "My little wife! My little wife! What shall I buy my little English wife, eh?"

And when Mr. Spokesly asked Evanthia if she would forget it all when she got to England she stood by the table, stricken to a sudden and mysterious immobility and regarded him with wide amber-coloured eyes. Then she lifted a finger to her lips.

There was a noise below. The iron gate banged. Evanthia, her finger to her lips, her eyes shining like stars, came to the window and leaned over.

"Art thou come back?" she called in Greek. And the voice of the young Jew replied:

"Here I am, Madama. I am returned from the city."

"Any news of the Franks at Aidin?" she asked, smiling at Mr. Spokesly where he sat in silent admiration.

"They are here, Madama. Three, one of them the man you described to me, young and full of laughter."

"*Aiee!* A good servant thou art. I will keep thee always." She turned to her lover.

"Ah, yes!" she sighed. "A house like this in England. And I have forgot Saloniki now. Supper is ready, *mein Lieber.*"

CHAPTER XVI

YEARS afterwards, when Mr. Spokesly, a cool and established person in authority in a far distant territory, would turn his thoughts back occasionally to the great period of his life, he would wonder how long it might have lasted had he not gone into the city that calm evening, had he never met that gay and irrepressible young man. There was no bitterness in his reflections. He saw, in that future time, how far removed from the firm shores of reality he and Evanthia were floating, his romantic exaltation supporting them both while she watched him with a suspicion of amazement in her eyes.

For there was a point in that period in the white stone house on the mountain side, high above the village in the quiet valley, when Evanthia herself wondered what was going to happen. She trembled for a while upon the verge of acceptance and surrender. They would go, she submitting to his command, and take that chance together which he was for ever picturing in his mind as a rush for freedom and ultimate happiness. Almost she lost that poise of spirit which enabled her to mystify and subjugate him. Almost she succumbed to the genius and beauty of the place, to the intensity of his emotions and the romantic possibilities of the future he desired to evoke. For one brief moment, so swiftly obliterated that he was hardly aware of it before it was gone, she saw herself united to him, thinking his thoughts, breathing his hopes, facing with her own high courage the terrors of life in an unknown land, for ever. He remembered it (and so did she) for many years, that one ineffable flash of supreme happiness when their spirits joined.

They had been down the steep hillside and across the Cordelio road to the shore where there stood a blue bath house built out over the water. As they had scrambled and slid among the shingle and loose boulders, the upper reaches of the mountains touched to glowing bronze by the setting sun while they were in a kind of golden twilight, there came a call from the next house and they saw a white figure at the heavy iron gate in the garden wall. And by the time they were among the houses of the village and stared at by the shy, silent housewives who were gathered about the great stone troughs of the wash house, they were joined by Esther, Evanthia's friend. And together the three of them, with towels and bathing suits, went down to the blue bath-house as the sparse lights of the city began to sparkle across the water.

Mr. Spokesly liked Esther. She traversed every one of his preconceived notions of a Jewess and of a Russian, yet she was both. She had come down from Pera with her Armenian husband, a tall, thin, dark man with a resounding and cavernous nose, who held a position in what he called the Public Debt. He had come over with her one evening and paid an extremely formal call, presenting his card, which bore the words "Public Debt" in one corner below his polysyllabic name. Mr. Spokesly liked Esther. She was a vigorous, well-knit woman of thirty, with an animated good-humoured face and capable limbs. He liked her broken English, which was uttered in a hoarse sensible voice. He liked her because she was a strong advocate of his. He heard her muttering away to Evanthia in a husky undertone and he was perfectly well aware that she was taking his part and proving to Evanthia that she would be a fool if she did not stay by him. She would talk to him alone, too, and repeat what she had said.

"You take her away," she urged. "Soon as you can. Me and my 'usban', we go to Buenos Aires soon as we can. This place no good."

"I want her to," he said. "She says yes, too."

"She say yes? She say anything. She like to fool you. I know. I tell her—you stay wis your 'usban'. Englishmen good 'usban's, eh?"

"Esther, tell me something. You think, when I say, Come, she'll come with me? You think so?"

For an instant Esther's firmly modelled and sensible features assumed an expression inexplicable to the serious man watching them. For an instant she was on the verge of telling him the truth. But Esther was empirically aware of the importance of moods in the development of truth; and she said with great heartiness: "I am tellin' you, yes! She come. I make her! But how you get away from here? You gotta wait till the war finish. And where go? Germany?"

"What for?" he had demanded with tremendous astonishment.

Esther looked at him then with some curiosity. She had all the news from Constantinople, and in the light of that news it seemed incredible to her that any one should doubt the triumph of the Central Powers. There would be nowhere else to go, in her opinion, unless one fled to America.

"Home, of course," he had said, and of a sudden had experienced an almost physical sickness of longing for the humid foggy land in the Northern Sea, the land of dark green headlands showing chalk-white below, of hedges like thick black ropes on the landscape, with sunken roads between, of little towns of gray and black stone with the dark red roofs and stumpy spires against the sky of clouds like heaps of comfortable cushions. He had been amazed at her cool suggestion that they go to Germany, and she had been amazed at him. For she had all the news from Constantinople, news that told her that the British fleets were at the bottom of the sea, that the millions in England were starving, the King fled to America, and that the great Kaiser in his palace in Berlin was setting out on his triumphal march to London to be crowned Czar of Europe. And why then should he not go to Germany? That was what she would do. She looked at him curiously as he said "Home!" not understanding, of course, the meaning of the word. She had a house, but the subtle implications of the word home, the word saturated with a thousand years of local traditions and sympathies, the word that is the invisible centre of our world, she did not comprehend. For her, patriotism was a dim and unfamiliar perplexity. She had no abstract ideas at all. She could not read very well. She personified the things in her heart. To her they were men as real as her husband and Mr. Spokesly himself. Husband, house, money, sun, moon, sea, and earth —on these concrete manifestations of existence she based an uncurious philosophy. And it must be understood that love was very much the same. Esther had none of Evanthia's untutored theatricality. She never saw herself as the Queen of Sheba or the mistress of a King. She had had a pretty hard life of it in Odessa as a child, and when she was fifteen she began to divide men into two main classes, the generous and the stingy. It never entered her head she could live without being dependent upon men. And then she made a fresh discovery, that generous men were often foolish and spent their money on women who were monsters of infidelity. Esther was faithful. Even when she was left with a baby and no money, when she was under no obligation to treat men with consideration, she remained one of those who keep their word out of an allegiance to some obscure instinct for probity. And now she was married to her Armenian, a serious creature with vague longings after Western ideas or what he imagined were Western ideas. She was conscious of both love and happiness as tangible facets of her existence. She had hold of them, and in her strong capable hands she turned them to good account. She liked Evanthia because she had that ineluctable quality of transfiguring an act into a grandiose gesture. When Esther's little boy came on Sunday to visit his mother, it was Evanthia who swooped upon him, crushed him to her bosom with an exquisitely dramatic gesture of motherhood, stroked his sleek dark head and smooth little face, and forgot all about him an hour later. Esther never did that. When she looked at her son she seemed to see through the past into the future. Her kind capable face was grave and abstracted as she watched him. She seemed to be apprehensive of their security. Her husband did not dislike the child. But if they could only get to Buenos Aires!

She came with them now and soon they were in the water racing to the end of the jetty and diving into the flickering green transparency towards the white sand bottom. He watched the two of them sometimes, while he sat on the jetty and they tried to pull each other under, noting the differences of their characters and bodies. Esther was something beyond his past experience. She had the sturdy muscular form of a strong youth and the husky voice of a man. As she climbed up towards him, the water glistening on the smooth sinewy arms and legs, and as she shook the drops from her eyes with a boyish energy and seating herself beside him accepted a cigarette, he was conscious of that delicious sensuous emotion with which a man regards the friend of his beloved without invalidating for a moment his own authentic fidelity. His love for one woman reveals to him the essential beauty of all women. And it was characteristic of Evanthia to swim back to the bath-house steps and go in to dress, leaving them there to talk for a moment.

"Say, Esther, where does your husband go every night? Why don't he come home and eat early?"

"He go to some club," she said, blowing a jet of smoke upwards. "He very fond of his club. He read plenty book, my 'usban'."

"What sort of books?"

"I don' know. Politics, Science, Philosophy. You go to that club, too. Your friend the Englishman, him with Armenian wife, he go there."

"I know he does. I was thinkin' about it. But it's a long way out here at night."

Esther laughed, a low husky chuckle, as she rose, flung away the cigarette and ran back to the bath house.

"Oh-ho! You love Evanthia too much!" she flung over her firm vigorous shoulder.

He knew by now that she meant "very much"; and as he followed her he agreed she was right. He had reached that stage when the past and the future were both obliterated by the intense vitality of existence. Only the never-ending desire to get her away into his own environment, to see her against a familiar background, held him to the plan he had worked out to get away. And it was the source of much of his irony in later, more prosperous years that he had come to see how essentially egotism and male vanity that never-ending desire happened to be. He saw the sharp cleavage, as one sees a fault in a range of cliffs at a distance, between his love and his pride. He saw that the fear in his heart was for himself all the time, lest he should not come out of the adventure with his pride entire.

But that evening he was absorbed in his emotions, saturated with the rich and coloured shadows of the valley, the tremendous loom of the mountains and the vast obscurity of the sea. And as they crossed the road he put his hand on her shoulder while Esther moved on ahead in the dusk to prepare the evening meal. And they stood for a moment in the road, facing the huge lift of the earth towards the great golden stars, silent in the oncoming darkness. They heard the deep booming bark of a watch-dog far up the valley, a sound like the clang of metal plates on earthen floors. She looked at him with a characteristic quick turn of the head, her body poised as though for flight.

"Promise you will come," he said thickly, holding to her tightly as though she were the stronger. "Can't you understand? I *must* go, and I can't go without you, leave you here. Promise!"

She watched him steadily as he said this, her eyes bright in the dusk and charged with that enigmatic expression of waiting and of knowledge beyond his imagining. It almost took her breath away at times, this consciousness of events of which he knew nothing. He wanted her to go with him to that terrible distant land where already the multitudes, starved out by the victorious Germans, were devouring their own children, even carrying their dead back in ships. . . . And he did not know.

"Promise!" he muttered, straining her to him. She looked up the dim dusty road, along which weary hearts had wandered for so many centuries, and a sudden wave of pity for him swept over her. She saw him for a moment as a pathetic and solitary being trembling upon the brink of a tragic destiny, a being who had come up out of the sea to do her bidding and who would sail out again into the chaos of tempests and war, and vanish. And it was her sudden perception of this dramatic quality in their relations that brought about the brief passionate tenderness. It was her way, to give men at the very last a perfect memory of her, to carry away with them into the shadows.

"Yes," she said gently, and her strong and vigorous body relaxed against his as he held her close. "How could you leave me here, alone? *Mon Dieu !* We will go!"

And for a moment she meant it. She meant to go. She saw herself, not in England it is true, but as the central figure in a gorgeous pageant of fidelity, a tragic queen following a beggar man into captivity in a strange land of her own bizarre imagining. They stood in the road for a while, he staring at the stars rising over the dark summits and she looking up the road into the dusk at a mysterious drama playing away in the brightness of the future. And then the moment was past, and neither of them comprehended just then how far their thoughts had gone asunder.

And she was sincere in that exclamation, when she asked how he could leave her there alone? For she was alone. The young Jew trotted to and from the town bearing fragments of news, like a faithful dog carrying things in his mouth, but he had given her nothing as yet that constituted certainty. She trembled within the circle of the arm that held her as she suddenly saw herself—alone. She must keep him there yet a little longer. And as they climbed up the gully and reached the iron gate in the garden wall, the tears started to her eyes. He saw them in the light of the lamp in the kitchen and kissed her with a fresh access of emotion. He did not imagine the cause of them. She stared at him through their brightness and smiled, her bosom heaving. She knew he would never never realize they were tears of anger, and were evoked by the perception of the helplessness of women in a world of predatory men.

But above and beyond this terrible abstract indignation

she found herself regarding him at intervals with smouldering eyes because of a certain subtle complacency in his manner. She could not know that this was the habit of years, or that men of his race are invariably complacent in the presence of their women. She could not conceive him in any rôle in which he had the right to be complacent. Yet he combined it with a tender humility that was very sweet to her in her situation out there on the hillside, playing for a hazardous stake. It was then she would look at him in stupefaction, wondering if she were going mad, and she afterwards would take the young Jew by the hair, dragging his head this way and that, and mutter between her clenched teeth: "*Mon Dieu! Je déteste les hommes!*" And he, poor youth, would assume an expression of pallid horror, for he had no idea what she was talking about, and imagined he had failed to carry out some of her imperious commands.

"Oh, Madama, what has thy servant done to deserve this?" he would whimper, less certain than ever of the solidity of his fortunes. And she would look at him, her hand dropping to her side as she gave a little laugh.

"Did I hurt you?" she would chuckle, and he would explain that she had not.

"But when Madama speaks in that strange tongue her servant is afraid he has not done his errand in the town as she desires."

"Tck! Go every day. You will find him soon."

"If Madama gave me a letter . . ."

"And some great fool of an Osmanli soldier would go through thy pockets, and lock thee up in the jail on Mount Pagos with all the other Jews. And who would write the letter? You? Can you write?"

"Very little, Madama," he muttered, trembling.

"And I cannot write at all, though I don't tell anybody. I could never learn. I read, yes; the large words in the cinemas; but not letters. Let us forget that. You have the picture?"

"Ah, Madama, it is next my heart!"

He would bring it out, unfolding a fragment of paper, and

show her a photograph about as large as a stamp, and she would glower at it for a moment.

"You are sure he is not at the Hotel Kraemer?"

"Madama, one of the maids there is of my own people, the Eskenazi, and she has assured me there is no one like the picture there. But the general will arrive in a day or two. Perhaps he is a general, Madama?" he hinted.

"He? Not even a little one! Ha—ha!" she chuckled again. "The dear fool! But hear me. He may be with the general. He may be what they call an *aide*. He may . . ." She broke off, staring hard at the youth, suddenly remembering that he might not come at all. "Go!" she ordered absently, "find him and thy fortune is made."

But the idea of a letter was attractively novel to her, and she immediately saw herself inspiring the dear fool with some of her own grandiose ideas. She even thought of sounding Esther upon the likelihood of her husband writing a letter. She stood by the window looking down into the garden where Mr. Spokesly sat smoking and gazing at the blue bowl of the gulf and the distant gray-green olive groves beyond the city. She was deliberating upon the significance of her courier's latest breathless news from the kitchen of the Hotel Kraemer. The general was arriving from the south. He and his staff had been as far as Jerusalem after the great victory over the British and were due to-morrow in the city on their way back to Constantinople. Evanthia's courage had suffered from the contradictory nature of her earlier news. It was part of her life to sift and analyze the words that ran through city and country from mouth to mouth. She had never had any real confidence in any other form of information. If she hired any one to write a letter, her words vanished into incomprehensible hieroglyphics and she had no guarantee the man did not lie. And when Amos had told her on the ship what he had heard in the Rue Voulgaróktono that they had reached Aidin, she had jumped to the conclusion that Lietherthal was with a party on their way from Constantinople to Smyrna. And now her quick brain saw the reason why they had not arrived before. He had joined the staff of the

general and had gone away south, through Kara-hissar, to
Adana and Aleppo to Damascus. And now they were on
their way back. She looked down into the garden, where
Mr. Spokesly, quietly smoking, was reflecting upon the
mystery of a woman's desires. Here, after all, she had forgotten all about that other fellow, who was probably having
a good time in Athens and who had no doubt forgotten about
her. And she was alone here, utterly dependent upon him,
who had made his plans for taking her away to a civilized
country, where he could make her happy. He smiled with
profound satisfaction as he thought of himself with her beside
him, in London. How her beauty would flash like a barbaric
jewel in that gray old city! He remembered the money she
had stowed away, ready for the great adventure. He called
it that in romantic moments, yet what was more easy than
running out after dark, with nothing fast enough to catch
him? Especially as he heard that there would be a review
in a day or so when everyone would be on their toes to see the
general. He thought of the money because even in his
romantic moments there was enough to live on for a year
"while he looked round." No more second-mate's jobs, he
muttered. He would pick and choose. He rose and stretched
luxuriously, noting the calm glitter of the city's lights like a
necklace on the bosom of the mountain. He would have to
spend an evening with that chap Marsh. Very decent fellow.
Had pressed him more than once to join them at Costi's in the
Rue Parallel. He was satisfied apparently, married to his
Armenian wife and teaching music and languages to earn a
living for a large family. Mr. Spokesly recalled a remark
made by Mr. Marsh one day at the Sports Club: "Oh!
Don't misunderstand me! For myself, as regards the war,
you know, I am a philosopher. What can we do? Ask any
fair-minded person at home, what could they do, in our
position? There's only one answer—make the best of it.
Don't misunderstand us."

And he had ventured a remark that possibly they, and the
fair-minded person at home, might misunderstand him, coming into an enemy port like that.

"Oh, no!" Mr. Marsh was untroubled by that. "You were like us, as far as I can make out. Had to make the best of it. Now your captain   . . ."

There was a fascination about the captain for Mr. Marsh. For twenty years he had lived in a sort of middle-class and inconspicuous exile, and destined, as far as he could discover, to remain for ever in the dry and unromantic regions of a middle-class existence. Nothing, he was often fond of saying to his friends, ever happened to him. The things one reads of in books! he would exclaim, with a short grunting laugh of humorous regret. Stories of fair Circassians, Balkan countesses, Turkish beauties, Armenian damsels. . . ! Where were they? He had married and settled down here, and remained twenty years in all, and yet nothing had happened. Yes, on the alert for twenty years to detect romantic developments—he had a daughter sixteen years old—and until that ship came in, not a chance! So he described it to his friends at Costi's and at the Austrian Consulate, an immense villa in a charming garden farther along in the Rue Parallel.

For somehow the arrival of that ship was a significant event in more than the accepted sense. It was reserved for Mr. Marsh to perceive the full romantic aspect of the adventure. For others it was a nine-day wonder, an official nuisance or blessing, as suited the official temperament to regard it. To Mr. Spokesly it was an exciting but secondary factor leading up to the greater adventure of departure. It was overshadowed by the more perplexing problem of explaining himself in a masterless vessel.

But Mr. Marsh, after twenty years, during which he had failed to detect anything resembling romance in his life, when he was called out of his bed at dawn that morning to go off as interpreter, saw the matter in a very different light. Indeed he saw it in the light of romance. His first comment when he found time to review his experiences was: "By Jove, you can't beat that type! We shall always rule, always!" and his bosom swelled at the thought of England. But it was his discovery of Captain Rannie which remained with him

as the great scene in the play.　He could not get it out of his
mind.　He told everybody about it.　He revealed a doubt
whether other people fully appreciated the extraordinary
experience which had been his when he went down that dark
curving stairway, "not having the faintest notion, you know,
whether I wouldn't get knocked on the head or perhaps blown
to bits," and found the door resisting his efforts.　An active
intelligent resistance! he declared, precisely as though the
man were trying to keep him out.　And as time passed and
the story developed in his own mind by the simple process of
continually repeating and brooding upon it, as an actor's part
becomes clearer to him by rendition, Mr. Marsh developed
the theory that when he first went down those stairs and
tried to get in, the resistance was in truth intelligent and
alive.

He was explaining this new and intriguing "theory," as
he called it, on the following evening when Mr. Spokesly
accompanied by the husband of Esther, who was "in the
Public Debt," entered the great room on the second floor of
the Consulate, a magnificent chamber whose windows opened
upon balconies and revealed, above the opposite roofs,
rectangles of luminous twilight.　Some half-dozen gentlemen
were seated on chairs in the dusk about one of the balconies.
As the newcomers arrived by a side door a servant came in
through the enormous curtains at the far end bearing a couple
of many-branched candlesticks and advanced towards a
table, thus revealing in some degree the elaborate design and
shabby neglect of the place.　Huge divans in scarlet satin
were ripped and battered, the gilding of the sconces was
tarnished and blackened, and the parquetry flooring, of
intricate design, was warped and loose under the advancing foot.　And above their heads, like shadowy wraiths,
hung immense candelabra whose lustres glittered mysteriously in the candlelight under their coverings of dusty
muslin.

Mr. Marsh was leaning his elbows on the balcony railing
and facing his audience as he explained his conviction that
the captain had intended to keep him out.

"I assure you," he was saying, and apparently he was directing his remarks at someone who now heard the tale for the first time; "I assure you, when I pushed the door and saw the man's shoulder, it moved. I mean it actually quivered, apart from my movement of the door. It gave me a very peculiar sensation, because when I spoke, there was no answer. Only a quiver. And another thing. When I finally did shove the door open and so shoved the captain over, the noise was not the noise of a dead inert body, if you understand me. Not at all. It sounded as though he had broken his fall somewhat! I can assure you——"

Mr. Marsh had enjoyed an excellent education in England. He had the average Englishman's faculty of expressing himself in excellent commonplaces so that every other Englishman knew exactly what he meant. But his hearers on this occasion were not all Englishmen, and suddenly out of the dusk of the corner came a voice speaking English but not of England at all. Mr. Spokesly, standing a short distance off, was startled at the full-throated brazen clang of it booming through the obscurity of the vast chamber. It was a voice eloquent of youth and impudent virile good-humour, a voice with a strange harsh under-twang which the speaker's ancestors had brought out of central Asia, where they had bawled barbaric war-songs across the frozen spaces.

"Broke his what? I don't understand what you mean," said the voice, and a fair-haired young man in a gray uniform, a short, thick golden moustache on his lip, came up suddenly out of the gloom into the radiance of the candles and began to stride to and fro. The interruption was trivial, yet it gave the key to the young man's character, courageous, cultured, precise, and impatient of inferior minds.

"His fall," explained Mr. Marsh politely. "The point is, I believe he was alive almost up to the moment, you know, of our entry. He even moved slightly as I stepped in—a sort of last gasp. I even heard something of that nature. A sigh. Good evening, gentlemen."

The last words were addressed to Mr. Spokesly and his friend in the Public Debt, who crossed the path of the young man striding up and down and were introduced to the company.

"You can corroborate what I say," said Mr. Marsh. "You know I mentioned it at the time—a sort of sigh?"

"What is a sigh, or a moment, for that matter, more or less?" demanded the young man striding up and down. "To me there is something much more important in his motive. Why did this captain of yours end himself? This is a question important to science. I am a student of Lombroso and Molle and the Englishman Ellis. Was this man epileptic? Did he have delusions of grandeur?"

"This gentleman," said Mr. Marsh, "was the officer on deck at the time," and he looked at Mr. Spokesly anxiously, as though waiting fresh details of the affair.

"Yes, he had delusions," said Mr. Spokesly, clearing his throat. "Thought everybody was against him. He took drugs too. My own idea is he took the wrong stuff or too much of it, in his excitement. He was down there in his room when we crashed. And he had another—delusion I suppose you could call it. He didn't like women."

"Didn't like . . . Well, who does?" challenged the vigorous metallic voice with a carefully modified yet resonant laugh. One or two laughs, equally modified, floated from obscure corners where cigar-ends glowed, and the animated figure paused in its rapid movement. "I mean, no man likes women as they are unless he is a true sensualist. What we aspire to is the ideal they represent. Your captain must have been a sensualist."

"Because his last breath was a sigh, you mean?" said Mr. Marsh. "I heard it you know. A long-drawn gasp."

"Precisely. The sigh of a sensualist leaving the world of the senses."

Mr. Spokesly stared at Mr. Marsh incredulously.

"I don't think you are 'right,'" he remarked, lighting a fresh cigarette. "The captain was not that sort of man. He was timid, I admit. He was scared of losing his life."

"Who isn't?" demanded the young man and was beginning another resonant laugh when Mr. Spokesly broke in.

"A good many people," he said sharply, "under the right conditions. Nobody *wants* to get killed, we know. But that does not mean they wouldn't take a risk."

"Well, didn't your captain take the risk?" said Mr. Marsh eagerly. "That was just what . . ."

"He did but he always wore one of these inflating things," said Mr. Spokesly quietly. "Vests you blow up when you want them. We had a collision, as you know, and he had it on then. And when he heard us crash I've no doubt he began to inflate it again."

"Then there is no use supposing he committed suicide," said a voice. "That would be absurd."

"Not altogether," replied Mr. Spokesly. "I don't know whether you gentlemen will think I am a bit mad for saying it, but after knowing him, it's quite possible he took something to kill himself and then tried to save himself from being drowned. There's a lot of difference between being dragged under in a sinking ship, and gradually getting sleepy and stiff in comfort, and don't you forget it. Humph!"

There was a silence for a moment when he ceased speaking, as though he had propounded some new and incontrovertible doctrine of philosophy. The young man who was walking up and down, almost vanishing in the gloom down near the great smoke-coloured velvet curtains, halted and looked interrogatively at Mr. Spokesly.

"But you have not explained why he should kill himself at all," he said. "A man as you say scared of losing his life."

"Well," said Mr. Spokesly slowly. "He may have seen himself. . . . I mean he may have realized he had lost his life already, as you might say."

"How, how?" demanded the young man, very much interested. "What do you mean by already?"

"You might call it that," muttered Mr. Spokesly, "with his ideas about women. Couldn't bear to talk about them. And he didn't like men much better. So I say he'd lost his life already. Nothing to live for, if a man hates women. And he did. That's one thing I am sure about."

"You are a psychologist," said the young man, very much amused. "You believe in the inspiration of love."

"Naturally," said Mr. Spokesly. "A man believes in what he understands."

The young man nodded and turned away with the slight smile of one who realizes he is dealing with a person of limited intelligence.

"You mean we believe in what we have cognition of," he amended in a harsh tone. "No doubt you are right. But your captain may have had beliefs and fidelities beyond your cognition. Perhaps he saw, suddenly, as in a flash, you understand, the ultimate futility of existence. He might. Englishmen don't as a rule. But if he had lived in the East a long while, he might."

"But surely you don't advance that as a tenable hypothesis," exclaimed Mr. Marsh. This man, who had contrived to retain the illusions and metaphysics of the comfortably fixed classes of England amid the magnificent scenery and human squalor of Ottoman life, was frankly appalled by the young man's ferocious gaiety while he advanced what he called his theory of philosophic nihilism. That was the disconcerting feature of the affair. This Herr Leutnant Lietherthal actually spoke with pleasure of a time when humanity should have ceased to exist! Mr. Marsh would almost have preferred a technical enemy to desire the extinction of Englishmen. It was more logical, and he said as much as they adjourned to a smaller room to supper.

"Oh, don't I?" exclaimed the Herr Leutnant, holding up his glass of Kümmel. That was his way of being revenged upon the country where he had lived many happy years. At Oxford, whither the munificence of Rhodes brought him, his sensuous mind had delighted in the apparently opposed but really identical studies of philosophy and philology. Following the example of his tutor at Leipzig, he had often neglected classrooms in his studies in English, and gone into the slums of great towns and on the dock-sides of London and Liverpool for idioms. And he got them. "Oh, don't I?" he exclaimed, laughing, and added: "I go the whole hog, my

friend." And only that subtle under-twang, that strong
humming of the vocal chords in his vowels remained to detect
him. He was addicted to saying that he had discovered the
secret of the English power, which was, he announced, their
mongrel origin. "A nation of mongrels who think of nothing
but thoroughbred horses and dogs," he had described them
to Evanthia, who could not possibly gauge the accuracy of
the sentence. Just now, as he set down his glass, he added
that he went "the whole hog, my friend, as your graceful
English expresses it." And then, in reply to Mr. Marsh's
shocked comment, he said:

"Why? It would be of no advantage to desire the extinction of any white race. This affair is only a family
squabble. But it is a symptom. You may be watching
now the first convulsions of the disease by which Europe will
die. Europe is dying. The war, the war is only a superficial
disturbance. The trouble is deeper than the mud of Flanders, my friend. Europe is dying because her inspiration, her
ideals, are gone. That is what I mean when I say Europe
will die. The old fidelities are departing. And when they
are all dead, and Europe is a vast cesspool of republicans
engaged in mutual extermination, what will happen then, do
you think?"

"Why do you talk that mad stuff here?" grunted one of
the guests, a quiet middle-aged person with a monocle. He
spoke in German, and Lietherthal answered quickly:

"What difference, Oscar? They don't believe me."

"What will happen, I ask you?" he continued in a vibrating tone. "When we have destroyed ourselves, and the
survivors of our civilization are creeping feebly about the
country, going back little by little to the agricultural age,
the yellow men from Asia and the blacks from Africa will
come pouring into Europe. Millions of them. They will
infest the skeletons of our civilizations like swarms of black
and yellow maggots in the sepulchres of kings. And in the
end humanity will cease to exist. Civilization will be dead
but there will be nobody to bury her," he concluded, smiling.
"Europe will be full of the odours of her dissolution."

"I cannot believe," said Mr. Marsh with energy, "that any one would seriously entertain such wild ideas. They imply the negation of all the things we hold dear. I should commit suicide at once if I thought for a single moment such an outcome was possible."

"Perhaps your captain had such a moment," suggested the young man, busily eating fish. "Perhaps he saw, as I said, the futility of existence."

"And you really believe there is no hope?"

"Hope!" echoed Lietherthal with a brazen-throated laugh. "Hear the Englishman crying for his hope! By what right or rule of logic can we demand an inexhaustible supply of hope, especially packed in hundredweight crates for export to the British Colonies? Hope! The finest brand on the market! Will not spoil in the tropics! Stow away from boilers! Use no hooks! That's all an Englishman thinks of if you ask him to consider a scientific question. Doctor, is there any hope? Hope for himself, not for anybody else."

There was a murmur of laughter at this, a murmur in which even Mr. Marsh joined, for he "could see a joke" as he often admitted. And as the meal progressed and the excellent red wine passed, the young man revealed a nimble mind, like quicksilver rather than firm polished metal, which ran easily over the whole surface of life and entertained them with the aptness and scandalous candour of its expression. To most of them, men like Esther's husband, Mr. Jokanian, who had absorbed European ideas through books, so that they had fermented within him in a black froth of pessimism and socialistic bubbles, he was a blond angel from heaven. "A man of remarkable ideas," he observed to Mr. Spokesly, who nodded.

"Remarkable is right," he muttered. He found himself withdrawing instinctively from the highly charged intellectual atmosphere of this community. As he ate his supper and drank the wine, he allowed his mind to return to his own more immediate affairs. It might very well be that civilization and even humanity would die out, but the urgency of the problem was not apparent to a man about to go out on a hazardous adventure with the woman he loved. Only that day he had worked with Mr. Cassar, the engineer, who had been making a silencer for the motor. Not that Mr. Spokesly was going to depend upon that. He had a mast and a sail, for he knew the wind was off shore and easterly during the night, and he could save his engine for the time when they had made the outer arm of the Gulf. Mr. Cassar agreed because he thought they might be short of gasolene in spite of the carefully stored supply. For Mr. Cassar had decided to go with his commander. It had been borne in upon Mr. Cassar that the family in Cospicua, for whom he was industriously providing, might perish of starvation while he grew rich beyond the dreams of avarice, if he could not send them any money—as he obviously could not so long as he remained where he was. Mr. Cassar was not at all clear as to the causes and extent of the war. All he knew was that he now earned more money, and he naturally hoped it would go on as long as possible. But he also knew enough of war to realize the limits set upon enterprise, just as at sea one had to submit to the ways of the elements. And he had inherited a placid contempt for everything Ottoman, which minimized in his mind the difficulties of departure. And it may have been also a sudden desire to see his wife in Cospicua. She had written him, in a mixture of Maltese and Italian, with many corrections and blots, which had caused the literary-minded censor in Saloniki much trouble, thinking they concealed a cipher; and she had implored him to come back to Valletta and get work in the dockyard. Then they could have a house in Senglea and the children could go to a better school. This was doubtless the underlying thought in Mr. Cassar's mind when he decided to go along with Mr. Spokesly. And Mr. Spokesly, before going over to the office of the Public Debt, to find Mr. Jokanian, had mentioned that he would be going back rather late to Bairakli.

He sat now, the wine stimulating his mind to unwonted activity, listening to the clever conversation of the blond young man. Mr. Spokesly was quite prepared to admire him. It was, he reflected, very wonderful how these chaps learned languages. He wished he could speak these lingos. Here they were, German, Austrian, Armenian, Jew, all speaking English. After all, there lay the triumph. As Mr. Marsh said, you couldn't beat that type. "We" went everywhere and all men adopted "our" language and "our" ideas. He heard the Herr Leutnant's tones as he told Mr. Marsh that he himself admired the English. He had lived among them for years. At one time was engaged to marry an *Engländerinn*. And his conclusion was that they had nothing to fear from any other nation. Their true enemies were within. The hitherto impregnable solidarity of the race was disintegrating. Mr. Spokesly was not clear what this signified. He knew it sounded like the stuff these clever foreigners were always thinking up. When all was said and done, they were all out to do the best they could for themselves. There was Marsh, living as calm as you please in Ottoman territory and making a very decent income in various ways. And there was a young fellow over there, with rich auburn hair flung back from a fine reddish forehead, who had been pointed out to him as the son of a rich old boy who had been there all his life as a Turkey merchant, with great estates and a grand house at Boudja where they were to hold a magnificent garden party to welcome the old General on his arrival from a tour of inspection in Syria. Mr. Spokesly had heard, too, of the way money was made just now, and he smiled at the simplicity of it. There was the material in the cargo of the *Kalkis*, hardware and flour and gasolene. A pretty rake-off some of these intellectual Europeans had made out of that in what they called transportation charges. And there was the Ottoman Public Debt they had taken up, paying for it in paper and getting the interest in gold. They were doing the best they could under the circumstances. He saw their point of view well enough. He himself had another problem. He had to get out of it. Mr. Spokesly, as he walked about that shining Levantine city, as he passed down those narrow tortuous streets into bazaars reeking with the strange odours of Asiatic life, as he watched the slow oblivious life of the poor, and the sullen furtiveness of the

Greek storekeepers and shabby French bourgeoisie waiting in line at the custom house for a chance to buy their morsels of food, saw with penetrating clarity how impossible it would be for him to remain, even if he did get a permanent harbour-master's job. No! He finished his glass of wine and looked round for the decanter. He saw that these people here, for all their intellectual superiority, their fluent social accomplishments, their familiarity with philosophical compromises, were simply evading the facts. They were variants of Mr. Jokanian, who was also reaching regularly for the decanter, and who was attempting to forget a national failure in high-sounding poppycock about the autocracy of the proletariat. Mr. Marsh was proud of being an Englishman, in a well-bred way, for he was always insisting "you could not beat that type"; but what was his idea of an Englishman?

A person who, strictly speaking, no longer existed. Mr. Marsh was fortunate in having his ideals and illusions preserved in the dry air of the Levant as in a hermetically sealed chamber. The type he spoke of was being very handsomely beaten in all directions and was being rescued from utter annihilation by a very different type—the mechanical engineer, who was no doubt preparing the world for a fresh advance upon its ultimate destruction. Mr. Spokesly, in a rich glow of exaltation, saw these vast and vague ideas parade in his mind as he listened abstractedly to the conversation. But as the wine passed, that cosmic quality passed, too, and he began to hear other things besides theories of evolution. He heard someone remark that they had a very fine piano, a Bechstein grand. Some consul had brought it from Vienna for his musical daughter. But it was impossible to take it with them when he was transferred to Teheran. Another voice desired to know what was done with the musical daughter, and amid laughter they began to push their chairs back, lighting cigarettes and lifting liqueurs to carry them to another room.

Looking down into a courtyard which contained, amid much rank vegetation, an empty marble basin surmounted by a one-legged Diana with a broken bow, and a motor car with only three wheels and no engine, Mr. Spokesly leaned out to watch the moon setting over the dark masses of the neighbouring roofs. Behind him the Bechstein grand was surrounded by some half-dozen gentlemen explaining their preferences, laughing, whistling a few notes, and breaking into polite cries of wonder. Suddenly there was a silence, and Mr. Marsh, seated at the instrument and running his hands over the keys in a highly versatile fashion, began "John Peel" in a high thin tenor that sounded as though it came from behind the neighbouring mountain. Thin yet sweet, so that the peculiar sentiment of the song, dedicated "to that type" which Mr. Marsh so much admired, reached Mr. Spokesly as he leaned out and noted the sharp, slender black shapes of the cypresses silhouetted against the dark blue vault of the sky with its incredibly brilliant stars. He smiled and reflected that the moon would be gone in a couple of hours, a red globe over Cordelio. In a few nights it would set before night-fall. He drank his liqueur. A moonless night and he would be away from all this. He wished he were back at Bairakli now. He grudged every moment away from her. He had caught her making little preparations of her own, and when he had chaffed her she had looked at him in an enigmatic way with her bright amber eyes, her beautiful lips closed, and gently inhaling through her nostrils. What an amazing creature she was! He would sit and watch her in the house, entranced, oblivious of time or destiny. He wished Mrs. Dainopoulos could know of his happiness. He never suspected that when Mrs. Dainopoulos at length heard of this episode, it was expressed in a single shrug of the shoulders and a faint vanishing smile. The song ended with a tinkle:

"*Oh, I ken John Peel, from my bed where I lay,
      As he passed with his hounds in the morning!*"

and there was a murmur of applause. Mr. Spokesly, looking out into the darkness, clapped and lit another cigarette. He was startled by a great crash of chords. The young man, a cigar in his teeth, his head enveloped in a blue cloud of smoke, was seated at the piano. Mr. Spokesly turned and watched him. Mr. Marsh came over to the window, smiling.

"D'you do anything?" he asked. "We should be delighted, you know, if you would. It relieves the tension, don't you think?"

"Not in my line, I'm afraid," said Mr. Spokesly. "I never had any accomplishments."

He stood listening to the full, rounded, clangorous voice, toned down to Heine's beautiful words:

> *"Die Luft ist kühl und dunkelt,*
> *Und ruhig fliesst der Rhein,*
> *Der Gipfel des Berges funkelt*
> *Im Abend Sonnenschein."*

"Wonderful voice," whispered Mr. Marsh. "Studied at Leipzig. Rather a talented chap, don't you think? By the way, I heard to-night they intend making an inspection of the outer harbour while they are here. Improving the defences. They don't want any more ships to come in the way you did. Of course it was luck as well as pluck. Probably lay fresh mines."

"Is that a fact?" asked Mr. Spokesly. As in a dream he heard the applause, himself clapping mechanically and then the booming of bass chords. And a voice like a silver trumpet, triumphant and vibrating, blared out the deathless call of the lover to his beloved:

> *"Isolde! Geliebte! Bist du mein?*
> *Hab ich dich wieder?"*

"Well it's pretty reliable. A friend of mine who is in the timber trade—got a saw mill up at Menenen and uses horses —has been given a contract to bring down a lot of stones to the harbour. Fill all those lighters, you know. That'll mean quite a lot of work for you, eh?"

Mr. Spokesly turned resolutely to the window and looked

out over the dark roofs at the lustrous and spangled dome of the sky. He would have to find Cassar and give him some instructions at once. It would be impossible to get away if they waited for a swarm of workmen and officials to come down and be for ever sailing up and down the Gulf. He ought to have thought of such a contingency. He must find Cassar. And then he must get back to Evanthia and tell her they must go at once. To-morrow night. He heard the heavy stamp of feet that greeted the end of the song and joined in without thinking. As he walked across to the door Mr. Marsh followed him, and Mr. Jokanian, his dark yearning eyes brilliant with the wine he had drunk, came over making gestures of protestation as another voice rose from behind the grand piano:

> *"Enfant, si j'étais Roi, je donnerais l'empire,*
> *Et mon char, et mon sceptre, et mes peuples à genoux,*
> *Et mon couronne d'or, et mes bains de porphyre."*

"I am coming back," said Mr. Spokesly, "but I must see if my boat is ready."

"You don't need any boat," said Mr. Jokanian. "We are going back in my carriage. Mr. Lietherthal goes with us. I have invited him."

"Pour un regard de vous !" sang the voice, and trembled into a passionate intricacy of arpeggios.

"I shall not be long," he repeated. "I must tell my man I sha'n't need it, in that case."

He felt he must get out of there at once, if only for a moment. This combination of wine and music was becoming too much for him. As he came out into the courtyard he heard Victor Hugo's superb challenge ring out:

> *"Enfant, si j'étais Dieu, je donnerais le Ciel !"*

He walked quickly along in the profound shadow of the Rue Parallel until he reached the great doors of the Passage Kraemer. Here he might have seen, had he been watchful, in a corner by the disused elevator of the hotel, the young Jew talking to a girl in cap and apron. The youth saw him and clutched his companion's arm.

"Madama's husband," he whispered. "The Englishman."

"Well," said the girl, bending her dark brows upon the figure hurrying out upon the quay, "I think your Madama is a fool."

"S-sh!" whimpered the young man. "She is the most glorious creature in the world."

"And a fool," repeated the girl. "That other upstairs in Suite Fourteen will desert her in a month. I know his style. He only left the last one in Kara-hissar, so his servant told us. I know if *I* had a chance of marrying an Englishman . . . Yes! She has got you anyhow," she added, laughing. "You are like a cony in love with a snake."

He put up his hand in warning, as though he feared by some occult power Madama would hear these rash and sacrilegious words. He took out a tiny piece of paper and looked at it.

"I must go," he said. "You are certain it is this Frank, who has come?" he urged anxiously.

"Yes," she said, smiling contemptuously. "When I passed him in the corridor, he put his arm round me and said he would love me for ever. You can tell your Madama if you like."

Mr. Spokesly, unaware of this conversation, made his way out, and was on the point of crossing the quay by the custom house when Mr. Cassar, who was drinking a glass of syrup at the café opposite, ran over and accosted him.

"Look here——" began Mr. Spokesly.

"I know," interrupted the engineer. "I've heard something else. Don't go over there now. I want to tell you this. Very important, Captain. Will you have a drink?"

"Coffee," said Mr. Spokesly, sitting at a table in front of a small café. "What is it?"

"I was working on the boat this afternoon, after you had been there," said Mr. Cassar, "and I got that silencer pretty good now, and some officers come up and say, this boat very good, we will want it. They make inspection of harbour, you understand. I say, all right, what time? They say to-morrow. The General he go round and make inspection. Want all three motor boats. I say all right. But I was waiting to see you. If I miss you I was going out to find you at your house. You understand?"

Mr. Spokesly nodded. He understood perfectly well. He reflected upon the wisdom of staying away from the Consulate after saying he would go back. He decided it would be better to return.

"You will have to get off," said Mr. Cassar in a matter-of-fact tone as he looked away towards the mountains. "Don't you think so, Captain?"

"Plenty of time," Mr. Spokesly muttered, "before daylight. Are you sure you are all right? Got everything?"

"Yes, everything," said Mr. Cassar positively.

"Right," said his commander. "Now you tell the customs guard I return to Bairakli at midnight. You go with me to bring the boat back as they want it in the morning. And if I don't come before one o'clock, you go alone. I shall be going by road. Some of them asked me to go with them. You go alone and wait for me at the bath-house jetty. Can you remember that?"

"Easy," said Mr. Cassar. "It is ten o'clock now."

"I'll go back," said Mr. Spokesly.

The evening was just beginning along the front as he passed once again through the great Passage beneath the hotel. There was no young Jew watching him now. That highly strung and bewildered creature was hurrying through the lower town on his way to Bairakli, bearing authentic news for his mistress. He had an uneasy suspicion that the person described by his friend in the hotel would not prove so good a friend as Mr. Spokesly. But he hurried on past the little Turkish shops, his fez on the back of his head, the lamplight reflected on the bony ridge of the large glistening nose that rose up between his scared pale eyes and sallow cheeks. All along the lonely road beyond the railway station he tripped and stumbled, muttering to himself: "Oh, Madama, he is come, he is come! I bring great news. He is come!" Sometimes he clasped his hands in an ecstasy of emotion and would almost fall into some unnoticed slough or channel by the way. All the griefs of the poor seemed to concentrate themselves upon him as he moaned and staggered. "Father of Israel, what shall I do if she abandon me? There is no food for a fatherless boy here. Oh, Madama!"

But when at length he scrambled up to the house on the hillside and saw his mistress and Esther Jokanian sitting in the window overlooking the sea, he took heart again. When Evanthia, leaning out in a loose robe that showed transparent against the lamp behind her, called, "Who is there?" he replied that it was her faithful servant with news. She came down like a swiftly moving phantom and unlocked the gate, pulling it wide with her characteristic energy and courage.

"Speak!" she said in a thrilling, dramatic whisper, all her soul responding to the moment. The youth held out his hand palm upward while he leaned his head against the rough wall.

"Oh, Madama, he is come," he replied in a low tone, as though he sensed the formidable importance of his words in their lives. She stood staring at him for a second and then, pulling him in, she closed the gate with a tremendous clang that jarred the very foundation of his reason. It was at times like these that this young man, born into a chaotic world of alien beings intent upon inexplicable courses of action, inspired by unknown and possibly sinister ideals, was upon the point of dashing his head with maniac energy against those heavy ancient stones which, by comparison, seemed less foreign to his distracted soul.

"Come," she said with a mysterious smile. "Your fortune is made. You must go back with a message."

"Oh, Madama!" he wailed.

She dragged him up the steps leading to the rooms above.

"Endlich!" she cried to Esther, who sat by the window, chin on hand, and muttering in her husky man's voice. "He is here. I must have been born with good fortune after all."

"You are throwing away the greatest chance in your life," growled Esther without looking at her. The young man gave a stifled yelp and choked, holding his arms out as though in supplication. They looked at him, but he could not proceed. His courage failed as his exacerbated imagination pictured the tigerish glare in Evanthia's eyes if he should tell her about the last one that was left at Kara-hissar. He put a hand to his throat and mumbled: "The message, Madama? It is late."

"You do not understand," said Evanthia crossly to her friend. "What do you think I am made of? Do you think I can go on for ever like this, pretending love? Men! I use them, my friend. The lover of my heart is here, and you ask me to go out on that cursed water to a country where it is dark wet fog all the time. What should I do there? My God, are you mad? Now I shall go to Europe, and for once I shall live. Ah! The message! Here!" She dragged a blank page from a yellow paper-covered volume lying on a cedar-wood console and hunted for a pencil. With a fragment of black crayon she began to scrawl her name in staggering capitals. "So!" she muttered. "Now I shall put the words *liebe dich*. Sacré! When I go to Europe I will learn this writing—or have a secretary. There! It is enough for my dear lunatic. Take it!" She folded it and gave it to the youth who stood by the door dejectedly. "Ask for the Herr Leutnant Lietherthal. Go down and eat first." She gave him a pat on the shoulder that seemed to put a fresh stream of life into him, and he disappeared.

"Take care, Esther, do not tell him a word of this. Or thy husband either. He might speak in forgetfulness."

"It is nothing to me," muttered Esther. "I like him, that is all. And fidelity is best."

"Fidelity!" said Evanthia slowly. "And is not this fidelity? Have I not followed the lover of my heart across the world? If the father of thy boy came up here and knocked at the gate . . . You talk! I am not a white-faced Frank girl to be a slave of an Englishman! He gives me all his money here, yes. But in his England, when I am shut up in the fog and rain, how much will I get, *hein ?*" her voice rose to a shout, a brazen clangour of the throat, and her hand shot out before her, clenched, as though she were about to hurl thunderbolts.

"Very well," assented Esther in a low tone, "but you don't know if the lover of your heart wants you any more. The lovers of the heart are funny fish," she added grimly.

"Prrtt! You are right," said Evanthia in an ordinary tone. "Did I say I was going away to-night, stupid?"

"I see the light of the boat," said Esther. "Perhaps my husband is with him. I must go back to my house."

"No! Stay here a little." Evanthia laid hold of her. "To-night I must have someone with me. I am shaken in my mind. I shall want to shriek. Stay."

"It is at the jetty," said Esther soberly. She looked out into a dense darkness, and in the lower distance she could see a tiny light where the launch had run alongside the old bath-house jetty. And then the light went out.

They waited in silence, smoking cigarettes, until their quick ears caught the sound of footsteps on the hillside. And then the grind of a key in the great lock of the gate.

As Mr. Spokesly came into the room he barely sensed the tension of the atmosphere. He broke breathlessly into his news at once.

"Quick!" he said in a low tone. "We must go to-night, dear. After to-night I may not have any boat. It is all ready. Come now. We have time to get out of sight of land before daylight."

"To-night!" exclaimed Evanthia, clutching her breast, and thinking rapidly. "Impossible."

"It will be impossible any other night," he retorted gently. "We *must* go."

Evanthia backed away, thinking clearly, concisely, and skilfully behind her astonishment. He turned to Esther.

"You tell her," he said. "We must go. It is our last chance. It was lucky I heard about it. They are going to fortify the Gulf. Go and get ready, dear. Bring me a blanket and I'll carry it down, and some bread and meat. Enough for a day, anyhow."

"Where is my 'usband'?" demanded Esther.

"He's coming by the road. He's got some friends with him, from the hotel. You mustn't mind them being a bit elevated. Plenty of wine to-night. They will be here soon, I expect. I want to get down and away before they arrive."

Evanthia, folding a blanket in the bedroom, stood perfectly still. She could hear her own pulses thumping, and she put her hand to her throat. She felt as though her heart would burst if she did not gain control of herself. She stood perfectly still thinking, her mind darting this way and that, as a trapped animal tests the resistance of the trap in every direction. For a moment she thought of killing him as they went down to the boat. She was strong: she felt she could do it. Under the shoulder-blades and in the throat. No, she must wait. Only as a last resource, that. She folded up the blanket and walked back into the room to give him the food.

He stood for a moment with the blanket and loaves of bread in his arms, unable to utter what he felt for her sacrifice for him. He could only say stumblingly:

"I sha'n't forget this. I know that much," and hurried away with his burden.

Esther sprang up from her seat by the window. Her misfortunes had not made her hard. She saw a light in Evanthia's amber eyes as she made her preparations, a light that frightened her.

"Nobody will ever be able to do anything with you," she muttered. "I must go home to get supper for my husband. You got a good man, and you throw him away like so much rubbish. You got no sense."

"I go!" said Evanthia, pausing with her hands full of things she was stuffing into a bag. "Do I not go?"

"You go!" said Esther savagely. "You make him take you to the town to see your fellow."

"Oh!" exclaimed Evanthia, stopping again and stifling a laugh. She had not thought of such a thing. "What you must think of me!" she murmured.

"And then tell him you are finished. You have a heart, yes, as big as that ring on your finger. You take everything from him, and now you . . ."

With a sudden gesture of rage the girl flung the things away and stood up to her friend.

"I'll kill you!" she growled through her teeth. "I know you! You are jealous, jealous, jealous! I see you talk, talk English to him at the bath-house. I see you go out with him for the walk through the village. I hear you talk to him about that girl Vera he saw once in Odessa. All right! Go with him! Go! Here are the things. Take them! I spit at you. You . . ."

She fell back, exhausted with the ferocity of her passion, her hands still making gestures of dismissal to the silent and scornful Esther who remained motionless yet alert, ready to take her own part.

"You are altogether mad!" she said at last in her husky tones. "Here is your husband. Tell him, tell him. . . ."

Evanthia spun round where she stood with her hands on her bosom.

"We must go, dear," said Mr. Spokesly and paused in astonishment at the scene. With a convulsive movement the girl tore at her dress and then flung out her hand towards the shore.

"Go then, go! Why do you come here any more? You want her. There she is, jealous because all the men want me. Look at her. She ask you with her eyes. Oh, yah! I hate you! I never love you. It is finish. Go!"

"Eh!" he called, swallowing hard. He looked at Esther in amazement. "What is this?" he asked. "What have you said to her? My dear!"

"You better go," said Esther sullenly. "She won't go with you. Can't you see?"

"But how can I go without her?" he exclaimed.

"I kill myself before I go. This is my place. Go back, you. I hate you."

Esther came over to him and, taking up the satchel, thrust him out before her. Down the steps and across the dark garden she went with him, and only when the great gate clanged did he make an effort to break through the dreadful paralysis of mind that had assailed him.

"What made her go on like that?" he demanded drearily.

"Go on. I tell you in a minute. You men, you got no sense."

"But what did she mean, about you?"

"Nothing. She's crazy. You no understand."

"You said yourself she'd come," he insisted.

"Yes, I *say* so. I tell her she better come. But you no understand women."

He was destined to find out, as years went by, that this was true. And when they stood on the jetty and looked down into the obscurity where Mr. Cassar sat in the boat patiently awaiting his passengers, Mr. Spokesly began to regain command of himself. For a moment, up there, he had been all abroad. The sudden emotional upheaval hardened his resolve.

"Well!" he said with a sudden intake of breath, and paused, once more overwhelmed by the change in his affairs. "I don't know what to say, Esther." He put his hand on her shoulder and she twisted away a little. "I feel as if I'd been having a long dream, and just woke up."

"Go!" she said huskily. "Good-bye. Good fortune. There is a carriage coming. My 'usban'."

"Anyhow . . . Esther. I did what I promised her to do . . . not my fault." He got down into the boat "Where's your hand? Good-bye . . . good-bye. . . . Push off, son, push off. . . . After all I done. . . ."

They saw, from a little way off, the white form of Esther spring forward and vanish behind the buildings as a feeble yellow flicker from a carriage lamp crawled slowly along the road and stopped. They heard laughter and confused arguments.

"Drunk!" whispered Mr. Cassar without either envy or malice.

"Full to the guards," assented his commander. "Hark!"

Someone was singing, a full youthful voice of brazen

vibrant quality, a voice with an ineluctable and derisive challenge to confident hearts. Though he did not understand the words, Mr. Spokesly was aware of this challenge as he listened:

> *"Auf, deutsches Volk, du stark Geschlecht*
> *Es schlug die grosse Stunde,*
> *Steh auf und sei nicht länger Knecht*
> *Mit Kraft und mut steh für dein Recht*
> *Im heilgen Volke bunde!"*

There was a pause, with protests and guttural amusement which were suddenly engulfed in a clarion shout:

> *"Die Freiheit bricht die Ketten!"*

"Go ahead," said Mr. Spokesly, looking back as he sat in the stern, "and make as little noise as you can."

Out of the darkness came the faint clarion call he had already heard that night:

> *"Isolde! Geliebte! Bist du mein?"*

and the sound, with its echoes from the mountain, seemed to stream out of that open window he had left. Suddenly, with a resolute movement, he turned and bent to the business of steering. The boat was moving through the water.

"Let her out," he muttered, looking at his watch. "We've got four hours to daylight."

And the dawn found him there, still crouching motionless at the tiller, while behind them the mountains of Lesbos rose enormous, the sun rising over Asia. And ahead lay the dark sparkle of an empty sea.

CONCLUSION

A LL I can say is," said the elderly lieutenant, and he
applied himself assiduously to the trimming of his
nails, "you were in luck all through."

"Yes," said Mr. Spokesly. "I suppose you can call it
that."

He was not entirely satisfied that this constituted an adequate description of his experiences. Luck is a slippery
word. As witness the old lieutenant, intent on his nails, like
some red-nosed old animal engaged in furbishing his claws,
who proceeded without looking up:

"Why, what else could you call it? You surely didn't
want that woman hanging round your neck all your life like a
millstone, did you? What if she did keep hold of the money?
I call it cheap at the price. And suppose you'd brought her.
How could you have squared things? *I* call it lucky."

Mr. Spokesly, however, did not feel that way. He looked
round at the green expanse of St. James's Park and up towards
the enormous arch which enshrines the dignity and cumbrous
power of the Victorian Age, and wondered if the taste of life
would ever come back. It was now eighteen months since
he had experienced what the elderly lieutenant called un-
common luck, when a sloop of war, hurrying on her regular
patrol from Lemnos to Malta had found him and Mr. Cassar
in their boat some ten miles east of Psara Island, a black
spot on a blue sea, over which there fluttered a patch of white.
And on coming cautiously alongside, the commander of that
sloop was surprised to discover a Maltee engineer somewhat in
disarray through his struggles with his engine, and under a
blanket in the bilge forward a sick Englishman.

For Mr. Spokesly had been sick. Looking back at it from
this seat in St. James's Park, with his demobilization com-

pleted, he saw well enough that the culmination of the spiritual stresses under which he had been existing had been suddenly transmuted into a bodily collapse. As the sun rose over the Ægean, he had given the tiller to Mr. Cassar and lain down without a word. He had not cared whether he ever got up or not. He lay staring up at the extraordinary brilliance of the sky, his throat very sore, his eyes tired and smarting, a feverish tremor in his limbs, refusing food, and even when the engine stopped, giving no sign that he was aware of any change in their fortunes. It had only been when Mr. Cassar informed him of the sloop bearing down upon them that he rose on an elbow and croaked hoarsely: "Show a white flag; handkerchief or something," and fell back, drawing the blanket over himself. He had been very sick. The surgeon, without waiting for a temperature reading, had carried him away into an extremely hygienic sickbay, where between a boy with tonsillitis and a stoker with a burnt arm, he had lain all the way to Malta. And after that, during weeks of dreary waiting, he had looked out of the high windows of the Bighi Hospital across the Harbour to Valletta, watching the ships go in and out, and seeing the great flame of the sunset show up the battlements of the Lower Barracca and die in purple glory behind the domes and turrets of the city.

For it seemed to him, in his intervals of lucid reflection, that the taste of life had gone, not to return. It had gone, and in place of it was an exceedingly bitter flavour of humiliation and frustrated dreams. It was almost too sudden a revelation of his own emotional folly for any feeling save a numb wonder to remain. He had told Esther that he felt as though he had had a long dream and was suddenly woke up. And while this was true enough of his mind, which maintained a dreary alertness during his sickness, his heart on the other hand was in a condition of stupor and oblivious repose. Even when sufficiently recovered to walk abroad and sit at the little tables in the arcades by the Libreria, or to journey across the Marsamuscetto to Sliema and follow the long smooth white beach, he moved slowly because he had no accurate means of gauging his intensity of existence. He would mutter to himself in a sort of depressed whisper: "What's the matter with me, I wonder?"

The surgeons had called it something ending in osis and prescribed finally "light duty." He remembered that light duty now well enough; a commission as lieutenant and the visiting of many offices in the formidable buildings which constituted the dockyard. And gradually, as the scope and meaning of this work became apparent, he found a certain interest returning, an anticipation of the next week and perhaps month. But of the years he did not dare to think just yet.

Because, once established there, he had sought, as a homing pigeon its cotes, to find Ada. He had written, full of weariness and a sort of gentle contrition, and implored her to write. He had missed all the mails since the *Tanganyika* had gone—she must make allowances for the hazards of the sea, and try again. He had put a shy, boyish postscript to it, a genuine afterthought—"I want so much to see you again," and mailed it on the Marseilles boat.

To that there had come nothing in reply save a letter from her married sister, who evaded the subject for three pages and finally explained that her own husband was missing and Ada was married. The paper had distinctly said all were lost on the *Tanganyika*. Ada's husband was a manufacturer of munitions in the Midlands, making a colossal income, she believed. They lived in a magnificent old mansion in the West Riding. The writer of the letter was going up to spend a week with them and would be sure to mention him. She had already sent on his letter and Ada had asked her to write.

There it was, then. Both ends of the cord on which he had been precariously balanced had been cut down, and he had had no interior buoyancy which could have kept him from hitting the earth with conclusive violence. And near the earth for a long time he had remained, very much in doubt whether he would ever go about again with the old confidence. Possibly he would never have done so, had not an accident sent him out to sea on patrol service. Here came relief in the shape of that active enemy he had preferred to his bureaucratic and scornful government. Here was an invisible and tireless adversary, waiting days, weeks, and possibly months for his chance, and smashing home at last with horrible thoroughness. This, in Mr. Spokesly's present condition, was a tonic. He got finally into a strange, shuttle-like contraption with twin gasolene-engines, a pop-gun, and a crew of six. They went out in this water-roach and performed a number of deeds which were eventually incorporated in official reports and extracted by inaccurate special correspondents whose duty it was to explain naval occasions to beleaguered England, an England whose neglect of seamen was almost sublime until the food-ships were threatened.

So he had found a niche again in life, and very slowly the dead flat look in his face gave way to one of sharp scrutiny. When he came ashore from his cock-boat he would go to a hotel in a street like a scene from the *Tales of Hoffmann*, and he would sleep in a great bed in a mighty room where papal legates had snored in preceding centuries, and the rulers of commanderies had dictated letters to the grand masters of their order. But even there, in that seclusion and fine repository of faith and peace, he dared not recall that last adventure at Bairakli, that catastrophe of his soul. Even the banjo of the occupant of the next room, a nice-looking boy with many medals and a staff appointment, did not mean much to him. He listened apathetically to the nice young voice singing a Kipling ballad:

> *"Funny an' yellow an' faithful—*
> *Doll in a tea-cup she were,*
> *But we lived on the square, like a true-married pair,*
> *An' I learned about women from 'er!"*

But the nice boy had never lived and never would live with anybody on such terms, and his clear young voice lacked the plangent irony of the battered idealist. It was perfectly obvious that he was entirely ignorant of the formidable distortion of character which living with people brought about. He evidently imagined marriage was a good joke and living with girls a bad joke. Mr. Spokesly would lie on his huge bed and try to get his bearings while his neighbour gave his version of "Keep the Home Fires Burning" and "I'd Wait Till the End of the World for You." He was visible sometimes, on his balcony overlooking the steep Via Sant' Lucia raising his eyes with a charming and entirely idiotic diffidence to other balconies where leaned dark-browed damsels, and dreaming the bright and honourable dreams of the well-brought-up young Englishman. Mr. Spokesly got no assistance from such as he. Even in his most fatuous moments he had known that for them the war was only an unusually gigantic and bloody football match, for which they claimed the right to establish the rules. When it was over we would all go back to our places in the world and touch our hats to them, the landed gentry of mankind.

Sitting on his park-seat, under the shadow of Victoria's triumphal arch, Mr. Spokesly saw this would not be the case. Behind his own particular problem, which was to regain, somehow or other, the taste of life, he saw something else looming. How were these very charming and delightful beings, the survivors of an age of gentles and simples, of squires and serfs, to be aroused to the fact that they were no longer accepted as the heirs of all the ages? How to make them see the millions of people of alien races moving slowly, like huge masses of rotting putrescence, to a new life? Indeed, they were very fond of using those words "rotten" and "putrid" for alien things they did not like. He felt sure they would apply both to Mr. Dainopoulos, for example, and those men he met at the Consulate. And with a twinge he reflected they might say the same thing about Evanthia, if they knew it all. Yet they must be made to know, those of them who were left, that the game was up for the cheerful schoolboy with no ascertainable ideas. The very vitality of these alien races was enough to sound a warning. "After all," Mr. Marsh had said in his throaty way, "you can't beat that type, you know." And the question looming up in the back of Mr. Spokesly's mind, as he sat on that seat in St. James's Park, was: "Couldn't you?"

He discovered with a shock that his friend the elderly
lieutenant, who had been visiting the Admiralty that morning and so had met Mr. Spokesly, was explaining something:

"I told him that taking everything into consideration, I
really couldn't see my way. Not now. You see, we aren't
getting any younger, and my wife is so attached to Chingford
she won't hear of leaving. And of course I couldn't go out
there alone now."

"Where did you say it was?" Mr. Spokesly asked. He
had not heard.

"West Indies. It's a new oiling station and they want an
experienced harbour-master. You see, I knew about it, oh,
years ago, when the place was first projected, and I put in for
it. And now he's offered it to me, I can't go. I don't have
to, you see. And yet I would like to put someone in the
way of it for the old chap's sake. So I say, why don't you
go round and see him? Three hundred a year and quarters.
It isn't so dusty, I can assure you. If I hadn't been rather
lucky in my investments I would be very glad to go, I can
tell you that."

And the odd thing, to Mr. Spokesly's mind, was that he did
not envy his elderly friend's happy position as to his investments. Here again luck masqueraded as a slippery word.
Was he so lucky? From where he sat now, beneath the Arch
of the great queen of the money-making, steam-engine era—
the era, that is, when the steam-engines made the money and
the old order fattened upon rents and royalties—Mr. Spokesly was able to see that money was no longer an adequate
gauge of a man's calibre. One had to grow, and that was
another name for suffering. In his hand was a newspaper,
and as he turned it idly, his eye caught an urgent message in
heavy type. The London School of Mnemonics pleaded
with him to join up in the armies of Efficiency. They urged
him to get out of the rut and fit himself for executive positions
with high salaries attached. His eye wandered from the
paper to the vista of the Mall, where the metallic products of
efficiency were ranged in quadruple lines of ugliness, the stark

witnesses of human ineptitude. He saw the children playing about those extraordinarily unlovely enemy guns, their muzzles split and dribbling with rust, their wheels splayed outwards like mechanical paralytics, and he fell to wondering if he could not find his way out of his spiritual difficulties sooner if he did what his friend suggested. He would have to do something. A few hundred pounds was all he had. And the chances of a sea job were not immediately promising. He recalled his visit the other day to the office of the owners of the *Tanganyika*, and the impression he had gained that their enthusiasm had cooled. They had done a big business with Bremen before the war, and they would be doing a big business again soon. Their attitude had contrasted oddly with the roll-of-honour tablet in the office where, printed in gold, he had seen the names of the officers of the *Tanganyika* "murdered by the enemy." All save his own. Somehow that word "murdered," to him who had been there, did not ring true. It was like the nice schoolboy's "rotten" and "putrid"; it signified a mood, now gone no one knew where. It was like Lietherthal's "*Die Freiheit bricht die Ketten*," a gesture which meant nothing to the millions of Hindoos, Mongolians, Arabs, Africans, and Latins in the world. "A family squabble," that sharp young man had called it, a mere curtain-raiser to a gigantic struggle for existence between the races. . . .

He rose and turned to his friend.

"It's the very thing for me," he said. "I don't feel any particular fancy for staying on in England."

"As soon as I saw you waiting in that corridor," said his friend, "I thought of it. Now you go and see him. You know the Colonial Office. He's a fine old boy and a thorough gentleman. There are prospects, too, I may tell you. It's a sugar-cane country, and I believe you'll have some very nice company in the plantations all round. And I believe there's a pension after twenty years. Well . . . not that you'll need to bother about it by that time. . . . As I say, it's a jumping-off place. Fine country, you know. But what about a little drink? I know a place in Chandos

Street—they know me there. And now about coming down
to Chingford. . . ."

Mr. Spokesly accompanied his friend through the great
Arch of Victoria into the Square and as they made their way
round by the National Gallery he reached a decision. He
would go. His elderly friend, toddling beside him, added
details which only confirmed the decision. That gentleman
knew a good thing. He himself, however, having more by
luck than judgment held on to his shipping shares, was now in
a position of comfortable independence. He had served his
country and sacrificed his sons and now he was going to enjoy
himself for the rest of his life. After drawing enormous
interest and bonuses he had sold at the top of the market and
was buying bonds "which would go up" a stockbroking
friend had told him. "A safe six hundred a year—what do I
want with more?" he wheezed as they entered the place in
Chandos Street. "My dear wife, she's so nervous of these
shipping shares; and there's no doubt they *are* a risk. Mine's
a large port-wine, please."

Yes, he would go, and it interested Mr. Spokesly to see
how little his tender and beautiful picture of two old
people "going down the hill together" appealed to him.
With a sudden cleavage in the dull mistiness which had
possessed his heart for so long, he saw that there was something in life which they had missed. He saw that if a man
sets so low a mark, and attains it by the aid of a craven
rectitude and animal cunning, he will miss the real glory and
crown of life, which by no means implies victory. He was
prepared to admit he had not done a great deal with his own
life so far. But he was laying a new course. The night he
received his instructions to depart he walked down to the
river and along the embankment to his hotel with a novel
exaltation of spirit. The taste of life was coming back. He
saw, in imagination, that new place to which he was bound, a
tiny settlement concealed within the secure recesses of a huge
tropical harbour. He saw the jetty, with its two red lights by
the pipe-line and the verandahed houses behind the groves of
Indian laurel. He saw the mountains beyond the clear

water purple and black against the sunset or floating above
the mist in the crystal atmosphere of the dawn. He saw the
wide clean space of matted floors and the hammock where he
would lie and watch the incandescent insects moving through
the night air. He saw himself there, an integral part of an
orderly and reasonable existence. He had no intention of
wasting his life, but he saw that he must have time and quiet
to find his bearings and make those necessary affiliations with
society without which a man is rootless driftage. He saw
that the lines which had hitherto held him to the shore had
been spurious and rotten and had parted at the first tension.

There was time yet. What was it the elderly lieutenant
had called her? "A mill-stone round your neck all your
life." No, he could not take that view. He did not regret
that supreme experience of his life. He recalled the swift
derisive gesture she had once flung at him as she spurned
his reiterated fidelity: "You learn from me, to go back to an
Englishwoman." Even now he delighted in the splendid
memory of her charm, her delicious languors and moments
of melting tenderness, her anger and sometimes smouldering
rage. No, he did not regret. It was something achieved,
something that would be part of him for ever. He could go
forward now into the future, armed with knowledge and the
austere prudence that is the heritage of an emotional defeat.
He looked out across the river and saw the quick glow of an
opened cupola in a foundry on the Surrey Side. There was a
faint smile on his face, an expression of resolution, as though
in imagination he were already in his island home, watching
the glow of a cane-fire in a distant valley.

And eastward, some five thousand miles, in the costly Villa
Dainopoulos on the shores of an ancient sea, Evanthia Solaris
pursued the mysterious yet indomitable course of her destiny.
She had arrived back from "Europe," as has been hinted
earlier, in some disarray, alighting from a crowded train of
frowsty refugees, silent, enraged yet reflective after her
odyssey. At her feet followed the young Jew, who in-
continently dropped upon his knees in the road and pressed

his lips, in agonized thankfulness, to his native earth. *"Je déteste les hommes!"* was all she had said, and Mr. Dainopoulos had spared a moment in the midst of his many affairs to utter a hoarse croak of laughter. Her story of Captain Rannie's sudden escape from the problems of living struck him for a moment, for he had of course utilized his commander's record and peculiarities in explaining the disappearance of the *Kalkis*. But the event itself seemed to perplex him not at all. He said, briefly, to his wife in adequate idiom: "He got a scare. He was afraid of himself. In wars plenty of men do that. He think and think, and there is nothing. And that scare a man stiff, when there is nothing." Crude psychology no doubt, yet adequate to explain Captain Rannie's unsuccessful skirmish with life.

But Mrs. Dainopoulos was not so callous. She suspected, under Evanthia's hard exterior, a heart lacerated by the bitterness of disillusion. Who would have believed, either, that Mr. Spokesly, an Englishman, would have deserted her like that? Mrs. Dainopoulos was gently annoyed with Mr. Spokesly. He had not behaved as she had arranged it in her story-book fashion. Evanthia must stay with them, she said, stroking the girl's dark head.

As she did. Seemingly she forgot both the base Englishman and the Alleman Giaour who had so infatuated her. She remained always with the invalid lady, looking out at the Gulf, watching the transports come and go. And when at last it came to Mr. Dainopoulos to journey south, when the sea-lines were once again open and a hundred and one guns announced the end, she went with them to the fairy villa out at San Stefano that you reach by the Boulevard Ramleh in Alexandria. It was there that Mr. Dainopoulos emerged in a new rôle, of the man whose dreams come true. His rich and sumptuous oriental mind expanded in grandiose visions of splendour for the being he adored. He built pleasaunces of fine marbles set in green shrubberies and laved by the blue sea, for her diversion.

He had automobiles, as he had resolved, of matchless black and cream-coloured coachwork, with scarlet wheels and orange

silk upholstery. He imported a yacht that floated in the
harbour like a great moth with folded wings. Far out on the
breakwater he had an enormous bungalow built of hard
woods upon a square lighter, with chambers for music and
slumber in the cool Mediterranean breeze, while the thud and
wash of the waves against the outer wall lulled the sleeper
to antique dreams. He did all this, and sat each day in the
portico of the great marble Bourse, planning fresh acqui-
sitions of money. His wife lay in her chair in her rose-tinted
chamber at San Stefano, looking out upon the blue sea
beyond the orange trees and palms, smiling and sometimes
immobile, as though stunned by this overwhelming onslaught
of wealth pressed from the blood and bones of the youth of
the world. She smiled and lay thinking of her imaginary
people, who lived exemplary and unimportant lives in an
England which no longer existed. And near her, hovering,
shining like a creature from another world, clad miraculously
in robes of extraordinary brilliance, could be seen Evanthia
Solaris, the companion of her hours. Often it was she who
shot away along the great corniche road in those cars of
speed and beauty, their silver fittings and glossy panels
humming past like some vast and costly insect. She it was
who lay in a silken hammock in the great houseboat by the
breakwater, and listened to the sweet strains from the disc
concealed in a cabinet shaped like a huge bronze shell. "*Je
déteste les hommes*," she murmured to herself as she wandered through the orange groves to the curved marble seats
on the shore.

Hearing these words as she passed, the young Jew, working
among the roses, would tremble and recall with an expression
of horror their experiences in Europe. Often, when in their
destitution she had taken him by the hair and hissed them
in his affrighted ear, and he would utter an almost inaudible
moan of "Oh, Madama!" For he loved her. He was the
victim of a passion like a thin, pure, agitated flame burning
amid conflagrations. He would have expired in ecstasy beneath her hand, for it would have needed more courage to
speak than to die. And now he was in paradise tending the

roses and suffering exquisite agonies as she passed, her beautiful lips muttering, "*Je déteste les hommes!*" As perhaps she did; yet she would sometimes look suddenly out across the waves with smouldering amber eyes and parted lips, as though she expected to behold once more the figure of a man coming up out of the sea, to offer again the unregarded sacrifices of fidelity and love.

THE END